MADS PEDER NORDBO is a Danish writer who lives in Greenland and works at the town hall in Nuuk. He holds degrees in literature, communications and philosophy from the University of Southern Denmark and the University of Stockholm. He is the author of five novels; his two latest books will be published in eighteen languages. *The Girl Without Skin* is the first to be published in English.

CHARLOTTE BARSLUND is a Scandinavian translator. She has translated novels by Peter Adolphsen, Mikkel Birkegaard, Thomas Enger, Karin Fossum, Steffen Jacobsen, Carsten Jensen and Per Petterson, as well as a wide range of classic and contemporary plays. She lives in the UK.

THE GIRL WITHOUT SKIN

MADS PEDER NORDBO

Translated from the Danish by Charlotte Barslund

TEXT PUBLISHING MELBOURNE AUSTRALIA

textpublishing.com.au

The Text Publishing Company
Swann House
22 William Street
Melbourne Victoria 3000
Australia

Originally published in Denmark as *Pigen uden hud* by Politikens Forlag, Copenhagen, 2017
First published in English by The Text Publishing Company, 2018

Cover design by Text
Cover photograph by Vadim Nefedov/iStock
Page design by Jessica Horrocks
Typeset by J&M Typesetting

Printed and bound in Australia by Griffin Press, an accredited ISO/NZS 14001:2004 Environmental Management System printer

ISBN: 9781925603835 (paperback)
ISBN: 9781925626803 (ebook)

A catalogue record for this book is available from the National Library of Australia

PROLOGUE

His skin was drenched in sweat. He wanted to cough but could only gurgle. Mucus had built up in his throat behind the cloth. He tried to bite down on the gag, to spit it out, but it had been shoved in so deep that he could barely move his straining jaws.

His temples throbbed. The overhead light cut through the flimsy fabric that covered his face. His breathing was shallow. Tense. His breath came in bursts. He tried to swallow the thick saliva in his throat and tasted metal. He gulped again, triggering a sensation of choking nausea. Everything was spinning. His stomach lurched and he had to tighten his throat and hold his breath to stop himself retching.

He didn't dare struggle. The pain in his hands was too severe. Every time he moved, screaming shafts of agony darted from the nail holes in his palms up through his arms to a point deep behind his eyes where everything imploded.

The air was irritating his nose. His lungs and head were pounding. He wasn't getting enough oxygen. His throat went into spasms. His muscles tried to suck in air but found only saliva and mucus.

He gave a hollow groan when he felt the edge of a cold blade sweep up his stomach, slashing his shirt and heavy pullover all the way to his throat.

Tears trickled through his beard. *Please*, he pleaded. *Please don't kill me*. But no words came out. Only a muffled growl.

He jerked when a finger softly traced a line up his taut stomach.

Then the blade carved a broad, stinging gash through the skin and tissue of his stomach. Steel crunched against bone as it hit his rib cage. Everything in his tensed body gave in. Skin. Flesh. Life. He gurgled a roar, the back of his head slamming against the floor as he pulled at his bloodied hands.

Snot bubbled up inside his nose, blocking the airflow. The cloth bled in his mouth. The light screamed. Disappeared. Screamed.

THE
NIGHTMARE

1

The red Mercedes came out of nowhere, and the moment its right front bumper hit the blue Golf, both cars were knocked off course and flung together. The Golf reared backwards and crashed onto the road, while the nose of the Mercedes drove into the tarmac before the car was flipped up like an empty can. The force of a fresh blow to the rear of the Golf caused the Mercedes to stop in midair and drop back to the road, where it slammed against the blue roof. The Golf buckled and its right side was flattened, while to the left the chassis held firm.

The Mercedes continued its fall and smashed into the barrier so hard that a section tore loose and sliced open the side of the car. The Golf skidded diagonally off the road and down the slope, rolling onto its side. The engine had cut out. Inside the Mercedes a man was screaming at the top of his lungs. There were no words. No language. Only screams.

Inside the Golf an ashen-faced man was staring into the eyes of a woman. She was trapped between the compressed roof and the dislocated floor of the car. The man was caught between his seat, the seatbelt and the hissing airbag. The woman's airbag had split open and deflated. The man was bleeding from several cuts to his head.

He reached down his hand to her, but she didn't take it. Her body was limp. Her eyes fading. His hand caressed her cheek. She was still there with him, her eyes locked onto his. Her gaze crept inside him, where everything was breaking and starting to trickle out. Down onto her.

His hand moved to her stomach. Rounding the bump. The little girl. The child inside. The woman's eyes closed forever. And with that everything disappeared.

Matthew woke with a scream and threw off his blanket. His T-shirt was soaked in sweat and clinging to his body. With a roar that came from deep inside his chest, he tore it off and hurled it away too. He smelt the acrid tang of his own sleep as he stumbled to his feet and made his way from the sofa to the balcony.

Outside the air was dense with evening mist. He could taste the sea and feel the moisture hiding in the cool North Atlantic fog while he rummaged around for his cigarettes. The packet in his jeans pocket was warm and squashed: he had been lying on it and sweating. He jammed a cigarette between his lips and lit it, then unbuttoned his jeans and kicked them off. His boxer shorts went too. Everything reeked of sweat.

The smoke seeped out between his lips, wafting down his face and naked body, then it merged with the fog—as did he. *You're a shadow child*, his mother used to say to him when he was little. *You're so pale you might dissolve in the fog.*

The mist from the cold sea around the headland wrapped itself around him. The chill tickled his skin, made the fine, blond hairs on his arms and legs stand up. The moisture grabbed them. He exhaled.

He still had trouble sleeping. His nightmares refused to leave him alone. They lay in wait and, when he drifted off to sleep, would ambush him and tear him to pieces. Night after night. Month after month. The same nightmare. The same eyes. Staring deep into his.

The cigarette found its way to his lips for the last time before he dropped it into a glass bowl containing a muddy porridge of several hundred cigarette butts and rainwater.

Somewhere behind him his phone buzzed. He picked up his jeans and took it out. It was his editor.

'Matt! Hi, it's me. Are you all set for the debate?'

Matthew looked down at his naked body. 'Yes.'

'The first debate with Aleqa Hammond and Søren Espersen is on now. Jørgen Emil Lyberth from the IA Party is taking part as well.'

Matthew flopped onto the sofa, grabbing the remote control to turn on the television.

'It's on KNR,' his editor said.

'I know, I know—'

'I want a summary of the debate on our home page as soon as it's over. Misu is ready to translate, so we're good to go. Have you found it?'

'Yes, yes…I'm looking at it now.'

'It's only just started.' His editor exhaled heavily. 'They're talking about the failed reconciliation commission and the ten million kroner.'

'I'm looking at it now,' Matthew said again, somewhat exasperated. 'Aleqa Hammond says we need to unite rather than divide. Greenland must come together. Lyberth disagrees—he thinks the ten million would have been better spent on the arts than on some expensive commission the Danish government can't even be bothered to take part in.'

'Exactly, good, you're watching it. Remember to get something online right away. You need to be writing while you're listening, okay?'

'Okay, I'm on it. I'm going to hang up now so I can make notes.'

The voice of Aleqa Hammond, Greenland's prime minister, filled the room. 'The ten million kroner isn't the problem—the problem is that Denmark can't be bothered to take part. We need this reconciliation.'

'We don't need reconciliation,' Lyberth interjected. 'What we need is to face up to some hard truths.'

A third voice joined in. 'Surely this commission is just another political scam to milk the Danish taxpayer for even more money while at same time clamouring for more independence?'

'It's the exact opposite,' Hammond retorted sharply. 'It's about solidarity and being part of a community, but we have a long way to go if the only politician we can get to come up here is some angry right-winger.'

'And yet here I am,' Espersen said swiftly.

'The Danish prime minister and the rest of her government are cowards for not wanting to reconcile,' Hammond said angrily.

'What is there to reconcile?' Espersen said. 'If it were up to me, Denmark would be running absolutely everything up here. It's grotesque that we send you billions of kroner every year and yet we don't have any say at all in what you do with the money. We would never put up with it in any other part of Denmark if it had the world's highest suicide rate or every third girl there were sexually abused.'

'And that's exactly the kind of rhetoric we've come to expect from the Danish People's Party,' Hammond sneered. 'You're reductive and racist.'

'Being against raping children wasn't racist the last time I looked,' Espersen said.

Matthew turned down the volume and the voices faded away. He didn't need to listen to Hammond and Espersen to know what they were saying. He had heard it all before. He grabbed his laptop.

The first of three planned political debates between Aleqa Hammond and Søren Espersen kicked off with the subject of the reconciliation commission, but was soon hijacked and led to sharp exchanges between the Greenlandic prime minister and the Danish People's Party's deputy leader and Greenland spokesperson…

Less than twenty minutes later his summary was ready, and

the very same second that a disgusted-looking Hammond shook hands with Espersen, Matthew sent the text off to the translator so it could be uploaded in Danish and Greenlandic simultaneously on *Sermitsiaq*'s website.

Less than five years ago, when Matthew had completed his degree in journalism, he had never in his wildest dreams imagined that he would end up here in Nuuk writing about reconciliation. His dreams had been bigger. He'd always seen himself chasing scoops. He wanted more, though. He had loved Tine, loved the idea of having a family. Emily. The car crash had put an abrupt end to that dream—and if he couldn't be with Tine, with their baby, the rest made no sense.

He flopped back on the sofa. The screams from his nightmare echoed in his thoughts. His fingers could still remember the curve of her stomach. He rubbed his eyes. It was late, but he wouldn't be able to sleep much more tonight. The town wouldn't get fully dark. The fog would probably lift. He pulled his laptop bag closer and stuck his hand into one of the pockets, where his fingers found a handful of old photographs. He studied them one by one and then arranged them on the sofa next to him.

All the photographs were dog-eared from constant handling. He'd had some of them since he was a child. Those of his father were the oldest. They had been taken at the US air base in Thule, in northwest Greenland, and his father wore a uniform in all of them except the one where he was sitting with Matthew's mother in what looked like a military mess hall. His father was smiling. They were both smiling. His mother with her big belly. One of the pictures wasn't a photograph but a postcard sent from Nuuk in August 1990. *I'm not able to come to Denmark as soon as planned*, it said. *Sorry, love you both.*

Matthew traced each letter with his finger. Those words were the only thing he had left of his father. The postcard had arrived a few months after Matthew and his mother had moved back to Denmark.

The last picture slipping through his fingers was that of Tine. Tine sitting down, watching him with a broad smile. She was smiling because they had learned that very same day that they were going to have a daughter. They had even seen their baby girl on the monitor at the prenatal clinic. *We'll name her Emily*, Tine had said. *Emily. And when she gets a bit bigger than my stomach, I'll read* Wuthering Heights *to her*. He had loved Tine. And she had loved him.

THE MAN FROM
THE ICE

2

The powerful helicopter rotors whirled the snow on the ice cap around the few men already present on the ice. The snow became a tornado of furious glass shards, and Matthew watched as the men raised their hands to their faces to shield themselves. Not that it would do them much good; once roused, the ice and the snow had a knack of finding their way into every nook and cranny. Nor did it help that the sun was high in the sky, and caught the thousands of tiny ice crystals in the dual fire of its rays and the reflection from the ice cap beneath them.

'Can you see anything?' a voice in front of him called out.

'Only some men,' Matthew shouted back, squinting and holding up his hand to shade his face from the sunlight. His fingers were trembling as usual, and he clenched his fist, pressing it against his forehead as he shut his eyes for a moment.

The huge Sikorsky helicopter flicked its tail and slowly turned on its own axis before starting its descent to the thick layer of compacted snow and ice. The sunlight was replaced by shade, and Matthew caught a brief glimpse of his pale face and blond hair reflected in the window.

The photographer sitting next to him leaned out so far that he risked plummeting to the ice. Matthew wondered why anyone would be mad enough to open the door before the helicopter had landed.

'There!' The photographer interrupted Matthew's catastrophising and quickly raised his camera to his face. 'Look! Over there!'

Matthew took a firm hold of the strap by his seat and leaned towards the photographer's shoulder, trying to follow the angle of the camera lens. Not many metres left to go now. The snow was being blown far away by the force of the downdraft from the blades, making the area immediately below them entirely smooth. Matthew's other hand brushed his jeans pocket, checking that he had remembered his cigarettes and lighter.

The men on the ice grew bigger, big enough for Matthew to see their squinting eyes and brown faces.

He had only been in Nuuk for a few months, and he had been sent to cover this story purely because there had been no one else in the office that morning when the editor called. *You need to be at the airport in half an hour. Some hunters have found a dead body that's been there so long it's been mummified. It might be a man from the Viking age. This is huge, I'm telling you. Huge!*

Shortly after his arrival in Nuuk, Matthew had been given the obligatory city tour, and had been shown the Inuit mummies at the museum in Kolonihavnen. It was rare for new mummies to be discovered these days, though, and this one, of Nordic appearance rather than Inuit, would be unique. It would be the first time a well-preserved Norseman had ever been found, and historians and archaeologists already had high hopes that this mummy would teach them more about the everyday life of the Norsemen.

Matthew had read that the Norsemen had disappeared leaving practically no trace after inhabiting Greenland for more than four hundred years—a disappearance shrouded in mystery, as it seemed odd that such an established population would vanish so suddenly.

Norsemen had also settled in Iceland and on the Faroe Islands, where their descendants still lived to this day, while in Greenland there was a gap from approximately 1400 to 1721, when the Dano-Norwegian missionary Hans Egede came in search of the Norsemen, found the old settlements abandoned, and so instead started his mission to convert the Inuit and laid the foundations for the Danish colonisation of modern Greenland.

Now a Viking had emerged from the ice. No one could as yet fathom what he had been doing so far out there in the white loneliness, but he was real, and it was him they had flown out there to see.

The editor's words kept going round in Matthew's mind: *We want to break this story. No one else. It's our news and our scoop, and we want the credit, understand? You can write in English, can't you?*

Of course he could. He had assured his editor of that many times during his job interview. English, German, Danish, Norwegian and Swedish, but not Kalaallisut, the Greenlandic language, although it had been a job requirement.

'Yes!' the photographer exclaimed as his massive camera clicked away. 'Bloody amazing.' He turned and looked at Matthew, wide-eyed. 'Do you think my pictures will be in all the foreign newspapers?'

'To begin with, yes.' Matthew nodded lightly without taking his eyes off the ice beneath them.

'Will they credit me?'

'We'll make sure they do,' Matthew said. 'But first let's just find out who he is, shall we?'

'This is insane,' the photographer exclaimed, ignoring Matthew's last words. 'I'm gonna be world-famous. Holy shit, it's insane! Yes!'

There was a jolt as the helicopter bumped against the ice. Matthew felt it sink as the wheels pressed into the belly of the heavy red body for one long second. It was his first trip in one of the big Air Greenland helicopters and, if his editor was to be believed, he might as well get his nerves and his stomach used to it, as many such trips awaited him—especially in the winter, when fixed-wing aeroplanes were often grounded by fog, storm, ice or thick snow.

None of that mattered right now. They had landed and were about to see the first Norseman mummy ever found. Dried out and preserved by the frost and the arctic air. Matthew could already visualise the headline: *The iceman from the past. The last Viking.* He tried to decide what would sound best in English, and how much drama he could inject into the story. A killing would be good. *The last Viking, wounded and dying alone on the ice.* That sounded intriguing. *The last Viking. Left behind. Dying from his wounds.*

3

The reflection from the ice was so bright that Matthew was almost forced to shut his eyes as he climbed through the helicopter door and made his way down the short iron ladder that had unfolded below his feet.

They were surrounded by a piercing whiteness more intense than anything he'd seen before.

The magic, however, was ruined by the still noisy rotors, which continued to chop the air into pieces above their heads with heavy, monotonous thuds.

One of the men signalled to the pilot, and soon the blades slowed as the engine was switched off. The din from the engine faded to a turbine-like drone before this tiny spot on the edge of the vast ice cap lay in deafening silence once more.

There had been three other men and a woman on board the helicopter. All were from Denmark originally, but as far as Matthew had gathered, they were now working at Ilisimatusarfik, the University of Greenland, except for one of the men, who was from the museum where Matthew had seen the Inuit mummies.

'Hi, are you the reporter?'

Matthew looked around and saw a police officer who, in contrast to the group from the helicopter, looked Inuit.

The photographer was also Inuit. His name was Malik. He had been leaping about on ice and rocks ever since he could walk, and he was one of the few people from the newspaper Matthew had made friends with.

'Yes,' Matthew said, still with his eyes almost closed. 'I'm supposed to write about the man found out here.' His fingers instinctively sought out the wedding band that he no longer wore.

The police officer nodded. 'He's over there, but that's not why I'm asking.'

'So what is it?'

'You mustn't touch him, but I'm sure you've already guessed as much.' He turned to Malik. 'And you keep your distance—are we clear?'

'Why?' Malik demanded. 'I mean, he's frozen solid.'

The police officer shrugged and nodded in the direction of the archaeologists from the helicopter. 'It's their call.'

'But it's all right if we take some pictures and write about him, isn't it?' Matthew said, hoping that the archaeologists might hear him and invite him to join them. 'This is big news, and we want to break the story before everyone else comes up here and steals our thunder. The whole world will want to know about this.'

He could see that his words hit home with the young police officer.

'What did you say your name was?' Matthew continued. 'I want to be sure I spell it right in my story. After all, it'll also go out in English.'

The officer pressed his lips together, but then he nodded. 'Ulrik Heilmann. With two n's.' He gestured briefly to the photographer. 'I went to school with Malik.'

'All right, Heilmann with two n's,' Matthew confirmed, and looked at Malik. 'Could you please take some pictures of Ulrik for the paper?'

Malik looked back at Matthew with his eyebrows raised, and then across to Ulrik. 'But I thought we—'

'Sure, sure, but we need the basics in place first,' Matthew interjected. 'We don't want to miss anything.'

Before Malik had time to protest, Matthew turned to Ulrik again. 'So can I write that you found him?'

'Well, some hunters discovered him and contacted us at the station, so they're the ones who found him.'

Matthew looked around. 'And have they left?'

Ulrik nodded, his eyes big and round. 'Yes, they've headed further up the ice to look for reindeer. Enok is getting married soon and they've gone hunting for meat for his wedding.'

'Enok?' Matthew echoed.

'One of their cousins,' Ulrik said with a shake of his head. 'It's not important. Only they were keen to move on.'

'There aren't many reindeer out here,' Malik whispered to Matthew. 'But they might come across a lost musk ox—you never know.'

Matthew looked at Ulrik. 'It's simpler if we write that you found him, but that you were acting on a tip-off from some hunters. It's better that it's your name in the paper when the calls start coming in from abroad. You're much easier to track down than…' Matthew looked across the fjords and the mountains, '…three hunters out there somewhere.'

Malik's lens caught the now beaming officer, who nodded to himself before he turned to the small cluster of archaeologists and the museum curator, who had gathered around a long, brown cocoon of old fur.

Matthew craned his neck but could see nothing but the brown fur. His thoughts were still juggling different headlines in Danish and English, and all the media attention he would soon be getting.

He shook his head and stamped his feet on the glittering snow carpet. It felt solid, and yet when he stomped hard his feet would sink in. The heat of the sun was intense—he could feel it nipping at his skin and tightening his face. The snow was porous and coarse-grained. Summer snow. Its density increased with every centimetre it went down. That was pretty much all he knew about glacier formation. Eventually the pressure grew so great that the snow was compacted into ice. Several kilometres of it. Over the years the cloudy ice became clear as the purest crystal.

He looked up again. There was a dark crack in the ice cap not far from them. 'Did you find him down there?' he asked Ulrik, pointing at the crevasse.

Ulrik nodded with a smile, then his face fell. 'They're saying I shouldn't have touched him before they'd had a chance to secure the discovery site, but we thought it was a dead hunter.'

Matthew smiled. 'Of course—how were you to know? I'm sure they understand.'

Ulrik shrugged. 'Perhaps…I hope so, anyway. It wasn't until I'd brought him up and had a proper look at him that I realised how yellow he was and how the skin on his face and feet had dried up like a hide that's been stretched out and hung up in the wind.' He unzipped his black uniform jacket, took it off and draped it over one arm.

'Feet?' Matthew said. 'He has bare feet?' Again he tried to catch the eyes of the archaeologists, but to no avail.

Ulrik sniffed hard. 'I didn't see everything, but I think he was naked inside the fur as well. It seems to be stuck to him. The fur, I mean. Almost as if it'd grown together with his skin.' He scrunched up his nose. 'He's been there a long time, let me tell you.'

'About six hundred years, if he's a Norseman,' Matthew said.

'I don't remember the dates,' Ulrik said.

'But they think it's a Norseman?'

'That's what I've been told, and there's nothing to indicate that the body is more recent or that a crime has been committed, but they've requested forensic pathologists and crime scene technicians from Denmark, just to be sure. I don't think they'll get here until next week. Until then our job is to secure the area.' He nodded towards the archaeologists. 'But they've been given permission to look at him.'

'This is global news,' Matthew said. 'BBC, NBC, *National Geographic, Time*. They'll all want to know. So do you think we could have a quick look?'

Ulrik nodded. 'All right—I'll see how far they've got. You can check out the crevasse in the meantime. But hey!' He caught Malik's eye. 'Watch your step. I don't have time to fly the pair of you to the hospital.'

'You've become really boring—did you know that?' Malik said with a grin. 'Before we know it, Lyberth will have got you voted into the Inatsisartut, and then all hope is lost. By next year you'll be just as dried up and wrinkly as that mummy.' Malik turned to Matthew. 'Ulrik is a Siumut Party candidate at the next election, backed by Jørgen Emil Lyberth. We're looking at a future minister for the environment or justice.'

'Whatever,' Ulrik mumbled, although he couldn't quite hide a smile that sent a red glow of pride to his cheeks. 'Let's just wait and see what the voters have to say about it, ilaa? It's only been sixteen months since the last election.'

'Oh, you'll get in. Lyberth has a seat in the cabinet with your name written on it.'

Ulrik shook his head. 'I think it'll take a bit more than just a sticky label.'

'I don't know about that.' Malik raised his eyebrows. 'Listen, if your ministry ever needs a photographer, promise you'll give me a call?'

'You just mind where you go and watch your step once you get down that crevasse, all right?'

'We will, mate—you know me.'

'Yes, that's my point precisely.'

Malik rolled his eyes. 'He's never going to let me forget the time I drifted out to sea on an icefloe and they had to dispatch several helicopters to find me.' He flung out his arms. 'But seriously, mate, the light on the ice that day was mind-blowing!'

4

Matthew perched gingerly on the edge of the crevasse as he watched Malik, who was already quite far down the ice wall. When Matthew had seen the crevasse from the helicopter, it had appeared like a dark slash in the ground, but now that he was staring right into it, it was more like looking into a luminous iceberg.

'You will be careful, won't you?' Matthew called out.

Malik turned and looked up at him with exasperation. 'This isn't an active part of the glacier. The crevasse is solid, and the footholds I'm using have been here forever. Don't worry. I'm only going to that ledge over there where they found him.'

Matthew looked down at him tentatively. Then he took a deep breath and stretched his neck from side to side a few times.

'Why don't you come on down?' Malik went on. 'We're going no further than this, so you'll be completely safe.'

Matthew rolled over slowly and let himself slide down until his feet found a foothold. He looked around. Malik was several metres below him, but the photographer was right—the ice felt safe and solid. Matthew looked to the side. Not far from him there was a vertical drop, and he couldn't see where the crevasse ended. Deep down, there was nothing but total darkness.

Malik had followed his gaze. 'We're not going down there today, but let me know if you want to do that sometime. The caves around here are absolutely insane. Mind-boggling. Completely turquoise. I can show you my pictures when we get back, if you like.'

Matthew nodded slowly. 'Another time, perhaps.' He was shivering, and regretted leaving his jacket in the helicopter. The moment they had climbed down between the enormous walls of ice, the temperature had dropped and their breath turned to wispy fog. 'So you've been down here before?' he asked.

'No, not here, but you find the same world in every crevasse and cave.'

There was silence for a moment. They could no longer hear voices from above. Matthew looked at Malik. He wore sturdy boots, thick orange trousers and a grey knitted jumper. A wiser choice than the sneakers and jeans in which Matthew had left his apartment.

'Are you coming?' Malik continued. 'This is the place. I can see where he was lying.'

Matthew didn't respond, but let himself glide down another level, grabbing hold of cracks and protrusions in the ice and compacted snow.

'Look, there it is!' Malik's camera clicked away first from this angle, then from that. Then he straightened up and looked towards the rim of the crevasse above them. 'The storm the other day must have uncovered him. We don't usually have such windy weather at this time of year, but you never can tell.'

'How would the storm have done that?'

'It must have swept away the snow to reveal him.' Malik tilted his head and ran a hand through his dense black hair. 'The wind here can move a mountain of snow in a matter of hours.' He glanced at Matthew. 'Let's head back up into the sunshine. I have some good pictures.' He hesitated. 'Do you want some mattak? I've got some in my rucksack.'

'Mattak? That's whale skin, isn't it?'

'Yes, and blubber. It'll warm you up in no time, I promise.'

Matthew shook his head. 'I think a bit of sun is all I need.'

'But it tastes fantastic and it's full of warming oil. Are you sure? You look like you could do with a cube or two.'

'I think I'll pass,' Matthew replied, and grabbed at the ice, preparing to climb back up. He placed one foot on a small protrusion while the other felt around for a good crack or a lump of hard snow to stand on. Getting down had been much easier than going up. It was like trying to climb up a slide, and the smooth soles of his sneakers weren't helping. His foot found a hollow and he pulled himself up with one arm, but soon he felt the snow shift, throwing him off balance. The void below reached out for him, and he had a vision of himself lying at the bottom of the turquoise deep with a hundred broken bones and a cloud of frozen breath hanging over him.

'What do you think you're doing?'

Matthew felt Malik's firm grip on his jumper, and allowed himself to be pulled back to his foothold in the snow.

'I thought we were being careful?' Malik reminded him.

The snow filled Matthew's hands as he dug his fingers into it. He was panting now, and could feel the cold ice wall against his face.

'That never would have happened if you'd eaten some mattak.' Malik grinned and slapped Matthew on the back a couple of times. 'And mattak clears your mind, so you can look into nature rather than just walk around it.' Still smiling, he pointed out a couple of holes in the ice wall close to them. 'Climb up over there. It's safer.'

'I just slipped, that's all,' Matthew grunted. He collapsed on the ice ledge and fished out his cigarettes from his jeans pocket. He looked up at Malik. 'Do you want one?'

Malik nodded and sat down next to him. Matthew took out two cigarettes and lit them both.

'Jørgen Emil Lyberth,' Matthew said, blowing smoke into the

cold air. 'He was the speaker of the Inatsisartut for quite a few years, wasn't he?'

'Yes, he was the longest-serving speaker ever. He served several terms, but he's been out for a few years now. When Ulrik gets elected, the old man will recapture some of his former glory.' Malik took a deep drag on his cigarette and pressed his chin towards his chest. 'I don't remember where Ulrik is from—one day he was just there. He came from some small village and Lyberth took him in. It's probably thanks to Lyberth that Ulrik was popular from day one, even though he was so strange and dark.' He took another deep drag on his cigarette, then tossed what was left of it into the void. 'And now he's married to Lyberth's youngest—would you believe it? Have you seen her?'

Matthew shook his head.

'She's seriously hot…He's done good, he has, the boy without a past.'

'Thanks,' Matthew said, and he tossed his glowing cigarette butt after Malik's. 'That'll help when I start writing my story.'

'That's kind of my point. Don't make an enemy of Lyberth—it's not worth it. Nuuk is a very small town.'

5

The sun was still beating down on the ice cap, and Matthew warmed up the moment he was free of the crevasse. Once again the snow blinded him with its thousands of tiny white mirrors, but his eyes soon adapted to the sharp light. The surface of the ice cap was rippled like a calm sea. Small hollows, mounds and frozen waves spread as far as the eye could see, formed over the years by the snow, the rain and the wind. All around them, steel-blue mountains stretched towards the azure blanket of the sky. At this time of year only a few peaks had any serious snow on them—although the snow had started to fall on the highest ones, it only stayed on the shaded sides, in ravines and crevices. There, however, it had been lying the whole summer. Matthew had yet to go hiking in the mountains, but knew it was only a matter of time. He had gathered that it was one of the things you had to do, if you were a new Dane in Nuuk and wanted to earn a little respect.

'So did you get some good pictures down there?' Ulrik asked.

Malik gave him a thumbs-up.

'Excellent,' Ulrik said. 'I've been told that you can have a look at him now, and that they're happy to answer questions.' He turned to Matthew. 'After all, we want Greenland's own media to be first with this news, don't we?'

'Absolutely,' Matthew said with a nod.

Ulrik smiled, possibly at the thought of the many pictures of him that would soon be beamed around the world on the strength of a story about the man they had found in the ice.

The archaeologists and the museum curator had retreated to near the helicopter, where two of them were on their satellite phones while the others were staring at a couple of open laptops.

'They'll be flying back shortly,' Ulrik announced. 'As far as I can gather, they need to pick up some equipment before setting up a camp out here, so they can examine the entire crevasse right down to the bottom. The police will guard the iceman tonight to make sure nothing happens to him. The archaeologists aren't allowed to move him until our people have examined him, but they've been given permission to put up a protective tent around him. They say he needs stabilising. I don't know why—he seems perfectly stable to me. When I pulled him out, he was stiff as a board.' He chuckled to himself. 'I can't imagine that lying in the sun will do him much good after all those years down in the cold, but he can't get any more dead, can he?'

'So will you be sleeping here?' Malik teased him. 'Next to the dead man?'

'I don't know if it will be me. Not that it matters.'

Malik gave a light shrug. 'Rather you than me.'

'Why?' Matthew frowned. 'Could you freeze to death out here?'

'Easily,' Malik said. He looked down. 'But I was thinking more about the spirits. They hate being disturbed. If he's been lying dead down there for all those centuries, many spirits will be attached to him...And they won't be the nice ones. They're from underground.'

Ulrik rolled his eyes. 'Ignore him. There are as many spirits out here as there are musk oxen.'

'A stray one might turn up looking for food,' Malik objected.

Ulrik threw up his hands in disbelief. 'There are no spirits or musk oxen on the ice cap!'

'It's full of spirits and demons underground,' Malik insisted. 'I've seen them myself.'

'When you play your drum?'

'*Before* I play my drum, obviously.'

'It's a part of our culture, and it's beautiful,' Ulrik told Matthew. 'But personally I don't believe any of that stuff. It makes no sense that the bedrock is full of spirits, and that we can use them against our enemies by carving little tupilak figures—but hey, each to his own.'

'Well, let's see if you survive the night,' Malik said with a broad grin. 'I could always come out here and play my drum for you, if you want me to? I could be back before it gets dark.'

'Oh no, I'm not having you getting under my feet out here. And I don't think I'll be the one staying anyway.' Ulrik clapped his hands. 'Right, why don't we take a quick look at the discovery before the others decide they're ready to fly back to Nuuk?' He nodded towards the group by the helicopter.

It took Malik only seconds to reach the brown bundle on the scarred surface of the ice cap. Matthew approached more slowly with Ulrik. They couldn't see very much of the dead man, but his face and feet were, as Ulrik had said, free from the stiff brown and yellow fur wrapped around him. It was impossible to tell whether the fur had been rolled around his body or whether he had pulled it tight around himself, but they guessed that he was naked beneath it, given that the feet and lower legs sticking out from it were bare. The fur itself seemed fossilised, almost like bronzed turf, the individual hairs having merged over time into a solid mass. The skin on the man's face had shrunk around his skull, and his eyes were long gone. All that remained were two deep hollows in the shrivelled, leathery skin, while his beard still bristled over his chin and halfway up the empty pouches of his cheeks. It was impossible to say whether he had been blond or red-haired, but his hair was definitely not black, and his facial features were far more Nordic than Inuit, so the theory that he was a Norseman seemed solid.

Malik bent over the mummified body with his camera, trying to capture every macabre detail. 'He looks like a tupilak with that demon face.'

The iceman's lips were nothing but two thin lines that had dried up and then pulled away from his jaw. It looked like he had died while grinning—a hysterical, angry grin, which had bared his teeth and torn his lips free from his face.

'Does it get dark out here at night?' Matthew asked.

Ulrik and Malik both looked at him. 'Not really,' Ulrik said. 'The snow lights up everything, and the sun isn't completely gone for very long at this time of the year.'

Matthew nodded. The snow. He had forgotten about that. Even so, he'd rather not sleep out here next to the dead man, no matter how light the night.

Malik had lain down flat on the ice to get a good shot of the iceman's shrivelled feet. He glanced over his shoulder. 'This is pure beef jerky, this is. Yuck, it's gross.' Then he smiled at Matthew, a mischievous look on his face. 'What those feet need is some whale blubber to make them baby-soft again.'

Matthew heaved a sigh and shook his head at his photographer, then headed back to the helicopter.

He stopped when he reached the archaeologists. 'Excuse me. Which one of you is from the museum?'

'I am,' said a middle-aged man of medium build.

Matthew couldn't decide whether he looked more Danish or Greenlandic. Not that it mattered. Genetically, Scandinavians and Inuit had been well and truly mixed up over several centuries.

'Can I ask you a question about the discovery?'

'Yes, of course. This find will give us a great deal to talk about.'

The man raked his fingers through a dense, greying beard. 'There's every sign that this is a unique discovery.'

'Yes, that was my question. Just how unusual is it?'

The man straightened his back. 'As far as I'm aware, no one has ever found a mummified Norseman from the Viking age. Bog finds and skeletons, yes, but none mummified, and that's crucial, because his skin, bones and possibly his stomach contents will have been extremely well preserved.' He paused, but Matthew could see he had more to say. 'Have you heard of Ötzi from the Tyrol? That's how important this discovery could be. The mummy might be a valuable source of knowledge once we open him up. But we need to proceed carefully or vital evidence could be lost. This is an exceptional discovery for Scandinavia, and possibly for the world.'

'So you're sure that he's a Norseman from a Viking settlement in West Greenland?'

'I find it hard to believe otherwise. We haven't collected samples for analysis yet—we need to wait for the police technicians—but I'd expect all our assumptions and theories to be confirmed in due course.'

'You compared him to Ötzi just now—is that because there might be some dramatic reason that he ended up all alone in the crevasse?'

'You're thinking murder, or death in battle?'

'Yes, something like that.'

'I haven't seen any marks on him yet, but we definitely can't rule it out. We know that the Norsemen disappeared completely from their many settlements after living here for about four hundred years, so something drastic must have happened. If this man lived during the Norsemen's last days in Greenland, then injuries from weapons or the contents of his stomach could certainly help explain their fate.'

'So he might have been killed?'

'Yes, he might easily have been killed.'

The sun was still high over the Atlantic when Matthew got back to his apartment. Both he and Malik had headed straight home from the airport to work undisturbed. They had agreed to meet early the next morning, so they could upload Matthew's story and Malik's photographs to *Sermitsiaq*'s website.

As Matthew began writing, he felt his skin tingle. It was a long time since he'd last experienced that sensation. It reminded him of the time he got top marks in his final exams, and when Tine had told him she was pregnant. A sense of being untouchably alive. The feeling was coming back to him now—not as strongly, but it was close. Before noon tomorrow, much of the world would have read his story, or heard about the discovery because of it.

> *THE RESURRECTION OF THE LAST VIKING—A more than 600-year-old Norse Viking emerged from the Greenlandic ice cap this week. His fair hair and a worn reindeer skin were all he had with him after a journey of several centuries. According to archaeologists, the mummified man is in such good condition that he will provide them with crucial information about the lives of the Vikings, and also, more importantly, may help them understand why the Norsemen disappeared from Greenland after having lived there for over four hundred years. Was it war, famine or the harsh conditions that drove them back to more densely populated areas of Scandinavia? And what about the Norsemen who reached North America?*

As soon as he had emailed his story to his editor, Matthew shut the lid of his laptop and flopped back on the sofa. He reached for a plate of crispbread topped with thin sheets of chocolate that he'd prepared before sitting down to write.

Crispbread was one of Tine's things, preferably served with a thick layer of butter and thin sheets of milk chocolate. During the early years of their relationship they would often go bike riding, and Tine would always pack crispbread for their trips. A white manor house had been a favourite destination. They would cycle along a path through the forest and picnic at the far end of the park. Tine rode a green bicycle with a white basket at the front where she kept the crispbread and bottles of water.

The crispbread crunched in his mouth. Dry, soft and sweet. He wished he could tell Tine that he loved her. Properly. Intimacy and openness had never been his strong suit.

6

The wind had changed direction overnight and dense fog had settled over Nuuk in the morning hours. Visibility was down to ten metres. Everything was swallowed up by this grey North Atlantic blanket, whose moist breath licked the houses and the mountains and caused everything to run together in a foggy, cold cloud.

Everything was obscured. Erased. Even the sea and the mountains Matthew could normally see from his flat. He inhaled the smoke from his cigarette deep into his lungs and let it take effect for a few seconds before releasing it into the fog.

When he first arrived in Nuuk, he'd imagined that he would just find himself a place to live. No private rentals had been available, but a company had offered him one of their apartments. It was on the second floor of a grey and yellow block with huge windows. Several items of furniture had been left behind, and he'd quickly decided to stay there as the place had everything he needed and more. There were two bedrooms and a living room with wonderful views over southern Nuuk, the sea and some distant mountains, and it was only a five-minute walk from the city centre.

He flicked away his cigarette butt and watched it fall towards the street, then he took a step back and closed the balcony door before returning to his bed.

He picked up his iPhone from the floor beside him and checked the time. It was only seven-thirty here, but eleven-thirty back home in Denmark. Home. Nuuk was his home now. He had taken the job with *Sermitsiaq* for an indefinite period of time because he had nothing to go home to. He opened his mailbox and skimmed the new emails. He had sent his story to his editor late last night so it could be uploaded early the next morning, once it had been edited.

The reply from his editor was short and to the point:

> Great work, Matthew. I've only changed a few minor things. Get it translated today, upload both the Danish and the Greenlandic version, and don't forget that I also want it uploaded in English today, so we can send links across the world. Tell me you got some good pictures? Please report back when it's online, then I'll take a look at it and send links to the major news agencies.

Matthew opened the edited document and carefully went through the text twice to make sure he hadn't overlooked anything, then he saved the new version and emailed it to the Greenlandic translator.

Then, with some reluctance, he untangled himself from the bedclothes a second time and sat up on the edge of the bed. He reached for his jeans and pulled them on, before going to the bathroom.

The man in the mirror looked exhausted. Pale, skinny and haggard. Coming to Nuuk hadn't put much colour in his cheeks, although the air here was clear and pure like nothing he had ever known. The problem was that he didn't spend enough time outside in it. His cheeks and chin were covered by a fine layer of reddish-blond stubble. He turned his head slightly and craned his neck to examine the stubble under his chin.

Some days his eyes were slate-blue, other days more green, and others again just grey. It depended on the weather, but he had noticed that they were blue more often in Nuuk than at home. He had never seen the blue in his eyes in Denmark in quite the same way. Close to his left pupil was a black dot, which made it look as if his eye had two pupils. He had never seen a doctor about it because his mother had told him that his father's eyes had been the same—it was nothing but a pigmentation error. Tine had called it an extra well in his eye. A place to hide his thoughts.

He had trouble hiding from his thoughts—couldn't hide from them anywhere—but since he'd come to Nuuk, they seemed to come together more easily. He'd started to feel like a human being again, for the first time since the accident. Or something close to human, anyway. He still had trouble sleeping, but it wasn't as bad as it used to be. Last night he'd managed five hours in total, which only six months ago would have been impossible due to the pain in his neck and the gloomy thoughts that refused to leave him alone for more than a few minutes. All that remained were the violent nightmares, some occasional pain and night sweats.

The sound of angry knocking roused him.

'Coming,' he called out and made his way to the front door. 'Malik! What—'

'I've been burgled.'

'Eh? What are you talking about?'

'My studio has been burgled. Everything is gone. The whole bloody lot!'

'Come in,' Matthew said. 'God, I'm so sorry to hear that. I didn't even know that you had a studio.'

An agitated Malik pushed past him and flopped down on the sofa. 'They've taken everything. All of it. My camera, computer… Everything.'

'How is that possible? I thought you kept your gear at home?'

'I do, but I spent the night with my girlfriend, and when I came home this morning…Bang. Gone.'

36

'Are you insured? I know that's not the point, but having the money for new equipment would be a start.'

'Yes, yes, everything's insured. What I want to know is why it was stolen in the first place. They also took all my USB sticks and every single memory card I had lying around. Why would anyone do that?'

Matthew shrugged. 'Have you spoken to the police?'

Malik dismissed the suggestion with a wave of his hand. 'Not yet. Listen to me, Matt, you can't sell stolen goods in Nuuk. Everyone would know it was my camera and my computer, so to get rid of it you'd have to leave town, which means sailing or flying, and you'd have to go a bloody long way to find somebody who doesn't know that stuff belongs to me. Forget it. I'll never see it again.'

'But why would someone take it if they can't sell it? I don't understand.'

'Neither do I. It makes no sense.'

'And the pictures really are gone?'

'Yes, it's all gone. My camera, my computer, my memory cards, photos. Everything.'

'Shit! The story's going up today.' Matthew slowly slid his hands over his face. 'I'll call the editor—there might be time for us to return to the ice and take some new pictures. And you need to call the police to report the theft.'

'Okay,' Malik said. 'Let's just get going. I'll stop off at the police station later.'

7

With a heavy drone from its whirring rotor, the Bell Huey helicopter from Air Greenland chopped its way to the edge of the ice cap.

Apart from the pilot, the passengers were the same four archaeologists, Malik, Matthew and Officer Ottesen, who would be replacing Officer Aqqalu, who had been guarding the mummy overnight. Matthew was sitting on the starboard side of the angular helicopter body, and he could feel the sun roast him through the large, square windows.

Grey-black mountains glided past underneath them in long, serrated, undulating rows. There were still several large patches of snow hiding in the darkness and cold of a gorge, while in other places the mountains were covered by green summer growth. The sea was a brilliant bright blue, speckled with white and turquoise growlers that had broken off the edge of the ice cap at the heart of the fjord.

The helicopter banked to the right, and Matthew's gaze was drawn down towards the shimmering surface of the sea.

'Do you see those two traces in the water right there?' Malik exclaimed, pointing.

'Where there's a little bit of foam?'

'Yes, that's it.' Malik nodded enthusiastically. 'Two whales just came up for air. Humpbacks, I think. They had broad, speckled tails.'

'So they won't be coming back up for a while—is that what you're saying?'

'No, I think they'll reappear a little further down, in the direction of the foam. There aren't any boats around to disturb them.'

The sea turned into sky when the helicopter straightened up. Then mountains and sea once more. They had followed the arm of the fjord most of the way, but now they changed course and were flying across a broad expanse of dark mountains. In front of them the patches of ice grew bigger and more frequent, and the bright white light from the ice cap began to intensify.

'Did you know that the ice cap is bigger than France and the UK together?' Matthew said, without taking his eyes off the window in the side door.

'Really?' Malik said. 'No, I've never heard that.' He had a camera borrowed from the newspaper around his neck.

Matthew turned his attention to the museum curator. 'Do you have more information about the guy who was found? The Norseman?'

The man shook his head. 'No, sadly. We still don't know if he's a Norseman, but I fail to see how he couldn't be. When you find a naked, mummified Scandinavian wrapped in reindeer skin at the very edge of the ice cap, what else could it be?'

'But I thought the ice cap was larger back when the Norsemen were here?'

The curator looked up. 'Yes, it was, and that's what's bothering me. My theory is that there might have been a mountain cabin some-where nearby.'

'But that doesn't change the fact that he was found naked and wrapped in fur in a crevasse...'

'You're still fishing for a violent death?'

Matthew nodded. 'He could easily have been killed fighting an

Inuit, or been chucked into the crevasse as a sacrifice, couldn't he?'

'A human sacrifice that late in the Middle Ages would be atypical, but living conditions were probably extreme in the last few decades the Scandinavians were here, so we can't rule it out.' He combed his dense beard with his fingers. 'When times are hard, people sometimes throw morality and ethics overboard.'

'But what about a battle?'

'You're suggesting he might have been killed by an Inuit?'

'Yes.'

'It just so happens there were no Inuit anywhere in south-west Greenland when the Norsemen arrived, so it was actually their country rather than the Inuit's, but the Norsemen's many trips to the north attracted the Inuit, who began coming south, and so in that respect the Inuit came closer. It's possible that the Inuit developed a taste for the Norsemen's sheep, which were easy to catch and very tasty…so different from the fish and seals which the Inuit had lived on for generations. And yes, it's also possible that it might have been the Inuit who expelled the Norsemen from their settlements.'

'Hang on,' Matthew said, taking out his mobile. 'Let me just make some notes in case we go for that angle…great. Okay, so you're saying that the Danes, who came later, didn't take the land from the Inuit, seeing as the Inuit had themselves stolen it from the Norsemen three hundred years earlier?'

'It's a plausible theory, but we can't prove it. Besides, if I kick you now, it doesn't give you the right to kick me in twenty years, does it?'

'So the Inuit arrived in Greenland *after* the Norsemen, and then *they* wandered down and into the land of the Norsemen?'

'Yes, that part we can prove. It's just the business with battles and wars which is dubious, even though the *Historia Norvegiae* states that Norse hunters came across small men in the north, whom the Norsemen named *skrællinger*, and that these small men got "white wounds" if they were slightly injured, but would bleed violently when fatally wounded.' He gave a light shrug. 'You might well ask yourself why it was so important to pass on to posterity the bit about superficial and fatal injuries, unless it was because it related to battle, especially if we bear in mind that the same passage states that these skrællinger used walrus tusks and sharp stones for weapons.'

'Hello, Ottesen?' The pilot's voice could be heard over the headsets, and attracted everyone's attention. 'Ottesen, could you come over here and take a look? I think we have a problem.'

The three Danish archaeologists started to look around the cabin, whispering and nodding.

'Is something wrong with the engine?' Matthew wondered aloud.

'It's not that,' Malik said quickly. His face was pressed against the window, his eyes aimed in the direction they were flying.

'Then what is it?'

'Look down.'

Matthew was aware of the curator leaning over him to get a look too, and moved his head close to the window. They were near the edge of the glacier. Beneath them the sea was dense with pack ice. In front of them the endless whiteness stretched out as far as the light and the eye could reach. It hurt his eyes. Millions of white crystals. Except in one place. One spot. Right where the Norseman mummy had been found and Aqqalu had kept watch. There the ice was glossy red.

There was silence in the cabin. The only sound was the chop-chop of the rotors.

'Is that...' Matthew's voice trailed off. 'Is that Aqqalu?'

'I know Aqqalu,' Malik stuttered. 'We were at school together.'

'But—'

'I don't know, but who else could it be?'

The curator sank back into his seat. 'Do you think it's him? But what happened?'

'Nanook,' Malik whispered. He didn't take his eyes off the ice beneath them. 'I kept saying I should have played my drum before anyone slept here. You can't just pull an old, dead soul into the light like that.'

'We're landing,' Ottesen's voice announced. 'You all need to stay inside while I get out and secure the area. A Sikorsky will take off from Nuuk in ten minutes and fly here to meet me. You'll stay in this helicopter and be sent back straightaway. Understand?'

Matthew leaned close against the window. The ice was glistening. The red was glistening. Growing. The body of the helicopter turned and prepared to land on the spot where Aqqalu should have been waiting for them. Matthew didn't know whether to look, but when Malik very slowly raised his camera and started pressing the shutter release, he too fixed his eyes on the ice beneath them.

Aqqalu was naked. His clothes had been dumped in a pile not far from his body. He was lying on his back with his arms stretched out to the sides. He had been gutted from his groin to his breastbone. The sides of his stomach had been pulled apart, and were hanging over the ice. His abdominal cavity was black from dried blood, as were his skin and flesh, which were exposed. The bottom of his rib cage shone white amid the darkness and the red. His organs had been ripped out of him and were lying on the ice, while his intestines seemed to be missing completely. There was blood spatter a metre away from the body. In one place several metres.

Malik gulped. 'This was no polar bear.'

The helicopter hit the ice unexpectedly hard, and they all jolted. Matthew's head bumped against the windowpane.

Ottesen jumped out and immediately signalled for the helicopter to take off.

Matthew's gaze settled on the small camp. He turned to the three archaeologists. 'Did you move the mummy yesterday?'

One of them shook his head. 'No.'

'It's gone now,' Matthew said, turning his face back to the cold glass. The red spot underneath them grew smaller and smaller. Aqqalu lay gutted in the middle of it, and Ottesen was kneeling close to him on the red crystals, which only yesterday had been Aqqalu's warm blood.

8

Matthew was at his desk at *Sermitsiaq*, scrolling through Facebook without taking anything in. Less than twenty-four hours ago he had held a global scoop in his hands, only for it to slip through his fingers as it turned into a violent murder.

His iceman article was open on the big screen, while Facebook was up on the smaller screen on his laptop in the docking station, where his mailbox was usually open. The article was ready to be uploaded, but it was impossible now. They had orders not to release any information about the two bodies. Not a single word, no photographs, about the iceman or the murder of Officer Aqqalu. These orders had come from on high, and his editor had stressed that they mustn't compromise the police investigation.

Matthew would still have liked to send his article about the Norseman mummy out into the world, and he had defended his position by saying that the archaeologists and the museum curator could all vouch for the discovery, but it made no difference to his editor. *It's out of my hands, Matt*, he had said. *This is a small community. We have to listen to one another, and right now I'm listening to the people who are trying to find a police killer. If you leak anything*, he had added with a weary look, *then you're finished here.*

Matthew sighed and closed the document with the article. Someone had left a plate with a piece of cake on his desk. A large, stale raspberry slice. The pastry was pale. Just like him. He rubbed his cheek. The stubble scratched his palm. Who the hell would gut a police officer and run off with a mummy? And in a town like Nuuk, of all places. Matthew pushed aside the plate.

Nor could they write about Aqqalu until his family had been informed, and that would apparently take some time, given that his older brothers had gone reindeer hunting somewhere out the back of beyond and wouldn't be home for days.

'Cheer up—it might never happen.'

The editor's voice made Matthew look up. His boss had a habit of pacing up and down between the desks and striking up conversations here and there.

'We'll find a solution, I promise. I'm sorry I came down so hard on you. It's just that…well, when we get orders from above, we tend to listen to them. It's the way things are done around here.'

'It's all right,' Matthew said, looking up at him. His boss was a short man around fifty. Fair-skinned, blond hair and at least twenty kilos heavier than his shirts could easily accommodate. 'What happened to that police officer was just awful. It…he had been gutted.'

'I know. I've never experienced anything like the last twenty-four hours here.' The editor arched his back. His second-last shirt button had come undone, revealing a patch of white skin. 'We'll be able to publish something soon. We just need to wait for the right moment.' He turned to leave, but then he stopped. 'Listen…if you need to talk to a psychologist, I can get hold of one.'

Matthew shook his head. 'No…no, but thank you. I just need to find another story, something else to focus on for a while.'

His editor nodded: 'If you want something to keep you occupied, there were some brutal murders here back in the 1970s that might be worth looking into. It was before my time, obviously, but someone mentioned them to me a few years ago. They've more or less been forgotten. I couldn't find anything much when I looked into them, but the archives are a nightmare up here. Paper only. For every decade you go back, it's actually more like a century. But there's something about the death of Aqqalu that made me think of them again. Check with Leiff downstairs, if he's in. He must have been a very young man back then, but he's been with the newspaper for a hundred years. At least.'

'Leiff? Okay. I'll head down there now and see if there's something in it. If there is, can I write about it?'

'Yes, I should think so. I mean, it's unlikely to create much of a stir after all these years, but if you find some hard evidence it might drag a few skeletons out of the closet and help make your name up here. After all, it's still one of the most violent unsolved murder cases in the Arctic.'

'Thanks,' Matt said. 'I'll head down now and take a look.'

His editor nodded and rubbed one eye. 'Sure, but don't get your hopes up. Sometimes it can be good to just lose yourself in a cold case. That's what I do when I want to take my mind off other things.'

Matthew turned his gaze back to his screen.

His editor patted his shoulder. 'How are things going otherwise? I mean, here in Nuuk?'

'Oh, I'm all right,' Matthew said, glancing up at the chubby man's pale face. 'I take it a day at a time. It's so different here. Amazing landscape.'

'That's good to know. And the apartment is okay?'

'Yes, absolutely. It's great. Thank you.'

'Let me know if you need anything, all right?'

Matthew nodded and grabbed his mouse. He googled the 1970s murders but found nothing, and sighed as he pushed his keyboard away.

If there really had been murders in Nuuk back in the 1970s that bore similarities to what had happened out on the ice, then he wanted to know more—if for no other reason than to have an angle when the time came to write about the murder of Officer Aqqalu.

9

Leiff was on his perch as always. No sooner had Matthew mentioned the murders than Leiff nodded, glanced around and suggested that the two of them go for a walk. That suited Matthew fine. He knew that, whatever Leiff told him, he could only benefit from the older man's years of experience with the newspaper.

Soon afterwards, the two men passed the big, rust-red Tele-Post building, and they continued along past the newest part of Brugseni supermarket. From there they took the pedestrian crossing between the supermarket and Hotel Hans Egede. The sun had moved well over the town and was bouncing off the long row of hotel windows, which flashed gold in the sun.

'When I was ten years old, they built a huge apartment block over there.' Leiff pointed to a large area of wasteland between the city centre and a row of shabby grey residential blocks. 'Ambitions were high—back then it was the biggest housing development in all of Denmark. Two hundred metres long, and with three hundred and twenty apartments. But, as is so often the case, ambitions failed to allow for real life.'

The area was now covered with colourful skateboard tracks, mounds of earth and climbing frames. At the far end were six light-grey housing blocks that had to be nearly as old and shabby as the one that had been demolished. On the end of one of the blocks someone had painted the giant face of a wrinkled, smiling old Inuit in shades of blue, turquoise and grey.

'Many of the families who were moved to Nuuk,' Leiff continued, 'came from small villages, and they never settled in the claustro-phobic apartment blocks miles from where they were born. I think it must be Denmark's most disastrous policy ever, wanting everyone in Greenland to be Danish. The Inuit were used to being at one with nature in their villages. It was where they lived, where they caught their food, where they could breathe freely. They couldn't breathe here, and the idea of living in a box high above the ground was foreign to them. Most people kept their windows open day and night, and some even lit fires in their living rooms. They were refugees in their own country.' He stopped. 'I know you didn't ask about that, but it's all connected.'

'That's all right,' Matthew said. 'I want to know more about Nuuk's history and its people, and nothing beats a guided tour like this…So what happened to the apartment block?'

'Many of the old apartment blocks in Nuuk are still standing, although they're falling apart. They're all numbered, except for the giant that used to be here. It was called Block P, and it became a troubling symbol of Nuuk's problems. It was demolished in 2012, so not all that long ago—but still fifty years too late, in my opinion.' He turned to Matthew. 'Have you had anything to eat today? You look a bit peaky.'

'No, I didn't have time, but it doesn't matter. I want to know how Block P is connected to the murders I asked you about.'

Leiff nodded and pointed to a cafe by Pisifikk supermarket on the corner of Hotel Hans Egede. 'Let's go to Cafe Mamaq.' He scratched his nose. 'It was in the early seventies, I believe…Yes, it must have been, because I turned eighteen that winter, so we're

49

talking late 1973. That was already a year of chaos. Everyone was up in arms about Greenland having to join the European Community as a part of Denmark, and about the oil crisis and everything else that was happening. But the murders still came as a bolt out of the blue, and it traumatised our small community. People were used to violence taking place behind closed doors, not out in the open for all to see. They found four men in their prime, flayed and gutted from their groins to their rib cages...their intestines ripped out of their bodies.' He frowned. 'When I think about it now, it was madness. Only it's so long ago that few people remember.'

'Flayed,' Matthew echoed. His thoughts had screeched to a halt at the word. 'Can you really flay a human being?'

'Well, I didn't see them for myself,' Leiff said. 'But, yes, the rumours were that they'd been flayed. The skin had been removed from their bodies with an ulo—a kind of flensing knife—and then pulled off them. And, like I said, their insides had been cut out.'

'Gutted and cleaned like a hunting trophy,' Matthew said. 'Just like Aqqalu.'

'Exactly, but he wasn't flayed—not as far as I've been told.'

Matthew shook his head. 'No,' he said. 'It didn't look like it.'

'Nor do I think anyone else here has been, since those four men in Block P.' Leiff furrowed his brow. 'But it's a long time ago, and I believe the point of those killings in 1973 was to cover something up.'

'What do you mean?'

'They were never solved, but I think the murders were motivated by revenge.'

'Revenge?'

'Yes, because two girls also went missing in '73.'

'And was this all part of the same investigation? I mean, the one with the dead men?'

'Yes, it was. Two girls aged ten or eleven years, as far as I recall. They were never found.'

'So why did people think the murders were related?'

'Because two of the dead men were the girls' fathers.'

Leiff and Matthew had reached the glass door to Pisifikk and Cafe Mamaq, and Leiff pushed it open. In the doorway Matthew brushed shoulders with a young woman with a shaved head. 'Sorry,' he said, briefly making eye contact with her. He could see no hint of make-up, but she wore an angry scowl. She looked him up and down. Did the same with Leiff. Then she pressed her lips together and marched on without a word.

She was slim and tall, her body sinewy and strong. Her black combat trousers fitted her legs tightly, and ended in a pair of scuffed army boots. She wasn't carrying a jumper or a jacket. She wore only a black sleeveless vest that was even closer-fitting than her trousers. An old rifle with a wooden stock and a telescopic sight was slung over one shoulder. In her right hand she carried an ulo. In her left was a bottle of water.

Matthew looked after her as she disappeared. At her rifle. Her ulo. Her muscles. The colours.

All the skin visible from her neck down was covered by tattoos of flowers and leaves. Not delicate and pretty, but lush and winding. He'd caught a brief glimpse of the soft crooks of her elbows, where on both her right and left arm a set of teeth grew from the deep foliage. Bared, snarling teeth. The size of fingers. Clenched in rage. A frozen, graphic flash of sneering skulls.

'She's something special, ilaa?'

Matthew felt a hand on his shoulder and turned his attention back to Leiff. 'Yes, she...Yes.'

Leiff patted his stomach. 'Right, let's get something to eat. All this running around makes me hungry.'

Matthew nodded slowly. 'I'd like to see the archives after lunch.'

'I'm sure we can work something out.' Leiff put his hand on Matthew's shoulder again. 'I'll show you where they are, but if we're

51

going to rake over this old case, we need to go about it quietly. A brutal murder like this one has only remained unsolved because someone important wanted it that way.'

10

The archives under *Sermitsiaq*'s offices were the darkest rooms Matthew had ever been inside, and he thought he had seen a few. The walls were of dark-grey concrete, and more than anything reminded him of Eastern European archives before the fall of the Berlin Wall. Rows of steel bookcases stood at right angles to the walls.

Leiff had shown him where in the basement he thought the relevant material might be kept—if there was anything at all. There were no records of the files in the basement. Whoever stored something there usually remembered where they had put it, but once that person left the newspaper, their knowledge was lost for good. Leiff had some idea of where the early 1970s files were, but he didn't have time to spend the whole day in the basement, as he had an interview to do. However, he had promised to contact both his wife, who worked at Nuuk Town Hall, and a good friend who worked at the Sana Hospital, to persuade each of them to search their archives for any information about the four murders.

After several unsuccessful hours alone in the basement, Matthew sat down on a pile of newspapers and looked about him with an air of defeat. A bare light bulb glowed above him; there was another closer to the door. Their light hung like yellow clouds of dust in the dry basement air, but further down there was nothing but darkness. He had no idea how far into the darkness the basement extended.

Next to his right foot was a newspaper facing upwards: *Air Greenland expands its fleet from three to eight Sikorsky S-61, and opens new helicopter base in Ammassalik this summer.* His eyes wandered upwards to the date. *May 1972.* He pushed the newspaper aside, reached for another pile and resumed skimming the headlines.

'Oh, no,' he whispered as he opened a newspaper dated 25 October 1973. A Sikorsky helicopter had crashed just south of Nuuk, killing all fifteen people on board.

His head flopped forwards, and he sat resting his elbows on his knees with his face buried in his hands. His fingers smelled of newspaper ink and cold dust. Aqqalu's bloody body haunted his thoughts. The gutted men. The little girls who had gone missing. The helicopter. Tine and the floor of the car. The smells of accident, metal, oil and death.

His world had imploded when Tine and Emily died. It hadn't been particularly eventful before. But without them it was completely dead.

It was a red Mercedes containing four Romanian men. They had overtaken him on a bend, but hadn't pulled out far enough and so collided with his Golf, which was crushed against the tarmac by the Mercedes and flipped off the road and into a field. He had been conscious throughout and felt every blow to his body, neck and face as the car rolled across the ground. His scalp and one hand had been lacerated by shards of glass, although he never knew exactly where it had come from.

He had been bleeding, and had to wipe his face constantly. Tine had been quiet. She hadn't even screamed. Or perhaps she had. It was all a blur until the car stopped rolling. That was when he saw her. Her eyes were open. She was bleeding from her ears. She was trapped. She died.

He had crawled through the window of the damaged front door, found a farm where he had dripped blood all over the floor. He remembered that vividly. And he had seen a horse. A horse in the field where the car was lying. He remembered that. And then the ambulance. The nurse at the hospital, who had picked the broken glass from his scalp without him feeling anything at all, although it had made a crunching sound like when you snap a bone to get at the marrow. He remembered the foam collar around his neck and throat. Tine's silent, grey face during the drive in the ambulance. They had fought to save her while he watched. But her blood had stopped pumping while she was still in the wrecked car. His heart had kept beating, and his wounds bleeding.

Then the darkness arrived. Darkness where every minute felt like a day. Sleepless days, nights tormented by the pain in his neck, which had started a few hours after the accident, never to go away again. The funeral. Months of daily rehabilitation with a physiotherapist. The machine pulling his neck. The warm compresses. Ultrasound. Countless reassurances that he'd be all right eventually.

Matthew took a deep breath and felt the tears running down the palms of his hands. He raised his head and sniffed loudly. The air still felt dry, and his eyes were stinging. He got up and walked down to a new wall of newspapers piled onto the overburdened steel shelving. He lit a cigarette, then picked up a few newspapers, trying to decide where to resume his search.

Having identified and pulled out the relevant piles, he sat down on the floor to go through them. Time passed at a snail's pace, as the cup by his side filled with cigarette butts and soon his head began to ache. Someone really ought to have transferred all the records in the basement to a digital archive, but it seemed a Sisyphean task.

When Leiff returned, Matthew was lying on the floor surrounded by stacks of old newspapers, too many to count, a cigarette dangling from the corner of his mouth. The sudden and unexpected noise from the door made him sit up.

'What time do you call this?' Leiff said with a frown. 'And I'm pretty sure you're not allowed to smoke down here.'

'I haven't checked the time, but I guess it's late,' Matthew croaked, quickly putting out his cigarette. 'I think this is pointless…I'm sorry.'

'Well, I did warn you. But listen, I've had a call from the hospital. They've found the post-mortem reports on all four men, and I persuaded them to scan and email everything to me. I forwarded it all on to you so you could print it out. You didn't pick up when I called you, so I thought I'd better check up on you myself.'

'There's no signal down here, but thanks, that's great news. Besides, I'm done here—my head is heavy from all that dust.'

'Hang on just a minute,' Leiff said. 'I had a peek at the post-mortem reports. Which year have you got there? Seventy-three, is it?'

Matthew looked at the newspaper in his hand and nodded. 'October.'

'You need November. That's when the first victim turned up. But let's get you something to eat. I can't have you stay down here all night. I bet you're thirsty too. My wife's going out tonight, but she's cooked spare ribs, so why don't you have dinner with me? There are too many ribs for one person.'

'Thanks, I'd really like that,' Matthew said. He reached for the cup with the cigarette butts and got up from the floor.

'Matthew Cave—now that's a funny name for a Dane,' Leiff said.

'My father was an American soldier,' Matthew said. 'I got my name from him…along with my quirky eye.'

'What you call quirky sounds shamanic to me,' Leiff said. 'An eye that can see into two worlds.'

'Thanks, but I think it's just a quirky eye.'

'Is that what your father would say?'

Matthew shook his head. 'I don't know. He disappeared shortly after my fourth birthday.'

'Where was he stationed?'

'At the air base in Thule, which is where he met my mother.' Matthew smiled. 'I was actually born in Greenland. Crazy, isn't it?'

'Yes,' Leiff said. 'But you've stirred my curiosity now. I'm like that. Did he stay up here?'

Matthew shrugged. 'I'm not sure. I believe he was in Nuuk at the time, and that he was going to join me and my mother in Denmark, but he never turned up. My mother had no idea what had happened to him, or where he'd gone. It's a big world, I guess.'

'Yes, but Nuuk is a small place. When was this?'

'The last news we had from him was a postcard sent from Nuuk in August 1990.'

'And what was his name?'

'His name?' Matthew hesitated and looked down. 'His name was Thomas. Tom Cave.'

'I love a mystery,' Leiff said. 'Mind if I take a look and see if I can find him?'

'No, I don't. But I doubt he's still alive.'

'You may be right,' Leiff said. 'But let's wait and see. People up here have a habit of disappearing, but they pretty much always turn up again.'

11

The body of Ari Rossing Lynge was discovered on Tuesday last week, but Godthåb Police have only now released the information to the press. *Sermitsiaq* has learned that his death was particularly brutal: Rossing Lynge was murdered and then gutted as if he were prey. Here at *Sermitsiaq* we have decided not to go into further detail, but on behalf of Godthåb Police we have agreed to report this killing, as well as two similar killings in Block P. Godthåb Police urge anyone with information to contribute to the case to get in touch with them. Please contact Jakob Pedersen at the Godthåb police station. We are publishing the full names of the three murdered men, along with pictures taken of them while they were alive.

Matthew put the article on the coffee table and reached for the post-mortem reports. After dinner with Leiff, he had returned to the basement and spent most of the night tracking down the relevant issues of the paper. He had eventually managed to compile all of November 1973, then he brought the papers home with him in the early morning hours when he had started to tire.

There were four post-mortem reports, but only three victims were mentioned in the newspaper article he'd found. The last man had been killed after the article was published.

He arranged the reports side by side on the coffee table. Four men. Three of them had a face. Matthew marked any recurring words in the reports with a yellow highlighter, trying to form an image of the victims in his mind's eye.

The men were all Greenlandic and had lived in Block P. They were aged between thirty and forty years, and there was no mention of any unusual features. They were, he presumed, men who had grown up in Inuit villages and spent more time hunting and fishing than going to school. Nor was there anything unusual about the men's height and chest measurements. They were smaller than your average Danish man, but that was to be expected.

Only the manner of the men's deaths was remarkable. All four had been flayed and gutted from the groin to the breastbone, and their insides cut from their body with a sharp tool—an ulo, according to the police investigation. So the intestines hadn't been ripped from their bodies, but cut free.

In the final report, which had been requested by a different police officer to the first three, several observations were listed. On closer examination, there was evidence that the last two victims had had a soft object stuffed into their mouths during the attacks. The earlier victims could not be examined for similar evidence as they had already been cremated. Further examination of the last two victims also suggested that the men had been gutted and had several of their internal organs removed while they were still alive. The skin, however, had definitely been flayed from their bodies after the intestines had been cut out.

His mobile buzzed and Matthew quickly answered it.

'Sounds like there might be a witness to the killing on the ice cap,' his editor said. 'Seeing as you were out there, I thought you might be interested.'

'What do you have in mind?'

'I want you to find him and hear what he has to say. He's a fisherman, and as far as I can gather he saw a man come ashore early this morning, covered in blood and carrying a black sack.'

'And where will I find him?'

'I believe he called the police while he was still at sea, but his boat will dock in about an hour. It's down by the little harbour behind the public swimming pool. Could you check it out? Not many boats come in there, so you can't miss him.'

Matthew rang off, got up and opened the balcony door while he lit a cigarette. A cool mist brushed his face and naked upper body before finding its way deep into his lungs. The fog came and went between the buildings.

He placed both hands on his stomach. The cigarette dangled from the corner of his mouth. He frowned, then went inside to the kitchen, pulled out the top drawer and brought a chef's knife back to the balcony. He closed his eyes and concentrated as he rested the tip of the knife just below his rib cage. Then he trailed the knife softly over his belly in one slow movement.

'What the fuck do you think you're doing? Have you gone completely mental?'

'Shit,' Matthew muttered and slipped the hand with the knife behind his back. The voice belonged to Malik. Matthew took the cigarette out of his mouth. 'I was just trying something out,' he called down towards the road, where Malik was staring up at him.

'Seeing as you live in a country with the world's highest suicide rate, could you not stand there wearing next to nothing and waving a knife around?' Malik called back, craning his neck to get a better view of the second-floor balcony.

Matthew shook his head. 'Sorry...Why don't you come upstairs and I'll tell you all about it?'

'No, get yourself down here now. You're coming with me. Some fishermen have found a body in the water out between the islands, and they think it's been dead for quite some time.'

12

The two men drove to the Atlantic Port in Malik's old Honda, which was in reasonable shape even if the exhaust fumes were practically black. Then again, the car didn't have too many miles on it, as Malik only drove around Nuuk, and the short distance out to Qinngorput, where his girlfriend lived. If you wanted to go further than the rocky outskirts of Nuuk, you had to leave your car on the last patch of tarmac, ice or gravel and make your way on foot or by boat. No roads led out of Nuuk. No roads led into it. This applied to every town in Greenland. Nuuk was Nuuk, and the only thing surrounding the town and its sixteen thousand residents was mountains, sky or sea.

'So do you know anything more about this body?' Matthew asked as he got out of the car.

Malik took the key out of the ignition and shook his head. 'No. Let's go find out.'

Matthew reached a hand behind his neck, grabbed his jaw and wrenched it back until it cracked.

Malik grimaced. 'That can't be good for you.'

'It loosens things up.'

'Oh, crap! The fog is coming back already.' Malik nodded towards the sea, where the fog had built up so densely that only the odd mountaintop could be made out. The sea had pretty much disappeared again.

'It seems to roll in from nowhere,' Matthew said.

Malik grinned. 'It's the sea breathing.' He raised a hand to his chest and inhaled deeply. 'In fifteen minutes, it might be completely clear again or the whole town could be invisible. It depends on her breathing.'

'Who?' Matthew said. 'The sea?'

'Yes, the mother of the sea.'

'The same mother who's pleased if you chop off your fingers so they can become seals?'

'Yes,' Malik said with a smile. 'That's one way of putting it, though that's not really the point of the story. It's more about how if you sacrifice something to nature, it comes back to you. In the myth you're talking about, fingers come back as seals.'

'So a hunter sacrifices his surplus to the sea—is that it?'

'Not everyone does it, but yes, it's always wise to sacrifice something you don't need. It goes against our culture and our respect for all living things to let anything go to waste.'

'Including intestines?' Matthew ventured.

'Yes. Say you kill a seal. You toss the intestines into the sea so the fish or the birds can eat them.' Malik looked at Matthew with a puzzled expression. 'But why would you ask that?'

'Four men were killed here in Nuuk in the 1970s, and when they were found, their intestines had been dumped next to their bodies. Perhaps a Greenlander would have done it differently?'

'I don't know,' Malik said. 'It's always possible, I guess, but I've got no idea what it means when you kill people like that.'

Matthew stared at the grey tarmac. 'Have you heard more about yesterday's killing?'

'Yes,' Malik said. He fished out his cigarettes and offered one to Matthew in silence.

Matthew took a cigarette and lit it. 'We don't have to talk about it, if you don't want to.'

'It's okay...He'd been gutted, we all saw that, but...' Malik stopped and closed his eyes. 'His intestines were actually missing.'

Matthew shuddered. 'We may have a witness, but I don't know much about him yet. My editor called to tell me just before you turned up.' Matthew took a long drag on his cigarette and looked at Malik, hesitant. 'Did you notice anything about his skin? Yesterday, out on the ice?'

'What do you mean?' Malik frowned.

'Those men back in the 1970s had been flayed...It was just a thought.'

Malik shook his head. 'That's sick.'

The sound of a car diverted them from their grim thoughts, and a big dark-blue four-wheel drive pulled up next to Malik's Honda. The police officer behind the wheel called something in Greenlandic through his open window. Malik replied, gesturing towards the fog across the sea a few times. The driver turned the engine off, and the two officers stepped out onto the quay. They greeted Malik and Matthew with a nod, and continued talking to Malik. One of them was Ottesen.

'They say the boat will be here in a few minutes,' Malik told Matthew, and beckoned him closer. 'The fishermen are too scared to look inside the black bag they've found, so it might be a false alarm. It might just be the remains from a hunting trip. A hunter wanted to tip something into the sea, say, but accidentally dropped the whole bag. Anyway, the fishermen are a bit freaked out because they're convinced it's a dead man.'

'Is it all right if we tag along?'

'Yes, I don't think the officers mind, or they'd have said.' Malik straightened up and raised his head. 'That'll be the boat now.'

Matthew fixed his gaze on the grey mass across the sea. He

couldn't hear anything, but a few minutes later the bow of a blue and white wooden boat ploughed its way through the fog in a long, smooth movement, cleaving it in two. The fog was so thick that they could see it peeling back against either side of the boat's hull.

There was a hollow thud as the boat docked. The two officers approached it.

'Let's follow,' Malik said, nodding towards the boat.

Three men were waiting on the deck. One of them called out to the officers, throwing his hands up in the air.

'He says they want to get back out as quickly as possible,' Malik translated. 'He thinks the dead body's spirit will curse their haul.' He pointed to the older police officer. 'Ottesen told him that was a load of rubbish, and they should just chuck the sack ashore, but they're refusing to even touch it, so now Ottesen and Minik are having to board the boat to get it.' Malik dropped his cigarette butt and squashed it under his boot. 'Bertelsen, one of the guys on the boat, is shit-scared of spirits.'

Both officers jumped on board, and Malik waved Matthew even closer. 'Come on—I want to see what's going on.'

Bertelsen called out again to the two officers.

Malik stopped. 'He says he doesn't want them to open the sack on the boat, so they're going to have to bring it ashore before they look inside.'

Ottesen bent down and picked up something they couldn't see from the quay. Shortly afterwards he called to his colleague.

'The sack doesn't seem all that heavy,' Malik said. 'He says that if it contains a dead body, it's likely to be a child.'

The sun had come out again and swathed the whole harbour in a blinding light. The fog kept to the sea for now.

The black plastic sack was wet and glossy in Ottesen's arms as he stepped back onto the quay. Malik took out his camera.

'Are you going to take pictures?' Matthew asked.

'Sure,' Malik said, then he hesitated. 'But not if it's a kid, obviously.'

Matthew fell silent, his fingers twirling the invisible wedding band. 'I'll be in the car,' he said, without looking at Malik.

'Eh? I thought you wanted to—'

But Matt had slammed the car door shut behind him before Malik could finish his question.

A red Dash-7 aircraft swept across the sea not far from them. The planes were waiting for breaks in the fog. Malik went to join the policemen.

From the car, Matthew couldn't see what was going on, but he saw the three men flinch as the bag was opened. An animated Malik ran back towards the car, beckoning insistently.

Matthew nodded, got out of the car and reluctantly went to join the others.

'It's insane,' Malik called. 'I've never seen a guy that rotten before. I nearly puked my guts out. You won't believe it. He fucking stinks.'

'Something doesn't add up,' Ottesen said when Matthew and Malik reached him. 'The plastic sack looks new.'

Matthew pinched his nose and struggled to control his stomach. The body had been gutted and the man's rotting organs stank, but he hadn't been flayed. The decomposing organs were fresh—but the skin was like tanned yellow leather.

Matthew drew Malik aside. 'I'm glad they've already called for a pathologist,' he said quietly. 'This is our mummy from the ice cap, only someone tried to get rid of him by throwing him in the sea.'

'What?' Malik leaned forward. 'Yes, you're right. That's him. But then why—' His eyes moved to the mass lying on the tarmac: a brown, greasy liver, two kidneys, a heart, lungs and intestines. Then he turned around and threw up. He slumped to his knees and kept retching in long spasms.

Matthew looked at Ottesen, struggling to put his suspicions into words. 'I'm sorry, I don't know how to say it…but I think the organs belong to your colleague, Officer Aqqalu.'

13

The road behind the public swimming pool was made up largely of potholes and granite chips. Several old dinghies lay scattered between the road and the bay. Sport fishermen would dock here when they had been out at sea.

Matthew expelled the smoke hard between his lips, and watched it disperse in the fog. His gaze scanned the small bay and continued down the arm of the fjord separating Nuussuaq from Qinngorput. Qinngorput wasn't far away, but the fog blocked his view of the buildings there.

He crossed a gravelled area where some boats had been pulled ashore. Two of them would definitely never go to sea again, while the other three looked in reasonable shape. A blue boilersuit on a coathanger was hanging from the gunwale of a boat, making it look as if an invisible man was standing next to the hull.

His mobile rang and he answered it. 'Matt, it's me,' his editor said. 'Have you reached the harbour yet?'

'Yes, I've just got here.' Matthew took another look around the small bay. 'There's no one here. Did you get my message about the sack that the police opened over at the Atlantic Port?'

'Certainly did. What a story. I can't make sense of it, but you just stick with it.' His editor hesitated for a moment. 'Don't forget, though, we can't write about it yet.'

'It'll leak out eventually,' Matthew argued. 'You can't keep things secret for very long up here.'

'Once it leaks, we'll leak with it, Matt,' his editor said. 'You've got a couple of stories ready to go, haven't you?'

'Yes, we're good to go.'

'Great.'

'This boat I'm supposed to be looking for,' Matthew said. 'Is it open or does it have a wheelhouse?'

'A wheelhouse, I guess. Perhaps he's not back yet? Are the police there?'

'No. I reckon they're still busy with the…black plastic sack.'

'All right. You find that fisherman and get him to tell you what he saw. I'm told he didn't see the killer's face, but he did see the boat the bloodstained man came ashore in, and he'll be able to identify it. You should be able to get something out of him. Keep at it, eh, Matt.'

There were only two boats with wheelhouses in the bay. One was about twenty metres out in the water, and the other very close to the shore. There was no way he could reach the one in the water without access to another boat.

The second boat lay near the low rocks. Matthew could hear it scrape against them, a grating, almost mournful sound. The waves were small, yet lively enough to cause the boat to bob up and down.

Matthew grabbed a rope hanging over the bow of the boat. He could see no signs that the boat was moored to the shore or that its anchor had been dropped. It was simply chafing against the rocks. When the tide turned, the boat would be carried out to sea in no time.

'Hello?' he called out, putting both hands on the gunwale. He tried calling out again, this time in Greenlandic. 'Halu?'

Matthew looked about him. There wasn't a soul to be seen who could help him. He managed to haul himself over the gunwale and roll onto the small deck.

'Halu?' he called out again tentatively. 'Is anyone here?'

Slowly he edged his way past the small wheelhouse in the middle of the boat. There was barely enough room to squeeze past it, and he would never have dared try this manoeuvre on the open sea. The waters around Greenland were so cold all year round that you would go into shock and die within minutes of falling in.

'Hello? Anyone here? I'm just visiting, all right? I'm looking for a witness who saw something this morning.' He hesitated, then continued cautiously, 'I'm working with the police. There's nothing to worry about. Officer Ottesen will be here in a moment.' That last bit was just a guess.

Carefully, he pressed down the handle to the small wheelhouse. The door opened with a click. He hesitated again before pushing it open. The room behind it was dark. Because the fog was so dense today, the portholes didn't let much light into the hull.

'Halu? Anyone here?'

He could smell fish and engine oil in the dark cabin. He made out some tins to one side, and a couple of half-full fish crates on the other. That didn't leave much floor space. He nudged the top crate. It was mostly cod and redfish, and none of it had been covered with ice, despite the fish being gutted and cleaned. There was a puddle of fish guts and blood on the floor by a tall cupboard jerry-built from masonite.

'Why would you abandon your catch?' Matthew mumbled to himself. 'Fish need to be kept cold, don't they?' He looked dubiously at the puddle of fish guts at his feet. He was baffled as to why the fisherman hadn't gutted his fish outside. Surely cleaning the wheel-house floor would create much more work for him than simply hosing down the deck?

A big wave jolted the boat, which crashed against the rocks. At the same time Matthew heard a bump from inside the cupboard. He looked down at the pink fish blood at the toes of his shoes. Then another wave hit, the cupboard flew open, and a short, heavy-set man lunged at him. They both crashed to the floor, knocking over a crate and scattering fish everywhere.

Matthew shouted and lashed out, pushing the man off him, and he didn't stop yelling until he had scrambled back to the door, where he collapsed. His hands, trousers and jumper were covered in blood. The man was lying on his back between the fish. He had been cut open from his groin to his chest. Just like the fish, he had been gutted.

14

There was a hiss as Malik flipped the cap off the bottle and handed the beer to Ottesen. By now there were quite a few empty bottles on the table in front of them. Malik had insisted that they needed sustenance so they had ended up getting a crate of beer and three large pizzas from Cafe Prego before returning to Matthew's apartment.

They had spent most of the evening discussing Aqqalu and the fisherman. Both were dead—killed and mutilated.

'This is my last one,' Ottesen stated firmly as he took the bottle. 'I'm not usually much of a drinker, but today I really needed a beer.'

Malik raised his own beer to his lips. 'It's just insane. The mummy, me being burgled, the murders…and Aqqalu.'

'Promise me you'll never board a boat on your own again,' Ottesen told Matthew, closing the lid on his empty pizza box. 'Anything could have happened.'

'How was I to know a dead man would fall out of the cupboard?' Matthew replied.

'Well, that's just it,' Ottesen grunted. 'Do you know who tipped off your editor?'

'No,' Matthew said. 'I was just told to investigate, but believe me,

I wish I'd never set foot on that boat.'

Ottesen took another swig of his beer. 'Still, I'm glad you called me straightaway.'

'I'm going outside for a cigarette,' Malik said, getting up. 'Are you coming, Matt?'

Matthew shook his head. 'Not right now.'

Ottesen picked up the printouts of the post-mortem reports, the notes and the newspaper cuttings from the coffee table and looked across at Matthew. 'May I?'

'Knock yourself out. It's an old case my editor suggested I look into.'

Ottesen skimmed the pages, nodding lightly. 'I know about this case.' He looked up. 'Four men flayed and cut open from their groins to their chests.'

'And now we have another two,' Matthew said, 'except that they weren't flayed.'

'True,' Ottesen said. 'But they're very different cases. The murders in '73 were of four very similar men with almost identical backgrounds. Our two victims are a police officer who was guarding a mummy and a fisherman who knew something about the murder of the police officer. Two very different men.'

'Sounds like you know the '73 case well?'

'Of course I do. They were the most brutal murders Nuuk had ever seen, and the killer was never caught.'

'Did the police have any idea who did it?'

'They certainly had a suspect, who went missing the same night that the last murder took place, but whether he did it I'm not sure. Not everyone thought he was guilty—that much I do know.' He put down the papers. 'Listen, we need an investigative consultant at the police station. Are you interested?'

'Isn't that a job for a police officer?'

'Normally, yes, but we've advertised the post for six months and haven't had a single suitable applicant. It's often like this up here, I'm afraid.'

'Sorry,' Matthew mumbled. 'But I don't think that's a job for me.'

'Never mind—it was just a suggestion. No harm in asking, is there? I think we could do with someone whose approach is different from ours.'

Matthew shook his head.

'Well, think about it,' Ottesen said, getting up from his chair. 'And let me know if you find out anything about the '73 murders. They baffled the police throughout all of Denmark at the time.'

'I promise,' Matthew said, looking at the papers on the coffee table. 'But there's not a lot to go on.'

'No, I agree, there isn't,' Ottesen said, and waved goodbye through the glass door to Malik on the balcony. 'I'd better be heading home,' he called. 'See you soon.' He turned back to Matthew. 'By the way, what's your surname? I need it for my report about the man you found today, and I didn't get all your details when we met down by the boat.'

Matthew hesitated. 'Cave. My father was an American soldier based in Thule.'

Ottesen raised his eyebrows. 'Matthew Cave. Right, catch you later. You take care, Matt Cave.'

The sun was in the sky above the sea and the mountains as he left, though twilight was falling. Nuuk still enjoyed many hours of daylight in August, but in just a few months the darkness would be so intense that the sun would come out only for a few hours each day.

'So Ottesen's headed home,' Malik said when he came back inside.

Matthew nodded. 'He wanted to hire me as a consultant.'

'Hah, he's always trying to hire people. Sounds like a boring job, doesn't it?'

'Probably.' Matthew looked down at the bottle in his hand. 'It's seven per cent alcohol. This…Musk Ox beer.'

Malik had flopped onto the black recliner. 'Did you know that the musk ox is a goat?'

'A goat?'

'Yes, it's a big, fat goat hidden underneath the most incredible fur.' He rolled onto his side. 'What happened today in the Atlantic Port? When you hid in the car?'

'Nothing. I just didn't want to see the body.' Matthew drained his beer and dropped his cigarette butt into the bottle. 'I knew I wouldn't be able to cope if it turned out to be a child.'

'No, they say that's the worst.'

The room fell silent.

'How old was your child?' Malik tried tentatively.

'My wife was six months pregnant when the accident happened. They both died.' Matthew slumped. 'They asked me if I wanted to see my little girl, but she was dead, wasn't she.' It was as if the falling darkness had crawled inside the living room and was now enveloping him. 'I had felt her moving in Tine's belly. Her kicks. What use would it be to see her dead? That wouldn't be the person I had been talking to and cared about.' Matthew's voice had grown weaker, until it was nothing but a whisper.

'Do you know something?' Malik said. 'I think everything has a soul. I think we can be together both before and after life, if our bond is strong enough.'

Matthew pushed himself up off the sofa. 'I'm going for a piss.'

THE
WOMAN

15

Matthew was deep into a complex and chaotic nightmare when his mobile started ringing. Without opening his eyes he found his phone and pressed the screen to take the call. 'Hello?' he grunted, hoarse and distant, as he pushed aside the sweaty bedclothes.

'Matthew, can you hear me? When might we have the honour of your company?'

The words snatched him brutally from the last remnants of sleep. His editor. The newspaper. Malik and the beers. His mouth tasted of stale alcohol and smoke. 'I'm on my way. I...I overslept. What time is it?'

'It's only just gone nine, but I want you to stop by the hospital because I've got news about your iceman. Turns out he's not an ancient mummy after all. Lots of things didn't add up once he'd been rehydrated, like a piece of dried fish. The preliminary analysis shows that he's only been dead about forty years.'

'Shit,' Matthew muttered. 'That's that story down the toilet.'

'I'm afraid so, but it could turn out to be another kind of news, so let's wait and see. Besides, we have the two murders to cover.' The editor was quiet for a moment. 'Could you stop by the police station as well? They've arrested somebody for the murder of both men.'

'Are you serious?'

'A young woman. A loner. Shaved head and tattoos. She's just been released from prison. She did twelve years for manslaughter.'

Matthew's hand with the mobile flopped onto the mattress.

'Are you still there?' his editor said. 'Can you check it out?'

'Yeah, sure. I'm leaving now.'

16

Just after midday Matthew and Malik walked up the steps to the Nuuk police station. Matthew hoped they would leave with more information than they had when they'd called in at the hospital earlier that day.

Their visit had lasted a couple of hours, but they had little to show for it. They had learned that the iceman had been dead for only forty years, rather than six hundred, but apart from that there wasn't much news. The precise year of the mummy's death had yet to be established, as had his age and nationality, but he was Caucasian, probably Nordic.

The man had been cut open and his guts removed; Matthew had already observed this for himself down at the Atlantic Port, because the salt water had loosened the animal fur in which he had been wrapped. In contrast to the four murdered men from 1973, this man's intestines were missing completely, and he still had his skin, so even if there was a connection to the other murders, there were things that didn't add up. The mummified man was also the only one whose body had been moved and hidden soon after death; in 1973 the victims had been left in situ after their violent deaths, as if for some grisly display.

Matthew grabbed a handle on one of the double doors and pulled it open. 'I'm pretty sure we're wasting our time here as well,' he told Malik wearily. 'They're never going to tell us anything about a suspect they've just arrested for the murder of one of their own.'

'We'll get something, don't you worry. I'll just ask for Ulrik.'

Matthew nodded and wandered over to a noticeboard covered with leaflets and posters. He still wasn't able to write about the murder of Officer Aqqalu, and the whole business with the iceman was so bizarre and confusing that it would take a miracle to get an actual story out of it—at least until he knew more about the dead man than he did now.

Malik soon returned. 'We're out of luck. Ulrik appears to be off sick today.'

Matthew nodded. 'That doesn't surprise me. He's had a rough few days.'

'He's not normally such a wuss,' Malik said. 'But you're probably right. He'll need to man up if he wants to climb the greasy pole as far as Lyberth has.' He looked towards the door leading to the offices. 'Ottesen will be out in a moment, though. They told me he has something for us.'

'For us?'

'Yes, I asked yesterday if he knew anything about those gruesome murders back in the seventies. I guess it must be about that.' Malik walked up to a vending machine. 'Fancy a brew?'

'No, thanks, and definitely not coffee.'

'I think I'll have a hot chocolate.' Malik sounded undecided.

'I still think I'll pass,' Matthew said. His thoughts felt muddled. About the 1970s case, the mummy, even the hot chocolate. But it was the woman who had been arrested for the murder of Aqqalu he couldn't stop thinking about.

'Oh, shit…'

Matthew looked at Malik, who was flapping one hand in the air while holding a steaming cup in the other.

Malik smiled towards the woman behind the reception counter. 'I'm sorry, but this hot chocolate is really…well, hot.' His face contorted in a grimace of apology. 'Sorry.'

The door to their left opened and Ottesen appeared. 'Hi, guys, good to see you again. This way, please.'

They walked down a short corridor to an office.

'I'm glad you're here because I've come across something you might want to take a closer look at.' Ottesen produced a brown leather notebook from a buff envelope and placed it on the desk between them. 'I was in our archives earlier, and I found quite a lot about the murders from 1973, but I can't give you access to our files because some of the information relates to people who are still alive. Relatives, witnesses and so on.'

'Of course,' Matthew said.

'But I found this,' Ottesen continued. 'It wasn't filed as a part of the report or logged as evidence or anything like that. It's a private diary.' He leaned forward. 'It contains notes on the case, but nothing official. It's just one man's thoughts, interspersed with various obser-vations about nature and life in Nuuk in 1973.'

Ottesen slid the notebook towards Matthew, who opened it care-fully and flicked through it. All the pages were yellow and densely covered with pencil.

'Just pop it back in the envelope before you go, will you?' Ottesen said. Then he added: 'I can't wait to see what you're made of, Matt.'

'Thanks,' Matthew said, his voice uncertain. 'Who's the author?'

Ottesen glanced towards the door, then looked back at Matthew with a determined expression. 'His name was Jakob Pedersen. He was one of the first police officers to investigate sexual assaults of girls up here. I think he'd worked on similar cases in Denmark, because men with that sick urge are found all over the world. Jakob became obsessed with the case of the men who were cut open, but he disappeared without a trace at the same time the murders stopped.'

Matthew tapped the notebook a couple of times, nodding to himself. 'Thank you so much.'

'You're welcome, but you didn't get it from me. I don't care what you do with it or what you have to say about it. Only you didn't get the information from this building—are we clear?'

'Of course,' Matthew said. 'I'll invent a source. An uncle or something. But can I ask you about the woman you've arrested in connection with the current case?'

Ottesen got up. 'There's nothing to tell.' The others took their cue from him and stood up too. Malik shook his hand and said something in Greenlandic. Ottesen's reply was brief.

Back at reception, Matthew stopped in his tracks. The woman he had bumped into outside Cafe Mamaq was standing at the counter. She was wearing the same tight black clothing. The same scuffed boots. The tattoos wound their way up and down her arms, over what he could see of her back and around her neck. Her head was just as smooth as the first time he'd seen her, only this time she wasn't armed.

Matthew tugged Ottesen's arm. 'I'm sorry—who is she?'

'Her?' Ottesen said. 'She's the woman you were just asking about. We arrested her in connection with the killing on the ice cap, but we had no evidence against her except her past, and the items we confiscated turned out to be clean.' He shrugged in exasperation. 'She's a wild animal. I'd like to keep her here but I can't, and she seems to know the law inside out.'

He said something in Greenlandic loud enough for the woman to hear. She didn't look up, but Matthew could tell from her back that she had heard it.

Ottesen fixed his eyes on Matthew's. 'If anyone asks, you came here today to talk to me about her, and I told you that you can't write anything yet. That's it.'

The woman disappeared through the door, showing absolutely no sign of acknowledging them, yet Matthew was convinced that she had noted every feature on their faces. He felt as if she'd looked inside him and penetrated his thoughts.

'Who is she?' he asked again.

'Her name is Tupaarnaq Siegstad,' Ottesen replied. He sighed. 'She's been in the care of Danish Social Services and the Prison Service ever since she shot and killed her mother and her two younger sisters and stabbed her father to death at the age of fifteen. They say she just sat in the middle of the carnage, covered in blood, clutching her mother's ulo. She had pretty much ripped out her father's guts. That's why we brought her in. She only moved back to Greenland a week ago, straight from serving a long sentence in Denmark. Oh, and one of the first things she did when she returned to Nuuk was to buy a rifle and an ulo.'

'Did she kill her family here in Nuuk?' Matthew asked.

Ottesen shook his head. 'No, that was in Tasiilaq, on the east coast. Her father had shot a polar bear three days earlier. I don't know why I remember that bit. He'd also shot a walrus that same month. He was something of a local hero over there. A highly respected hunter and fisherman who ignored quotas and restrictions. Then again, global warming is a far greater threat to polar bears and walruses than hunters are.' He shrugged. 'Anyway, I've got work to do.'

They said goodbye to Ottesen and left through the doors in the middle of the long, black and brown building.

'What did Ottesen say just as Tupaarnaq left?' Matthew wanted to know.

'That it was a woman who had injured Ulrik during an arrest, but they'd had to let her go.'

Matthew frowned. 'Injured? How?'

'Search me,' Malik said, throwing up his hands. 'I think he only said it so that she would hear it.'

Matthew nodded.

'Do you want a lift home?' Malik offered.

'No, I'm happy to walk.' Matthew's eyes followed Tupaarnaq Siegstad down the street. Her back was straight, her footsteps hard and firm. He shook his head. 'I need to get a couple of things over at the Nuuk Centre.'

'Okay, I'll see you tomorrow, then. You take care, won't you?'

'Yes, you too…Oh, hang on. What did you ask Ottesen about when we were in his office?'

'I asked him why he gave us the notebook.'

Matthew looked at him quizzically. 'And?'

'He said, "Karlo was my father."'

'Karlo?'

'Yes, Karlo. Apparently he's mentioned in the notebook.'

17

As soon as Malik had left, Matthew tried to catch up with Tupaarnaq. She walked briskly and steadily, her stride long and determined. Even from a distance he could sense how hard her heels hit the road.

She had a jumper tied round her waist. The rays of the sun played with the colours of her tattoos.

She turned down the road that led to the apartments on the edge of the headland. To their left was a series of more modern, six-storey blocks with impressive, colourful decorations the full height of the buildings, while to their right, where the rocks sloped steeply down to the icy waters of the North Atlantic, lay clusters of wooden houses of various colours, sizes and shapes.

Matthew was forced to jog to get closer to her. He was well aware that his noisy footsteps had long since given him away and she knew she was being followed. Her back spoke its own language. Everything she didn't show or say was expressed through its muscles and movements. It listened. It watched. He guessed that the tattoos also covered the skin under the black clothing. Perhaps not a single inch of her body was free from the chokehold of the plants.

The road ended abruptly after a few hundred metres, but Tupaarnaq carried on across the glittering blue-grey rocks and the tufts of grass between them. The sun was low in the sky, and Matthew watched his own shadow jump from rock to rock.

The two long housing blocks at the edge of the headland were shabby, bordering on derelict. The facades were patchy and stained from decades of neglect. A scaffold-like structure of concrete, red-painted wood and iron railings ran alongside each block, providing every apartment with its own narrow balcony. These blocks stood in stark contrast to the new ones further up the road, where everything was attractive and beautifully maintained. These dying buildings were known as Blocks 16 and 17, and Matthew remembered reading about several violent incidents here. Fires and a murder in 2013, when a young man was thrown from Block 17 and broken by the bedrock in front of it.

Tupaarnaq walked on across the rocks. Her stride had grown longer and more aggressive. Then she stopped and turned around. She wasn't very far from Matthew. She stared right into him.

'Tupaarnaq?' he asked tentatively, to break the awkward silence and to give himself a vague alibi. *If all else fails*, his editor always said, *just play the dumb Dane.*

Tupaarnaq was still silent, but she continued to stare at him. Her face was tilted slightly forwards.

He didn't look away, although he desperately wanted to. He had such a powerful urge to look at her, and yet at the same time couldn't bear to.

She stepped towards him. 'You reek of man,' she said angrily. 'Get lost, you disgusting pig.'

'My name is Matthew,' he began. 'I work for *Sermitsiaq* and I'm investigating an old case where some men were murdered and cut up with an ulo.'

Her eyes burned into his; the feeling was so intense that he could no longer keep his eyes fixed on hers. His gaze drifted over her face, over the pale freckles around her nose and on her cheeks. Her eyes were not black, but brown. A shade of brown so deep that, up close, they gleamed like polished teak with a hint of gold.

'Why are you telling me that?' Her voice was low—it felt as if it were crawling along the ground and wrapping itself around his legs.

'Because…'

The corner of her mouth twitched briefly. 'Tell me,' she snarled.

'Because you know what happens when a man is killed with such a knife.' His thoughts stumbled over one another. 'How long it takes him to die. The agony.'

In a flash, she reached out and pinched the sinew stretching from his neck down to his left shoulder. He slumped to his knees instantly, his face contorted in pain. Her fingers dug into his flesh.

'I damaged my neck in an accident,' he managed to croak.

She merely tightened her grip in response. The muscles in her arm tensed all the way to her shoulder and across the sinews of her neck before she released him.

He curled up, then, after a moment, rested one hand on the ground and tried to push himself up.

'This conversation is over,' she snapped, yet she stayed where she was, watching him as he struggled to a sitting position. 'You dropped your notebook,' she added, nudging it towards him with the toe of her boot.

'Take a look at it,' he said, his voice still strangled.

She hesitated, but turned her gaze from him to the brown notebook on the ground beside him. 'Why?'

'A police officer here investigated four murders committed with an ulo. He ended up being the prime suspect, and then disappeared into thin air. I'm wondering if it's his body that has just been found on the ice cap—if he was murdered too.'

She pressed her lips together and inhaled deep into her lungs. Then she leaned forward and picked up the notebook. 'Four unsolved murders,' she whispered to herself. Carefully she opened the notebook, and her fingers trailed its pages as she skimmed them, pausing at certain sections. 'Read it yourself, and you'll find your killer.'

Matthew looked up at her in surprise. 'What do you mean?'

'I know who did it,' she said, tossing the book down to him. She turned around and started to leave.

'Wait,' Matthew called out. 'Will I see you again?'

'Maybe.' Her back did the talking. Her face was done with him for today.

He watched her walk to the corner of Block 17, where she disappeared behind the grey and white concrete. Shortly afterwards, she reappeared on a second-floor balcony. She didn't look at him. Only at the sea.

Matthew fished out his cigarettes from his jeans pocket and lit one. The first drags were long and deep, until he started to calm down. Tupaarnaq was no longer on her balcony. His gaze scanned the rocks and then the sea. It travelled as far as the mountain peaks several kilometres away. Then he looked down at the notebook and placed his hand on its ageing cover. His fingers crawled right to the edge and under the leather.

18

He began by skimming through the notebook. Every now and then he would look up towards the balcony where Tupaarnaq had been standing.

The contents were as Ottesen had described them: one man's private scribbles about the cases he had worked on, and the landscape and culture that surrounded him in early 1970s Nuuk—which back then was always referred to by its Danish name, Godthåb.

Jakob Pedersen had several theories about the killings, and gave detailed descriptions of the way each murder had been executed: where the intestines were, and how the injuries had been inflicted. At the very back a large drawing had been glued in place. Before it were some pages written in another hand.

There were several short lists dotted around the notebook; one of four male names caught Matthew's attention. Each man's age and address were listed next to his name, and a little further down was the name of a girl, whose age was also listed. All the girls were under twelve. The obvious conclusion was that two of the girls were the ones Leiff had mentioned. The ones who were never seen again. The names of the four men matched those in the post-mortem reports, and the three in the November 1973 newspaper article.

One page in the notebook was mostly blank, except for these words:

A box was left outside my home tonight. After the rock was thrown through my window, I think. It contained a projector and some film reels. I have viewed the first two.

That was all. There were two marks that looked as if they had been made with the point of a pencil, as if Jakob Pedersen had wanted to write more, but couldn't.

However, there were also several other pages that Jakob had covered densely from top to bottom with beautiful, poetic thoughts and observations about nature. The more Matthew read, the keener he became to know more about the author of the diary.

I have lived here once. In this place. Drawn every breath of the North Atlantic air and sought refuge in a stone cottage—half buried in the ground with grass growing across its roof. I have lived here once. Slept under heavy blankets and furs. Felt the cold dance on my face and sear my lungs, spreading to every fibre of my body. I have lived here once. Lived with a new god in my thoughts, but with the words of the old gods pulsating in my veins. I have lived here once—marked by nature's toughness. Allowed myself to be shaped by the wind, the breeze and the frost. Loved the mountains and the sea because they were my body and my blood. Loved the fog because it was my breath. Loved the cold because it was the grey and blue colours of my eyes and the soaring wings of the soul. I have lived here. I live here.

Matthew flicked back to the list of the four men and the names of the girls. The girls had to be their daughters, if Leiff's comments about sexual abuse were to be believed. The men had to be those mentioned in the newspaper and the post-mortem reports, and there was also something about two of the daughters that hinted at a link. Jakob had put a cross and a question mark next to the name of the first victim's daughter, Najak Rossing Lynge, which made Matthew wonder if Jakob had had his doubts about whether or not the girl was in fact dead. There were no marks by the names of the next two victims' daughters, while a small heart had been drawn beside the last one, Paneeraq Poulsen. There was nothing by the men's names.

Matthew's fingers found the final page, and carefully unfolded the drawing. In the background were two sombre, slate-grey mountains, and between their round, worn peaks a sky of grey clouds, with the odd long streak of a delicate, endless turquoise. A porous fog floated over the blue and black sea at the foot of the mountains, a third peak erupting through the mist from the dark grave of the deep. It wasn't a mountain like the others, though. It was a woman. Her shoulders lay beneath the mirror of the sea, but she was visible from her collarbones up. Her neck was arched, and her head leaning backwards, exposing her throat. Her blue-black hair flowed like wide rivers from her head and merged with the sea, right where the tops of her shoulders could be made out as they broke the surface. Her eyes were two bottomless wells, and her lips as black as her eyes. Her skin glowed grey and yellow, like smoke. She looked like a craggy mountain. Like a dead body found in the icy sea. But she was alive. At the bottom right-hand corner, someone had written *Najak*.

Matthew massaged his sore shoulder gently and glanced up at the deserted balcony, the girl's name echoing in his thoughts. He put down the notebook, pulled his woollen jumper over his head and made a pillow of it against the rock so that he'd be more comfortable while reading the notebook properly from the start. He would have to delve right down between each line to get to the bottom of Jakob's life and musings, and rather than go home or to the newspaper office, he might as well do it while sitting here in the sun.

BREATHING
ICE

19

'There's a well-known saying that a fairy is born whenever a child laughs, and yet few of you know what happens when an angel cries. But I do because I've seen it. Whenever the tears of an angel touch a newborn child, that child becomes special. The angel cries because it knows that this child's life will be so hard that the child is unlikely to survive. So the angel weeps its strength and love into the tender soul, grafting the divine power of love into the infant. A power that will one day lead that poor, damaged child from the darkness and into a brighter life.'

Jakob looked up from his folded hands as the vicar's words pierced his tired mind and demanded his attention. Rarely had the vicar's sermon been so true and so pertinent to his own life. He was up to his neck in damaged children, and yet he rarely saw them.

He took his eyes off the vicar and looked up at the wooden ceiling of the Church of Our Saviour in Kolonihavnen. The vicar knew the truth, as did Jakob. Knew without a shadow of a doubt what it was like for the children here. For the girls. The girls suffered the most.

Jakob stood up and sat down automatically as the vicar spoke. He let the last hymn seep out between his lips without singing the words.

•

Outside the red wooden church the snow was falling heavily, but not a breath of wind was stirring. Godthåb was already covered in a thick, white blanket.

Jakob turned his face towards the city, obscured by grey fog, and shook thousands of soft snowflakes off himself. His skin tingled every time a snowflake landed on it. He pressed his eyes shut and took a deep breath. The air felt cold. Alive.

Two days earlier he had been summoned to the first murder. *You can deal with it, Pedersen*, the chief of police had told him, and Jakob hadn't minded. No one else had thought it warranted much attention. *Probably just a couple of drunken locals having a go at each other*, Benno had piped up, shaking his head. *Let them sort it out among themselves. They always do.*

But there had been more to it, and Jakob had had a bad feeling from the moment he learned the name and address of the deceased.

The man they found in the apartment had been cut open from his groin to his chest, and the skin had been flayed from his body. His guts were spilling onto the floor around him, not in a neat pile but spread out like a halo, the intestines circling his body. His skin was missing from the scene, and so far they had had no luck finding it.

Lying next to him they had found an ulo: a crescent-shaped flensing knife used by the local women to scrape the blubber from the inside of a sealskin. Jakob had picked up the knife and immediately knew it was the murder weapon. The raw, undulating cuts to the man's tissue and muscles made that clear. This bloodstained ulo had been plunged into him and cut him up so badly that his insides could be ripped free and pulled from his body. It was a brutal execution, like something from the darkest years of the Middle Ages, a time when removing the skin and disembowelling a person still alive was a favoured method of torture.

Jakob had brought Karlo Lange, a Greenlandic colleague, to the crime scene. Karlo was one of the few police officers who took his job seriously and genuinely cared about the lives and the safety of all residents in the district. The two men had quickly agreed that the killer had to be a man. Although the ulo was traditionally used by women, there was a rage and a force to the killing that they couldn't see coming from a woman—and besides, a Greenlandic woman would never dare commit so violent an act as to cut open a man.

I think, Karlo had said, *that it was probably a confrontation between local men, but it's certainly not just another stabbing. I've never in all my life heard of someone up here gutting another human being as though he were an animal.* And then he had added something to which Jakob had paid extra attention: *You must remember that we never kill an animal except when we have to. We only kill what we eat and need. We respect the creatures around us and we apologise whenever we take a life. Even that of a fish. This killing hasn't been followed by an apology.*

But no matter how disturbing that might be, it wasn't the most distressing aspect of the case as far as Jakob was concerned.

Just under a week ago, Jakob and Karlo had visited the very same apartment, and had filled in a survey together with the parents and their eleven-year-old daughter. Now the girl was missing. She wasn't at home. She wasn't at school. She wasn't in the neighbourhood. She appeared to have vanished into thin air. They had fifty volunteers out looking for her all over Nuuk and in the surrounding area, but they had found no trace of her. The police had even dispatched a helicopter, but the girl had proved impossible to find. The heavy snow and sparse daylight didn't help.

20

The moment Jakob turned up at the station the next day, he was summoned by Mr Mortensen, the chief of police, whose office, as always, was foggy with grey smoke from the cigars in the ashtray on his desk near the room's only window.

'Pedersen, God damn you,' Mortensen grunted. 'What have you got us mixed up in this time?'

'I don't quite follow...Good morning, sir.'

'And good morning to you too. They've found another one. Another dead man. His skin gone and his stomach cut open. This is turning into a real mess. And it's not for this sort of thing that we're up here, is it?'

Jakob picked at one of his shirt buttons, not sure how he was supposed to respond.

'Don't just stand there fidgeting, man. Do something!' Mortensen slid a piece of paper across his desk towards Jakob. 'It's Block P— again. Here's the address.'

Jakob picked up the note and stuffed it into his trouser pocket.

'Take Karlo. He understands all that local hullabaloo. Now get out of here. One skinned and gutted man we can handle, but two? Whatever next?'

'I'll handle it, sir. If the two deaths are connected, we'll know and we'll intensify our search for the killer.' He hesitated. 'Any news about the missing girl? Najak?'

Mortensen shook his head. 'I'm afraid not.'

'But we'll dispatch people to look for her again today, won't we?'

The fat, balding man nodded and picked up one of his stumpy cigars from the ashtray. 'Yes. Of course. I'll see to it.'

Mortensen had come from Horsens, a provincial town in Denmark where he'd been a superintendent, before ending up in Godthåb as chief of police.

'Get out of here,' Mortensen growled, and puffed on his cigar, smoke trailing down his chin like heavy evening clouds over a mountain range. 'I'll have the bloody mayor and the provincial council on my back before the day is over.'

•

Less than thirty minutes later Jakob and Karlo had reached Block P, where, as expected, a crowd of locals had gathered outside one of the stairwells in the long concrete building.

Karlo led the way and told the onlookers, whose number included young children with grimy faces and big black eyes, as well as toothless old women and men, that they needed to keep back. When that didn't have the desired effect, he added that the killer was still at large and might summon evil spirits from the underground.

Whether it was his words about the killer or the bit about the evil spirits that made the dark eyes and red cheeks disperse and seek refuge behind posts, doors and curtains, Jakob couldn't tell, but scatter they did. Karlo pressed on, taking long strides up the steps to the apartment where the new victim had been found.

He swore loudly the moment he went through the door. Jakob was close behind him. The living room seemed filled with dark shadows and deep, brief cries, as if they were being attacked by demons, but it took Jakob only seconds to realise that it was just a couple of black ravens flitting around the room. Karlo was trying to shoo them out. The birds seemed angry, but Karlo managed to herd them out of the open windows.

'Bloody birds,' an agitated Karlo yelled across Store Slette. 'Who leaves their windows open in this weather?' He shook his head.

'Perhaps the killer let the ravens in?' Jakob ventured.

'Perhaps,' Karlo said. 'But I don't think so. It's just so typical. Many of the residents don't understand these big apartment blocks. My grandmother lives here, and she often has the heating on full blast in the living room while leaving all the windows open.' He shook his head again and closed one of the windows. 'I've told her that it's stupid and a waste of money, but she just says that she misses the feel of the wind and the scent of the sea, which always came into her house back in the village. Here the walls are too thick and solid.'

All this time Jakob's gaze was fixed on the flayed body on the floor. It was a Greenlandic male, like the one they had found yesterday. Muscles, sinews and fat glistened through membranes of congealed blood.

'He was killed in the same manner,' Jakob said quietly, and he squatted down on his haunches next to the mutilated corpse. He carefully placed his fingertips on the man's exposed chest muscle. 'He hasn't been dead for very long.'

'He's been cut open just like the other one,' Karlo said. 'But this is messier.'

'I think we can blame the birds for that,' Jakob said, picking up an ulo. It was smeared with a red and brown substance. 'My guess is that the intestines were laid out as they were with the first victim, until the ravens helped themselves.'

Karlo straightened up and looked around the living room. 'So we've got our very own Jack the Ripper.'

'We might have.' Jakob put down the ulo. 'Except Jack the Ripper's victims were women. But it's true he cut open their stomachs and took out their intestines.'

Karlo knelt down by the bloody corpse too, slowly nodding to himself. 'Whoever did this knew what he was doing. This skin wasn't pulled off or hacked off by some amateur.' He looked at Jakob. 'This man's skin was removed by someone who has been doing it for years. It's routine work. Smooth, clean cuts. If we had the skin, I'm sure we would find that it was intact and without holes. Ready to be tanned.' He looked down. 'Pardon my choice of words, but that's what it looks like.'

Jakob felt a shiver down his spine. The skinless face stared at him. The bared teeth. The holes that had once been the nose. The big, staring eyes. 'It's all right,' he said. 'But isn't it unusual for a hunter to be that good at skinning?'

Karlo nodded. 'It is. Every hunter knows how to do it, but most regard it as women's work.'

Jakob sighed. 'So all this was done by a steady hand, someone completely unaffected by death?'

'I wouldn't know about that,' Karlo said. 'But it's good, solid work. They've even left the skin behind on the victim's hands and feet.' He looked at Jakob again. 'When this man was flayed, he was nothing but a dead seal in the killer's hands.'

Jakob was still staring at the corpse's raw face. 'When we leave, would you please ask if anyone has seen this man's daughter today?'

Karlo got up from the floor and nodded. 'As far as I know, the rest of the family is with one of the wife's sisters. She lives right over there, in Block 6. I can follow it up if you want me to?'

'Yes, please, and I'll deal with the report.' Jakob looked through the windows across Store Slette, which was not only covered by snow, but also hidden by heavy clouds and shadows from the feeble setting sun.

21

The aroma of freshly brewed coffee spread like life in a fjord valley in the summer. Jakob looked up from his report and spotted Lisbeth, who had just entered with a tray filled with steaming mugs.

'I thought you boys could do with some afternoon coffee—am I right?'

Jakob looked around. There were five of them in the office. Him, Karlo, Benno, Fransen and Storm. A couple of the others had gone out with the police boat, and one was dealing with a domestic dispute at one of the blocks.

As always, Benno jumped up like a peacock when Lisbeth entered the room, but she was rarely impressed by his preening. Her trips always ended at Jakob's desk, after she'd cut Benno down to size with a few cheeky but devastating remarks.

The mugs disappeared from the tray one after the other. Benno took his with a grunt and rolled closer to his desk. Jakob heard him say something to Storm about the snow outside his apartment.

'Fancy a brew?'

Lisbeth's voice was very close. Jakob looked up and into her hazel eyes. She had an oval face with pale freckles, most of them dotted across her small nose and round cheeks. He reached out his hand and took the last mug.

'I've added a dash of milk,' she said, 'just the way you like it.'

'Thank you,' he muttered, embarrassed.

She placed her hand on his shoulder and leaned over him so that her lips were close to his ear. 'I brought in a cake as well, but don't tell the others or there'll be a stampede.'

Jakob smiled bashfully and stared down at his desk.

Karlo nodded in Lisbeth's direction as she disappeared out of the door, the tray dangling beside her leg. 'I think you have an admirer.'

'Er, it's just...just coffee and cake,' Jakob stuttered, raking a hand through his hair. 'No, it's—'

'We have a saying up here: a woman like that will keep you warmer than ten reindeer skins on a cold winter's night.'

Jakob stared at Karlo with a frown. Benno sniggered.

'Thank you, that'll do,' Jakob said firmly, drumming his fingers on his finished report. 'I think I'll take this to the boss.'

●

After Jakob had briefed the chief of police on the facts about the two violent deaths that had occurred only a day or so apart in one of the city's less desirable neighbourhoods, he walked down to the small sand and rock beach by Kolonihavnen, where a couple of growlers had washed ashore. It was a little outside the season for that, yet here they were, glistening in the twilight.

Not far from him, an old Inuit was playing a traditional qilaat drum, shifting his weight from foot to foot, his upper body swaying. He was standing on a rock worn smooth and stripy by the forces of the sea. The old man held his flat, round drum in one hand and beat it with the palm of the other while singing his mournful, quiet prayer across the icy, charcoal-grey sea.

Jakob looked away from the drumming dancer and placed his

hand on the growler in front of him. Its chill instantly penetrated deep inside his skin. He was mesmerised by the drumming and the singing.

A hundred thousand years ago, the water that now made up the core of this huge block of ice had fallen as the softest snow over an as yet unnamed Greenland. In time the snow had been compressed into the hardest ice, pure and beautiful like nothing else.

'If you breathe on the ice, you can feel it breathe back.'

The voice had come out of nowhere, and it was not until then that Jakob realised that the singing and drumming had stopped. He turned around and looked into the eyes of the Inuit man who had sung to the sea.

The old man nodded his head at the enormous growler in front of them. 'Try it!'

Jakob took a hesitant step forwards and moved his lips close to the ice. He exhaled deeply, and felt in that same moment an icy breath reach out for his face. He exhaled again and closed his eyes. The ice was alive just as as he was.

'It's the breath of life,' the old Inuit said.

Jakob turned and looked at him again. He was at least a head shorter than Jakob. His face was brown and wrinkled, like a prune, while his eyes were alive and seemingly bottomless.

'Do you mind me asking who you were playing for?' Jakob said.

The old man grinned from ear to ear, revealing stumpy teeth. 'For the ice there,' he said. 'For the sea. The mountains. For all the life that surrounds us.'

Jakob's gaze shifted across the water.

'Your soul is troubled,' the old man said, putting his hand on Jakob's arm. Jakob looked down at the wrinkled hand, the size of a child's.

'I'm a police officer,' he sighed, shaking his head. 'So many ugly things go on behind closed doors in this town.'

'Yes, I know,' the old man said softly. 'I also know where you will find your demon, but you need to think very carefully whether catching it is the right thing to do. Demons aren't released without good reason.'

22

The heavy snow had come early, and the ice had taken hold long ago. First all the little brooks, then the faster-flowing waterfalls. They all froze from the outside in, and for a long time you could see and hear the water still running underneath—sometimes like babbling little melodies, which occasionally found their way up through a hole and spewed bubbles of freezing water across the ice, and sometimes as wild, whirling currents that carried off stones and gravel underneath the crystal-clear surface of the ice.

In one place the frost had taken the water so completely by surprise that it looked as if several waterfalls on their way down the tall mountainside had frozen mid-flow. Even the foam on the water had frozen, the knobbly bubbles reflecting the sun's rays like thousands of crystal prisms in an old chandelier.

Jakob was sitting on a rock, gazing across Kolonihavnen. In his hands he held his small brown notebook and a yellow pencil.

He and Karlo had recently visited every household in Block P, on the pretext of carrying out a survey of children's school habits. It was just a cover, but even so, such data gathering wasn't really a job for the police. Three hundred and twenty apartments. School-age children didn't live in all of them, of course, but as there was no register of the residents, they had no choice but to knock on every single door. Jakob and Karlo had suspected child abuse in forty-three apartments. In four of them there wasn't the shadow of a doubt.

Jakob had made a list of the fathers in the forty-three apartments, and recorded the names and ages of any young daughters living at the same address. In addition, he had written down the names of the four worst offenders in his private notebook. Two of these men were the two victims they had found killed—the first one only a few days after Jakob and Karlo had shared the results of their survey at the police station, to Mortensen's immense irritation. *We're not going to get involved in this, Pedersen,* his boss had declared. *You don't have any evidence. If we jailed anyone we didn't like the look of up here, everyone in this godforsaken place would be behind bars.* Karlo just stared at the floor, but Lisbeth from reception had marched out of the room. Later, she had come over to Jakob's desk and nodded affirmatively at his list of names. Her eyes had been as sad as those of the girls he had seen in Block P.

Jakob shook his head. Now two men had been killed, and an eleven-year-old girl was missing. If they had got involved sooner, perhaps it wouldn't have happened.

23

Jakob woke up abruptly from a dream so distressing he'd almost fallen out of bed.

He staggered from the bedroom and into the living room, where he flopped into a deep velvet armchair that had been there when he moved in. He gazed out of the large windows that overlooked the bedrock between his house and the next. There were no gardens in Godthåb. All that grew here was grass, tundra flowers, dwarf willow and arctic angelica—short things.

His breath formed a faint cloud in the air. There had to be something wrong with the heating. It had never worked at night in the living room, and the closer they got to the darkest time of the year, the more he felt the cold force its way through the wooden walls of the house, as if the frost and the arctic wind were trying to eat the wood, chew it up with their toothless but steadily grinding jaws.

His hands found a glass and a bottle. He poured some and sniffed at it. Johnnie Walker. Red label.

He opened his notebook and started jotting down his dream, but meandering thoughts soon took over, and before he knew it an hour had passed. As he shut his notebook, he heard a strange sound and thought he saw a shadow glide past the windows. It could have been any number of things, of course. Except that no one in their right mind would be outside at this time on a winter night. He heaved a sigh, put down his notebook and got up to check the windows. There were no streetlights, but the moon had found a way through the clouds, and its glow lit up the snow, giving him a clear view of the nearby houses.

He shook his head, despairing at himself. The town was just as dead as the grass under the snow. Then he narrowed his eyes. A shadow had appeared on the wall of the neighbouring house. He stepped closer to the window to get a better look. At that moment the shadow stepped away from the wall, and moved towards him. Jakob was startled. He took a few steps back and squinted again, but only caught a fluttering movement a short distance from the house before he heard the glass splinter and felt a hard blow to his face. He slumped to his knees. Blood started pouring down his face, and he touched his forehead, confused. On the floor was a lump of rough granite, the size of a fist, with a note tied around it. He pressed one hand against his bleeding forehead and made his way to the broken window to look outside, but the shadowy figure had gone.

He staggered to the kitchen, turned on the light and wrapped a tea towel around his head to stop the bleeding, but he wasn't entirely successful. He needed to see a doctor and get seen to. If he could get hold of a doctor, that is. Even thinking about it was exhausting, so instead he picked up the rock and the note, returned to his armchair and collapsed back into it.

Mind your own business or she is done for.

'Who is *she*?' he muttered to himself. Who on earth would write such a thing? The note fell from his hands and floated to the floor. He loosened the tea towel and dipped one end of it in his whisky. Then he pressed the wet fabric against his injured forehead, letting the alcohol seep into the wound. It stung so fiercely that he could barely sit still. He got up and walked over to the broken window. He could feel the frost reaching out for him.

The wound was throbbing, but the worst of the bleeding had now stopped. He poured himself another large Johnnie Walker, and this time he knocked it back in four big mouthfuls that almost made him gag. But he kept it down and sank deep into the armchair, breathing heavily. He pulled a woollen blanket over himself.

24

'What the hell is this? Hello! Hello! Pedersen, what the hell do you think you're doing?'

Bit by bit the words made their way to Jakob, together with the sound of crunching glass. It sounded like a distant scattering of ice.

'Jakob? Are you all right?' The voice belonged to Karlo. 'You look terrible. What happened? Can you hear me? Jakob?'

Jakob opened his eyes, but he struggled to gather his thoughts. His temples were throbbing, as was his forehead. His mouth and throat tasted of iron and alcohol. He was shaking violently all over, and not a single sound escaped his lips.

'Sir, would you fetch some more blankets?' Karlo said. 'And make some coffee right away.'

Mortensen was about to bridle at the bossy tone from his Greenlandic junior, an officer of the lowest rank, but when he saw Karlo strip down to his underwear and climb under the blanket to join the near-naked Pedersen, he understood the gravity of the situation, fetched some extra blankets and made some coffee.

Jakob felt the heat from Karlo's body and his hands rubbing his skin. Slowly, he regained enough control over his own hands that he could sip some coffee from the cup Mortensen was holding to his lips.

'I can't leave you alone for a single minute,' Mortensen growled.

Jakob looked up at his boss's round, balding head. In many ways it had all been worth it just to see Karlo order the boss around. He smiled. His fingers clutched the cup.

'What happened?' Mortensen demanded.

'There was a man outside my window last night,' Jakob stammered. His head was pounding, and his body was still stiff after being so close to hypothermia. 'He threw a rock through my window with a threat. It hit my head, but I don't think that was part of his plan, because I was standing here in total darkness.' Jakob took a big gulp of the steaming coffee. 'I ended up in this chair, and I tried to clean my wound with whisky.'

Mortensen patted him lightly on top of the blanket. 'Right. Let's take the note to the station and see if it tells us anything.' He looked about the living room. 'And I'll get a couple of men to tidy up this mess for you.' He turned back to Jakob. 'This *she* the note refers to— do we know who *she* is?'

Jakob shook his head. 'I've no clear idea. Najak, possibly. But no, I don't know.'

Mortensen nodded. 'Apart from that wound, are you fit for duty?'

'I think it's best that I stay here today,' Jakob said.

Mortensen clenched his teeth and looked at Karlo. His chubby fingers patted the pockets of his long, beige coat.

'What's wrong?' Jakob asked.

Mortensen produced a packet of cheroots from his inside pocket, and turned to Jakob.

Karlo took over. 'There's been another murder. Another man was killed and left in exactly the same way.'

Jakob closed his eyes. 'What was his name?'

'Anders Umerineq.'

Now only one of the four men on Jakob's list was still alive.

'In that case I'm coming,' he said, struggling out from under the blankets.

'Are you sure?' Karlo asked as Jakob put his clothes back on. 'You look like you need a trip to the hospital.'

'If Pedersen says he's ready, he's ready,' Mortensen grunted. 'I haven't got time to run around Block P.' He heaved a sigh. 'This is the third brutal murder, and I've no doubt that the mayor, the chairman of the provincial council and the idiot chairman of the Home Rule Committee have been ringing my office nonstop in the last hour while I've been out. These bloody murders.'

Jakob wrapped the blanket around himself and disappeared into the bathroom.

'We'll deal with it, sir,' Karlo said.

'I bloody well hope so, Lange,' Mortensen growled, and took a deep drag of his cheroot, letting the rich smoke glide around his tongue and the roof of his mouth. 'Do you think the rock and the note have something to do with the murders?'

Karlo looked at the rock, then at Mortensen. 'I do, sir.'

Mortensen raised an eyebrow and looked at the young Greenlandic police officer. 'And what might that connection be, Lange?'

Karlo steeled himself. 'I'm thinking it might have something to do with child abuse, sir.'

'Ah,' Mortensen snorted as he walked over to Jakob's dining table and studied the almost finished jigsaw puzzle there. 'All those visits to Block P that I never approved.' The fingers on his left hand tapped the jigsaw puzzle box. 'This education survey the two of you have carried out here in Godthåb.'

Karlo look at his boots, and then at the jigsaw puzzle. On the lid under Mortensen's fingers it said *Godthåb*. 'I don't think so,' he mumbled to himself. 'It might be some Scottish or Norwegian town, but it's definitely not Godthåb.'

Mortensen turned and walked back to the armchair where Jakob had been sitting. He dropped the butt of his cheroot into the empty whisky glass. 'I don't want to hear another word about that survey... from anyone.'

'I'm ready,' Jakob called out as he reappeared. He smoothed his brown tweed jacket and gave his tie an extra tug at the knot.

'Glad to hear it,' Mortensen said. He glanced at the gash on Jakob's forehead. 'That really needs stitching, though I'm guessing it's a bit late now.'

Jakob gave a light shrug.

'It'll leave you with a lasting memory,' Mortensen said, and he clapped his hands. 'Are you good to go?'

Jakob nodded. 'I'm ready, sir. Lange and I will take it from here. You go back to the station. I'll just take a couple of painkillers, and we'll be at the crime scene in a few minutes.'

Mortensen left, grumbling as he went about the amount of snow on the slope leading to Jakob's house.

'Sit down for a moment, will you?' Jakob said, pointing to the dining room chair next to where Karlo was standing. 'I just need to get some painkillers from the bathroom.'

Karlo nodded and sat down on the wicker seat, and then looked around the room. There were two tall wooden candleholders, a small blue porcelain cat and a rubber tree on the windowsill. The window was framed by curtains of some sort of velvety material, dark red with broad lilac stripes. Over the sofa was a big painting of a fjord on a late autumn day, and there were several wooden masks, tupilaks and rock samples on the furniture and the shelves. An old harpoon made of wood and iron was mounted on the wall over the sideboard by the dining table. Karlo strolled over to take another look at the puzzle.

'I've put in some more pieces in your jigsaw,' he said when Jakob returned.

'Oh, that was here when I moved in,' Jakob replied.

Karlo looked up with a smile. 'It's almost done now.'

Jakob smiled back. 'Pretty much all the stuff was here when I moved in. A couple called the Hemplers used to live here. They were killed when that Catalina crashed into the sea during a landing in '64.' He looked around. 'I haven't changed it much. If they came back, I bet even they couldn't tell the difference.' He turned to the bookcase and picked up a delicate porous stone. 'Except for all the geological specimens. I'm the rock collector.'

'I think you've gathered one too many,' Karlo said, nodding towards the rock that had been thrown through the window.

'I don't believe it was meant to hurt me,' Jakob said, slipping an arm into the sleeve of his warm coat. 'If it was, I'd be on the floor right now with my stomach cut open.'

'You're probably right about that,' Karlo said, looking at the gash on Jakob's forehead.

Jakob pointed to a half-open cardboard box by the door to the hall. 'Did you bring that?'

'That box?'

'Yes.'

'No, it was on your doorstep.' Karlo shrugged. 'I thought it was yours.'

Jakob walked over to it and pushed one of the flaps aside. 'A film projector.' He looked back at Karlo. 'I've never seen it before in my life.'

'It was just sitting there.'

Jakob frowned. 'There's no film. Only an empty reel.'

'How odd.'

Jakob nodded. 'I'll keep hold of it. Maybe the owner will turn up.'

WHISPERING
SEA

25

High above Block 17, the sun was halfway through its journey to the mountains on the far side of the cold fjords.

Matthew put down the notebook and rubbed the corners of his eyes with one hand, while the fingers of his other hand sank into the ground underneath him. The scent was alive, spruce-like and sharp.

A world of dwarf plants was hidden among the rocks. Grasses, crowberries, blueberries, thyme, dwarf willow, yellow lichen and small arctic flowers crawled densely in and out of every crevice, like a soft, prickly quilt covering the rock. Sometimes the growth was so deep and springy that his feet sank into it as he walked; in other places it was merely a thin membrane, adapted to survive the long, harsh winter.

His fingers closed around a tiny flower made up of even tinier flowers, the size of pinheads, each complete with pink petals and a yellow stigma. Somewhere in his notebook Jakob had described such a flower. Maybe not quite the same one, but it was close.

Matthew took out his mobile and pressed Malik's number.

'We need to rattle some cages,' he said the moment Malik picked up. 'Are you able to set up a meeting for me with Jørgen Emil Lyberth? Tell him that I've found Jakob Pedersen's private diary from the winter of '73. That should do it.' He hung up.

A shadow broke the light around him. 'You still here?'

Matthew turned his head towards the voice, which he recognised immediately. Tupaarnaq's face and body were in deep shade with the sun behind her.

'Have you found your killer?'

He shook his head.

'You will.'

She stepped out of the shadows and became a living woman, her gaze so intense that he had to look away. She had scattering of light brown freckles—one on her nose looked like a heart. She held a laptop.

'Where are you going?' he asked tentatively.

'To pick up my stuff from the police before they close for the day.'

He nodded and pressed his lips together, then said: 'I'm heading the same way. Can I walk with you?'

'That's up to you,' she said, and stepped past him.

Matthew grabbed his jumper and Jakob's notebook as he rose to follow her. Her movements were calm. Not quick and angry, like earlier. 'I need to speak to Lyberth,' he said.

'Why?'

'I think he's one of the big villains in all of this,' Matthew said, holding up the notebook.

'They won't like that at the top. One of their national father figures with his dick buried in little girls.' She shook her head. 'Ah, well. He wouldn't be the first politician here who can't keep his dick in his pants.'

Matthew felt a tingling under his skin. 'I've let him know that I have this notebook.'

Tupaarnaq glanced at Matthew. 'Then you'd better start looking over your shoulder.' She let out a deep sigh. 'Bunch of bastards. All of them.'

Her footsteps were angry again, but she wasn't walking any faster. Her heels just hit the tarmac harder.

They reached the new, fashionable apartment blocks not far from the police station.

'Why did you buy a gun when you came back?' he asked, not daring to look at her.

'So I could go seal hunting.'

'Just like that?'

'Yes, just like that. Surely it's better than hunting men?'

There was no challenge, no aggression in her voice. It was a statement. Nothing more. Gutting a seal was certainly better than gutting a man.

They followed the road around the corner, where Tuapannguit and Kuussuaq streets meet. Mount Ukkusissat loomed far off on the horizon between the houses in midtown, the Nuuk Centre and Nuussuaq. Back in Jakob's day, Mount Ukkusissat had been known by its Danish name, Store Malene.

'I'd like to hike up there one day,' Matthew said, pointing towards the mountain. There were a few patches of snow on the peak. From this distance they looked like frozen puddles, but up close they were probably several hundred metres long.

'Then do.'

'I don't know the way. And I've been told that you should always hike in pairs…for safety.'

'Okay…and when you eat something, do you also have someone watching you in case you choke?'

'Eh?'

She shook her head. 'It'll take you a couple of hours, max, to reach the top from the city centre, so if you want to go there, then do it. It's as simple as that.'

She sounded impatient, but he noticed her footsteps had grown quiet again. 'Are there any seals near where you live?' he asked her.

'Yes, but when I go hunting I'll take a boat, so I can get away for a bit.'

Matthew's eyebrows shot up. 'You have a boat?'

'Tell me, just how thick are you?'

'But you just said—'

'I'll borrow one and then I'll return it. You're really not from around here, are you.'

'I've been here two months.'

'Time to get you blooded.'

'Blooded? What do you mean?' Matthew nearly tripped, but managed to keep up with her.

'I'll take you hunting later—see if it makes you run home to Denmark.'

By now they had reached the police station.

'Is this where you're going as well?' she asked him.

He shook his head. 'No, I…I don't know what I'm doing.'

She nodded towards the door. 'Come with me, then. Can't do any harm, given how nice and Danish you look.'

Five minutes later they were standing in front of the counter. The petite woman on the other side had called an officer to deal with the matter.

'We can't release your weapons,' the officer said, nodding at the computer monitor, which was facing away from them. 'The case hasn't been closed, and there's a note here saying that your items can't be returned.'

'Like I've just explained to you,' Tupaarnaq said, 'there was no case, so—'

'That's no use to me,' he said. 'We're talking about weapons that haven't been signed off for release.'

Tupaarnaq took out some papers, which she placed on the counter. 'Here are my receipts for the rifle and the ulo...And here you have my proof of residence and my tenancy agreement.'

He looked at her quizzically.

'Were my rifle or my ulo used in the commission of a crime?'

The officer stared stiffly at the screen.

'I'm happy to help you,' Tupaarnaq said. 'They weren't, nor were they illegally in my possession.'

'You were just arrested for murder,' he mumbled.

'Unlawfully,' Tupaarnaq said calmly. 'I was released the same day because the charge didn't stand up. It didn't. And you know it.'

The officer sighed. 'Your property, however, was listed as potential evidence, and it'll take time to get it released.'

'Not in Nuuk, surely?' Matthew heard the anger in her voice now, but she kept her cool. 'Now, listen to me. I'm not an idiot, though you may think I am. My rifle is just around the back, and you know that not a single shot has been fired from it, or you would never have released me so fast. So if you could just go out and get it for me, that would be great.'

'Your rifle is in our possession.'

'Why?' She leaned her upper body across the counter.

He looked back at the screen. When they'd arrived, the reception area had hummed with quiet office life. Now it was silent.

'Unless you can produce a valid reason for retaining my property, or you can show me, in writing, that the *Weapons Act* here in Greenland has been tightened within the last few minutes, then you must give me back my belongings. If you won't, please provide me with details of your complaints procedure, together with a form to be completed when reporting a case of theft.'

'But—'

'No buts. Make your mind up. Those are your choices. I can always get hold of the forms myself, and then I'll write to the authorities and the media in Denmark about how you are personally obstructing the rehabilitation of a recently released, traumatised young woman, who would like to return to her life as a hunter and fisherwoman after being locked up since she was fifteen years old. And of course I'll mention the brutal arrest and police harassment based on nothing but misogyny and circumstantial evidence. So what's it to be?'

26

Matthew held Tupaarnaq's laptop while she swung her rifle over her shoulder. 'There are few things on this earth I hate more than men,' she said. 'None, in fact.' She took out her mobile and checked the time. 'It's too late to go hunting today.'

'Today? You were going to go hunting today?'

She nodded and took her laptop from him. 'Absolutely, but it's too late now. Spending the night at sea would be stupid.' She took a deep breath and nodded resolutely. 'We'll go early tomorrow morning.'

'I—'

'What?' she said, glancing sideways at him. 'You have something better to do?'

He shook his head hesitantly.

She sighed. 'Listen, if I wanted you dead, I would have flayed you by now. You're coming with me so that we can see what you're made of. I can't work with a wimp.'

Matthew frowned. 'We're working together?'

'Yes. Your notebook, the murders and me being arrested—they're all connected. Only I don't know how yet.'

The thought of their paths merging was dizzying, and he felt something unravel inside him as they walked. 'You were pretty impressive back at the police station.'

'He had no idea what he was doing,' she said. 'This is Nuuk, not Copenhagen. If the police want to act within the law, they have no grounds on which to retain my property.'

'You certainly sounded as if you knew what you were talking about.'

She stopped. They were on the path that went over the steep rocks in between the apartment blocks where she lived.

'I was locked up for twelve years. While I was in prison, I sat my finals and then I read law. You could say that I had plenty of time to study.'

She started walking again. Matthew looked briefly at her back before following. 'You're a lawyer?'

'Well, I've got the degree, but I don't expect I'll ever practise as a lawyer, with my background.'

The long, grey apartment blocks emerged from the rocks. Solid concrete. Rows of dark windows. Matthew followed Tupaarnaq up a weathered wooden staircase and into a shabby gallery that ran along the building's ground floor.

'I want to show you something,' she said. 'You can come with me up to my place, but you'll have to wait outside the door. I don't want anyone coming inside.'

Matthew followed her through first one heavy swing door and then another. Both were old and wonky, and it looked like it was a long time since either of them had shut properly. Behind the doors were concrete stairs that led up to the first floor. Matthew tried in vain to close the second door before he followed Tupaarnaq up the steps. There had to be a massive draught in the winter once the storms and the frost got hold of the headland—especially in this block, which bordered the dark deep of the North Atlantic. The walls around them were covered with simple graffiti. Names. Years. Profanities. There was a skull with the caption: *xixx—u wil di in 12 day—c u in hel.*

Matthew and Tupaarnaq went out through the door to the first-floor gallery and upstairs to the second floor. This door was even more damaged than the ones downstairs. Its plastic window had been torched, and had shrivelled into long, brown, melted scars.

'This is it.'

She stopped in front of a white door to the right of the stairs. Above the door someone had written in red spray paint: *Abandon hope, all ye who enter here.*

'Wait here.' Tupaarnaq looked at him sharply to make sure he had understood before she took out a key and let herself in. She gave him a last look from under her eyelids before disappearing into the apartment. All Matthew had time to see was a totally empty hall. Absolutely nothing but the floor and the walls had been waiting for the woman who had just entered.

He walked on as the door closed with a quiet click, and continued towards the external gallery. This heavy door wasn't as damaged as the previous one, but it couldn't be closed properly either. He pulled it open and looked across the rocks and the sea. He identified the spot where he had been reading Jakob's notebook earlier that day. The fingers of his right hand instinctively moved to his left collarbone, and he glanced back towards the closed door.

After a while Matthew returned to Tupaarnaq's apartment. It was quiet behind her front door, not that he had expected anything else. He had no idea what it might be like inside. Or what it must have been like to be locked up at the age of fifteen and not let out for twelve years.

He jumped when the door opened. She looked at him, nodded and handed him a USB stick. 'Take a look at this.'

'What is it?'

'Just some stuff. Remember, there are two sides to every story, always, and the truth is often found in the details of a lie.'

'Thanks,' he said. 'I'll have a look at it when I get home.'

'Good. See you tomorrow. Be here at eight.'

Matthew steeled himself and nodded. 'Okay. Eight o'clock it is. See you then.'

'Put on some old clothes. Killing is messy.'

•

As soon as he got home, he inserted Tupaarnaq's USB stick into his laptop. It contained several folders with files saved either as PDFs or JPEGs, and as he opened them he realised that they were all pictures of articles about the killing of her family in Tasiilaq in 2002.

Matthew read the files one after the other. There was no doubt that Tupaarnaq had been convicted even before the first news reports reached the public. The murders were brutal and the newspapers explicit in their coverage of the tragedy in the east Greenlandic village. A picture of two dead girls lying on a double bed was published in several papers. The blood from their bodies had soaked into the quilt and mattress. A woman was lying on the floor not far from them. The pictures of the father had all been taken when he was alive, but according to the papers he had been shot with his own gun and then cut up with an ulo. The newspaper *Politiken* wrote that it was the most gruesome murder ever on Greenland's east coast—a tragedy in which the family's oldest daughter had killed everyone except her younger brother, who hadn't been at home that afternoon.

Matthew continued looking through the files. The intervals between the stories grew longer until the verdict came. Tupaarnaq had only ever admitted to killing her father, and had refused to speak about anything else throughout the entire trial. She was convicted of all four counts of manslaughter: guilty of killing her father, mother and two little sisters. Contrary to the advice of her legal counsel, she had not appealed the sentence.

Matthew picked up his mobile and checked the time. Then he

found Leiff's number and texted him. *The girl who killed her family in Tasiilaq. Do you know anything about her younger brother who survived?*

Once he had sent the message, he texted Malik as well. *Have you heard from Lyberth?*

Outside, the sun had set fire to the evening sky over Nuuk. The orange light from the flaming clouds cast a glow so strong that it looked as if the living room walls were burning.

He found his cigarettes and went out onto the balcony. His thoughts circled tentatively around the notebook, the landscape, Tupaarnaq, and the many loose ends, wondering how they were all connected. The cigarette smoke soothed him, allaying his unease.

He finished smoking and went back to the sofa, where he picked up his mobile. He had two messages. Leiff had written: *No, but I will look into it*, while Malik's reply was more comprehensive. He hadn't heard from Lyberth, but Ulrik had written to him saying that the police wanted the notebook back. Malik had replied that he didn't know where it was, which had prompted Ulrik to call him and complain bitterly. Malik could tell that Ulrik was calling from home rather than the police station, because Lyberth's daughter had said something in the background.

Just then a new message from Malik appeared at the top of the screen. *Ulrik has spoken to Ottesen and knows that you got the notebook from him. Just so you know.*

27

The sea was calm and reflected the scarred, round peaks of Mount Ukkusissat the next morning when Tupaarnaq and Matthew sailed out between the rocks in the small harbour by the public swimming pool. It hadn't taken Tupaarnaq many minutes to pick a boat and get it started. On the way to the harbour she had told him that it was better to borrow one without a steering wheel, as such boats always required a key. She couldn't be bothered to short-circuit one when all they needed for a quick trip was a low dinghy with an outboard motor and a tankful of petrol.

The boat slammed against the waves, and the wind swept across the open hull. Matthew shivered in his blue anorak and zipped it all the way up to his neck, while he looked enviously at Tupaarnaq's thick woollen jumper and black boots. The forecast had promised sun all day and up to twenty degrees Celsius, but out at sea the conditions were different. The bouncing of the boat caused his half-empty stomach to lurch, and the wind whipping across the sea was so cold that it felt like frost against his skin.

At the bottom of the boat lay a long stick with an iron hook on one end. The dark stains on the hook bore witness to the animals who had bled before they were pulled out of the sea. Tupaarnaq's rifle lay next to it, gun-metal grey with a wooden stock.

The boat listed to the right, and Matthew's body moved in the opposite direction. He had no idea where they were going. Tall mountains grew out of the sea around them.

Tupaarnaq sat next to the motor, the tiller under her arm and behind her so she could look ahead and steer them between the arms of the fjord.

Matthew's thoughts returned to the files on the USB stick, and he reviewed the information in his mind. Why hadn't she appealed her sentence? Surely an innocent person would have appealed a conviction for murdering their own mother and little sisters?

Tupaarnaq knocked on the hull to get his attention, then pointed at the sea in front of the boat. He turned and saw a lump of ice the size of a truck pass close by. 'They can be several hundred metres tall, if you go further up the coast.' She was practically shouting to drown out the engine and the wind. 'Above the water, I mean. Below the surface they can be one kilometre.' She pulled the tiller and the boat made a soft arc around the lump of ice, which shone white and turquoise in the morning sun.

'It's the first time I've been this close to an iceberg,' he shouted back. 'It's amazing.'

'It's not an iceberg, it's a growler. Icebergs are bigger.'

'But it's still beautiful,' Matthew whispered to himself. The growler had a long shelf right below the surface of the sea, and the water over it glowed turquoise and was so pure that he felt like jumping in.

The mountains continued everywhere. In some places they rose steeply. In other places there were long slopes covered with grass and shrivelled shrubs. They were going in the direction of Kobbe Fjord, in between Mount Ukkusissat and Mount Kingittorsuaq. Or Store Malene and Hjortetakken, as they were called in Danish.

Tupaarnaq switched off the engine, and once the boat settled on the sea, the icy wind mostly eased off.

Matthew started to relax. 'Aren't we going ashore?' He looked briefly at her before turning his gaze to the plain at the foot of Mount Kingittorsuaq.

She shook her head. 'No, we shoot seals out here. If you want to go reindeer hunting, you'll have to wait. It can take days before we spot any.'

'No, no…This is quite enough for me.' He stretched his neck, which had grown stiff and sore from the wind and the bumping waves. 'I was just wondering if we could go ashore and take a look at the landscape instead.'

'There,' she said, pointing across the sea. 'And there!'

'What are you looking at?' he asked, his gaze scanning the waves in vain.

'The small black dots on the sea. Can't you see them? They're seals. There are lots of them.'

She leaned forward and picked up the rifle with one hand. The other slipped into her pocket and reappeared with a small black magazine filled with cartridges.

'I can't see anything.' He narrowed his eyes and continued his search.

'They pop up and then they disappear again,' she explained and raised her rifle to her cheek. 'They come up for air.'

The slim rifle seemed a part of her. As if she was born to have this long weapon close to her body. The butt was pressed against the thick jumper covering her shoulder, and her left hand merged with the wood and metal in a firm grip. She lowered the weapon and smiled contentedly. 'Plenty of seals.' Then she cocked the rifle. The bolt clicked in place, with a cartridge in the chamber.

She raised the rifle to her face again and wedged it against her shoulder, while she pressed her cheek against the glossy wood of the butt and closed her left eye. Her right eye stared into the telescopic sight.

He heard how her breathing slowed and became heavier. He couldn't see any of her tattoos. Not a single leaf or a flower. No skulls baring their teeth. No deep shadows. There was only her face and shaved head. The freckles around her nose.

Suddenly a shot rang out. Her body was rigid. Frozen in the shot. She continued to stare into the solitary eye of the telescopic sight, then she put down the rifle and grabbed the tiller. The engine awakened from its slumber with a roar and the boat began leaping across the sea, wave after wave, until she released the tiller and let the boat coast until it came to a standstill.

'There,' she said, pointing diagonally to her left. She nudged the tiller slightly with one knee, so they were heading straight towards the animal in the water. It wasn't dead, but it was struggling. Its head and eyes were above the water, while its body lay just below. It tried to swim but its body refused; the water along the left side of the animal was red from blood.

Matthew looked up at Tupaarnaq. 'Aren't you meant to kill it outright?'

'Hang on.'

She turned and switched off the engine, before straightening up and pushing the boathook towards him with her boot. 'You jab the hook into its neck once I've shot it a second time.'

'Eh? But…it's—'

She looked at him. 'Are you going to help me or what?'

The seal splashed about in the water. It was trying to escape, but the bullet in its body and the onset of paralysis trapped it at the surface of the sea. Its small black eyes stared backwards. It waved a flipper.

'I…'

She took aim and fired the rifle. The seal's body jerked. The amount of blood in the sea grew explosively. The rifle ended up at the bottom of the boat again, while Tupaarnaq grabbed the hook and plunged it into the seal. 'The least you can do is help me land it.'

Matthew reached out nervously. They had to employ all their strength to haul the smooth, wet body over the gunwale. The seal flopped down into the bottom of the boat in a sudden gliding movement. Its eyes were still two staring black beads, but there was no life left in them. Blood flowed quietly from the two dark holes in its skin.

Matthew slumped back in his seat, while Tupaarnaq grabbed a flipper and turned the seal onto its back, baring its speckled silver and black belly. The sun's rays played in the hairs of the wet fur. She produced a hunting knife from her side pocket and stuck it into the seal, deep between its tail flippers. She tightened her fingers around the handle as the blade opened up the seal to its middle. The fat layer of blubber glowed pink; it looked like an open eye in the animal's lower body. The meat was dark, black almost. Her hands delved into the warm body and pulled out a long ribbon of pink intestines. Somewhere deep inside the animal, she managed to loosen them so they came out in one piece.

Matthew watched the intestines go over the gunwale and plop into the sea. 'You're just going to throw them away?'

'Well, I've no use for them.' She turned to look at him. Her stare was hard. 'You need to join in.'

'It's so gory.'

She gave a light shrug. 'It's just hunting.' Then she turned her attention back to the seal, and carried on removing its organs and throwing them overboard. Only a quivering dark lump was dumped in the bottom of the boat.

When everything had been cut out and disposed of, she sank the knife back into the seal near its tail flippers and cut the skin around them free from the skin on its body. She did the same with the two flippers along the animal's sides. Then she slipped the knife under the skin by its belly and started separating the skin from the fat and the body in soft movements, until only the glistening, flayed body remained. The skin itself she rinsed in the sea, then she tossed it at Matthew's feet.

He looked at her, stunned.

'It needs cleaning.'

'What do you mean?'

She took out her ulo and grabbed the skin. Carefully but steadily, she used the round blade to remove any blubber still attached to it. 'This is how you do it.'

Matthew took the ulo and bent hesitantly over the fur. The blubber was warm and greasy. Softer than he had expected, but viscous and tough to cut. It stretched, before snapping back like an elastic band.

'You need to get right down to the fur, leaving absolutely no blubber,' she told him. 'But be careful. The skin is worthless if you cut holes in it.'

He hesitated. He squished a piece of skin and blubber between his fingers. 'Do you eat this the way you eat whale skin?'

'You mean mattak? No, this stuff tastes like shit.' She took the ulo from him and let it glide in rocking movements along a piece of skin, leaving it clean and smooth. 'Like this.' She passed the ulo back to him.

'Will you be eating the meat yourself?' he asked, looking at the bloody body resting near him. She had even flayed its head, exposing the flesh and the sinews. The black eyes stared out at him from the flayed face.

'No, I don't eat meat. I'll sell it down at Brættet. I need the money to buy a few things.'

The ulo rested in his hand. His fingers were glossy with fat and blood.

'You need to taste the liver,' she said, holding out a piece of the dark, quivering lump she had saved earlier.

He wrinkled his nose in disgust and felt his throat contract with nausea. 'No, thanks.'

'It wasn't a suggestion,' she snapped. 'You can't come home after your first seal hunt without having tasted warm liver. Those are the rules, and they apply to you too.'

'I can't,' he croaked, staring at the small piece of raw seal liver. 'I'm going to throw up.'

'Not my problem. Eat it!'

His eyes sought refuge at the bottom of the boat. His sneakers were soaked with salt water and smeared with blood and guts. Her knee slipped into the picture, and when he looked up, she was squatting down right in front of him. A distant yet also present smile was playing on her lips.

'You either eat it yourself or I shove it down your throat.'

'Okay, okay, okay. I'll eat it. Relax.' He exhaled, then he frowned. 'Have you ever tasted it?'

'We all eat it. Some even by choice. As if it were candy.'

He took the liver from her hand. It felt soft, grainy and delicate between his fingers.

'It's just blood,' she said, and she ran two fingers down his face, leaving broad, dark traces on his skin.

The liver grew in his hand. His eyes were drawn to the flayed, dead body of the seal. The skin and the blubber at his feet. The ulo. The intestines. The seal's belly as it had surrendered to the knife and sprung open in a fleshy wound.

He started hyperventilating. He swallowed saliva that wasn't there. Suppressed his nausea. His fingers found their way to his mouth. The liver went in. His teeth cut through the soft, jelly-like substance. The meat burst. A taste of metal filled his mouth. His throat tightened.

'Go on, spit it out,' Tupaarnaq said with a short grin. 'I need you to be able to walk. You'll be carrying half the seal to Brættet.'

He spat into the sea. 'I think I just failed your test,' he spluttered.

'No, you didn't. I don't want a companion with a taste for blood.'

Matthew looked at what was left of the seal with a frown. 'But you…We just…'

She nodded grimly. 'It's the easiest way to make money right now. It's how I was brought up.'

28

The black plastic bag with the large chunks of freshly killed seal weighed heavy on Matthew's back. He could feel the bones from the animal digging into him through the plastic and pressing into his back. His shoes and trousers were stained with salt water and seal blood, and he had no idea whether he had successfully washed the blood off his face.

Tupaarnaq walked alongside him in her old, thick jumper, with a bag similar to his slung over her shoulder. Rust-coloured patches were drying on the light-grey wool; her rifle hung from the same shoulder and bounced slightly with every step she took.

'How far is it?' he said. The weight of the meat was sending jolts of pain up his crooked neck. He gave in to it and shifted the bag, so that it rested against his shoulder.

'You don't know where Brættet is?'

'Is it next to Brugseni?' he ventured.

She nodded. 'We'll be there in a few minutes.'

He only had himself to blame. He had refused to get on the bus with the bags. Blood was dripping from their seams, and the thought of sitting on the bus and watching blood run across the floor was more than he could handle. When she told him how far it was to walk, she hadn't mentioned how many rocks and steps they would be going up and down. He was worn out already, and his back hurt as much as his neck.

Sweat trickled down his forehead and under his jumper. He looked back at the path they had walked. When he'd switched shoulders, more blood had run out of the bag, leaving on the gravel a small, dark puddle of death.

·

Brættet was busy when Matthew and Tupaarnaq entered through the glass door. To their left were several steel tables with big lumps of dark meat, and very close to them lay two heads and the fins from a couple of porpoises. To their right were several white plastic crates with different kinds of semi-gutted fish.

'I'll just find a buyer for this,' Tupaarnaq said.

Matthew let the bag slip from his shoulder so it dangled from his hand and arm. There was blood on several of the steel tables. Puddles on the floor below them. The two small whales looked as if their heads had been chopped off with one violent blow. The display seemed to have been set up so that you could see the porpoises' smile. Further into the market was a seal, gutted like theirs. Its bloodstained body had been spread out into flat halves.

Tupaarnaq was busy talking to a man, who rummaged around in her bag.

The biggest tables were at the back of the market, and on them lay large chunks of dark meat. He had never before seen such big, firm pieces of meat without any bones in them. They looked like the thigh muscles of a dinosaur. On a sign taped to the table he read the words 'fin whale'. The man behind the desk had a solid hold of a chunk the size of his own torso while he spoke to a woman in Greenlandic. He nodded and started slicing the meat with a long, thin-bladed knife.

'Give your bag to that guy over there.'

Matthew jumped. He spun around and looked at Tupaarnaq. 'Okay. Did you manage to sell everything?'

'Yes. As I expected.'

Matthew turned back to the man with the big lumps of meat. 'Is he cutting whale steak?'

'Yes, and we can buy one, if that's what you fancy.' She took the bag from his hand. 'Only not for me—I'm not having any.' Then she went over to the man who had bought her seal meat and chucked the bag on the table next to the other one.

The man in the white coat pushed down the plastic bag to get a good look at the reddish-brown lumps of meat. He picked up a broad piece with the ribs exposed and turned it over a couple of times, then nodded contentedly and looked at Tupaarnaq. He put the meat down on the table again, where it left a bloody outline on the steel.

Tupaarnaq nudged Matthew's shoulder. 'You're completely away with the fairies. You're quite sure you don't want some whale?'

He shook his head slowly without turning to her.

'Just ask the guy over there if you fancy trying some. He'll cut you a steak…my treat.'

'I…' Matthew hesitated as his thoughts moved back and forth between the dying seal in the sea and the flayed, fleshy skulls staring emptily at him from the steel tables. 'No, not today. I think. Neither seal nor whale.'

'Okay—it's up to you. You can always come back another time.' She nudged him again. 'I'm off. Are you coming?'

'Yes,' he gulped and raised his eyebrows. 'Where are we going?'

'I'm going home,' she stated firmly. 'Alone. I'm not used to being outside, so I need some time on my own now.'

He smiled and followed her out of the door.

She turned to him outside in the square. 'I just need to get a few things.'

'From Brugseni?'

'Yes, but I'll do it on my own.' A short grin crossed her lips. 'I'm glad you tasted the liver today. If you hadn't, I would have thrown you into the sea.'

She was smiling but he wasn't at all sure that she was joking. His gaze moved to the small, simple stalls put up on the square outside Brugseni. Low tables, rugs and cardboard signs. The hawkers sold everything from figures carved out of reindeer antler to knitwear, seal mittens and old DVDs. They also sold pink frozen prawns, and one sold second-hand toys.

'Why did you give me the USB stick?'

'You wanted to know who you were going hunting with.'

'But the articles don't tell me that, do they?'

She exhaled deeply and looked him in the eye. 'I gave it to you because you wanted to understand about murder and what it means to kill. And that was also why I took you with me today. Perhaps it'll make sense when you switch off your light tonight.'

He frowned.

'Causality,' she went on. 'If you want to understand why a ball is rolling, you need to find out what set it in motion. The rest is nothing but effect, and the effect is visible to everyone. The explanation is found in the cause.'

29

The smoke seeped slowly out of the corner of Matthew's mouth. He was lying on the floor with a pillow under his neck near the balcony door, and could feel the cool air creep in around him. In one hand he held an almost empty Musk Ox beer, and a cigarette rested between the fingers of the other.

Tine was never a fan of smoking. *Everything reeks of smoke*, she would say when they had been among smokers.

He took a deep drag and let his hand flop back to the floor.

He had bought his first packet of cigarettes the day after the accident. He had been standing by the till, looking at his shopping, and when the cashier had smiled to him he had asked her for a packet of twenty Prince. *With or without filter?* she had asked. Back then he had still worn his ring.

To begin with, he had been so numbed by the smoke that he experienced a mild rush. Even the smoke filling his lungs had a calming effect he had never expected. He couldn't explain it. Sometimes he would take a break from smoking for several days in order to experience again the feeling of getting high on the smoke.

His mobile buzzed in his pocket, and he leant over to drop the cigarette butt into the beer bottle and read the message.

Are you home? Tupaarnaq. That was all it said.

Yes, he replied, and pressed send. He heard nothing for several minutes. *Why?* he added eventually.

I'll be there in five minutes.

He got up immediately and pushed the balcony door fully open. He tossed the beer bottle into the kitchen bin and stacked his dirty cups and plates in the dishwasher.

You need to be alone. Am almost there.

He pulled out a drawer, found some pink tea lights, put them on a plate and lit them. Like pretty much everything else in the apartment, they had been here when he moved in. Now their time had come. The smell of warm candle wax began to spread immediately, and he set the plate down on the small dining table between the kitchen and the sofa.

His mobile buzzed. *Let me in.*

He put down his mobile and went out to the entry phone.

The pale-yellow walls and large, light-grey tiles shone more brightly than the ceiling lamps out on the landing. The lift hummed behind the steel doors, and he reached for the ghost wedding band on the ring finger of his right hand.

'Inside,' she commanded the moment the lift door opened.

He allowed her to push him backwards. 'Okay…'

She had already marched past him and into his hallway. 'I need to borrow your bathroom and a T-shirt.'

Her thick jumper was draped over her arm, but this time it wasn't the dark tattoos on her arms and shoulders that attracted his attention. It was the blood on her fingers and hands. They had washed off the seal blood out at sea, and after Brættet her hands had been as clean as his. Now they were smeared with dried blood.

'I'll find you a top. What happened?'

'You won't be talking to Lyberth,' she said hoarsely. 'He's lying on the floor at my place, gutted.'

Matthew had to grab the doorframe for support. The words echoed in his mind. 'What?' he managed to whisper.

'I don't know why he's there, but he's very dead.' She heaved a sigh. 'You're not expecting any visitors, are you?'

'No,' Matthew said. Then he wondered whether it might not be wise to text Malik and tell him not to come over, in case he was planning on it, but concluded that doing so would probably arouse more suspicion, given everything else that had happened. 'Can I get you anything?'

'Yes, a T-shirt—but first let me tell you about Lyberth.'

'And you're quite sure that he's dead?'

'More sure than I was about the seal we sold down at Brættet.' She turned on the kitchen tap, squirted washing-up liquid onto her hands and started rubbing them together under the water. 'It's the first time I've seen a dead body since…' Her back arched and her head slumped a little. 'It has been a while.'

'But why would you kill Lyberth? I mean, the two of you didn't even know one another, did you?'

'It just so happens that I didn't kill Lyberth. But no, I don't know him, and that, if nothing else, would be a requirement for my having a motive.'

'So someone killed him in your apartment, thinking that you would be the obvious suspect and that they would get away with it?'

'Perhaps. I don't know. It seems far-fetched, but then again it's what very nearly happened when they brought me in for the murder of those two men.'

'Aqqalu and the fisherman?'

'Yes, of course. Them.' She paused and carefully dried her hands on a tea towel. 'The three murders are connected.'

'Are you sure?'

She nodded and sat down in the black recliner at the end of the coffee table. 'Lyberth had also been gutted.'

Matthew buried his face in his hands. 'And he's in your apartment right now? And no one else knows?'

'The killer knows he's there. As do you. But apart from that, yes.'

'Shouldn't we call the police?'

She shook her head slowly. 'They'll bring me in immediately. He was killed in my apartment in the same way as...' She ground to a halt. 'I touched the body. I don't know why. I'm such an idiot. I mean, I could see that he was already dead. This time I'll get life.'

'But you were with me all day, and—'

'I could have killed him afterwards,' she cut in. 'There'll be forensic evidence implicating me. The location. Fingerprints.' She looked up at the ceiling. 'It was exactly what happened when they found my...father.'

'But what about motive? It was you who told me always to look for the cause.'

'Yes, for the defence. Not for the prosecutor. There, it's the burden of evidence that weighs most heavily.'

They were silent for a few minutes. Her upper body rocked back and forth a little.

'If you don't go back to your place when there's a dead body inside it, that could also look bad during a trial.'

'The police just need to find the killer quickly.'

'But they're not going to do that if they believe you did it. They'll just keep looking for you until they find you.'

'Then I'm going to have to find the killer myself.' She shook her head. 'It's like I told you. Our cases are connected. Oh, shit.'

'You mean they're connected to the murders in the seventies?'

'Maybe. I don't know. He...arghhh!'

Matthew looked at her. Sitting in the recliner she suddenly seemed smaller than ever. 'What will the police find at your place, if they discover the body themselves?' he asked.

'Well,' she said, staring vacantly into the air. 'What will they find?' She got up and went over to the balcony door. 'This is so messed up. His hands and feet are nailed to the floor, like some crucified Jesus. A sock was stuffed into his mouth, and he was blind-folded. He's completely butchered.'

The sofa felt cold and dead under Matthew.

'His stomach was cut open,' she continued. 'Right from his groin and up to his breastbone. His skin had been pulled out to the sides, and everything in his abdomen had been ripped out and thrown onto the floor around him.'

'Was there an ulo?'

'No, there wasn't. And he wasn't killed with an ulo. The cuts are far too straight and clean.'

'And he's lying there now?'

'Yes, I think so. I don't remember locking the door behind me. I just grabbed my stuff and got out of there.'

'And where are your things now?'

'It doesn't matter.' She narrowed her eyes and rubbed her scalp. 'Mind if I have a shower? I…it's gross. All of it. I…I've been kicked twelve years back in time.'

'Yes, of course,' he said, and got up immediately. 'Let me get you a towel and a T-shirt.' He hesitated. 'I accidentally smashed the door to the bathroom, so it doesn't close properly.'

'Idiot. Well, I'm still going to have a shower, but don't you dare come near me, do you hear?'

'I'll go for a walk,' Matthew said, handing her an old black T-shirt. 'It's all I've got.'

'You can't leave while I'm here,' she said. 'Or I won't be able to stay. The police might turn up. Anything could happen.'

He slumped and looked down. 'I was just going down to the cemetery to smoke a couple of cigarettes.'

'You can smoke inside, if you like. But if you leave now, I'll leave too. I have to.'

'It's okay,' he replied with a nod. 'It was a stupid idea. I…I'm just shocked.'

'Smoke your cigarettes in here. It's your apartment.' She tried to fix him with her eyes. 'So are you staying or what?'

'Yes…Yes, of course.'

'Okay. Then I'll have a shower.' She finally made eye contact with him. 'And you stay in here or you're finished.'

'Okay.'

He waited behind the recliner until he heard the water being turned on. Then he took out his cigarettes and lit one. His hands were shaking so much that the tip of the cigarette quivered.

Matthew had only just flopped onto the sofa when he remembered that he hadn't given her a towel to take to the bathroom.

The door hung crooked on its hinges and revealed most of the bathroom. The shower was concealed behind a thick pane of glass that reached from the floor to the ceiling. The steam had already clouded the glass, so he could only see her silhouette. He looked at the towel in his hand. He could see her body in the mirror.

It wasn't just her arms, shoulders, chest and neck that were tattooed. Everything had colours. Her body was completely covered by flowers and leaves. Not delicate and pretty, but lush and winding. Camouflage.

Her toes were free. Her feet almost. The growth started around her ankles where it blossomed, reached out and covered most of her. Concealing her. She wasn't there. She didn't exist. There were just plants winding and curving. The flowers breathing. The shadows and the two mouths of death. Everything was covered up, and the dark didn't release its grip until her neck. That was her existence. She was two feet, two hands, and a face. That was all. The rest was a dark wilderness.

The water in the shower must have been boiling hot, given how much steam it generated. She stood still under the jet. Picked up the soap and started soaping herself. She covered every part of her body before she grabbed a razor and let it grip her. She followed the movements of the plants along her muscles and shaved her legs, her groin, her belly, arms, armpits, her throat, her face and her scalp. She scraped away the outer layer of herself in slow, viscous movements, and let it wash away down the drain.

Only the colours remained.

Her body was slim. Sinewy. The muscles in her arms tensed. They stood out in all the colours that were her. That was all she was. Muscles and colours.

Matthew took a step forward in order to leave the towel just inside the open door. She reacted to the movement and turned her gaze on him at that very same moment. It burned. Forcing him to the floor.

'You're finished,' she hissed.

Matthew disappeared into the living room, where he turned on the TV and ended up watching an English TV series.

He could hear Tupaarnaq muttering harshly while she got dressed, but he couldn't hear what she was saying. Not until she came back to the living room.

'You're no better than the rest of them,' she said, hurling the damp towel at him. 'Fucking pig. You're a bunch of perverts…all of you.'

He wanted to say something. Defend himself. But she was gone.

THE LIGHT OF
DARKNESS

30

A spell of milder weather had arrived, something that Jakob had not expected, but which in an ideal world would have occurred a few hours earlier, when he had stupidly sat by the broken window and the dead radiator and nearly frozen to death in his own living room. He glanced at Karlo. If it hadn't been for his colleague's prompt response, he might easily have died. Just before they left, Mortensen had added insult to injury by asking them not to mention to anyone that the two of them had been practically naked under the same blanket. Two men. Police officers at that. *The people of this town shouldn't start having thoughts like that about the forces of law and order. We'll keep all of that in-house.* Their boss had been unable to look at them as he spoke.

Jakob slipped in something outside the stairwell they were about to enter, and Karlo grabbed his arm.

'Where on earth did that change in the weather come from?' Jakob said. 'And thank you.'

'Oh, it'll be frost again in a moment,' Karlo said, sniffing the air. 'I think we've escaped the big chaos of the melt for now.'

Jakob smiled and looked up at Block P. 'Is this it?'

'Yes, it's on the second floor.'

'Have you been up there?'

'Not yet, but the door has been locked and I have a key. His wife and children have gone to stay with her parents.'

'Including his daughter?'

'Yes, she's in the same place.'

'Only now she's safe,' Jakob muttered quietly. It troubled him that he hadn't ignored the rules and Mortensen's words about the girls, but what else could he do? It was winter. There was nowhere to move them to.

Jakob remembered the apartment clearly. As he did all four apartments where he believed the police must take immediate action to save a minor from abuse. He sighed to himself. Save was the wrong word. These girls were already damaged for life, but at least they could have stopped any further abuse.

And now it had stopped for this man's daughter, and for one of the others, while Najak had gone missing and Paneeraq was still trapped in her living hell. He patted his trouser leg and said, 'Right, what have we got here?'

'It's exactly the same,' Karlo said. 'The ulo is lying in the middle of his intestines. He's covered in blood. And he has been flayed. The Nuuk Ripper strikes again.'

The dead body had indeed been flayed like the other two; it looked like a bloody hunting trophy someone had tossed on the floor. The flayed face stared back at them. The bared teeth. The muscle fibres. Pale sinews. Blood. The belly had been brutally slashed open in the most agonising way that Jakob could imagine. The ulo wasn't a stabbing tool or a knife to cut something open with. It was a tool designed to remove fat from skin, and the nature of the cuts to this man's stomach indicated that the blade had ripped up his skin and flesh in slow, tearing movements. But it had been operated by a skilled hand. A hand that knew precisely where every cut should be made. The pain must have been excruciating.

Jakob got up and did a tour of the apartment's two bedrooms. His stomach lurched when he looked at the beds in both rooms. Right there, the man's little daughter had had to submit to her own father's adult body, and no one had said or done anything to help her. No one. Except one person. And now it was Jakob's duty to catch this someone and put them behind bars.

'Doesn't Anguteeraq Poulsen live nearby?' He looked towards Karlo.

'Two stairwells from here,' Karlo replied, getting up from the floor, where he had been setting out small numbered flags for the forensic pathologist from Denmark, as well as for the photographer who would take pictures of the dead body before it could be moved.

'I think we ought to visit him right away.'

'And warn him? He's the last man on your list.'

Jakob touched the cut on his forehead carefully. Then he shook his head. 'I just want to see him.'

Karlo checked his watch. 'You want to go over there now?'

'Yes—if it's all right with you?'

'It's not a problem, but I'm concerned about you. Your forehead is starting to go blue—maybe you should rest? And I still think you ought to see a doctor. You could easily be concussed. Perhaps you should sleep at my place tonight so you're not alone?'

Jakob smiled. 'My mother is eighty-one,' he said, looking across to Karlo. 'I believe I'm old enough to take care of myself.'

'I know, I know. I was more thinking you might lose consciousness.'

'Well, I'll probably wake up again if I'm meant to.' Jakob patted Karlo's shoulder. 'Don't worry about me. It doesn't feel like a concussion. But it's kind of you to care.'

'And we're having pork chops tonight,' Karlo said hungrily. 'Big, fat, juicy ones.'

Jakob took a last look at the gutted man on the floor. 'I'll take a raincheck, thanks, Karlo. Once we're done here, all I want to do for the rest of the evening is hide under my blankets.'

31

The stairwells looked pretty much identical. All were made from concrete, had the same doors and the same orange-red wooden banisters. The only difference was the names on the letterboxes and the stuff left outside the front doors or littering the communal areas. In some places shoes and boots were carefully arranged, while in others bags, clothes and fishing gear covered half the floor space.

Outside Anguteeraq Poulsen's place, the boots were lined up neatly and they were clean, as was a pair of snowshoes, old and worn, but greased and ready for use.

'Hello,' Karlo said in a cheerful voice the moment the door was opened and a subdued-looking woman peered out from the crack. 'We're here to follow up on the police survey of children's school habits. I'm afraid we didn't manage to complete our form when we were here last, so we were wondering if we might trouble you with a quick visit.'

The woman closed the door as she nodded, and it grew silent on the landing as the two men stared at the closed door. Soon it opened again, and the man they had spoken to the last time they had visited popped out his head. He glared at Jakob, then turned his attention to Karlo and muttered something in Greenlandic. Karlo replied, and the two men spoke for just under a minute before Anguteeraq Poulsen finally took a step back and opened the door fully. He was wearing jeans and a stained and faded green T-shirt. His hair was messy.

'He says he can't be bothered to speak Danish today,' Karlo whispered to Jakob as they entered. 'So I'll talk to him in Greenlandic and tell you what he said afterwards.'

Jakob inhaled the smell of the place through his nostrils. 'Ask him if he knew the other three men, but don't let on too much...Just ask a bit about everything.'

Karlo nodded and sat down on a brown sofa that the man had pointed to. Jakob sat down next to him, and they were each given a cup of black coffee.

The two Greenlandic men started talking, while Jakob studied Poulsen's facial expressions and the apartment around him. Poulsen clearly resented Jakob's presence. Anger exuded from his eyes, from the frowning of his forehead and from the restlessness of his body. In Jakob's opinion, though, it was more than just anger. They weren't welcome. Not just because they were police officers and because Jakob was Danish. No, they were people who had entered his home, which didn't bear close scrutiny.

Jakob nearly burned himself when he raised the cup to his lips. He looked into the steaming coffee, before nodding politely to the woman sitting on a light-coloured chair by the door to the kitchen. There were another two doors leading from the living room, but both were closed. Between the two brown sofas was a pine coffee table, with a brass lamp above it that sent out its light through a series of yellow oval glass discs. The walls were bare except for a single, simplistic painting of a man in a kayak on the sea in front of Mount Sermitsiaq.

Jakob turned his attention back to Anguteeraq Poulsen. His trousers. His T-shirt. His gaze. The cowed wife sitting by the door, staring at the floor, her hands resting on her legs, which were pressed together.

'Karlo,' he sighed, 'would you please tell Mr Poulsen that we have a few questions for his daughter, because we didn't manage to complete the form the last time we were here.'

'She's asleep,' Anguteeraq Poulsen interjected in Danish.

Jakob sniffed the air and picked up the aroma coming from the kitchen. 'It smells like you're about to eat.'

Anguteeraq Poulsen scowled at them both, then got up and disappeared into one of the rooms. A few minutes later he emerged with the girl in his arms. He put her down on the sofa and sat beside her, keeping his hand on her shoulder all the while.

'She's not quite herself,' he said. 'She went to the hospital today for an injection.' For a moment his gaze seemed more apologetic than angry. The girl's body was floppy. She wasn't making eye contact, but just stared down at herself. Her hands were gathered like her mother's.

'Sorry to wake you up, Paneeraq,' Jakob said. 'It's just that we forgot a few things the last time we were here, and we want to make sure that our survey is perfect so we can build the best school for you children.'

The girl nodded. According to Jakob's notebook, she was eleven years old. Her father was the last of the four men on his list of people who should never be allowed near a girl or a woman for the rest of their lives. He struggled to contain his emotions.

'Paneeraq…'

The silence after her name shaped a question in the air, and the girl looked up.

A shiver went down Jakob's spine as all the blood and life inside him froze. 'Paneeraq,' he repeated in a croaking voice. 'Do you like going to school?'

She didn't say anything. She just looked down again, but she nodded lightly.

'And if you have any problems, do you get plenty of help?'

She shook her head very slowly.

'So no one helps you?'

'No one,' she whispered.

Jakob watched as tears trickled down the girl's chubby cheeks.

Her father tapped her shoulder and her whole body flinched. 'You asked her that the last time,' he growled. 'She's tired.'

'Sometimes you get different answers depending on when and how you ask the question,' Jakob said, without taking his eyes off the girl. 'Paneeraq, it's always okay to ask for help. Don't you ever forget that, ilaa?'

She didn't say anything, and he realised that he had to release her from her father's grip. 'That's enough. Paneeraq, you're free to go back to bed if you want to.'

The girl got up so quickly that her father didn't have time to stop her. She kept her eyes firmly on the floor, but shook hands with both Karlo and Jakob before she limped with some difficulty towards the door to the bedroom and disappeared.

Jakob could no longer bear to look at Anguteeraq Poulsen. His face spoke volumes now, and all of it was ugly.

•

'I'll bloody well kill him myself,' Jakob fumed when they were back outside Block P, looking up at the closed windows of the apartment. 'I'll bloody well kill him and gut him myself.' Everything whirled around in his mind, and he struggled to keep hold of the many loose ends. 'Oh, damn,' he then exclaimed. 'I need to go back to Ari Rossing Lynge's place. Do you know if his wife is still living there?'

'You want to go there now?' Karlo checked his wristwatch as he stepped further away from the apartment block, and his eyes moved from the watch face to the front of the building. 'The light is on, so

I'm guessing that she is.'

Jakob rubbed his face with a weary expression. 'I have to have another look. Around the living room and the bedrooms.'

'But—'

'It's all right.' Jakob raised his eyebrows. 'You don't have to come with me. It's okay. I can hear the pork chops calling you.'

'Is it really all right?'

'Of course. It's late.' He sighed and shook his head. 'I just need to check something. I won't be long.'

'Sure. Mind how you go.'

32

'Hello?'

Jakob had only just entered the brightly lit stairwell where Ari Rossing Lynge had lived when a voice called out to him.

'You're a police officer, aren't you?'

The voice was coming from the first door to the right. Its white surface was ajar, and through the gap he could make out a strip of a female face. An eye, a cheek and a little of her mouth.

'Yes,' he said, stepping closer to the door. 'My name is Jakob Pedersen, Godthåb Police. I'm looking for Mrs Rossing Lynge.'

'Is this about their daughter?'

Jakob hesitated. 'I'm sorry, but why do you want to know?'

The door opened fully so that he could look in. A petite woman about thirty years old was standing on the tiled floor just inside the door. Her face was short and broad, and her eyes as black as her hair.

'My name is Inge-Lene,' she said with a timid smile. 'Would you mind coming in for a moment?' She glanced around and listened briefly to the silence in the stairwell. 'There's something I've been meaning to tell the police for a long time. About the night Najak disappeared.'

'You know something about Najak's disappearance?' Jakob said, looking at the woman with consternation. 'It's really important to pass on such information to the police immediately.'

She nodded. 'Yes, and that's what I'm doing now. Come inside for a moment. I don't want to talk out here.'

'Of course.'

When Jakob had taken his boots and coat off, she showed him into a small living room and invited him to sit on a green sofa with wooden armrests and several embroidered cushions. Inge-Lene herself continued into the kitchen, where he heard a clatter of plates and cupboard doors open and shut. He had hoped that she would just tell him what she had to say so that he could get home to his own armchair, but he didn't have the heart to refuse her hospitality.

There was a lamp hanging over the coffee table. The shade consisted of three lime-coloured glass panels; on the table below was a magazine and some knitting. There was no TV in the room, but several drawings in pale wooden frames adorned the walls. All were pencil sketches, sensitively coloured so that the colour didn't steal the attention from the subjects. Jakob got up and went over to the longest wall in the living room to study the artworks. The first one depicted two girls, both wearing Greenlandic national costume. The younger girl was sitting at a table, while the older girl—with some effort, it seemed—was trying to put a kamik boot on the foot of the smaller one. The older girl's hair was piled up on top of her head in the shape of an ulo, while the little girl's hair was short and loose.

'Here we are.'

Jakob turned around. 'What impressive drawings.'

'Thank you,' Inge-Lene said with a big smile as she set down an orange enamel tray on the table and picked up her knitting. She looked about her, then placed the yarn and the knitting needles in a basket next to the sofa. 'They're of my sister and me when we were little.'

Jakob was surprised and took a closer look at the drawing, and then at the pictures near it. 'You're the artist?'

'Yes. I've always loved to draw, so people in my family don't have a lot of wall space left.' She laughed briefly. 'I've just made a pot of coffee, so I got you a cup and…some cake. Well, it's just fruit loaf, really.'

Jakob was given a slice on a plate, then he sipped his coffee. He had long since grown used to coffee always being drunk black in Godthåb. Especially during the long, dark winters. 'I hate to ruin the nice mood,' he began, 'but please tell me what you saw and heard the night that Najak went missing.'

Inge-Lene retreated slightly down her end of the sofa. 'Let me just…' She chewed and swallowed.

He smiled and took a bite of his fruit loaf. The butter was thick, and his teeth left marks in it.

'I don't know what to think,' she said quietly. Her eyes had grown serious and glum. 'I'm scared that something has happened to her.' She took a sip of her coffee and swallowed it with a slight shudder as she put down the cup. 'Anyone can see that she's not a happy child. She has had a bad life so far. When I think about her eyes and the way she moves, I feel awful. It's like she's invisible. I've never seen her cry, but then again, I've never seen her smile either. Not once.'

Jakob took another bite of his fruit loaf and leaned back on the sofa. 'So you know her well?'

Inge-Lene shrugged. 'I invite her in from time to time, but not very often because she's pretty much terrified of her own shadow.' She looked at the walls. 'She likes my drawings, and I know that she's fond of drawing. I told her once that it was like being in another world when you draw, and she understood that, I could see it. So I try to get her to come here to draw as often as I can.'

'So the two of you draw together?'

'That's probably an exaggeration, but she has given me one of her drawings, so I know how good she is. I mean, she's only eleven years old.' She got up from the sofa and went over to a brown sideboard with three doors. 'Just a moment. Here it is—her drawing, I mean.'

Jakob reached out and took the paper she was holding out. It was coloured right into every corner with shades of blue, grey, yellow and black, which together produced a sombre image of a woman's head and neck breaking the flat calm surface of the sea in between two dark mountains. He turned to Inge-Lene. 'Did Najak draw this picture?'

She nodded with a sad smile.

The room fell silent.

'I want you to have it,' Inge-Lene said.

Jakob cleared his throat and put the picture down on the coffee table. 'No, it's yours. I don't know Najak the way you do. I can't accept it.'

'Please take it with you,' she urged him. 'You can give it back to me when you find her.'

'Are you so sure that I will find Najak alive?'

She stared at the floor. 'No.'

'I'll do whatever I can,' he promised. 'Not just for her, but also for the others.'

'That's what I'm hoping.'

Jakob slowly massaged his upper lip with his thumb. 'Are you ready to tell me about that night?'

She inhaled deep into her lungs, and then expelled the air. 'It was the night before Ari was murdered. Several men had gone up to his place, and there was a lot of screaming and shouting. It was mostly Nukannguaq, Ari's wife, doing the screaming, while the men were shouting. In Greenlandic and in Danish. A little later it grew quiet again. With hindsight it was probably an ominous silence, but I didn't think so at the time. I didn't hear Najak's voice at any point either, so I don't know if she disappeared that night, but I have a feeling that something terrible happened, and because of that Ari

165

ended up getting killed.'

'Did you see any of the men?'

'I saw them.' She gathered her hands in her lap. 'And that's why I didn't contact the police.'

'But you're talking to me now?'

'This is different. You wouldn't be sitting here, talking like we are now, unless I trusted you. Besides, nobody knows that you're here.'

Jakob leaned closer. 'You should only tell me more if it's what you want.'

'I do want to talk to you,' she said. 'I feel I must.' Her eyes shone with sincerity. 'It was dark, so I couldn't see clearly, but I saw three men come down from upstairs, and once they were outside this block, they met up with a fourth man. He was a thick-set, red-haired man with a bushy beard. When the others left, this man entered the stairwell, and I heard him walk up the stairs. Later that night I heard thumping from Ari's place, as if someone was banging on the floor, but I ignored it because it was now several hours since I had last heard or seen someone in the stairwell. Later, I fell asleep, and the next day all hell broke loose when Ari was found murdered. Nukannguaq was in shock and Najak was gone.'

'Could you identify any of the first three men you saw?' Jakob didn't want Inge-Lene to know that what she had heard was undoubtedly a dying Ari's hands bashing the floor as he was being gutted alive.

She shook her head. 'Only one of them.'

33

Jakob had only managed to sink a few centimetres into his armchair before there was a knock on his front door. He scowled at the dark windows and heaved a sigh. The knocking persisted, and he closed his eyes in an attempt to disappear so deep inside himself that only the silent night would remain.

The next sound to reach him came from the window. Fingers tapping the glass lightly. 'Wake up, Jakob.'

The voice was female. It belonged to Lisbeth. He opened his eyes and hurried to the door.

'Lisbeth, do come in,' he said, smiling, with a glance at the folded blanket in her hands.

She stared at his forehead. 'Good heavens—does it hurt?'

'Hurt?' Jakob touched his forehead. 'No, it's fine. Nothing to worry about. I hope you haven't—'

'I've brought you some rissoles,' she interrupted, nodding at the blanket. 'I didn't think you should be on your own after being attacked yesterday.' She looked down. 'Or have you already had dinner?'

'Why don't we eat together?' he suggested, taking a step backwards. 'I love rissoles.'

He followed her into the kitchen, where she unwrapped a dish from the blanket.

'Is it all right if we eat at the coffee table?' he asked. 'There's a jigsaw puzzle on the dining table.'

'Yes, yes, of course. You're in charge.'

He looked at her back and at her long, black plait hanging down. 'It smells good.'

'Thank you. I hope it tastes even better.' She turned around and looked at him. 'If you don't mind setting the table, the food will be ready in just a sec.'

Jakob found a couple of plates and carried them to the living room. 'Do you drink wine?'

'Yes, indeed I do.' Her voice was soft and vibrant. 'But I'm not sure it's a good idea with that cut to your head.'

Jakob opened a door in the sideboard behind the dining table, and took out two wineglasses.

'Do you have a trivet?' She had appeared from behind, holding the steaming dish in two oven gloves.

He nodded and put the glasses on the coffee table, then rushed back to the kitchen. 'I can't find one,' he called out, reappearing in the doorway. 'We'll just use a book.'

She smiled and set down the dish when he placed a book on the table. 'Shall I do the honours?'

He nodded while he poured the wine.

'Cheers,' Lisbeth said, raising her glass. 'And thank you for inviting me.'

He looked up at her with a frown.

She smiled and winked. 'I'm just teasing you, Jakob.'

'Cheers…And thanks for the rissoles. It was kind of you to think of me.' He put down his glass. 'Have you always lived in Godthåb?'

'No, I'm from Qeqertarsuatsiaat.'

'Qeqertarsuatsiaat,' he echoed. 'I haven't been there yet.'

'Only a few hundred people live there now,' she said. 'But my grandmother is still there. She doesn't want to move to Godthåb.'

'We could go down there one day in the police boat,' he said. 'I mean, if you would like that.'

'You know how to sail?' A big smile had spread across her face, all the way into her eyes. 'I'd love to, but I don't want to cause problems for you. Promise? It would probably take us all day.'

'I have a lot of time on my hands,' he said.

She sipped her wine and smiled. 'That would be wonderful. I miss my grandmother. She's the kindest person I know.'

'I can imagine.' Jakob topped up their glasses and raised his own to his lips. He rarely drank wine, even though he enjoyed the taste.

'Are you getting anywhere with your investigation?' She put down her cutlery, which clattered softly.

He shook his head in despair. 'We're not getting anywhere at all.'

'I guess I shouldn't ask you about it.'

He took a big gulp of his wine. 'It's not the killings. Well, don't get me wrong, the murders are terrible, but they're just men. Grown men who weren't good people in any sense of the word, and frankly I would happily have beaten Anguteeraq Poulsen to a pulp myself, although it's very wrong of me to think like that.'

Lisbeth tilted her head and tucked up her legs underneath her. He could see her black tights where the grey marl skirt ended around her knees.

'I understand,' she said quietly.

'I just don't get men like him. I mean…' He ground to a halt as he tried to articulate his thoughts. 'Surely the most natural feeling in the world is to love your child?'

'It certainly ought to be,' Lisbeth said.

'Yes, it should, shouldn't it? Surely nothing is more important than that. I wish it was like that for all children. No child should ever suffer abuse.'

Jakob reached out and grabbed the bottle in order to share the last of the wine between them.

'The same goes for adults,' she said softly. 'The older we get, the more introverted, fearful and frightened of love we become.'

He nodded. This wasn't his area of expertise at all, but the wine and the food had loosened his tongue. 'Adults carry their childhood sorrows with them all their life. That's why it's so important to love your child, so that it can grow up knowing that love exists, and that it's safe to accept that love and to love in return.'

She looked at him with a gaze that was simultaneously wistful and warm. 'Do you have a child back home in Denmark?'

He looked down and shook his head.

'Only suddenly it sounded as if you had. I'm sorry, I didn't mean to pry.'

'That's quite all right. However, I'm very concerned about child abuse.'

'You would make a good father,' she said, and drained her glass. 'I used to go hunting with my father. It was always me who butchered the seals. My mother taught me how to slide the ulo in between the blubber and the skin, and slowly remove the skin from the body. I was ten years old when I flayed my first seal. My father had cut open its belly so the intestines spilled out—the rest was my job. I cut free its guts. Intestines, heart, lungs. Everything. We always had to taste the liver. *It makes you strong*, my father would say.' She shook her head. 'My arms could barely reach right round the seal while I cut it.' She looked at her hand. 'The warm sensation of the blubber…and of the body.' She looked down. 'My father nudged the seal with his boot. He never really helped me. *It's women's work*, he would say. *You're a woman now*.' Her gaze disappeared in the deep-pile rug. 'I knew that he saw me as a woman. Whenever I cut up an animal, I would think of him. Sometimes I would be covered in blood all over. In some strange way I enjoyed it.'

Jakob looked at his plate. He pushed his empty wineglass further onto the coffee table.

Lisbeth shook her head. 'I talk a lot of nonsense. I'm sorry. I think I had better be going.'

'It's not nonsense,' Jakob said, looking at her face. Her freckles and her black hair gleamed in the electric light. 'Many people have deep wounds that no one ever sees. I'll walk you home, if you don't mind. It's a dark and cold night.'

She smiled to him. 'Thank you, but I've lived with this weather all my life.'

'I don't mind walking you home,' he offered again. 'Maybe we'll see the northern lights.' He had seen the northern lights many times, but she didn't have to know that.

Lisbeth looked at his face. Then she reached up and kissed him lightly on his cheek. 'Thank you.'

34

When Jakob returned after walking Lisbeth home, he could see from the path leading up to his house that someone had left a small bag on his doorhandle. He freed the bag from the handle and turned to look out into the night, where the snow lit up the darkness. There were too many footprints in the snow by his door for him to see if any of them were fresh. His fingers had detected immediately that the bag contained two reels of film.

Once inside, he kicked off his boots and pushed the door shut. He hung up his coat and cap on the old pine coat stand in the small hall.

'Now, what's going on here?' he muttered to himself.

He picked up the box Karlo had brought in. It didn't take him long to plug in the small grey projector and turn it on. The two reels were labelled *1* and *2*, so he assumed that he should watch number one first. He glanced at the glass with Mortensen's cheroot butt and fetched a clean glass from the kitchen. The aroma of whisky reached his nostrils before the taste spread inside his mouth and, for a brief moment, numbed his tongue before the heat exploded. He put the glass on the armrest and pressed the play button.

The film began rolling with a monotonous clicking sound, and the light flickered on the white wall in front of him.

The camera appeared to have been mounted in the corner of a large shipping container. The walls were covered with a metallic material that reminded him of tinfoil, but it was thicker, more substantial. The floor looked like plywood. Uneven sheets. From the ceiling hung a single naked light bulb that turned on and off all the time. Sometimes it would be dark for a few seconds. At other times for longer. The light was bright when it was on. Everything went pitch-black once it disappeared. It was stressful for his eyes to look at.

His fingers tightened around the glass on the armrest. The tinfoil room was completely empty. Except for one thing. In a corner furthest from the camera, a small girl was curled up. There were no sounds in the light and the darkness. Just the clicking rhythm of the projector in Jakob's living room. The girl disappeared and came back again with the light. She didn't have any shoes on. No boots. Only tights covering her legs. Red tights. Her dress was dark brown. It was covered by a green jacket that fitted her tightly. She held her arms close to her body. Her hands were by her mouth. She was gripping something dark and knitted. A hat. Pressing it to her face as if it were a teddy bear. She would chew the hat. Her eyes were closed. Her body twitched. The light coming and going clearly distressed her behind her eyelids.

The girl sat like this for the whole film, which lasted about twenty-five minutes. Afterwards there was darkness in his living room. The reel rotated with the loose filmstrip flapping.

Jakob was hyperventilating. He had never seen Najak but it had to be her. She had gone missing eleven days ago, and now someone had sent him a film of her. His thoughts were all jumbled up. There were no containers of that size in Godthåb right now. Very few large container ships called in here in the winter, especially given what the weather was like at the moment. Then he remembered the bag on the doorhandle. He jumped up from his armchair, found the bag and took out the second reel of film. Along with the film was a note that looked similar to the one that had been tied to the stone. *If you tell anyone about this film, she dies. Stop your investigation or she dies.*

He let the note slip from his hand and put the second reel on the projector. He drained his glass of Johnnie Walker in two big gulps and refilled it.

The film crackled and clicked like the first one. It was the same room. Tinfoil walls and plywood flooring. The naked light bulb dividing up the time. Najak curled up in a corner with her woolly hat pressed against her mouth. Her hair was more tangled and messier than in the first film. Her tights were stained with dirt.

Jakob jumped when the camera suddenly came to life. It moved towards the huddling girl. The light disappeared. Came back. Disappeared. She flinched even more. Shaking. The camera was very close to her now, and a hand reached out and snatched the hat from her.

Jakob jumped up, swiping the glass so hard from the armrest that it smashed against the wall.

Her mouth opened and it looked as if she was screaming. She buried her face in her hands. Her short fingers were stiff and quivering. Her lips sucked the skin on one hand. The film ended.

Jakob ran out into the hall and tore open his front door. 'I'm going to bloody well kill you all!' he roared.

Everything was quiet around the house. The frozen air settled around him. The night was black. The windows in all the houses were black. He looked over to where the shadow who had thrown the stone had come from. 'I'm going to bloody well kill you all,' he vowed quietly.

35

The frost intensified dramatically after the last hint of autumn warmth had soaked the town in slush for half a day. The cold returned with a vengeance and everything froze, even the sea around the more sheltered parts of the headland, and that meant it was a severe frost, because the morning and evening tides did their best to break up the ice and allow the moon to continue gazing at its own reflection in the black sea. And yet it turned to ice. Large, white sheets formed by layers of trapped, turquoise seawater.

The frozen water gained a foothold even in the centre of town, climbing up and down the buildings. In some places the icicles were so thick that not even a man could get his arms round them. The snow on the square between Hotel Godthåb, the police station and Brugseni was shovelled into high piles by a rusting yellow bulldozer, leaving the square itself open and clear.

Jakob took a sip of his coffee. He stared absent-mindedly at the black liquid. If he had trusted Mortensen more, he would have shown him the films, but he didn't dare run the risk. The threats in the notes and the official indifference towards Najak made him fear that it would do her more harm than good, were he to open his mouth. She was alive for now, he kept telling himself. He didn't know where she was. He didn't know who she was with. But if he continued investigating the case—discreetly—he would catch a break eventually.

His eyes moved from his coffee across the many papers and files on his desk and out through the window, where his thoughts slipped past the orange supermarket walls and up towards the white peak of Store Malene and Hjortetakken's stubby top. His gaze stopped abruptly and came crashing down to earth by the piles of snow near his window. He shifted so he could see past the mother-in-law's tongue on the windowsill.

There was a small girl out on the square. All alone. Well hidden in a shabby, dark green coat with a hood and a black fur collar. On her back she had a black and orange satchel. Her hands were bare and as red as her cheeks, which he could just make out inside the hood.

'Paneeraq,' he whispered to himself, then he turned in his office chair to look at the others in the room. He wished that Karlo had been here, but he was on a job down by the harbour and it would take time to get hold of him. He looked back at the girl. She couldn't just stand there. Why was she standing there? He knew that the other officers would complain if he brought her in, but he couldn't leave her outside all on her own.

He took a deep breath and got up from his desk without looking at the others.

'So, Pedersen,' Benno called out, 'are you off to see Lisbeth?'

Storm leered like an idiot. 'Get me a cup as well, will you?'

'It's...' Jakob pushed open the door to the reception area. 'There's a little girl outside in the cold. I think she wants to talk to me.' The door closed behind him, and he stopped talking. He didn't give a damn about them. About any of them. Except for Karlo. Karlo was the only Greenlandic police officer there, and the only one he could trust when a case got to him.

'Paneeraq,' he called out, even as he walked down the front steps. The cold crept through the fibres of his knitted jumper. 'Paneeraq, what are you doing out here in the cold?' He looked at her red fingers. 'Why don't you come inside for a bit?'

She didn't move. She just stood there. Like a pillar of stone.

He bent down and looked at her face inside the fur-lined hood. 'It's far too cold for you to be out here, sweetheart.'

'I don't want to go home,' she said quietly.

'Come inside with me,' Jakob said again. 'And I'll see what I can do about it.' He struggled to force the last words up through his throat. What if there was nothing he could do for her? What if he had to send her home, even though she had asked him for help? 'We'll work something out—you come inside with me.'

He didn't dare touch her, so he sufficed by pointing towards the door. 'Lisbeth will get you some hot chocolate,' he said. There was no way the child could be in the office with the other officers when Karlo wasn't there, Jakob had already decided. Benno's frequent derogatory remarks about Greenlanders made Jakob sick.

Paneeraq didn't say anything else, but she took some small, tentative steps towards the door.

Jakob smiled. Not on the inside, but to her. Then he smiled imploringly at Lisbeth as he explained that Paneeraq had got very cold and needed a cup of hot chocolate. He smiled when Lisbeth got up to look after Paneeraq with a maternal gaze and the promise of yummy hot chocolate. And he smiled as he walked through the door of the chief of police, closed it behind him and accepted being enveloped in the stench of cigars that lingered in the room.

He continued to smile as he told Mortensen about Paneeraq. He still didn't tell him about the films and Najak. What if her abductors carried out their threat and killed the girl because of him? He only allowed himself to talk about Paneeraq. Who she was. Her father. His well-founded suspicion that she was a victim of incest. Her limping.

Her cry for help outside in the cold. He even smiled as Mortensen started getting het up, but only because his smile was so fixed at this point that he had no idea it was still plastered across his face.

'This case,' Mortensen practically shouted. 'Dammit, Pedersen, as if we didn't have enough problems with the gutted men, and now you come here…You have to drive the girl home. We can't keep her here, can we? What the hell were you thinking?'

Jakob rubbed the scab on his forehead. 'But, sir, that child is probably being raped every day. We can't just turn a blind eye. There must be something we can do for her. We can't let her down now that she has finally plucked up the courage to come here. She's just a little girl, for God's sake! If we had removed Najak, then she wouldn't have… vanished into thin air.' He stared down at his shoes.

'That's what life is like up here, Pedersen. You can feel sorry for them, but that's all. There's nothing we can do. It goes too deep. Drive her home.'

'Is this a police station?' Jakob exploded. The blood was boiling in his veins. 'Or a slaughterhouse?'

'That's enough!' Mortensen screamed so loudly that his high-pitched voice slipped into a falsetto shriek. 'Have you completely lost your mind? You solve your murders and leave the politics to the rest of us.'

'I'm trying to prevent murders!' Jakob said, still shouting.

'Are you really? Are you sure about that? You're the one stomping around a slaughterhouse. After all, the murdered men are all from your so-called school survey. Eh? You drive that girl back to her parents, who are probably out of their minds with worry, and don't you dare go near anything that involves children from now on. If I hear another word about those girls, I'll suspend you immediately and put you on the first flight back to Denmark. Do you understand?'

Jakob stared briefly at the small, balding man. Then he turned on his heel without saying a word. He disappeared down the corridor and went out into the reception area, where Paneeraq had just finished her hot chocolate and had pushed back her hood, so her face was visible. Her eyes were black and round. Her cheeks still red. Her hair dark, smooth and short. She smiled cautiously to Lisbeth, who had given her the hot chocolate, and handed the cup back to her. 'Thank you,' she whispered politely.

'I've found a place where you can stay for a little while,' Jakob said to her, and in response got the same anxious smile from the girl that Lisbeth had received.

Lisbeth took his hand gently and gave it squeeze, nodding lightly. Then she let go.

He fetched his coat, his files and the notebook from his desk and took Paneeraq with him as he left the police station. There was no help to be had there, but even so, there was no way that girl was going home to her father.

36

The heating was turned up in the small living room, where an aroma of fried sausages and boiling potatoes had spread and now lay like an enticing, transparent quilt around the girl on the black sofa at the far end of the room. She was holding her maths exercise book. Her open satchel lay by her side. Jakob had spent more than two hours helping her get started on her homework, and when she finally understood it, she had continued doing sums in the book. Jakob had wondered whether they shouldn't move on to another subject, but in a strange way it seemed as if the logic and repetition of maths were absolutely the right thing to calm their thoughts.

Paneeraq had decided that they should have sausages for dinner. He had asked her what she would like, and after a long pause she had replied: *Sausages*.

The curtains were closed. Outside, the dark had settled around the house and all of the town, and Jakob had decided to draw all the curtains so that no one could look in. He had even locked the front door, something he rarely did. After the murders and the stone with the threat, security had become a priority—and now, with the girl here, it was crucial.

The sausages sizzled in the frying pan. The potatoes were nearly ready. It wasn't often that he cooked a proper hot meal, but he had been lucky today and got fresh sausages in the supermarket.

From the kitchen he could see Paneeraq on the sofa. She wasn't very tall—about one metre twenty would be his guess. Shorter, perhaps. She had tied back her short hair with an elastic band she had found in his kitchen. He smiled to himself at the memory. She wore a dress that reached just below her knees, where a pair of thick yellow stockings took over. There were polka dots on her dress. Big dots in different colours. The dress was buttoned right up to her neck and had a Peter Pan collar.

She was too short to sit the way she did. Her feet couldn't reach the floor, but stuck out into the air under the coffee table. Her eyes were deep into the maths book. One hand held the book, while the other controlled the pencil from sum to sum. Jakob was delighted to see her working. She was a bright child, and he was surprised at how swiftly she had picked up the logic behind her homework.

'Are you hungry?' he asked into the air.

She looked up from her homework and nodded. He could feel her eyes on him. They were filled with something that simultaneously contained calm and scepticism. Distance and hope.

He couldn't possibly imagine how her day would normally have unfolded. Nor did he want to. He wanted to protect his thoughts from the images that invariably followed. Then he reproached himself for being so sensitive. What right did he have to shield himself from what this little girl had to subject her body and her mind to so often? Her thoughts must be plagued by nightmares, day and night. Jakob felt powerless and guilty. His hatred for her father knew no bounds. No limitations. As she sat there in her dress, doing her homework, it was absolutely beyond him that an adult would ever want to hurt her.

'I'll put two sausages on your plate,' he went on, giving his attention back to the frying pan. He turned off the stove, drained the potatoes and added some cream to the fat in the frying pan. 'Do you fancy eating your dinner on the sofa?'

She shrugged, and he could tell from her eyes that she didn't know what to say.

'Yes, let's eat there,' he said, answering his own question. 'Would you like me to cut up your food for you?'

She shrugged again.

'Does your mum cut up your food?'

The girl looked at him quizzically. A small frown appeared on the fine skin on her forehead. 'Not often,' she said.

'Do you like it when your mum cuts your food into bite-size pieces?'

Her frown grew deeper and her eyes widened.

'I mean, in small bits?' he explained.

The wrinkle disappeared as she nodded quickly.

'Then I'll cut it up for you,' Jakob said with a smile, and plated the food.

He covered her dress with a clean tea towel, put the plate on top of it and handed her a fork. His mother would have turned in her grave, had she seen it, but he had been eating like this for a long time now. Besides, he thought the girl might feel safer if she was allowed to stay on the sofa, rather than having to sit at the dining table with him. On the sofa she had a small spot where she had sat for several hours with her homework and been left alone.

She ate slowly. Carefully and tentatively. As if each bite needed examining before it could be swallowed. He tried eating at her pace, so she wouldn't feel out of place, but found it hard because his tongue couldn't wait so long before swallowing once it had tasted the food.

Halfway through the meal she looked up. 'Will I be sleeping here?'

He hesitated and tried to read the expression in her eyes. 'Yes—if you'd like to?'

She looked down at her plate and skewered a piece of potato. 'I would like to. You are nice and you help me.'

'You can sleep in the bedroom,' he said. 'In the big bed. I'll be sleeping here in the living room, so you'll be all on your own in there, but if you want anything, just give me a shout. I can easily hear you.'

Jakob knew very well that the situation wasn't sustainable. Paneeraq couldn't continue to stay with him. It was Lisbeth who had suggested that he bring her home when he'd asked her advice, and she had pointed out how odd it was that Paneeraq wasn't scared of him, given that he was a man. *Many girls here have a tough father because we've pretty much always lived in a tough culture, surrounded by a tough environment. Perhaps she's just glad to have met a nice man. It's good for her to experience that. Why don't you take her home so that she can calm down and have a nice evening where she's treated well? But be careful—if she gets a taste for it, she won't want to go home. I've seen that happen so many times.* She had said the latter with a glint in her eye. *I found it hard enough to go home myself.*

He had asked Lisbeth if she would like to join them, but she was hosting a kaffemik party for her sister. *It'll probably do you good as well,* she had said, and now Paneeraq was ensconced in the middle of his sofa.

37

Jakob flicked through his book on rocks and fossils. He had decided that Paneeraq might like a bedtime story, and now she was snuggled up under the big, airy quilt in his bed, while he perched on the edge with his book.

The idea of reading aloud to her was a good one, but he had forgotten that his library contained mostly non-fiction and police magazines—and while educating the young about the value of police work mattered greatly to him, it probably didn't appeal to an eleven-year-old girl. He had finally settled on his geology book, but was only halfway through Igaliku sandstone in the sedimentary rock chapter when he was forced to concede that it might not be of interest to the little girl either.

He slammed shut the book. 'This is really boring, ilaa?'

She nodded and smiled feebly.

'I don't mind you saying so,' he said. 'In this house you can say whatever you like, and even I have to admit that rocks can be a bit dull.'

Her smile widened. She had pulled up the big, white quilt so far that her face was only visible above her nose.

'Wait here,' he said. 'I'll just get something from the living room.'

He returned with a fossilised sea urchin and the shell of a more recent sea urchin. He placed them both on the mattress next to her pillow so she could see them.

'These are both sea urchins,' he said, giving each of them a little push. 'One became fossilised, while the other is like a seashell. The sea urchin itself was probably eaten by a seagull or a raven in the summer.'

Paneeraq looked curiously at the two objects on the mattress. The shell was lying on its back, so it was easy to see that the two objects were very similar. The furrow on her brow reappeared, and she looked up at Jakob.

'You're allowed to touch them,' he said, nodding towards the fossil and the shell.

Her small fingers closed around first the fossil, and then more delicately around the shell. She turned them over and studied their backs and their stomachs. The fossil was solid, the shell hollow and delicate. 'How did it turn into a stone?'

'It was probably buried in the mud of a big ocean more than three hundred million years ago, and it was slowly fossilised and turned into flint stone. Its shell has long since disappeared, so what you're looking at is the soft animal inside the shell.'

She didn't say anything, but clutched the fossilised sea urchin.

'It's incredible, don't you think, that these little creatures crawled around in the sea all those millions of years ago? And that they look and function in exactly the same way today as they did thirty or a hundred million years ago. On the beaches back home in Denmark, where I come from, you can bend down and pick up a living sea urchin with one hand and a fossilised one with the other.'

Her hand enclosed the fossil. 'Can I turn into a stone?'

He rubbed one eye. 'Yes, you can, as a matter of fact, but it would take many more years than there have been people on this earth, so no one would ever know.'

She smiled contentedly and nodded softly, while she opened and closed her hand. 'It feels warm.'

'It's your hand warming it up. Rocks love heat, and if they get plenty of it, they become liquid.'

She looked at him in disbelief.

'It's the truth. Once, all of Greenland was liquid. It's called lava and comes from the core of the earth.' He could see that she recognised the word *lava*.

He stopped speaking, and she let her head sink back on the pillow, but she continued to clench the fossilised sea urchin in her hand. 'You can keep it, if you like,' Jakob said.

She looked at him without really daring to look.

'It's yours now,' he added, and got up from the bed.

Her clenched fist disappeared under the quilt, as did the rest of her face. Only a little tuft of hair continued to stick out. He wished he could stroke her hair, but he didn't dare touch her.

'Good night,' he whispered, and turned off the light. 'I'll leave the door ajar.'

The quilt said nothing. It didn't even move.

Jakob carefully pulled the door to, leaving a gap. He went over to the sideboard and got out the projector. When he had brought Paneeraq back to his house, another bag had been hanging on the doorhandle. Jakob had removed it and opened the door as if nothing had happened. Through the thin plastic he could feel the box with the reel between his fingers, and had known that the contents were important. But he had set the bag aside and concentrated on Paneeraq's homework and dinner instead.

Now he set up the small projector next to his armchair again, and mounted the new reel. He looked at the door to the bedroom for a long time before starting the projector. Light filled the room, as did the clicking sound from the motor, feeding the film from the reel through the heart of the projector.

The camera was static. Mounted in the corner that was facing Najak. The light came and went. Jakob jumped every time. Not because the light and the darkness were frightening in and of themselves, but because every interruption came without rhythm or order, and so felt like a shock. Because the little girl was still curled up in the far corner of the shiny tinfoil hell, which would alternately scream in light and reflection and then be lost in total darkness. Her body was scrunched up. Wrapped around itself. Her hair was messier. Uncombed. Rat-tailed. It was several days since the last recording, it would appear. Her feet were bare now. Her tights were gone. Her legs bare and stained with dirt. The seconds stood still. Najak looked lifeless.

Jakob tried to keep his gaze fixed on the glowing square with the girl in the corner. The room around him came and went in time with the light on Najak. He could see only a little of her face. She was chewing monotonously, sucking one hand. There was no other movement. Traces of tears on her cheek. Smeared. Dried.

The film kept on playing. It was the longest one so far.

Jakob got up and fetched himself a large whisky and four painkillers, before collapsing back into the armchair. The film continued playing, but there was no movement other than the light going on and off, and the child sucking her skin.

He disappeared inside himself. The film carried on. As did everything else. Without noticing it, he slipped into an uneasy, shallow slumber.

38

Jakob shot up from his armchair so fast that he nearly blacked out, but he grabbed the back of the armchair for support and regained his balance. The spots stopped dancing in front of his eyes. He could tell from the clock on the wall near the kitchen that it was ten-thirty in the evening. The reel had run out. Someone was knocking on the door and, still dazed, he looked towards the hall. It was the knocking that had woken him up. No one ever visited him at night. Especially not on a winter's night when the cold was this fierce.

He looked about him, then quickly unplugged the projector and hid it in the sideboard. More knocking on the door. He took a few steps towards the hall.

There was another knock. This time it was hard and insistent, and Jakob felt his terror pulling at the cut on his forehead. He swore softly under his breath, and grimaced before he took the last few steps towards the door, which he unlocked and opened. The cold air swept inside immediately and enveloped his upper body, like the breath of an icy demon.

He recognised two of the three men outside, but the third, who was still standing with his fist raised to knock, he had never seen before. He was a broad, ruddy-faced man with messy red hair, a bushy red beard and two gruff, ice-blue eyes hidden under thick eyebrows. He wore an Icelandic sweater, jeans and black clog boots.

'Jakob,' one of the other two men said, putting his hand on the red-haired man's shoulder to move him aside. 'We'll just come in for a moment.'

Jakob wanted to protest, but the three men had already pushed their way past him.

'I'm sorry that you've had a wasted journey in this cold,' Jakob said, following the three men into his living room. 'But can't it wait until tomorrow?' His heart was pounding.

The two men stared at him, while the man with the red beard walked around, inspecting the furniture and the jigsaw puzzle on the table. Jakob knew one of the two men, a young Danish lawyer called Kjeld Abelsen. He was thin, bordering on gangly, and so light-skinned that the contrast between his black hair and his pale face made him look like a black-and-white photograph stripped of any softer shades. He was clenching his jaw so tightly that his lips almost disappeared, and his eyes were shiny and piercing. He had only been in Godthåb for a few years, but had already earned himself some status and respect. He had—in Jakob's opinion—an uncanny ability to always know on which horse to bet.

The other man he recognised was Jørgen Emil Lyberth, and his round body and head made him Abelsen's physical opposite. He was an Inuit, and one of the members of the Greenlandic Provincial Council who made the most noise when debating secession from Denmark and leaving the European Economic Community.

Jakob knew exactly what the two men represented, both individually and together, but he had no idea what they were doing in his house with a red-haired Icelander late one night with biting frost and wind. To the outside world, Lyberth and Abelsen were opposites in terms of politics and vision, but behind the scenes they were, as far as Jakob had worked out, a strangely secretive pair who might very well turn out not to sing the same songs in darkness as in daylight.

'What do you want?' Jakob demanded to know, unable to hide his irritation that the young men and their older, red-bearded attack dog had forced their way into his home.

'Why don't you sit down, Jakob,' Abelsen said with a cold look.

'I'm fine standing.'

'I think you should, or I'll have to ask our friend from the Faroe Islands to help you.'

Jakob looked at the robust man, who had moved close to him. 'I'm fine standing,' he reiterated angrily.

'Suit yourself,' Abelsen went on. 'Then again, you've never seen him gut a pilot whale, but never mind, the fall will be the same wherever he drops you.'

Lyberth had sat down on the sofa, but he got up again. Abelsen looked towards him and made a quick gesture with one hand. Lyberth nodded grimly.

'You have a nice home.' Abelsen picked up a rock from a shelf and tapped it against his forehead. 'But I see that you keep injuring yourself. Then again, being a police officer is a dangerous job, isn't it? And we're up to our necks in murders right now.'

Jakob thought frantically about the murders, the film reels and Najak. He did his best to keep an eye on the bedroom door and Paneeraq, while at the same time trying not to send even a fragment of his attention in that direction. 'What's this about?'

'We have a conflict of interests, Pedersen,' Abelsen said, almost without moving his narrow lips. 'And you would do well to keep your nose out of our business. Some investigations end up being shelved, as you well know. In the public interest.'

'I don't follow.'

'Wind up your investigation.' Abelsen had walked right up to Jakob so their faces were close. 'Conclude that the murders were committed by a Greenlandic man, and people will lose interest.'

'But we don't know that they were,' Jakob objected, looking to Lyberth. 'We can't just pin the blame for three murders on an innocent man.'

'Thomas Olesen from Block 16,' Abelsen went on, still eyeballing Jakob. 'There's your killer. Pick him up tomorrow after the morning briefing.'

'Thomas Olesen,' Jakob exclaimed. 'But he's just a lonely drunk.'

'Charge him with the murders and close the investigation tomorrow morning. Thomas Olesen?' Abelsen snorted with contempt. 'Who is going to miss him? He drinks, he gets into fights all the time, he's known for being the first to pull his knife, and he can gut a seal like no one else. Bring him in and close the case so the rest of us can get on with our lives.'

'I'm a police officer,' Jakob said, his gaze jumping between the two men. 'I'm not a mercenary or an executioner. What on earth do you think you're doing? I'm going to have to talk to Mortensen about this.'

'You charge Olesen with the murders tomorrow morning or suffer the consequences.' Abelsen turned his upper body slightly, and nodded towards the Faroese man. 'Either we make you the next victim or we charge you with the murders.'

'Well, you clearly can't do that,' Jakob said, aware that his voice was quivering. His gaze shifted from Kjeld Abelsen's eyes to his narrow lips, which looked even whiter and deader than usual. If he was right in his suspicions, these men might kill Najak. He clenched his fists, digging his nails into his skin while staring stiffly at the men, one after the other.

'Jakob, he's just an alcoholic hunter. He doesn't matter.'

'Everyone matters. We can't just jail an innocent man so you can get political breathing space. I won't be a part of it, and I'm not going to let it happen.'

'Okay.' Abelsen beckoned to the Faroese. 'You're finished, Jakob

Pedersen. You're a danger to Greenland.'

The broad Faroese with the piercing blue eyes reached Jakob in seconds. He grabbed Jakob's neck with one hand and his right wrist with the other. Jakob was so stunned by the man's strength and speed that he did nothing to defend himself.

The man released Jakob's neck and ripped open his shirt, exposing his chest and stomach, while with his other hand he took out a knife. Before Jakob had time to think, the knife was pressing against his ribcage.

He breathed in short, shallow gasps. It was too late to fight back. His thoughts were chaotic. Najak, who was being held a prisoner. Paneeraq, who, more than anything in the world, mustn't make the slightest sound. Not one. This wasn't about politics or breathing space.

The room closed in on him. He could feel the three men. The knife against his skin. The furniture. Karlo sitting by the jigsaw puzzle. Karlo was missing from the living room now. The snow outside. The drumming dancer. The beat of the drum merged with the beating of his heart, only centimetres from the tip of the blade.

'I'm a police officer,' he croaked. 'You can't—'

'It's up to you,' Abelsen cut him off. 'You decide who lives and who dies.'

TRACES OF
BLOOD

39

During the night Matthew had checked his mobile repeatedly, but there was nothing from Tupaarnaq. His thoughts kept returning to Lyberth's part in everything, though the blood-soaked images Tupaarnaq had planted in his mind were a distraction.

It was light outside. He turned over in bed and reached for Jakob's leather notebook, which was lying on the bedside table. Something in between the lines had got Lyberth killed, and now Tupaarnaq had been caught up in it, probably because she was an obvious scapegoat. She had nothing to do with the murder, Matthew was sure of it. The motive was to be found in Jakob's notebook. Not directly, but because in it he had described something that someone had been prepared to kill to keep secret. Forty years ago as well as today.

He looked at the list of the girls. The lost girls. Maybe he could find them? Go back in time and discover the fates of the people Jakob had written about. The four men were all dead, but what about the girls? Next to the first victim's daughter, Najak Rossing Lynge, Jakob had drawn a small cross and a question mark, but Matthew couldn't be sure that she was dead. And then there was a near blank page about some films Jakob hadn't felt able to write about. The notebook's unanswered questions had lingered on in time after Jakob's disappearance, but it should be possible to track down the girls. Especially Paneeraq Poulsen, whom Jakob had brought to his house.

Matthew didn't have Ottesen's mobile number, so he texted Malik asking him to ask Ottesen if any eight-millimetre films relating to the murders in 1973 had ever been found.

He checked his watch. Leiff must be at work now.

'Hi, Matthew—what are you up to?' Leiff sounded cheerful, as always. 'You missed the morning briefing...again.'

'No, I...Leiff, I was wondering, could you help me find some people who lived in Nuuk in 1973?'

'You're thinking about the people from the case I told you about, the four murders?'

'Yes, that's it.'

There was silence for a few seconds. 'We'll probably have to rummage through the Town Hall archives for that.'

'Okay. Is that possible? I mean, right away.'

Leiff cleared his throat. 'Yes,' he began tentatively. 'In theory, yes, but their archives from the seventies are even more chaotic than the ones here at the paper.' His voice brightened up. 'But listen, my wife works at the Town Hall, and she looked up some of them last week when we first asked about the murders. I'll check with her. I'm sure she knows her way around every nook and cranny.'

40

Leiff and Matthew walked the short stretch from *Sermitsiaq*'s offices to the Town Hall. The rectangular building grew rust-brown, green and concrete-grey from one of the city centre's T-junctions.

The sun shone warm and bright, as it had done yesterday, and there was nothing to suggest that autumn was coming. The arc of an almost cloudless firmament rested across the mountains except for a few flimsy, white tufts that stretched across the top of Mount Ukkusissat like snakeskins.

Matthew was dreading the phone call he would inevitably get once Lyberth's body was discovered. If it hadn't been found by tonight, he would have to do something. Lyberth couldn't just lie there, rotting. It was unacceptable. The man had a family waiting for him, and the fact that Lyberth was lying there hidden away, crucified and gutted, wouldn't make it any easier for them. Matthew was also very worried about Tupaarnaq by now. Perhaps she had gone back to her apartment. Or maybe far away. He looked down at his feet and kicked a pebble out of the way.

'We'll take the door to the right,' Leiff said. 'The main door is closed until noon.'

Matthew pressed his hand against his chest and breathed lightly a couple of times as he followed Leiff up towards the tall concrete building, whose height and pale colour were in stark contrast to the dark-brown and green extension.

'Are you all right?' Leiff said, looking at the hand Matthew was pressing against his chest. 'You don't seem yourself.'

Above them, Greenland's flag flapped alongside Denmark's, two red and white sails against the deep blue sky.

'I'm all right,' Matthew said, lowering his hand. 'I think I got too much fresh air yesterday...I'm all right.'

Leiff put his hand on Matthew's shoulder. 'I've lived here for sixty years,' he said, his voice mild and warm. 'Every year new Danes arrive, their heads full of themselves and their romantic dreams about Nuuk and nature. Six months later more than half of them are back in Denmark—for good.' He patted Matthew's shoulder. 'Danes who actually care enough to dig up a cold case and attack deep-rooted problems are few and far between...I'm always here for you, if you want something.'

'Thank you,' Matthew said. The way things were going, he couldn't even be sure if he would still be in Nuuk next week, let alone in six months. If Tupaarnaq went down for Lyberth's murder, he would be dragged down with her and he would be finished here.

The glass door opened inwards and took them into a narrow but tall corridor lined with glass and grey concrete. Leiff greeted a couple of women cheerfully and patted a young man on his shoulder. From the angular hall they continued into a low passage with glass walls that terminated in a new, bigger hall two floors high. In the middle of the hall was a shallow, rectangular turquoise basin containing clean water. An old leather kayak was suspended above the basin.

'We're going up those stairs over there,' Leiff said, pointing to the far side of the basin.

'Did she tell you what she has found?' Matthew's gaze lingered briefly on an oil painting of a mountainous area in a soft, arctic winter light.

'No, but we're about to find out. Have you made any progress since we last spoke?'

'I don't know.' Matthew looked down at the orange-brown tiles below them. 'I think I'm going round in circles, so I'm hoping that we can track down someone from the seventies case—someone who's still alive.'

'Fingers crossed.' Leiff's gaze followed Matthew's down to the tiles. 'Did you really not bring anything other than those sneakers?'

Matthew shook his head. 'I promise to get myself a pair of boots soon.'

'Hi, guys.' A tall, sturdy woman popped her head over the white-painted wrought-iron bannister. A long row of slanted windows in the vaulted ceiling cast so much light over the steps and the basin that the hall felt more like an atrium.

'Hi,' Leiff called out and waved to her once. He turned to Matthew. 'This is my wife, Ivalo.'

'I'm Matthew,' Matthew said, sticking out his hand as they reached her.

'And I'm Ivalo,' she said, and showed them into her office. 'Nice to meet you, given that I missed you when you came round for dinner. I've looked up the names Leiff sent me, and I have to say that there wasn't much, but I found a few things. Do sit down.' Her fingers tapped the keyboard. 'It's only recently that we're starting to get a proper handle on what data we have here. It's all thanks to a series of IT grants.' She shook her head. 'You won't believe this, but before computerisation we had no real cross-referencing of basic information, so not only was it difficult for people to have their cases dealt with efficiently, it was also easy for people to disappear. Especially anyone whose details were still on paper. We didn't bring the past with us when we went digital. However, all is not lost because the information is still in the archives. All you need is an old woman who knows where to look, and I'm that old woman.'

Matthew found it difficult to judge Ivalo's age, but thought she was probably around sixty. She was taller than Leiff and more robust. Not fat, just robust. Her hair was black and cut in a short, wavy style.

'I found them all in the basement archives, but only one of them has made it to our new IT system. All the men died in '73, and I can find absolutely no trace of Jakob Pedersen after that year, but as far as I recall he was a police officer and was regarded as deceased. Isn't that right, Leiff?'

'Yes, I believe so. He disappeared during the investigation into the killings, and when neither he nor his body was found, he was presumed dead. Murdered. As you know, the whole thing was very suspicious. Some people thought that he was the killer, others that the murderer had killed him.' Leiff shrugged. 'Whatever the truth, neither the murders nor Pedersen's disappearance was ever solved, and nobody seems to have wanted to delve deeper into it until you came along.'

Matthew was tempted to tell them about the notebook, but decided to keep the information to himself for a little longer.

'It was pretty much the same when I started looking for the girls,' Ivalo said, unprompted. 'Two of them died of cancer when they were still in their early thirties, while one vanished without a trace in November 1973. The last girl also disappeared, but she turned up again. We have no information on her in the period from 1973 up until 2012, when she suddenly reappeared here in Nuuk, saying she had just moved here. She claims to have lived in a village one hundred and thirty kilometres south of here, but even so I still can't find anything on her between 1973 and 2012. Like I said, it's only recently that we have digitalised our basic data, and we still have many villages to add—maybe we'll never get round to it. So she could easily have lived in some coastal village for all those years. She had no parents, as they died shortly before she herself went missing.'

'They were killed,' Leiff corrected her. 'They were buried here in Nuuk.'

'And the girl is in Nuuk now?' Matthew was on the edge of his seat. 'She's alive?'

'Yes—I've made a note of her address for you.' She handed him a piece of paper.

Paneeraq Poulsen, it said at the top. Matthew looked out of the window by Ivalo's desk. The daughter of the fourth victim. The one with a heart next to her name in Jakob's notebook. 'Thank you so much. You've been a huge help.' He hesitated. 'Are you sure it's the right person?'

'Yes. I don't believe there's any doubt about that.'

'Paneeraq,' Matthew whispered to himself. She would be over fifty years old now, and no longer a little girl hiding under Jakob's blankets with her sea urchin.

Outside the windows, the weather had changed dramatically— more so in such a short space of time than any place Matthew had ever experienced. The sky had turned from blue to black, and the rain was sheeting down in dense, grey curtains.

'What's on your mind?'

Leiff's voice scattered Matthew's thoughts.

'Sorry, I...I...What did you just say?'

'That you'll get your feet wet in this weather.'

'Yes—how did that happen? Only a minute ago it was sunny.'

'The North Atlantic is more fickle than a newly married Greenlandic woman,' Leiff chuckled.

Ivalo looked at him sternly. 'Watch it!' She shook her head, then bent down to examine Matthew's sneakers. 'Are those your only shoes?'

'Yes...I haven't got round to buying anything else yet, but I'm sure I'll be all right. I wear these all year round.'

'I'm sure you do, my dear—in Denmark, but not in Greenland. You've no idea how quickly it can turn cold and wet here.'

'Or how deep the snow can be,' Leiff added.

'What size are you?' Ivalo was looking at her husband. 'Leiff, you must have some boots in the basement? Let's see if you have a pair that would fit Matthew.'

Matthew looked at his sneakers. 'I can just go and buy myself a pair in the Nuuk Centre, if it becomes necessary.'

'It has just become necessary,' Ivalo said. 'But let me check our basement first. There's no need to spend money on new ones, if Leiff has a pair that will fit you.'

'Why don't we drive home and take a look now?' Leiff said, his voice brightening up. 'Anyway, it's time for lunch.'

Matthew's mobile buzzed in his pocket, and he quickly took it out. 'I'm sorry,' he said to no one in particular. 'I've just got an email, and I was expecting—' He ground to a halt. In his inbox was an email from jelly@hotmail.com, but there was no information about the sender other than a name at the bottom of the message.

Meet me by Nipisa Friday evening at 10 o'clock. I won't be in Nuuk until then. It's about a notebook belonging to Jakob Pedersen, which you claim to have. I would like to see it. I haven't heard his name for a long time. Regards Jørgen Emil Lyberth.

The email had been sent only ten minutes ago.

'Bad news?' Leiff asked him.

'No, it...Sorry, it just threw me.'

'Was it work?'

'No, it was someone I haven't heard from in a long time, so it caught me off-guard. Never mind—it really doesn't matter.' He felt a shiver run down his spine.

'Yes, that can give you a bit of a shock,' Leiff said, smiling, while he took out a note and handed it to Matthew. 'I left this on your desk today, but as you didn't come into the office, I brought it with me instead.' It was an address scribbled on a piece of paper, just like Ivalo's note, and below it the words: *I think your father lived with this woman for a long time.*

'Eh?' Matthew burst out. 'Are you serious? He...I...'

'Give it a try,' Leiff went on. 'It's just an address, but you never know.'

41

Less than thirty minutes later Matthew was dropped off outside his building with two pairs of boots in a bag. A pair made from black leather and a pair of blue Sorels that had never been worn. Leiff continued to the office to let them know that Matthew would be working from home on his story about the information they had unearthed from the Town Hall archives. This was technically true, but the moment Matthew got in, he put on the Sorel boots and went straight to Tupaarnaq's apartment. The addresses on the two pieces of paper were burning a hole in his pocket, but they could wait. Or they could wait more than Tupaarnaq and the recently deceased Lyberth, who was apparently still sending emails.

Rather than walk back through the town, around Tele-Posthuset and down Samuel Kleinschmidtip Aqqutaa, he took the footpath behind the blue community hall and emerged close to Lyngby-Tårbæksvej, which ran past a large area of low, white apartment blocks before reaching Block 17.

The weather was still bad, and he soon felt the water penetrating every opening in his clothing. He wasn't even halfway there by the time his jacket and trousers were soaked. Only his feet in his new boots remained dry.

He could see the Atlantic Ocean most of the way, but it was grey and hazy due to the dense rain that fell between the houses from moisture-rich, foggy clouds. The water soaked his head and dripped from his hair and nose.

It was only one o'clock in the afternoon, but the cloud cover over Nuuk was so thick that it felt more like early evening. Water swept in from all sides. The wind tossed the fog and the water around. It tore at his jacket and he had to lean into the gusts so as not to be knocked over.

The rain and the wind also tore at the damaged doors and howled up the stairwell leading to Tupaarnaq's apartment. On the first floor, where some of the glass in the door to the gallery was missing, there were puddles of water on the floor. There was a heavy, clammy smell. Like damp cardboard, or wet mortar.

The fingers of his right hand closed around the cold steel handle on the door to Tupaarnaq's apartment. The handle responded. It moved down with a quiet, light click as the locking mechanism let go of the doorframe.

Matthew's heart was pounding. His blood was roaring, swelling the veins under the skin on his hands and arms. He swallowed a couple of times and forced himself to slow his breathing.

The hallway was bleak. As empty as if no one had ever lived in this place. On either side of him were two closed doors, while the middle door was open. It was from there that the sparse light entered the small space. He closed the front door behind him, almost without making a noise, and listened for any sounds. The wind was still howling, but not as crazily as out in the stairwell.

He wanted to leave. Reverse out of the door. Walk backwards all the way down the stairs and far, far away.

The apartment smelled of sewage. Sewage and damp. He closed his eyes and listened. He stood very still, taking deep breaths. It was so quiet. So empty. He couldn't imagine how anyone else but him could be here. And certainly not a dead body. Nor could he smell death. Death smelled differently. It was dry. Medicinal. Not rotting. It is an indeterminate smell seeping out of every pore only minutes after the blood has stopped circulating. Colour fades from the skin. Everything turns grey. Then the smell arrives. He had seen it with Tine in the wrecked car. Felt it in the ambulance. He was getting that sensation now.

A door slammed in the stairwell and he almost jumped out of his skin. He looked over his shoulder in order to see the front door. The sound of stomping boots on the stairs grew louder, then rapidly faded. Matthew turned back towards the light in the living room and entered it.

Without thinking, he took out a cigarette from the packet in his jeans pocket and lit it. The warm smoke slipped deep into his lungs. 'Oh, shit,' he whispered, and took another drag so deep that he ended up coughing up the smoke.

Lyberth was positioned like a Christ figure, with a big nail bashed through each palm. His palms were facing upwards and were filled with dark, congealed blood. The flesh around his nails was frayed.

He had been a short, compact man with stumpy legs and a fat belly. Now he had been gutted. His skin, fat and flesh had been pulled aside and nailed to the floor so that his belly opened up like a crater. Inside, only the pale bones and the muddy, dark flesh remained. Everything else was gone. A coagulating brown lake surrounded the body. But no intestines. When Tupaarnaq had told him about the dead Lyberth on her floor, his abdomen hadn't been nailed to the wooden floorboards; she had described how the dead man's intestines were lying around him. Nor had she said anything about there being a sock in his mouth or a piece of fabric draped over his eyes. She had said that his mouth had been smeared in blood and saliva, and the blood vessels in his eyes had burst.

A flimsy fraying cloth was flapping outside on the balcony. It had probably hung there in all kinds of weather for years. The light played with the holes torn in the sun-bleached fabric and cast fleeting shadows and patterns across the wooden floor around Lyberth. Apart from the shadows, there was nothing in the living room. This apartment stood empty, as did so many others in these blocks, which had been condemned due to mould.

Suddenly Matthew caught a glimpse of a face on the balcony. For the second time he nearly jumped out of his skin, and he ducked immediately. The face was gone as quickly as it had appeared, and the flapping curtain had obscured every recognisable feature in the brief second the face had been visible.

Matthew turned and stared at the front door. He knew that the balcony reached as far as the kitchen door, and that it was possible to reach the hall that connected the living room and the front door through the kitchen.

His eyes swept across Lyberth's bloated and emptied abdomen.

Footsteps in the kitchen caused him to look up. They were rapid. Running feet. His heart beat wildly in his chest.

'Hello?' he called, and cleared his throat. 'Tupaarnaq?'

The front door slammed. Matthew ran towards the noise. The hall was empty. The kitchen was empty. He ran outside to the gallery. Somewhere below him he could hear footsteps jumping down the stairs.

He bent down and picked up a damp cloth lying on the gallery floor, then went back to Tupaarnaq's apartment, where he opened the door he guessed led to the bathroom. He dropped his cigarette butt into the toilet bowl and lit another one. Then he tore off a large wad of toilet paper from the roll and started walking through the apartment and wiping off any possible fingerprints. Every handle, door surface, kitchen cupboard. Including Lyberth's skin. He looked in every cupboard in every room, but found no trace of Tupaarnaq. Not one. Finally, he flushed the cigarette butts, the toilet paper and the cloth down the toilet.

On his way out of the apartment block, he paused on the first floor and took out his mobile to reread the email from jelly@hotmail.com. Then he pressed reply, and started typing with one finger:

Deal. We will meet as you suggest, Friday night. I'll bring the notebook.

Next he opened a web browser and went to jubii.dk, where he created a new account and wrote:

Jørgen Emil Lyberth lies murdered on the second floor in Block 17, stairwell J, behind the door with the words 'abandon hope all ye who enter here'.

As soon as he had sent the email to Nuuk Police, he deleted the account.

At the bottom of the stairwell, a man was sitting up against the wall on piles of junk mail and old newspapers. He looked to be in his mid-fifties, but it was hard to tell as he was wrapped in several layers of filthy clothing, and his face was grimy and weather-beaten.

'Piss off home to Denmark,' the man grunted as Matthew went past. His eyes followed the cigarette on its way to Matthew's mouth. 'Give us one,' he said.

Matthew hesitated and took another drag. The man hadn't been here when he arrived. Then he took out his cigarette packet and gave it to him. 'You can have all of them, but if anyone asks, I was never here—understand?'

The man nodded as he pushed open the packet. Fifteen cigarettes were left in it.

'Did you see someone run past just now? A woman, possibly? No hair?'

The man on the floor shook his head as he took out a cigarette. 'I won't tell anyone.'

Matthew's mobile buzzed in his pocket. He nodded to the man and pushed open the door. 'Yes?'

'It's Tupaarnaq. Can you pick me up from the police station?'

'Yes...Pick you up? Why?'

'The idiots have brought me in again. They just don't get it, morons.'

Matthew looked up across Block 17. 'Why have they arrested you?'

'I can't be bothered to explain that now. So are you coming or what? They'll let me go as long as someone agrees to keep an eye on me...and I don't know anyone else.'

42

Ottesen was the first person Matthew met at the police station. The officer smiled as he shook his head. 'I get where you're coming from, Matt Cave, but be careful. She's a she-wolf.'

'A she-wolf?' Matthew echoed.

'She's a wild one. I would watch my back if I were you.' Ottesen hesitated and tilted his head. 'It was her who bit Ulrik the first time we arrested her.'

'What happened?'

'We were chasing her across the rocks...she runs like an arctic hare. Anyway, we reached the edge of the rocks, and I guess the drop was too steep so she turned around and slumped to her knees...just like one of those Olympic sprinters. And when Ulrik tried to grab her, she lunged at him with such force that they rolled a fair way down the rocks, and then she bit him. We heard them both snarling like wild animals.'

Matthew rubbed his upper lip. 'So what has she done this time?'

'She beat up a man behind Brugseni. She wanted us to arrest him because she had seen him groping his daughter, but there were no other witnesses and the girl clammed up. In the end we had no choice but to bring Tupaarnaq in so that she could calm down. We never intended to keep her very long.' He patted Matthew on the shoulder. 'Are you getting somewhere with your story?'

'I've been out and about looking for information. I think I might be close to finding a witness. Fingers crossed.'

'A witness? I hope you'll keep me in the loop.'

Matthew nodded. 'When I asked you about the eight-millimetre films and the 1973 case…are you absolutely sure you've never seen any film reels here at the station?'

'Totally,' Ottesen said. 'Now, I can't know what happened forty years ago, obviously, but I've never heard about any films, and I'm sure we haven't got them now.'

'Okay,' Matthew said. His gaze wandered past Ottesen without ending up anywhere.

'Are you all right?'

Matthew shook his head lightly. 'Yes, yes.'

'Good. I'll go and get the she-wolf,' Ottesen said with another smile, and he disappeared through the door to the corridor where Matthew and Malik had met with him earlier.

Matthew could hear her footsteps in the corridor before the door was even opened. Angry footsteps attacking the floor.

'She's all yours,' Ottesen said with a friendly sweep of his arm towards the double doors.

'I'm not anyone's,' Tupaarnaq snarled. 'Can I go now?'

'Yes,' Ottesen said. 'Absolutely, but a word of friendly advice: it's a short road back to prison for someone who has only just been released.'

She eyeballed him until he looked away.

Tupaarnaq shoved Matthew aside and pushed open the glass door so hard it banged against the porch outside.

Matthew looked wearily at Ottesen, then traipsed after the incandescent woman, who was already well ahead of him. 'Where are you going?' he called out to her.

'To talk to a man.'

'About what?'

'That's none of your business.'

'I went to take a look at Lyberth.'

'Idiot. Why?'

'He can't just lie there, and they haven't found him yet.'

'I'd guessed as much, you halfwit, or those morons at the station would never have let me go.'

'I've emailed the police to tell them where he is.'

'You really are an idiot.' She stopped for a moment and slapped his forehead hard with the palm of her hand. 'What if they had found him while I was still in custody? Eh? You really don't think things through, do you, caveman?'

'How was I to know you'd beaten someone up? I thought we had agreed to keep a low profile.'

'And you think emailing the police telling them that their venerated statesman and major pervert lies murdered in my apartment is keeping a low profile?' She slapped Matthew's forehead another three times. 'I've just spent twelve years in prison for killing some other sick bastard who couldn't keep his disgusting dick in his pants, for fuck's sake.' She spun around and continued her furious march towards the low housing blocks in the distance.

Someone had written 'Fuck the state' with green spray paint next to the door they went through. She continued up the stairs. Her strides were so long that she took the steps two at a time. She stopped on the second floor and checked the name on the letterbox before she started banging on the door.

'How did you know his name?' Matthew wheezed.

'The other officer who attended mentioned it, and I bet there aren't many men called Sakkak Biilmann living around here.'

Matthew didn't have time to say anything else before the door was opened.

'Is Sakkak in?' Tupaarnaq demanded to know.

The short woman who had appeared in the doorway nodded quietly, then looked anxiously up and down Tupaarnaq's tattooed arms, where the two skulls snarled at her.

'Good,' Tupaarnaq hissed and pushed the woman aside.

'I'm so sorry,' Matthew exclaimed and grabbed the woman, who was about to fall over.

'What does she want from us?' the woman whispered.

Matthew shook his head. 'Not much, I hope. Did your husband go into town with your daughter today?'

The woman nodded. 'Yes, and he was angry when he got home because some drunken thugs had pushed him into a ditch.'

Matthew could hear furniture being upended in the next room. He let go of the woman and rushed inside. Tupaarnaq had knocked over Sakkak Biilmann, who was lying on the floor beneath her, shrieking. She had a firm grip on his throat with one hand and was punching him with the other. His face glowed red from the beating and the lack of oxygen. Matthew had no idea what the man on the floor was saying, but he could tell from his panic that he was struggling for air.

'If you ever touch your daughter again,' Tupaarnaq screamed at him, 'I'll come back and kill you. And that's not an idle threat. I'll be watching you. Every day. One wrong move and you're dead. Got it?'

The man yelped, but didn't say anything.

Her hand reached across to his groin and gripped his testicles through his trousers. She squeezed them so hard that his yelp turned into the howl of a dying animal. Matthew watched her fingers tighten ever more. The man continued to scream, and then started to cry. Snot flowed from his nose as he whined and squirmed. She jerked her hand violently from side to side before getting up.

Whimpering, the man coiled into a foetal position. He was trembling as he rocked himself back and forth.

'Touch her again,' Tupaarnaq hissed, kicking his ribs hard with her booted foot, 'and you're a dead man, you piece of shit.'

43

Outside the apartment block, Matthew stopped and looked around. 'What's this place called?'

'You mean the area?'

'Yes.'

'Radiofjeldet, I believe.'

Matthew took out Leiff's note and handed it to her. 'Then we're not far from this woman.'

'What about her?'

'Someone from work gave me this address. He thinks my father used to live with her.'

'Your father?'

Matthew shrugged. 'He disappeared when I was four years old. My mother and I never heard from him again. Someone from the paper offered to look into it, and earlier today he gave me this address.'

'But why on earth would your father be in Nuuk?'

'He was stationed at the Thule air base. That was where my mother met him.' Matthew looked down at the paving slabs. 'I was actually born in Thule, as it happens.'

'You're kidding me?' Tupaarnaq nudged his shoulder. 'You're made in Greenland? Shut up! You're a dark horse.'

He returned her smile cautiously. 'I was thinking of going to see her.'

'And so you should.' Her brow furrowed. 'That is, if you can control…what's going on inside.'

Matthew nodded distantly. 'I stopped being angry when… nothing mattered. Including him.'

'Do you want to see him—if he's still alive?'

'Yes…I'm just not sure if I want him back in my life after all these years.'

'You have to go see her,' Tupaarnaq said, looking up at the sky. 'I hate men. I hate fathers. But that's just me.' She let out a quick sigh. 'In ten years you'll hate yourself if you don't knock on that door, now that you know it's there.' She patted his shoulder. 'I'll catch you later. It's only two blocks from here.'

He watched her back as she disappeared down the path. The black boots. The black combat trousers. The dark jumper. At the end of the path she gestured with her right arm towards the next apartment block, while she herself turned left without looking back. Matthew shook his head. He hadn't kept his promise to Ottesen to keep an eye on Tupaarnaq very long.

Soon Matthew was walking across the rocks between the buildings, and before long he was standing outside the stairwell where Else Kreutzmann lived.

He had only knocked twice when the brown door opened. A petite woman peered out. She had salt-and-pepper hair and wore spectacles with oval lenses. She looked Matthew up and down before her eyes settled on his face. 'Yes?'

'Are you Else Kreutzmann?'

'Yes.'

'I got your name from a friend.' Matthew shook his head. 'Forgive me. My name is Matthew Cave, I work for *Sermitsiaq* and I live here in Nuuk. I've been told you might know my father?'

Else looked at him. 'Your name is Cave?'

Matthew nodded. 'Yes. Matthew Cave. My father's name was Thomas Cave, but I haven't seen him since I was four years old.'

'You had better come in,' she said with a weary sigh, and turned around.

Matthew followed her through a narrow passage and into a rectangular kitchen with a small table and two chairs.

'Can I get you anything?' she said, looking across the kitchen table, which, apart from some plastic tubs, a knife block and a microwave oven, was empty.

He shook his head. 'No, thank you, but it's kind of you to offer. I hope you don't mind me coming here. I thought he might be here as well—Tom, I mean.'

She found a tin from a tall cupboard, put it on the table, pushed open the lid and took out a biscuit. 'No, he's not here, and it's been a very long time since I last saw him.'

Matthew looked down at the smooth white tabletop.

'He never mentioned a son,' she went on. 'Not once during the almost ten years I knew him…Have a biscuit.'

'He was stationed at the Thule air base,' Matthew said. 'He was a soldier. We lived there until I was four years old, then my mother and I moved to Denmark. The plan was that he would follow us.'

'That sounds just like him.' She looked into Matthew's eyes. 'Not that I had any doubts. When I opened the door, I knew immediately.'

Matthew smiled. 'The eye?'

She nodded. 'Yes. There's no doubt that the two of you are related.'

Matthew looked away again. 'The last time I saw him was in 1990.'

'That was when he came to Nuuk,' Else said. 'I knew him for almost ten years, then he disappeared. I'm sorry he never got in touch with you. I didn't realise he had another family.'

'That's okay.'

'He was always running away from something, so perhaps it should have crossed my mind. His invisibility.'

'What do you mean?'

She sighed as she helped herself to another biscuit. 'He was hiding from the army...the US Army. I don't know why, but he was certainly hiding, always working under a false name. He never told the authorities his address.'

'What did he do for a living?'

'Well, while he was here in Nuuk, it was mostly cash-in-hand jobs. Sometimes it would be carpentry, other times he would work on the trawlers. But he made good money, so that was never a problem. He was strong and a hard worker.' She shrugged. 'I don't know what he did when he was in the army, but it troubled him—often he'd be in a world of his own.' She looked at Matthew. 'Then again, he could have been thinking about you. I don't know.'

'But he never mentioned me? Or my mother?'

'I genuinely don't think I'm wrong when I tell you that I never heard him utter a word about the time before I met him.' She glanced at her watch and then at Matthew. 'I'm sorry, but I need to be some-where. I was just getting ready to go out when you knocked.'

Matthew leapt up from his chair. 'Yes, I need to get going too. I...I was just curious.'

Else looked at him and ran a tired hand across her face. 'Hold on.' She turned around and removed a picture from the fridge door. 'This is my daughter, Arnaq,' she said, passing the picture to Matthew.

He took it and studied the young girl. She seemed taller than her mother, and with hair a little lighter.

'We had her in '98, Tom and I. He left us two years later.'

Matthew closed his eyes. He could feel icy shivers running up and down his arms and his back.

'She's at school in Denmark, but if you want me to I can tell you more about her.'

Matthew slumped. His throat felt constricted and closed.

'Give me your number, if you like,' Else continued. 'And we'll see.'

Matthew nodded.

SHATTERED
LIFE

44

'Are you awake?' Jakob asked as he knocked softly on the bedroom door. He gave the door a light push and peered inside.

Paneeraq pulled the quilt over her head.

'I've fried you an egg,' he went on. 'If you come into the living room, you can eat your breakfast there. There's also yoghurt and apple juice.'

He watched her peek out of the small crack between the quilt and the mattress.

'Ah well,' he said in a loud voice, retreating. 'It doesn't look like she's here. I think I'll go to the kitchen to get some cutlery, and we'll just have to see if a girl drops out of the sky meanwhile.'

Back in the kitchen he could hear Paneeraq dash through the living room and over to the sofa. The sound of quick footsteps and a big quilt being dragged across the floor.

'Good heavens,' he exclaimed in mock surprise when he came back from the kitchen. 'Did that quilt crawl in here all by itself?'

The quilt giggled.

'I wonder,' he went on in a pensive tone of voice, 'if quilts like fried eggs and rye bread, or whether they just drink juice? I've never seen a quilt with a mouth, and I don't think I really would want to, because it would be difficult to sleep if you're worried about your quilt nibbling at your toes.'

A head appeared. Two black eyes surrounded by bed hair.

'Oh no, it's a troll!' Jakob shrieked.

Her eyes widened.

He narrowed his eyes and inspected her closely. 'Aha! It's you, Paneeraq. Phew, you had me worried for a moment.'

She held out her hand and opened it so that he could see the fossil.

'And the sea urchin. Are the two of you hungry?'

She nodded.

'Then make your way to the table and eat your breakfast. I've read somewhere that fossilised sea urchins absolutely love fried eggs.'

She scrunched up her nose and looked sceptically at her fossil, but then she put it on her plate next to the rye bread and the fried egg.

They couldn't see out of the windows, which were completely covered by the snow that had drifted up against the house overnight. Jakob could hear the wind still raging and tearing at everything.

'I think we're snowed in,' he said, nodding towards the front door. 'Have you ever tried that before?'

She nodded and looked towards the windows on either side of the front door.

Jakob got up and walked over to the front door. 'I'll be looking through that window in a moment—if I can clear the snow away, that is.'

Paneeraq nodded again. She reached for her juice.

The front door opened with a hollow sound, and Jakob muttered to himself as he stepped outside and a long, cold gust of wind found its way into the living room.

Paneeraq looked alternately at the door and the window. 'Jakob?' she called out tentatively after just under ten minutes. She frowned.

'Jakob?' she called out again, louder this time.

A windswept face covered in snow appeared in the doorway. 'Yes?'

He saw her dive back under the quilt while he brushed the snow off his face. 'I'm almost done,' he continued. 'You'll be fine here. I'll leave some food out for you, and I'll lock the door behind me.'

Paneeraq's eyes scanned the living room, and Jakob tried to follow her gaze. It was completely different from the living room she was used to at home. The dark furniture and the many fossils and books must have seemed strange to her. He remembered what Lisbeth said: that many little girls in Greenland didn't know love and affection in a way that was natural to him. He looked at the quilt and the girl. She might well prefer to be with him because it was safe and fun, but he didn't have to think too hard before realising it could never happen. There was no physical evidence against her father, and her mother was doing her best—despite the father's long shadow. Jakob sighed to himself. Mortensen would have a heart attack when he found out about it. *You kidnapped a child, Pedersen. A potential witness in your own crackpot investigation!*

'Would you like some more juice before I go?'

'Yes,' she said from under her quilt. 'Can stones not feel anything at all?'

'No, I don't think so,' Jakob replied with a smile, while he put two cups on the table. 'After all, it wouldn't be very good if we always had to apologise to the rocks for walking on them.'

Paneeraq looked down at her clenched fist and smiled almost imperceptibly.

'What do you think its name was?' She opened up the palm of her hand so that he could see the small, dotted piece of flint.

He exhaled and raised both eyebrows. 'I really don't know what those creepy crawlies were called all those millions of years ago, but... well, why don't we call it Paneeraq, just like you?'

She turned her gaze towards him. 'Do you think that was its name? Is it a girl?'

'Well, I know it's not called Jakob, because that would be a silly name for a sea urchin.'

She turned her hand slightly so that she could study the sea urchin from another angle. Her eyes had grown sad again. Her fingers closed around the fossil. 'They'll come back.'

'Who?' Jakob pressed his lips together.

'The men. They always come back.'

'We don't know that,' he responded as swiftly and as calmly as he could, but he struggled to hide his agitation. He had been hoping that she had slept through it all. 'They were just angry. That happens to grown-ups like them sometimes.'

'They always come back.' Her voice had slipped deeper into the embrace of the quilt.

Jakob looked at her. 'Do you mean those specific men?'

She nodded. Slowly. Without looking up.

'Do you know them?'

'They visit my dad sometimes,' she said in a voice so small it was barely audible. 'And the last time they brought an old man from Denmark.'

'Old?'

'Like you...*The minister, that bastard*, my dad called him when he had gone.'

There was total silence in the room.

Jakob wanted to sit next to Paneeraq and give her a big hug, but he was scared to even touch her hair.

'They'll never come back,' he said. 'And that's a promise.'

45

It proved quite a challenge for Jakob to get to work that morning. The storm continued to rage around the houses, snapping up anything left lying on the ground, and it felt as if snow was being hurled at the town from all sides.

Paneeraq was alone in his house with plenty of biscuits, crackers and juice, as well as comics, pencils and paper, should she want to draw. He had told her that she was free to move about his house and that she could touch anything she wanted to. There was nothing dangerous or forbidden in his home. She was even allowed to play with the fossils. She had been upset when he left, but he had promised her that he would be back and that he was going to find out where she would live from now on. She had said that she would like to live with him. He had had no answer to that.

Jakob looked about uneasily as he walked through the entrance to the police station. His recent row with Mortensen was unlikely to be a secret, and he was afraid that everyone would know that he was hiding the girl.

'Did you return the child, Pedersen?'

He turned his head and saw Mortensen's chin. 'I need to speak to you about Jørgen Emil Lyberth and Kjeld Abelsen. It's serious.'

'Really? I'm rather busy today.'

'But they—'

'I hope you haven't upset those fine gentlemen for no good reason?'

Jakob shook his head. 'No, but they—'

'Good, then it can wait. I have meetings with the Home Rule Committee, the Greenlandic Provincial Council and the Minister for Greenland, and I haven't got time to listen to your conspiracy theories. You understand that, don't you?' Mortensen rubbed his eyes. 'We need to put a lid on all that nonsense before the minister flies back to Denmark tomorrow—that's the way it is. Frankly, it's like herding cats.'

Jakob shook his head and took a very deep breath all the way down to his stomach.

'Take Karlo with you, then go and apologise to the girl's parents,' Mortensen said. He went back towards his office, but turned around in the doorway to make sure that Jakob had taken his message on board. 'I mean it.'

'Yes, sir.' The air seeped out of Jakob. 'We will.'

He could smell wet clothes inside the office. His fellow officers, their snow-caked boots, trousers and jackets were thawing in the heat. The steam from the melting snow made the office smell like a damp basement.

'I'll keep my coat on, shall I,' Jakob grunted when, at that very moment, he spotted Karlo, who was waiting for him, already dressed for the outdoors.

The two men went outside and let the snowstorm embrace them. Jakob patted Karlo on the back. 'The more decorations they get on their shoulders, the less they remember what it means to be a police officer.'

'The responsibility probably weighs heavily on them.'

'I wish. No, I think it's about not wanting to lose what you've got, so you switch your allegiance upwards rather than remember those down on the ground.'

'I don't think the world is as black and white as you make it out to be.'

'You may be right, but our boss would rather be a friend to politicians than a protector of children at risk—that much I know.' Jakob's voice sharpened. 'Right, we had better get a move on, although this is yet another deeply idiotic idea. Why are we having to suck up to a rapist instead of pursuing him all the way to hell?'

'Let's wait and see how the case pans out,' Karlo said, looking straight into the hissing polar wind. 'We still have to solve the murders.'

Jakob leaned towards Karlo. 'Jørgen Emil Lyberth and Kjeld Abelsen paid me a visit last night. They want us to arrest Thomas Olesen from Block 16 for the murders and close the case.'

'Thomas Olesen? But surely he has nothing to do with this.'

'And they know it, but they want the case closed now. They brought with them some thug from the Faroe Islands and they threatened me.'

'Are you serious? Please tell me you're not.'

'I am—although no one will ever believe me. But I'm telling you, they were there, I swear.'

'Yes, of course. I believe you. So what happens now?'

'We apologise to that bastard in Block P, and when we get back to the station, Mortensen will tell us to arrest Olesen for the murders.'

'Mortensen? Do you think that—'

'It's entirely political,' Jakob interrupted. 'The last thing anyone up here wants is an investigative commission from Denmark turning up while the hullabaloo about the EEC is still a gaping wound and the newly minted Home Rule Committee is trying to find its political feet and its identity.' He heaved a deep sigh and watched it linger in the cold air as tiny frozen particles. 'I'm thinking in particular of all the Danish civil servants who have been up here for years, acting like petty monarchs. They don't want to hand over their power to Denmark, or to a new, independent Greenland.'

'And Mortensen and Abelsen are two such monarchs?' Karlo said.

'You bet they are. And when it comes to politics at that level, some damaged girls and a few murdered men don't count for much. Until they start to attract unwelcome attention—something that threatens the status of the monarchs, that is.' Jakob kicked a pebble along the road. 'There's something about this case that can bring down Abelsen and Lyberth, and possibly the Minister for Greenland as well. And unless I'm very much mistaken, the crux of the matter has nothing to do with politics and everything to do with the minister, who has a taste for little Greenlandic girls.'

Karlo stopped. 'What? Are you serious?'

Jakob nodded. 'I am, but I can't prove it yet. I...' He exhaled. The wind was pulling so hard at their clothes that they both struggled to stand still. 'I think that's the connection, but right now it's just a theory.'

Karlo rubbed his forehead and the snow scattered from him. 'Once this storm dies down, the Minister for Greenland will fly back to Denmark.'

'I know.' Jakob shook his head. The gusty snow stabbed his face like icepicks. 'But there's not a lot I can do about that. I simply haven't got the evidence.'

'And we can't arrest the three of them purely on a hunch.'

'I know that too.'

'So what happens, then?'

The wind took hold of Jakob and he missed a step. 'It'll play out like I said. We'll be ordered to arrest Olesen so that he can be convicted of the murders, and if we don't, then I'm finished.'

'And the girls?'

'No one gives a toss about the girls.'

Block P was starting to emerge from the snowstorm in front of them. Jakob heaved a sign of resignation and glanced at Karlo. 'We'll have to see what happens.'

46

Karlo knocked on the door to the apartment they had already visited twice.

Jakob wondered how best to handle the conversation. He couldn't very well apologise for having kept the girl, because there was no way he was giving her back to such a father. It was out of the question. But then again, Karlo didn't know that Paneeraq was back at his house. No one knew, nor had the parents reported her missing, which proved Lisbeth's point.

'I don't think they're in,' Karlo said, knocking so hard the whole stairwell could hear.

Jakob grabbed the handle and pushed it down. The door made a small click and opened. He looked at Karlo and raised his eyebrows. 'Let's take a look around.'

'Are you sure? After all, Mortensen—'

'—isn't here,' Jakob cut him off, pushing the door wide open and taking a step inside. 'Something's wrong.'

Karlo nodded slowly and moved past Jakob. 'It smells like someone has been hunting.'

The two men looked at one another, and the reality dawned on them simultaneously.

'Oh, no,' Jakob exclaimed, and with long strides he followed Karlo into the living room, where he came to an abrupt halt. Anguteeraq Poulsen was lying on the floor in front of them. His intestines had been cut out and left around his body in a bloody circle of death. His skin was gone, except for that on his hands and feet. His facial features had been erased. All that remained were brown muscle fibres and pale sinews. His teeth grinning. Exposed and hysterical.

Jakob raked his hands through his hair, all the way to the back of his neck.

Karlo had already squatted down by the body. 'Jakob,' he said slowly. 'The four men we listed as the worst offenders are all dead now. No one else.'

Jakob stared straight past Karlo and down at the dead man's forehead. They had both seen it.

'There's a piece from your jigsaw puzzle on his forehead.' Karlo's voice was hoarse.

Jakob closed his eyes and pinched the bridge of his nose. 'It must be the man from the Faroe Islands who put it there…He was messing about with my jigsaw puzzle last night. The one I told you threatened me with a knife.'

Karlo nodded, but he looked away.

'Surely you don't think…?' Jakob ground to a halt and his shoulders slumped.

'No…no.' Karlo shook his head.

'Where's his wife?' Jakob heard his own voice say the words, but it was Karlo's body that moved. Past the dead man. Past the blood and the stench of gutted prey. Around the sofa, where he stopped. He looked up. Stared at Jakob, who stepped past the body of Anguteeraq Poulsen so he too could see the dead woman on the floor behind the sofa.

She hadn't been killed in the same manner as the men. Far from it. She had suffered a single injury to her head. That was all.

Someone had hit her hard, and the blow had killed her. It might not even have been intentional.

'There's one thing I don't understand,' Karlo said, interrupting Jakob's train of thought. 'You don't seem to be worried about the girl at all.'

They both looked towards the door to the bedroom from where, a few days earlier, Poulsen had carried his daughter.

Jakob knew he had to react quickly to the question. Say the right thing. But his thoughts were so disjointed that all words deserted him.

Karlo took three long strides towards the door, pushed it open and disappeared inside. 'She's not here,' his voice called out from inside the room. 'But then, you already knew that, didn't you?'

47

Paneeraq smiled contentedly. Jakob's coffee table was covered with rocks. Not as densely as the shore of a pebble beach, but more like a display in a shop. She had arranged them on the stripy wood, pretty much in order of size. Only one had received special treatment. The small, fossilised sea urchin lay at centre stage, with plenty of room around it.

She had spent hours lining up the stones, and was finally satisfied with her efforts. It had been a big job because there were so many colours, shapes and patterns, and no two of them were alike.

She trailed her hand across the stones, and tapped them lightly with her forefinger one by one while she reeled off an endless list of names. 'Hansiina. Nivi. Aviaaja. Rebekka. Olga. Julianne. Nuka. Najak.' The finest of them all was Paneeraq, in the middle. It was also the softest and had been found in Denmark, which was far away.

At school they had seen many pictures and movies from Denmark. It was a country with tall trees with fruit on the branches, and it was warm. In the summer the children could run around and play outside—for a whole day, if they wanted to—without getting cold. It was hard for her to imagine, but she thought that it might explain why the little sea urchin was so smooth and fine. All that heat. After all, stones could melt if they got very hot.

She was wearing her white dress with the big coloured dots that she had worn yesterday, and the same yellow socks. She had nothing else, but Jakob had said that he would get the nice lady from the police station to help find her some clothes. They could also get some from her mum at home, but she didn't want to leave yet. Being at Jakob's was fun and peaceful.

Outside it was daylight, and the snow glowed white and bright through the windows. Jakob wouldn't be back until it was dark again. Completely dark. Just after five o'clock, he had said, but he had also promised her that he would try to be home sooner than that.

She was startled by a sharp noise. She tumbled to the floor and disappeared into the grey woollen rug under the coffee table world of soothing rocks.

The noise came again—three hard knocks. Someone was outside. There shouldn't be anyone outside. No one should be knocking on the door. Jakob had said so. No one comes here. Jakob had said so.

She clutched the sea urchin in her small fist. Mumbled to herself into the rug, telling herself that no one was knocking on the door. But they were. And they did it again. Three fresh knocks. Hard. Exploding against the wooden door.

Don't open the door to anyone, Jakob had said. But someone was banging on it now. The handle rattled. Up and down. She tried pushing herself into the deep pile of the carpet. Hiding in the grey, dusty world.

On the shelf below the coffee table was Jakob's book about rocks. The boring one. She could see its spine and the words on it. She closed her eyes. She tensed her body. Praying to turn into a stone herself.

The hammering resumed, and a voice reached the living room through the window near the coffee table. The voice called out to her.

It spoke her name, but it wasn't Jakob's voice. It was angry. She had to open the door, the voice ordered her, or they would break it down. But she wasn't going to open the door. She didn't want to let the angry men in. She didn't want to leave Jakob's house and the stones.

The noises by the door changed. One crash after another. Paneeraq's fists were clenched in front of her mouth, while a monotonous, hoarse sound seeped out between her lips. Her body rocked back and forth.

The door gave in with a heavy splintering and slammed into the wall. She shook her head. Cried out *no* on the inside. *Where is Jakob? Where is Jakob?*

Her dress grew wet. As did the rug. And her face. The chanting between her tightly pressed lips grew louder and more panicked.

Voices jumped around her like snarling dogs. They spoke but said nothing. A big hand grabbed her and spun her around. She didn't want to look.

Relax, the hand said. *We have you now. You're safe. He can't hurt you anymore. You're free.*

Did he hurt you? another voice said, but she didn't want to see or hear them. These men were wicked. They had come to take her away from the stones. And Jakob's sofa.

Bloody hell—she's pissed herself!

Two big hands grabbed her and picked her up. *You're coming with us,* the voice behind the hands said. The hands were very strong. She fought but she wasn't strong enough.

The voice shouted at her and the hands squeezed her tight. They shook her. She lashed out with her feet. The hands tightened their grip. She couldn't breathe. She dropped the sea urchin. She was slung over someone's shoulder and restrained.

The shoulder was hard. The back below it broad. Her eyes followed the small sea urchin as it rolled across the floor. It fled towards the bedroom, but lost speed before it got to safety and ended up lying on its side, its fossilised stomach pointing diagonally up into the air.

Paneeraq stopped moving. Her hands were clamped together, and her legs held in place. Then she screamed her own name. She cried out for the sea urchin, which grew smaller and smaller with every step taken by the body below her, until it disappeared.

They left the house. Everything around her grew cold. The frost nipped at her arms, her face and her legs. The urine froze on her thighs. As did the tears on her cheeks. Her eyes stung.

A car door opened and she was plonked onto a cold plastic seat. Someone tossed in her jacket, boots and satchel. The door slammed shut. She pushed against it and pressed her face against the icy glass. Her mouth wide open. Her teeth grinding against the windowpane. She was still screaming. Screaming deep inside herself.

48

The moment Lisbeth saw Benno and Storm arrive at the police station with Paneeraq, she jumped up and ran to the little girl. She knelt down in front of Paneeraq and tried to look into the girl's red eyes.

'What have you done to her?' she challenged the two officers.

'We just went to fetch her,' Benno said casually, attempting to maintain his status in front of the angry secretary. 'Out at Jakob's. She was like that when we found her.'

'Yes,' Storm piped up. 'There's no way we're taking the rap for this. The girl was already lying on the floor screaming when we came in.'

Lisbeth gently pulled Paneeraq close and could feel the child shaking all over. She turned her attention to Benno. 'And how did you get in?'

He shrugged. 'She was lying on the floor without moving, so we broke down the door.'

'Standard procedure,' Storm added. 'We were sent to pick her up, and she was just lying there on the floor. How were we to know what he had done to her?'

'Have you completely lost your minds?' Lisbeth was whispering in order not to frighten Paneeraq even more. 'Have you no idea how traumatic that would have been to a child?'

She got up slowly and guided Paneeraq carefully to her chair and desk. 'Now, you sit here for a moment,' she said softly, pulling open a drawer and finding some chocolate. 'I'll get you some cocoa in a minute, and afterwards I'll take you home with me. This isn't a place for children.'

'But we…' Benno cleared his throat. 'She's in our care, and we need to get her seen by a doctor today.'

On hearing this, Paneeraq flinched.

Lisbeth squeezed Paneeraq's arm and shook her head dismissively. 'Just ignore them. I'll go and get your cocoa now, and we'll leave very soon.'

Paneeraq nodded. Her eyes had started to liven up a little.

'If I hear either of you say another word to that girl, I'll bloody well kill you.'

Benno looked at the small, incensed woman. 'Listen, we were only doing our job.'

'Your job? What kind of a job is it to scare the living daylights out of an already broken little girl? Eh? Can you tell me that? Have you really no idea what this child has suffered? Not just for one night, but for years.'

Benno stared down at the wooden floor, as if an answer could be found in its cracks.

'You're only a secretary,' Storm sneered. 'So perhaps you should let us do our job—especially if you want to keep your own.'

'Oh, shit,' Benno grunted with resignation as he stepped in front of Storm and felt Lisbeth's blow hit his chest with full force. For a moment he was winded, but he kept his gaze fixed on the irate woman's eyes. 'That's enough for now,' he said with a quick nod, then he turned around, grabbed Storm by the arm and dragged him into the office.

Lisbeth could hear Storm complaining bitterly, but she could also hear Benno, who, in an even louder voice, shouted, 'Just shut your mouth!'

She waited to make sure that the two men were not coming back, then rushed to Mortensen's office, where she knocked while pushing open the door without waiting for an answer.

'Mrs Ludvigsen,' the small man exclaimed in surprise. 'You nearly gave me a heart attack.'

'I apologise, sir,' she said, her voice trembling. Lisbeth was so angry that the words got stuck in her throat. 'But Benno and Storm have just terrified a little girl who is already utterly broken. What the hell is it that you men don't understand about girls and women who have been destroyed by men? Do you think we just wake up the morning after we've been raped and everything is fine? Can you really not imagine that it hurts forever, and we're eaten up by anguish and grief every hour of the day and night?'

Mortensen stubbed out his cigar in the ashtray and rubbed his pale chin. 'I know what you're saying,' he said. 'But we must never let personal feelings cloud our objectivity as law enforcement officers.'

'We're talking about a little girl. A child!' Lisbeth threw up her hands. 'There's nothing objective about that. She needs love, and your men are stomping all over her like a herd of elephants.'

'I was referring to the objectivity between you and Pedersen,' Mortensen said. 'We couldn't leave the girl with him—it wasn't lawful. And being a police officer, he should have known better. Besides, the whole investigation has taken a very unfortunate turn for Pedersen, and the worst-case scenario is that the girl might have been staying with her parents' killer. So you see, we had absolutely no choice other than to pick her up. You have to understand that. I promise to have a word with Benno and Storm, so we can establish whether they acted in accordance with procedure.'

'Thank you,' she said, forcing herself to stay in control. 'I would appreciate that.'

He nodded with a dry smile. 'Is there anything else?'

She shook her head. 'Yes…I'll take the girl back to my place now. She needs a bath, clean clothes and some TLC. If you try to stop me, I'll go straight to the papers with everything I know. And the same applies if you sack me.'

Mortensen drummed his fingers on a small brown notebook that lay on the desk in front of him. 'You don't scare easily,' he said with a nod. 'I like that.'

49

The smoke from Mortensen's cigars was so thick that Jakob couldn't remember the stench in the small office ever being worse. There were three half-smoked cigars in the ashtray and one dangling between Mortensen's yellow fingers. Around the ashtray were stacks of files, loose sheets of paper, newspapers, a few pots with pens and an old, grey typewriter. Jakob's notebook lay in the centre of the ash-stained green blotting pad. Mortensen's fingers rested on the closed cover.

'Pedersen, Pedersen,' his boss sighed behind the grey and yellow fog. 'What the hell am I supposed to make of all this?' He aimed two probing eyes at Jakob.

Jakob shrugged.

'Yes, I took the liberty of flicking through your notebook, seeing as it was lying around here at the office. I had started to realise that it might be worth having a look at it.'

He paused again to allow for objections, but Jakob remained silent.

'It contains four names,' Mortensen sighed. 'You wrote down four names. Yes, I acknowledge that there are many other names on your lists, but you have identified these four men as being particularly evil. Four men who are now all dead.' He turned his head slightly, without taking his eyes off Jakob. 'We can agree on that, can't we?'

'What do you mean?'

'That it's your notebook, and that you appointed yourself judge, jury and executioner of these four men.'

'That they are four men who repeatedly raped their own daughters—yes, on that we can agree.'

'And you wrote the list, didn't you?'

'It's in my notebook, yes.' Jakob looked down and adjusted his shirt nervously. 'But listen—'

'And you stated publicly that you would be willing to kill Anguteeraq Poulsen,' Mortensen cut him off. 'And in secret and against my express orders, you took in his daughter the night before her parents' murder—am I right?'

'Her name is Paneeraq.' Jakob looked up at Mortensen again. 'What have you done to her?'

Mortensen rubbed his septum. 'The air is so bloody dry up here.'

'Where's Paneeraq?'

'She's in safe hands now.'

'Not if she's in this building,' Jakob snapped. 'This whole town is rotten to the core.'

'Pedersen...' Mortensen summoned his attention. 'She's in safe hands, trust me. She has no family left, but I can promise you that she's safe. I can't tell you where she is, obviously, as we don't want you running straight over there. You've become obsessed with this case.' He cleared his throat and hawked violently. Drummed his fingers on the notebook a few times. 'This reads like the work of a madman. Not a police officer.' He looked up. 'What the hell is this? Poetry and conspiracies all muddled together? What has got into you? Has the darkness finally pushed you over the edge? We have four flayed bodies, but you're busy philosophising about the taste of the ice cap and conspiring against our leading civil servants.'

'Those notes are private,' Jakob said. 'Surely the only madness is that I predicted who was going to die, and as I still believe the deaths are related to the sexual abuse of children, then I was also right about the four men being the worst offenders in this town.' He flung out his arms. 'I've nothing to do with the murders themselves, obviously. Do you want me to come up with an alibi for the nights of the murders—is that what you're saying? Now that would be truly mad. And since when is it illegal to write poetry and to love nature, or is that the preserve of murderers? I don't know what it's like back in Horsens, but where I come from we still have free speech.'

'I happen to be from Stensballe, not Horsens, not that it matters.' Mortensen nudged the brown notebook. 'And the jigsaw puzzle piece? What about that? A signature? You know how this works. No serial killer ever wants to get away with his crimes—deep down he's desperate for the world to admire his work. Am I right?'

'I agree, but that knowledge doesn't turn you or me into a serial killer. And as far as the puzzle piece goes, I've no idea how it ended up on the deceased.'

'The deceased? You mean Anguteeraq Poulsen? That's true. Now, what did you say again? That you would bloody well kill him and gut him yourself?'

'For God's sake, sir. We had just left the apartment. The girl could barely walk. He...he had just...Karlo was angry too. Men like Anguteeraq Poulsen shouldn't get away with destroying children. Surely you agree?'

'Of course, Pedersen, but it's something we have to let the law deal with. Our job is solely to collect the evidence, if there is any.'

'Also to prevent crime, surely,' Jakob objected angrily.

'Yes, that's correct, but did you see a crime in progress while you were there? Did anyone report anything? How about witnesses?'

'I knew he had raped her! I could tell from all their faces. From their eyes. The way she walked and her body language towards her father. She hurt all over. They were covering it up.'

'But has anyone reported it? Where's the evidence? There might be another explanation, don't you think?'

'Everyone is too bloody scared to speak out,' Jakob yelled. 'And even if they do, who will help them? The kids are simply sent back to their families. For God's sake, we need to protect those children.'

'And who will protect men against false accusations, if we start acting purely on a hunch?'

'Men? Protect men?' Jakob stared at the chief of police in disbelief. 'The men...they—'

'Deserve to die?' Mortensen completed Jakob's sentence.

Jakob looked at the floor. 'To hell with the men. We ought to be protecting the girls.'

'Work with me here, Pedersen. You have this bizarre notebook where you've written down the names of four men—before they were killed. You have publicly expressed a desire to kill one of them. You removed that man's daughter from her home shortly before he was killed. And a piece from your jigsaw puzzle was found on the dead man's forehead.' He exhaled heavily. 'Can you see where I'm going with this, Pedersen? We have, as far as I'm aware, at no point had another suspect under consideration, but if you look objectively at the facts I've just listed, what would you call the man hiding behind them?'

'I do have some suspects now,' Jakob remarked dryly.

'I would call such a man a suspect,' Mortensen continued, pushing his own argument. 'Wouldn't you?'

Jakob shook his head. 'I had a visit last night. Actually, "intruders" would be more accurate. Jørgen Emil Lyberth and Kjeld Abelsen. They forced their way into my house, along with a strong, ruddy-looking man from the Faroe Islands.'

Mortensen frowned and picked up a cigar stump. 'Are you still going on about that? Didn't I say I wanted to hear nothing more about it?'

'With all due respect, sir, you need to let me speak, because all these events are connected.'

'Very well—get it off your chest, then.'

'Like I said, they entered my home last night, and they brought this big, red-haired man with them. They threatened me, told me to abandon my investigation into the children, and said I should charge an innocent man with the murders. They told me to arrest Thomas Olesen from Block 16 today. *After* the fourth murder, that is, but at the time they were probably the only ones who knew that a fourth murder had been committed.'

'Pedersen, why would Jørgen Emil Lyberth and Kjeld Abelsen threaten you and have a random man go to jail for murders he has nothing to do with?'

'Because they have something to do with the murders. The man with the red hair ripped up my shirt and pressed a knife against my chest, while Abelsen told me that I could easily end up gutted as well.'

'Tell me *why*, Pedersen. Why would Lyberth and Abelsen want all these men killed? Yes, and on top of that, why would they threaten you, a police officer, with your life, unless you agreed to close the case?' He shook his head. 'I simply don't see the logic, my good man.'

'I don't know.' Jakob heaved a sigh and his shoulders slumped. 'I think they're involved in the assaults on the children. Perhaps they take part. Perhaps they establish contact with the fathers, who then hire out their daughters to high-ranking politicians or civil servants from Denmark. Perhaps the four men got greedy and wanted more money for their silence. Paneeraq mentioned that Lyberth and Abelsen had previously been to her parents' apartment together with an older Danish man, and that this man was addressed as "Minister".'

'And did she say exactly what had happened?'

Jakob shook his head slowly. 'She's only eleven years old.'

Mortensen slammed both palms against his desk and drummed his fingers. 'I'm not about to accuse two prominent citizens and the

Minister for Greenland of murder and sexual assault just on your say-so. We work with evidence here, and if I've understood you correctly, you have nothing to support your accusations. Nothing. I wouldn't even go to the trouble of telephoning them.'

'I have another witness.' Jakob stumbled over his words. 'A woman who saw, among others, Lyberth and the man from the Faroe Islands near Ari Rossing Lynge's place on the night that Lynge was killed and Najak disappeared. She saw them out in the street and heard them argue upstairs. I believe…I have reason to believe that she heard the murder itself.'

'So she saw these people through a window at night when it was dark and it was snowing, and heard something through the ceiling?' Mortensen held up a hand in order to stop further protest. 'It won't stand up—not without evidence, Jakob. And even if your crazy theories are right, you're still not in the clear. I have your notebook here, you've made threats in public, and you made sure that the girl was out of the apartment on the night of her parents' murder. So…I'm suspending you for now. I need you to hand in your warrant card and your key to the police station immediately. I'll try to get a handle on what's going on today. There's going to be one hell of an outcry from the powers that be.'

Jakob removed a key from his key ring, and tossed it and his warrant card onto the desk next to his notebook. 'You can all go to hell.'

'Thank you, thank you. We'll get there eventually.' Mortensen picked up Jakob's warrant card. 'Please go home and stay there until further notice. That's all for now.'

Jakob stopped halfway to the door. He was seething with rage. 'Najak may still be alive!'

'We all hope that,' Mortensen grunted, and looked up at him. 'Anything else you want to tell me?'

'There are some films where I think you can see her.'

'Films? Here in Godthåb?'

Jakob nodded. 'I think they were recorded at the location where she's being held…by Abelsen or the Faroese.'

Mortensen shook his head and stood up with effort. 'That's the final straw, Pedersen. You bring me your films—if they really exist, that is—and then stay the hell away. You're suspended no matter what, and it won't help your case if you have evidence lying around at your house.'

Jakob stared at the floor.

'Now get out of here,' Mortensen shouted. 'Get out of here before I tell your colleagues to walk you home and tear your house apart.'

50

The snow was several metres high along the roads, so few rocks managed to peek out from underneath the glittering carpet. The moonlight bounced back from it, making the earth look as if it were bathed in phosphorescence. The wind had suddenly died down so even the tiniest movement could be heard from afar. It was only six o'clock in the evening, but the sky over the city was already black and infinitely deep. Millions of stars sparkled over Jakob's head, and even more crystals under his feet. The cold bit at his nostrils and throat; it felt like it was minus fifteen Celsius already. He inhaled deeply through his nose. It stung, and the hairs in his nostrils froze instantly.

The houses lay scattered along the road, and light shone from the small windows. Except for his own house, which was just as dark as the sky. The moment he had thrown his warrant card on Mortensen's desk, he had known that his days in that house were numbered, but he didn't mind. It was never his home. Two people had once lived there, and they had died together and left everything as it was. A mausoleum. He had merely borrowed it. Now it would be passed on to the next person. He was moving on.

From a distance of several houses, he had seen that his front door was ajar, and as he took the last few steps across the snow towards the building he realised that the door had been forced. It was ripped from its frame, and the wood around the lock was splintered.

He had known that the house would be empty. As the day had dragged him deeper and deeper into a bottomless void, he had realised that he wouldn't be able to keep his promise to Paneeraq to come back and take care of her. She had been removed by force, and the thought of how that must have been for her was unbearable. He had no idea where the child was now, or if he would ever see her again.

Jakob pushed open the front door and entered the hall, where he picked up a small plastic bag from the floor—another reel of film. He closed the door as best he could, and continued into the living room.

The coffee table had been upended, and pretty much his whole rock collection lay scattered in a crescent shape on the grey rug beside it. He touched the table. There had never been a single scratch in its glossy wood, but now the veneer was crisscrossed with fine lines and dots. His hand continued across the rug and brushed a couple of rocks. Behind the coffee table a section of the rug pile had been squashed down, and in the middle of the flat area was a wet patch.

He hooked up the new film in the projector and fed it through the machine. The beam of light revealed dust motes dancing in the air. The square on the wall flickered. She was still in the container. Curled up in her corner. But even in the brief flashes of light, he soon realised that her condition had deteriorated. Her hair was unkempt. Dirtier. Matted. She wasn't wearing any tights. No dress. No underwear. Only the jacket, which she had wrapped tightly around herself. Her body was trembling. Twitching. Light turned to darkness. Then it exploded again in life. Her bare legs were soiled. Filthy. The light and the dark no longer affected her closed eyelids. Her hands were pressed against her mouth and nose. There were trails of several layers of dried tears in the grime on her cheeks.

She sat like that, completely still. Jakob lost track of time. He just waited. There had been a new note with the film. *Last warning,*

Jakob. Close the case. She dies tomorrow. Jakob stared at the girl in the darkness and the light. Suddenly a shadow appeared and slipped in front of everything. Without the camera moving. It was a tall, thin man. Black hair. Wearing a long, dark coat. He was pale and stern, although his face was seen only in profile for a brief moment. He threw a blanket over Najak, but she didn't stir or open her eyes.

The film ran out. The camera hadn't moved. Nor did it have to. The man who had appeared had answered all Jakob's questions.

His temples were throbbing. 'She's only eleven years old,' he screamed into the air. He stared at the projector and shook his head. Then he looked at the wall clock near the kitchen. It was just past eight o'clock. 'Shit!'

He got up and put on his coat. There was no telephone in the house, so if he wanted anything done, he would have to go out. He picked up the projector and put it in the cardboard box in which it had arrived. He put the films down alongside it.

The cold bit his face hard. The wind had increased again; given the density of the darkness, a thick cloud cover must have crept over the headland. The frost and the whirling snow cut his face, so he struggled to see. His eyes were smarting and his cheeks hurt. He carried the box in both hands, and was constantly on the verge of stumbling because he couldn't see the road.

Before he reached the police station, he tripped and fell to his knees three times, sinking into the snow. His fingers were numb even though he was wearing gloves. From time to time he carried the box with one hand only, so he could wiggle the fingers on his free hand and get his circulation going again. In summer the walk from his house to the police station took only a few minutes, but on this pitch-black winter's night in a snowstorm, it took him more than a quarter of an hour.

The police station was just as dark as the night, but unlike the sky it stood out in clear contrast to the white snow, which covered everything around the long, dark-brown wooden building. Jakob took the last few steps up the stairs, set down the box and got his breath back. Then he tried the door. It didn't even budge. He had hoped that someone would be there. Anyone. Even Mortensen. He tried a few more times, then started banging on the window frame.

He waited several minutes, but all he could hear was his own breathing. Then he picked up the box and walked down the steps. He waded through the deep snow and looked through some of the windows. The station was dark and empty.

His boots were filled with snow under his trousers. His gloves were covered in lumps of ice. He continued past Mortensen's house, which lay close by, but it was just as dark as the police station. In the end he was forced to walk all the way back home. He would have to wait until tomorrow. Besides, they couldn't start looking for the container until it got light.

Back in the house he took off his icy outdoor clothing and put the cardboard box away in the sideboard. Then he went to the kitchen and poured himself a brimming glass of Johnnie Walker Red Label. He opened a drawer and took out the big chef's knife. Another remnant from the days of the previous tenants. It was heavy and felt good in his hand. Its blade was almost as long as his forearm.

He picked up the glass with his left hand and sipped the cool whisky. He pulled a face and took another slug, then returned to the living room and the armchair, where he sank into the soft upholstery and placed the knife on the armrest. There was an icy draught from the damaged front door.

51

Jakob woke when his empty glass fell to the floor, but it was something else that had caused him to drop it in the first place. He coughed hard, inhaled deeply through his nose into his lungs, and felt the cold air clear the sleep from his thoughts.

The chair squeaked feebly beneath him. He straightened his stiff back and extended his legs along the floor until they were so taut that they started to quiver. Slowly he reached for the knife on the armrest, but his fingers found only wood. He fumbled along the armrest and continued down to the floor. Nothing.

The darkness moved and Jakob froze.

'Can't you find your knife, Dane?'

Jakob recognised the Faroese accent immediately, and heard contempt and hatred drip from every syllable.

'I decided I'd better look after it for you. A little Dane like you can't handle a big knife like that.'

Jakob sat up straighter in his chair and stared blindly about the room.

'What's that?' the man from the Faroe Islands said. 'You can't see me? Let me help you.'

Jakob jumped when the man turned on the lights. The muscles

in his arms and legs contracted.

'There! Better now?'

Jakob rubbed his eyes.

'You're very quiet, Dane.'

The voice now came from behind him. Jakob turned around in the armchair and saw the red-faced man standing by the door to the bedroom. He was leaning against the doorframe, and had folded his arms across his chest, which was covered by a thick, patterned jumper in shades of white and brown. In one hand he held the chef's knife, with the edge pointing away from him.

'What are you doing here?' Jakob demanded, slowly getting up from the armchair.

The Faroese dropped his arms by his sides, while the knife rotated once in his hand, so its edge was now pointing downwards. His thumb seemed to caress the top of the handle.

The man's ginger hair flowed like his beard. His face was freckled. His shoulders broad. His arms seemed as strong as ship's timber. Jakob didn't doubt for one second that the man was stronger than him.

'Yes—what am I doing here?' The Faroese took a couple of calm but carefully measured steps forward. His eyes were locked on Jakob's.

'I imagine your friends sent you?'

'Friends?' The man looked at him with scorn. 'I've no friends here.'

'You're right about that,' Jakob said. 'You're just as finished as I am, given how much you know.'

The man let out two short laughs, which sounded more like grunts. 'This concrete village doesn't scare me.' He shook his head. 'And neither does a Danish lawyer whose balls have yet to drop, or a Greenlander whose balls never will.'

Jakob heaved a deep sigh. 'Just tell me where you're keeping

Najak, and I'll forget about everything else.'

'You just don't get it, do you? Your job was to keep your mouth shut and close the case. The girl is already dead. But there are three more girls, remember?' He looked around the room. 'Where have you hidden the films? I'll find them sooner or later. If you tell me now, I'll let you die quickly.'

'You don't want a child's blood on your hands,' Jakob said hoarsely.

'All blood tastes the same, you pathetic little Dane.'

Jakob's eyes scanned the room frantically. There was no escape. He took a step back towards the upended coffee table, and then another one, all the while keeping his eyes pinned on the Faroese, although without looking him directly in the eyes. When his foot touched the edge of the grey rug, he spun around and in the same movement snatched two big rocks from the floor, and then stood up again. The rocks, the size of a man's fist, now weighed heavily in his hands. His fingers clutched their rough surface and found a grip in the small hollows.

'What's this?' the Faroese said. 'You want to play with rocks now?' He pointed to the wound on Jakob's forehead. 'I thought you'd had enough of that.'

Jakob's arms were slightly bent. Ready to attack. 'Go back to your masters and tell them that I'm not one of their dogs.'

The man from the Faroe Islands grunted angrily. 'I have no masters, Dane. Don't you get it?'

'Just piss off home to your masters,' Jakob hissed, and bashed the two rocks together in front of his chest. 'You're nothing but a miserable lackey.'

The red-bearded man's eyes burned with rage. 'I'm from the Faroe Islands,' he shouted, taking two long strides towards Jakob, brandishing the knife. 'I'm my own master.'

Jakob took his movement as an attack, and lunged at the man. He swung his right arm, but the Faroese had stopped. Jakob's hand with the heavy rock continued through the air, pulling him with it and exposing him to his opponent. He only had time to make a half-turn with his head before a hard blow collided with his temple.

52

Jakob's head was pounding so fiercely that he could barely open his eyes. The light from the ceiling lamp cut him like the repeated slashing of a sharp blade. Mixed with the pain and the metallic taste that filled him to bursting, the light triggered a wave of choking nausea in him. He felt the air going in and out in gusts between his lips. He tried to swallow the viscous lumps of saliva in his throat. He gulped again. Pressed his lips together until they grew white.

He opened his eyes a little. Two narrow slits. Pupils sweeping across the floor. He recognised the floorboards. The grey rug. The furniture. One side of his face lay flat against the floor. It was one with the floor. His body felt heavy. As if it was stuck to the floor. Everything was spinning. His nausea surged and he had to tighten his throat and hold his breath in order not to give in to it.

Not far from his face, he could see a hand. It was alive. Or it seemed alive. It reacted when he thought. The fingers twitched. Not much, but enough. His eyes closed. His gaze contracted behind his eyelids into two black points surrounded by burning red. Then he looked again. Shifted his focus. In little gusts. Like his breathing. Blood was growing from the floor close to the hand. Behind the blood lay an ulo. Its blade was stained with dried and fresh blood.

The handle was completely dark.

His thoughts were alive.

He could see and feel.

He was able to breathe.

His gaze followed the floor. Past the hand, the ulo and the blood. Until it reached the body. The body, which lay so far from his face that it couldn't be his. His concentration failed him. His gaze zoomed helplessly in and out as he attempted to focus. The blood. The pale body. The red hair. The beard. The bloody lumps along the white skin.

He tried to work out if he was still in one piece. It felt like it. Stuck but intact.

The sound of something living pierced his thoughts. Footsteps. Shoes moving across the floor not far from him.

His gaze searched the floorboards again until it found the shoes and the two legs moving them around. He looked up. Two hands drying themselves on one of his tea towels. The face. The dark eyes.

FOSSILISED
LIFE

53

Matthew briefly considered going home and changing his clothes, but decided against it. Instead he walked straight from Radiofjeldet and down to Block 2. As he walked, he texted Tupaarnaq about Else and Arnaq. She replied straightaway that it was probably better to have a sister than a father, given that fathers were invariably idiots.

A few minutes later Matthew had reached the address Ivalo had given him. The long building was almost as derelict as Block 17, but it was constructed differently: each front door here opened out onto a shared gallery that ran the full length of the block.

On entering from the yard, he noticed a round sign in red and white with a red line across a black outline of a man taking a piss. The message could not be misinterpreted, and yet a strong stench of urine still lingered.

The front door was blue. The paint was cracked and discoloured, but what he could see of the apartment through the windows looked fine. There were floral curtains in the windows on either side of the door; through one window he could see right into a clean and neat kitchen.

The second time he knocked, the door was opened by a petite woman in her early fifties, who peered out from the crack between the door and the frame.

'No junk mail,' she said wearily when she saw his face.

'Junk mail?' he echoed, perplexed.

'Yes—that's what you're handing out, isn't it?'

'No.' He frowned. 'I'm a journalist and I have some questions for you.'

'Oh, are you? I thought you were one of those parents who go round with their children raising money for school trips because they think it's too dangerous for the children to be out on their own.'

'My daughter is dead.' Matthew felt his heart plummet inside him so fast that his knees nearly buckled. He had no idea where the words had come from, and he wished he could take them back. 'I'm sorry, that was a stupid thing to say. My name is Matthew and I'm looking for Paneeraq Poulsen. Do you know her?'

'Yes,' she said tentatively. 'That's me.'

'I work for *Sermitsiaq* and I'm investigating an old case—four murders committed here in Nuuk in 1973.'

Paneeraq said nothing, but she studied him closely.

His fingertips on his left hand gently enclosed the ring finger on his right hand and started rubbing it. 'As far as I've discovered, it was a case where the murder victims were possibly even more evil than whoever killed them, although the murders were brutal.' He struggled to find the right words. 'I got your address from a woman who works for the council, and now I'm here. It's not an easy case to investigate. Everyone clams up like oysters.'

Her silence caused his hands to shake again.

Eventually she nodded slowly and pressed her lips together. 'Just a minute,' she said and closed the door.

A few doors further down, three young Greenlanders had come out into the gallery from another apartment. They were all smoking, and Matthew felt the craving for a cigarette. He went over to the gallery railings and leaned over to look down. There were only three cars parked in the yard between Block 1 and Block 2, and one of them was a wreck. Diagonally to his left, he could see a corner of the Arts Centre.

The door opened again, and he quickly turned around.

'Do come in,' Paneeraq said, and opened the door fully. 'I've never told anyone what happened, but I'm fifty-three years old now, and I've nothing to live for except my grandfather. If I'm going to die, I might as well die shriven, and my grandfather is well into his eighties so he doesn't cling to anything either.'

Matthew didn't know what to say, so he bent down to unlace his boots.

'We discussed it just now, before I let you in,' she continued. 'Once someone from the government hears about it, it'll be common knowledge soon enough.'

'I haven't been talking to them,' Matthew interjected. 'It was an older woman I know from the council. She feels strongly about the appalling...' He hesitated. 'The appalling attitude towards women in so many villages.'

Paneeraq nodded with an empty smile, and then ushered him into the living room. 'Well, let's see.' She pointed out a chair by the dining table. 'We can sit there.'

The living room was divided into three small islands: the dining table, the sofa and the television, and a comfortable armchair in which an old man was dozing. He was slumped in his chair and almost hidden in an anorak like those Matthew had seen worn by the Greenlandic men who ran the stalls down on the square. A round, flat drum of the kind used for drum dancing was leaning against the armchair.

'That's my grandfather,' Paneeraq said, placing two cups of steaming black coffee on the table. 'He doesn't say a lot these days.'

She pulled out a chair and sat down opposite Matthew. Her face was round, her eyes small and her eyebrows sparse. Her hair was thick and short, and brushed to the left. There were traces of grey in the black.

'What would you like to know?' she said, without looking at him.

'I'm working on a case from the seventies,' he began hesitantly. 'The four murders I mentioned just now. The way I see it, the murders happened because of child abuse within the family. Now, the girls didn't kill their own fathers, of course, but someone close to them had had enough and took action on the girls' behalf.'

'And you think I'm one of the girls?'

Matthew's fingers traced the side of the hot cup. 'Yes, I do. But it's okay if you don't want to talk about it.'

The old man in the armchair let a wrinkled hand fall from the armrest and down onto the drum, where it tapped the taut skin. Not hard, but enough for it to catch Matthew's attention.

'I don't mind talking about it.' Paneeraq interrupted the drum, which fell silent immediately. Then she got up and went over to a small, dark-brown chest of drawers, where she lit two large white candles with Christian images. On one candle was a picture of Jesus in the style of an icon, and on the other the Virgin Mary.

Matthew spotted a small, fossilised sea urchin between the candles. 'Do you have such fossils up here?' he asked, smiling at her.

'No, it was given to me a long time ago by a good friend.' She returned to her chair at the table and took a sip of her coffee. 'What would you like to know?'

Matthew shifted in his seat. 'When I started my investigation, I thought it was an unsolved murder case, but that has changed.'

'Changed to what?'

'Child abuse.'

Paneeraq heaved a deep sigh and stared at the table.

'It really is quite all right if you don't want to talk about it,' Matthew said.

She shrugged. 'Well, you're here now.' Her gaze moved towards the candles. 'Every girl who is abused remains a lost and lonely child her entire life. The pain of being betrayed so profoundly by the very people who should have protected her never goes away. The pain is there every day, and it hurts just as much now as it did back when she was nine or twelve years old and crying herself to sleep every night.'

'Do you mind if I record this?' Matthew asked, taking out his mobile.

'No…but if you publish your story, I would like to see it first, especially if you mention my name.'

'I haven't decided yet. Would you prefer me not to mention your name?'

'Do what you think is best.' She stared emptily at his mobile. 'I wasn't abused at home, but many other things happened.'

Matthew looked up. The words in Jakob's notebook about Paneeraq, who could barely walk and was terrified of her father, had had a profound impact on him, but he didn't want to bring up the notebook or Jakob. 'Oh? I thought the killings were some sort of reprisal for the sexual assault of—'

'Us girls?'

He nodded slowly.

'They might have been, but there was more to it than that. I don't know what it was like for the other three girls at home, but I do know what the four of us had been through and were still a part of after we returned to Nuuk, just under a year before my parents were killed.'

'I thought you lived in Nuuk? With your parents?' Matthew felt Jakob's suspicions about the girls and their fathers crumbling between his fingers.

'It doesn't sound like you've got very far with your investigation, but that's probably just as well. We've been forgotten. Everything has been forgotten.'

'Not quite,' Matthew protested. 'After all, I'm writing about it now.'

'But not because of us girls—am I right? Because of the murdered men. Everything relating to us has been misplaced or lost, so you won't find any evidence.'

'Perhaps the evidence will turn up once the genie is out of the bottle. After all, you're a witness and you can testify.'

Paneeraq sipped her coffee and moved back a little in her chair. 'There were four of us. Me, Najak, Julianne and Nuka. We were all about nine years old when we arrived at Ammassalik. That must have been in 1969. There was a children's hospital there and we were being treated for tuberculosis.' She shook her head. 'Frankly, I think it was nothing but an orphanage, but someone wanted an excuse to test pharmaceutical products on us, and TB provided a convenient pretext because no one paid much attention to little girls with a chronic cough.'

'So you spent two years at the orphanage in Ammassalik? That's not at all what I had imagined.'

'Yes, I guess we were there for about two years. The days merged together. I think we had given up hope that we would ever go home again, then suddenly it happened, and on the same day the four of us were flown back to Nuuk. We were told that we had been cured, but that we would need ongoing treatment to stay healthy, and that treatment would be best provided in Nuuk. It was more than a year since I had last coughed, so it made no sense to me at the time, but today I know why. But whatever the reason, it was a huge relief to get out of that place. Or so we thought.'

'All right,' Matthew said hesitantly. 'So no one had been assaulted before the murders were committed?'

'I didn't say that.'

The silence settled around them.

'I wasn't raped at home, but I was raped at the orphanage.' Paneeraq's eyes closed. Her face was distorted by distant pain. 'It was a dreadful place. Rapes. Humiliation. Medical experimentation. They gave us pills and injections from the very first week. Amphetamines, I believe today. But also lots of other things—I didn't know what they were then and I still don't. We were never told anything, except that it was part of our treatment. Some drugs gave me such severe pain in my back and legs that I could barely walk. And we slept much more than we ought to have done. Some days we were given pills that would give us our energy back, but they couldn't do anything about the pain.'

Matthew cleared his throat. 'Are you telling me that being raped was a part of life at the orphanage?'

'It was for me and those three other girls. There was an old doctor from Denmark. He had been there for years, and there was a rumour that he had once got a girl pregnant. Today, I believe that was why we were sent away when we reached the age of eleven or twelve. Not only because we were starting to understand what was going on, but also because we might get pregnant.'

'What a bastard. Why didn't anyone stop him?'

'A Danish doctor in Tasiilaq in the sixties and seventies? If you're a man, you can get away with anything in Tasiilaq. You could then and you can now.'

'Tasiilaq? I thought you said Ammassalik?'

'Tasiilaq used to be called Ammassalik. It's perhaps one of the most beautiful places on earth, but only if you're a man...or a rock.'

Matthew rubbed the bridge of his nose. 'Did you ever meet the doctor again once you returned to Nuuk? Or other people? I'm thinking of civil servants who wanted to make sure you kept silent.'

She nodded with a light smile that hid behind two sad, black eyes. 'So you do know something after all. We continued with our treatment after we came back to Nuuk. Once a week we would go to the hospital to get an injection in our thigh. I don't know what it was for, but I was knocked out for hours every single time. Except that twice I woke up and found the doctor between my legs while I lay semiconscious in a hospital bed.'

'The doctor from Tasiilaq?'

'Yes.'

'So he had also come to Nuuk?'

She nodded. 'Yes, he had. I don't know how that came about, but at the time I thought he must be stranded in Nuuk for the winter, because there were very few winter flights by helicopter in those days.'

'Did he also rape the other girls after they came back to Nuuk?'

'Yes, he did, and that was where things went really wrong because he was found out. Nukannguaq Rossing Lynge, Najak's mother, came to pick up her daughter at the hospital after treatment one day, and when she entered the ward she saw him lying on top of her naked child. Najak was awake and started screaming and crying when she saw her mother. I don't know if any of the other girls were also raped by their fathers. But the doctor was another matter, and suddenly all hell broke loose. Some men from the Town Hall and from Denmark turned up, but they had no intention of exposing the truth—they were there to silence us. That was when we realised that all the drugs we had been given weren't entirely by the book. They were experimenting on us, and that was the big secret. That was the real reason for the cover-up. Not the rape of four little girls.'

Matthew had put down his mobile. 'Do you know what happened to the other girls?'

'Najak went missing. I think her body is hidden somewhere in Nuuk. Julianne and Nuka got ill and died as a result of the treatments we were subjected to as children—I'm sure of it. I'm the only one of us still alive, but there are hundreds of other orphanage children from those days.'

'Do you think those men killed Najak?'

Her eyes slumped into an even deeper darkness. 'Yes, but not with their bare hands. I think they gave her an overdose of something.'

'And what about the girls' fathers?'

'I don't know,' she said, staring down at the table and shrugging in resignation.

'Please forgive my many questions. Only the murders were so brutal, and the events aren't connected in the way I expected.'

'That's quite all right.' She looked up again. 'There were probably powerful reasons why the murder investigation was stopped.'

'Those reasons being that the men who visited you at home and who were mixed up in it all were Jørgen Emil Lyberth and Kjeld Abelsen?'

'I don't know how you got those names, but you're on the right track. They came to our place a couple of times and argued loudly with my father, but I've no idea if they murdered my parents. Most of the row was about the doctor and the years of medical experimentation.'

Matthew drummed his fingers on the table. 'If they wanted to silence you, it makes no sense to kill only the fathers of the other girls—and why did the murders have to be so brutal?'

'Perhaps the brutality was to paralyse people's thoughts, and divert their attention away from the real reason.'

Matthew traced the side of his coffee cup, which was getting cold. He still hadn't mentioned Jakob and neither had she, but he didn't want to ask her about theories that were still disjointed in his mind. Jakob was dead and gone, and wiped from every archive. If he asked Paneeraq about Jakob or anything specific from the notebook, he would have to admit that he had it, and he wasn't ready to do that yet. He couldn't risk her getting upset with him for not owning up to just how much he already knew when he knocked on her door. Nor was he sure who to believe. Paneeraq's and Jakob's stories didn't match. The motive for the murders—as Jakob had seen it—might be gone, but Jakob was unlikely to have known that when he made his notes.

Matthew looked at Paneeraq out of the corner of his eye. 'Have you heard that they found the body of a man out on the ice cap?'

She shook her head, and didn't seem troubled by this news.

'I heard this morning that it might be a fifth victim from 1973,' he said. He paused and looked in vain for a reaction in her eyes. 'There were only four girls—is that right?'

'Yes, we were four.'

Matthew shook his head. 'It's just too much of a coincidence. The man on the ice cap was killed in the same way, but his body was hidden. And if he was also murdered in '73, you would think there'd be a connection.'

'I wouldn't know.'

There was no expression in her eyes. No fear, anxiety or grief. Not even relief. Matthew looked at the brown chest of drawers, where the candles glowed over the small fossil.

'Do you know where the Hemplers used to live? I believe they died in the 1960s, in a plane crash near Kolonihavnen, but as far as I know they had a house here in Nuuk. I'm curious about whether the house is still there.'

Paneeraq hesitated, then nodded. 'I visited that house myself as a child, but I don't want to talk about that now. Perhaps some other time.' She smiled distantly. 'It was where I got my sea urchin.'

'But do you know if the house still stands?'

'Oh, it does. It's near Kolonihavnen.'

Matthew's mobile interrupted her. *Leiff—newspaper* said the display on the screen.

'Go on, answer it,' she said. 'I don't mind.'

Matthew pressed *Answer*. 'Hi, Leiff.'

'Hi. You need to meet Malik out by that Tupaarnaq's apartment.

They've found Lyberth inside it. Dead. More than dead, as far as I can gather.'

'Dead, really? Are they sure it's him?'

'They're quite sure. Hurry up.'

'Okay, I'll be there in ten, fifteen minutes max.' He checked the time on his mobile. 'I'll be there before eight o'clock.'

'All right—but there's something you need to know first.'

'Go on…'

'You know I can never let sleeping dogs lie? I decided to find out what became of the surviving boy in the Tasiilaq murders. You know, the ones involving Tupaarnaq?'

'I'm with you.'

'Now, it just so happens that Ulrik Heilmann came to Nuuk a mere three days after the Tasiilaq murders. And not only is he the same age as the surviving boy, he also shares the same birthday and has no known family. Are you thinking what I'm thinking?'

'You're saying that he—'

'Yes. I'm trying to get a copy of his birth certificate, but it's not easy. Perhaps Lyberth helped him out—he was the local vicar back then. But, yes, I'm pretty sure that Ulrik is Tupaarnaq's brother. How he met Lyberth I've yet to find out. By the way, I think we can safely assume that he knows who Tupaarnaq is. In such a small police station, everyone is bound to know when a convicted murderer comes to town.' He paused briefly. 'Right, you had better get going. I'll keep digging. Just bear it in mind in case you see them, will you?'

'I will,' Matthew said. 'And Malik is already out there, you said?'

'Yes, he's waiting for you. Oh, by the way, how did your meeting with the woman who knew your father go?'

'She said that she lived with him for ten years, but that she doesn't know where he is now. She also said I have a sister who is at school in Denmark.' Matthew shook his head. 'This day just gets more and more bizarre.'

54

As Matthew farewelled Paneeraq, she told him he could visit her again if he had any more questions, or if it became necessary for her to read his article before he posted it.

After reaching the yard between Blocks 1 and 2, he hurried through the centre of town towards Tupaarnaq's apartment, which was less than a ten-minute walk away. Red and white police tape had been put up around the stairwell by Block 17. Near the tape a couple of police officers in black trousers and light-blue shirts were talking to a group of people—perhaps curious onlookers, or maybe residents now denied access to their own homes.

'Hey,' a voice called out to Matthew. 'Got any cigarettes? I seem to have forgotten mine.'

'What's going on in there?' Matthew asked as he lit two cigarettes and handed one to Malik, who accepted it and took a drag deep into his lungs.

'It's mind-blowing,' Malik said, smoke seeping out of the corners of his mouth. 'Batshit crazy. It's none other than Lyberth—would you believe it?'

'Ulrik's Lyberth?'

'Yes, that's the one.'

'Have you been inside?'

'No, they've restricted access to the whole area, but we know it's Lyberth.' He nodded towards the police officers by the tape. 'I've taken a few shots of the guys over there, and a few more from the other side, up towards the balcony and windows.'

'Great—that'll do for now.'

'Oh, no, it won't.' Malik shook his head. 'We'll hang around for a bit longer. They'll have to bring him out at some point.'

'I don't know,' Matthew said, staring at the wet car park in front of the apartment building. 'We might be in for a long wait.'

'So what? We're talking about Lyberth! Don't you want to see what happens?'

'Yes, of course I do.' Matthew closed his eyes. The wind had eased off, and the rain was no longer quite so intense, but the smell of a wet world still hung around them like a thick, damp fog. 'Only I have some stories I need to finish writing.' He took a long drag on his cigarette. 'And I need to check out the garden of a house down by Kolonihavnen.'

'A garden—in Greenland?'

'Yes, or whatever you have here. Rocks. Heather. I just need to take a look around.'

'Today? Why?'

'I think an eleven-year-old girl was buried there in 1973, and that her skeleton might still be there.'

Malik threw aside his cigarette butt. 'Seriously? Is this a joke?'

'No. That notebook Ottesen gave me hints at something like that.'

'Bloody hell, what a day!' Malik exclaimed, and he slapped Matthew on the shoulder. 'I'll join you later, if that's all right. I want to see what happens here first.'

'Someone's trying to get our attention,' Matthew said, nodding towards the tape.

'Ah, I know her,' Malik said. He waved back and started marching down the gallery towards the officer. 'Come with me. We're about to be allowed in.'

'Hello.' The young female officer's voice was mild but firm.

'Hey…Can we come in now?' Malik tried hopefully.

'No, that's not why I waved you over.' She looked at Matthew. 'Ottesen would like a word with you.'

'With me?' Matthew said, every muscle in his body freezing. 'Why?'

'I don't know, but in you go.'

'Right, we'll do just that,' Malik said, putting his hand on Matthew's shoulder.

'Not you, Malik,' the officer added swiftly. 'Just Matthew.' She took a small black walkie-talkie from her belt and raised it to her mouth. 'Matthew is on his way.'

The walkie-talkie crackled briefly before a voice broke through: *Okay, I'm coming down.*

Matthew avoided looking at her. The short distance to the heavy, wonky swing door felt like a funeral march.

'Hello again,' Ottesen said the moment the door had slammed behind Matthew.

'Hello,' Matthew squawked, with absolutely no control over his voice.

'You may have heard that we've found Jørgen Emil Lyberth dead in Tupaarnaq's apartment.'

Matthew nodded slowly, while he tried to steady his breathing. His gaze scanned the junk mail on the floor, where the vagrant to whom he'd given his cigarettes had been sitting.

'I told you she was dangerous,' Ottesen said, and he pressed his lips together for a few seconds. 'We can't say anything for certain yet, as there are several things we need to establish, so…Whatever you reporters may hear, please would you restrict yourselves to just writing that he was found in Block 17, and that police are treating his death as suspicious? Just until tomorrow. Then I promise you there will be an official press briefing at the police station or the Town Hall.'

'Sure,' Matthew said, and he inhaled air deep into his lungs. 'We'll hold off. It's all right.'

'Thank you.' Ottesen rubbed his upper lip between two fingers. 'You know that notebook I gave you?'

Matthew felt the sweat break out all over his body.

'I know that Lyberth was keen to get his hands on it. Do you have any idea why?'

'I think he was mixed up in some scandal in the early seventies.'

'Does it say so in the book?'

Matthew nodded again. 'I thought you had read it?'

'I have.' There was silence. 'We should probably put that note-book back.'

'All right—I'll go and get it.'

'Okay. Matthew,' Ottesen hesitated. 'About Tupaarnaq…You've seen quite a lot of her recently, haven't you?'

'Yes,' Matthew croaked.

'You went seal hunting together, and now you're the guy she calls when we pick her up?'

'She asked me. I…I…'

'Yes?'

'I'm just trying to work out who she is.'

'And who is she?'

'She's not who everyone thinks she is.'

'Good.' Ottesen inhaled deeply through his nose. 'Because right now there's a lot to suggest that you're wrong. Have you ever been inside her apartment?'

'No…No, she wouldn't let me.' He ground to a halt and stared at the floor.

'Wouldn't let you?'

'She's not ready for visitors yet. She has just been locked up for twelve years, don't forget.'

Ottesen smiled briefly. 'You're right. It does funny things to people.' Then he shook his head. 'I've never liked prisons. Right— you bring me that notebook, okay? And if you see Tupaarnaq, please tell her that we really want to talk to her.'

'Okay.'

'And you need to stay here in Nuuk.'

'What do you mean?'

'Don't leave town until we say so.'

55

The twilight was slowly gathering in the long shadows of the fog around the houses in Kolonihavnen when, just under two hours later, Matthew and Malik stood in front of the house where Jakob Pedersen had lived forty years earlier.

Matthew tried to visualise the layout as Jakob had described it in his notebook. He knew that the living room with Jakob's armchair must be behind the windows to the right of the front door.

'Are you sure this is the place?'

Matthew saw a glowing cigarette pass his face.

'It's the address that Paneeraq gave me, and it fits the description in the notebook.'

Most of the houses around them could easily be more than forty years old. The distance to the nearest neighbouring house also matched the information in the notebook.

'Let's take a closer look,' Malik said, making a beeline for the front door. 'It doesn't look as if anyone lives here now.'

'Are you sure?'

'What would I know? Only it looks empty.' His eyes scanned the exterior. 'And it could seriously do with a lick of paint.'

The path towards the house was narrow and obscured. It had

been wider once—they could tell from the gravel strip winding in and out between the rocks—but the walkway didn't look as if it was in use much now, having been overrun with low grasses.

The rain had almost ceased, but the cloud cover had grown heavier and lay so densely over the roofs and the rocks that it felt as if the clouds had merged into one with the moisture between the rocks and the brown and green shrubs. The house, which had been visible only a few minutes ago, now vanished into a fog so intense that it felt like cold, damp breath on their skin. Matthew watched Malik dissolve halfway up the path and hurried after him, wiping the moisture from his face with one hand.

A loud knocking penetrated the fog and Matthew jumped. 'What are you doing?'

'I'm knocking on the door. The place really does look abandoned.'

Matthew could barely see his own feet, but he walked in the direction of Malik's voice, which sounded close by. The house emerged from the fog with its red, peeling paintwork. 'You can't just knock on the door!' he protested.

'We can always do a runner if anyone is in,' Malik grinned. He stepped past Matthew and up to the window, where he cupped his hands around his face. 'It's pitch-black in there. Hold on.' His fingers rummaged in his trouser pocket and he pulled out his mobile. Soon the torchlight from the phone was shining through the window. 'What are we looking for?'

'I don't know yet,' Matthew said, stepping up beside Malik.

The light wasn't powerful enough to penetrate every corner, but it was enough. An old-fashioned living room was hidden behind the window. Nut-coloured, glossy Brazilian rosewood furniture. Deep-pile rugs, one blue and one grey. Along one wall was a bookcase with books, Greenlandic figures, an ulo and lots of rocks.

'Could you point the light towards the bookcase again, please?'

Malik tilted the mobile so the light shone brightest on the

bookcase with the stones.

Matthew nodded to himself. 'The guy from the notebook,' he whispered. 'He lived in this very room.'

'You mean this house?'

'Yes, but also this living room. It's a perfect match for the description in his notebook.'

'Okay, all right. So you're saying the guy—who might be our mummy from the ice cap—used to live here, and everything has just been left as it was?'

'The living room certainly has.'

'You're kidding me! It must be forty years ago.'

'Forty-one, almost.'

Malik turned to Matthew. 'Bloody hell! This place gives me the creeps.' He stretched out his arm and pushed up his sleeve. 'Do you think he's still in there?' he added, and resumed peering through the window. 'Or what if his spirit is?'

'Of course it's not.' Matthew took a few steps back, and then walked up to the front door. 'If he's inside, it'll be because he's still alive, but no one can hide in a house in the middle of Nuuk for forty years. Hang on.' There was a letterbox near the door, and a small nameplate in the top right-hand corner with the name *Abelsen*. 'One of the men who got him killed lives here now.'

'Holy shit! Then I'm one hundred per cent sure that his spirit is in there,' Malik exclaimed, looking about him. 'I'll just take a walk around the house.'

'What? Why?'

'I need to check something.'

Matthew grabbed a shovel that was by the door and walked down the front steps and onto the gravel. The fog had closed around Malik the moment he moved, and nothing but moisture remained. 'Malik?' Matthew called out nervously.

'Over here.'

His voice came out of the fog. Possibly from the other side of the house. Or maybe it was nearer. The sound was bouncing around the drops of dense air.

'Oh, screw it,' Matthew grunted and stuck out a hand. He found the wooden cladding of the house and started moving in the opposite direction to the one Malik had taken, in order to find the kitchen. On the day Jakob was hit in the head by the stone thrown through the very window they had just been looking through, he had seen a silhouette approach the house. And the next day he had written in his journal that the snow outside his kitchen had been severely disturbed—that there had been pebbles and soil mixed up in it.

His hands fumbling across the rough wood, Matthew edged his way around the house. The fog held him in a firm grip. If he let go of the house, he would have no idea in which direction to walk. His feet searched for a foothold between stones, rocks and low scrub. He set down his shovel, took out his mobile, and switched on the torchlight. It wasn't a huge improvement, but it was enough for him to see his feet and the red wooden wall. He turned a corner, and a few metres later another dark window appeared. He carefully moved right up to the glass, and pointed the mobile's light inside.

He couldn't see much, but it was definitely Jakob's kitchen. Matthew recognised the hard, marled plastic kitchen table with the dark-brown edges from the notebook. Even the white kitchen cupboards with the grey metal handles looked the same.

Matthew jumped when someone put a hand on his shoulder. His mobile slipped from his grip and glittered as it whirled towards the ground where it landed face-down in the gravel.

'Relax,' Malik said with a grin. 'It's only me.'

Matthew bent down to pick up his phone. 'Shit, Malik. I'm standing here staring into a dead man's home.' He straightened up and breathed out, patting his chest softly a few times with his left hand. 'You nearly gave me a heart attack.'

'Sorry, mate. And I didn't even mean to.' Malik grinned again, but stopped quickly. 'There's nothing to see here, and there's definitely no one at home.'

'No, I agree. But Abelsen does live here, and there's probably a reason for that. I just don't understand how he could live here for forty years without making any changes at all.'

'He's always working,' Malik said. 'He doesn't have a wife or children, and he's known as the coldest and most powerful man in Greenland.'

'I think it's a trophy.'

'A trophy? You mean, like a pair of antlers?'

'Yes, exactly. This house is Abelsen's hunting trophy. Acquired through a chase that cost many people their lives, and helped him up the last few steps to the throne.'

Malik turned up his nose. 'An old house like this is hardly what I would call a trophy.'

'It probably looked better in '73, but it's not the house as such that's the trophy. He moved into it purely to demonstrate his power. He was untouchable even to the police and the politicians.'

'I believe he still is,' Malik said. 'What are you doing with that shovel?'

'It was just a daft idea. Somewhere underneath us is the skeleton of an eleven-year-old girl who was killed by an overdose in November 1973. Abelsen and Lyberth were both involved in the girl's death.'

'And now Lyberth is dead.'

'And now Lyberth is dead.' Matthew stared at the house. 'If this is Abelsen's trophy, then I want to get inside.'

'Inside the house? Now? You mean, we break in?'

'Yes. Now. We need to get inside that house while Abelsen is out.'

'And you're quite sure that he's out?'

'Yes, for a little while. Come on. You were the one who was all gung-ho about knocking on the door a minute ago.'

Malik nodded. 'There are no open doors or windows. I checked when I walked around the house.'

'Maybe there's another way in.' Matthew glanced around. 'I'll just take another look at the front door.'

Back outside the front door, he grabbed the handle and pushed it down hard a few times, before he gave up and started looking for a key in the porch. It didn't make sense for a man like Abelsen to leave the key in such an obvious place, but you never could tell. While Matthew searched under some boxes stacked against the wall by the door, his ear picked up a sound. It was coming from the inside. Behind the door. He jumped up, and when the door opened at the same time, he stumbled back down the porch steps.

'We've finally made a breakthrough,' Malik stated proudly, beaming at Matthew from the doorway.

'What? How did you get in?' Matthew grabbed the railing and pulled himself back up.

'Those old windows are so brittle…I'm afraid one of the kitchen windows just came apart in my hand.'

'We'd better get a move on.' Matthew walked past Malik, through the hall and into the living room. 'We're looking for anything from '73. Film reels and so on.'

'All right, but everything in here is from the seventies.'

'Just start looking. Check the cupboards.'

Malik got to work immediately, opening cupboards and drawers and rummaging around in them. 'How about magazines, cups, stuff like that?'

'No, I think we're looking for films, or something technical, like a notebook…' Matthew ran his hand across Jakob's coffee table, and looked at the grey rug underneath it. 'Possibly a jigsaw puzzle of Godthåb.' He continued towards the tall bookcase, which was laden with police magazines, books and rocks. There was nothing that pointed directly to the case.

'Did you say films?' Malik asked. He was sitting on the floor near the sideboard, and in his hands he held an old film projector. 'I've also found four reels of film,' he said, reaching his arm into the sideboard. 'Is this what we're looking for?'

'Yes, I think so. Very much so.' Matthew glanced about the living room again. The harpoon. The figures. Everything that was Jakob's. The Hemplers' things. 'Right, let's get out of here.'

'With the reels and everything?'

'Yes—we'll keep them at my place.'

56

Matthew had only been back in his apartment for a few minutes when his entry phone buzzed. He looked down into the street. Darkness was starting to settle on Nuuk, but it felt lighter because the fog had moved up towards the night sky.

'It's me.' He heard Tupaarnaq's voice in the handset. 'Are you alone?'

'Yes,' he said, and buzzed her in.

The lift hummed and the door opened with its clicking sounds.

'You're back late,' she said, marching past him and into his apartment.

'Yes, I…Have you been waiting for me?'

She unlaced her boots and kicked them off. She was wearing a new jumper—a black knitted rollneck. Her trousers were the same black ones with pockets down the sides. On top of her head was a thin, dark membrane of millimetre stubble.

'They've found Lyberth,' he said.

'I know.' She held up a black rucksack. 'Do you have wi-fi?'

He watched her narrow back disappear into the living room, and went to get the code for the router from the bedroom.

'What's happening out there?' she asked when Matthew returned to the living room, where she had sat down on the sofa, cross-legged, balancing her laptop.

He handed her the small white router lid with the code. 'There were quite a lot of police around, and someone asked me why I had come to the police station with you and why we had gone seal hunting.'

She nodded slowly without looking up.

'They want to talk to you,' he added.

'That'll have to wait,' she said, and looked up at him. 'Do you have anything to eat?'

'Food?'

'Yes, food—what else? I haven't had anything to eat all day.'

'I don't know what there is,' he said, and went to check the fridge. 'Do you eat eggs?'

'Yes, I don't mind eggs.'

Matthew took out a bowl and put a frying pan on the stove. 'I'll make you an omelette, then.'

She fell quiet behind him. He stood for a moment, looking at her hunched body in the yellow glow by the sofa. Her nose was small, and from where he was standing he couldn't see a single freckle. She had pulled off the black rollneck jumper and was wearing a dark sleeveless vest underneath, like the first time he saw her at Cafe Mamaq. Her tattoos seemed alive in the artificial light, and the swirling, dark-green leaves reminded him of a dragon's scales.

He looked away, and turned his attention back to the food. After whisking the eggs he poured them into the hot frying pan. He chopped up a couple of tomatoes and a red pepper, and added them to the mixture before the eggs started to set.

'Salt? Pepper? Rosemary?'

'I'm in now.'

'In where?' He turned around with a frown.

'The server of the Greenlandic government.'

'What?'

'Their security is a joke.'

Matthew tipped the omelette onto a plate, which he brought her. She looked up. 'Aren't you having some?'

'I shared a pizza with my photographer a few hours ago…What are you doing on the government's server? Can't they trace you?'

'I didn't even break a sweat. And they couldn't trace their own nose. Right, let's take a look at Abelsen's emails.'

'What?' Matthew exclaimed again, straightening up. 'Is it all right if I sit here?'

'Sure—it's your sofa.'

She scrolled down a row of lines that looked like email subject headings. 'I've searched for any emails he has received from Lyberth.'

'Open the one with no subject heading from the day before yesterday.' Matthew pointed at the screen.

'You can look at it yourself,' she said, passing him her laptop. 'While I eat this. I would also like to use your shower.' She eyeballed him. 'And this time you stay away—understand? I can't keep letting you live if you're going to be such a moron.'

'I'll stay here, I promise.' He looked up. 'I can't believe you managed to hack his emails. There are quite a few from Lyberth… most of them after the iceman was found.'

'Anything about the murders?'

'Lyberth seems worried that the old investigation might be reopened because of the iceman. Abelsen writes that he needs to calm down and let him fix things, as he always does. He sounds rather arrogant. Lyberth is afraid of how much might be revealed.' Matthew opened another email. 'Okay. Lyberth wants out, but Abelsen threatens him and says he needs to stick to their deal. Wow…'

'What?'

'Here Abelsen writes that Lyberth and Ulrik are both going down for the murder of the man on the ice.'

'Does it say which man?'

'No, just *the man*.'

'So that could be the mummy or Aqqalu.'

'Exactly. That's the problem. But the tone is harsh, and there's a lot of intimidation and threats.'

She put her fork down on her empty plate and moved closer to Matthew.

'Fuck, he's in Tasiilaq,' he murmured.

'Abelsen?'

'Yes, right now. He writes here that they need to meet before he leaves for Tasiilaq.'

'Does it say anything about where they'll meet?'

Matthew opened another email and then another, but both times he shook his head. 'They must have arranged that some other way. But it says here that they're going to meet, and that was written on the same day Lyberth was killed.'

'It's not enough to acquit me,' she said, rubbing the stubble on her scalp.

'Not even the emails?'

She shook her head. 'There's no hard evidence of a crime. It's all circumstantial. It's not enough.'

Matthew closed his eyes. 'Lyberth's pet, Ulrik, is from Tasiilaq. Perhaps that's relevant.' He considered sharing Leiff's discoveries with her right then and there, but he couldn't. Instead he said, 'I met with a woman today. She's the only person, apart from Abelsen, who is still alive from the '73 case, which I'm sure is what Lyberth and Abelsen were arguing about.'

Tupaarnaq turned her upper body and looked at him. 'Can she link the two men directly to the murders? Or the man on the ice?'

'Ultimately, it's about medical experiments on Greenlandic children, but also sexual assaults and child abuse at an orphanage in Tasiilaq. In late 1973 it threatened to become a major scandal, but

Abelsen cleaned up the mess.'

'Any physical evidence?'

'I don't think so, but I have a witness who was subjected to it all.'

'I need to speak to her. What time is it?'

'Eleven-thirty. It's too late now.'

'Then it'll have to be tomorrow,' she replied. She got up from the sofa, shut her laptop, and put it on the coffee table. 'I'm off to take a shower.'

'Yes, all right.' He hesitated for a moment. 'There's another thing.'

'Go on.'

'I got an email from someone claiming to be Lyberth, but it was sent after Lyberth was murdered. He wants to meet with me down at Nipisa.'

She frowned. '"Nipisa" means lumpfish.'

'It's a restaurant down by the old quay in Kolonihavnen. It'll be deserted after closing hours.'

'Do you think Abelsen sent it?'

Matthew nodded. 'I'm pretty sure it was him. I have a notebook belonging to that police officer they killed in 1973. Abelsen wants it. As do the police.'

'When are you meeting him?'

'Friday night. Do you have your gun?'

She nodded. 'My stuff is across the road. In the blue building.'

'The small block scheduled for demolition?'

'Yes, I've picked the lock of one of them. We can sleep there, if your place becomes too dangerous.'

57

The sound of running water from the bathroom was reassuring. Somewhere in the middle of it, Tupaarnaq was standing behind a wilderness of tattoos that seemed to move under the spray of steaming water and the purifying razor.

Matthew took out his own laptop and turned it on. From the sofa he could see the top of the building Tupaarnaq had broken into. He closed his eyes for a few minutes to organise his thoughts, and then began writing his story, basing it on Jakob's notebook and the information he had gathered from Leiff, Ivalo and Paneeraq.

The words came quickly, and it took him just over an hour to finish the piece. Meanwhile, Tupaarnaq had emerged from the bathroom and sat down with her own laptop at the opposite end of the sofa.

He included everything. The abuse at the orphanage in Tasiilaq and in Nuuk. The brutal murders. The medical experimentation. The Danish doctor. The murder of the police officer investigating the case. The widespread sexual assault suffered by Greenlandic girls. He stated that he had interviewed a girl from the orphanage, and had access to Jakob's notes about his investigation.

It was just past two in the morning when Matthew emailed the article to his editor. The bad weather over Nuuk had eased off, only to return with a vengeance. Outside his balcony door, the wind was shaking the houses again.

Matthew felt a craving for a cigarette as soon as he pressed *Send*, but he didn't want to smoke when Tupaarnaq was with him. He clenched his fists, relaxed them, then clenched them again. 'I'm just going downstairs for a moment.'

She looked up. 'I'll come with you. Don't look so scared—I know perfectly well you're going for a smoke. I don't want to sit here on my own and wonder who's trying to get in.'

'But we're the only ones here, and it's the middle of the night.'

'Yes…and I'm coming with you.'

Matthew found his cigarettes and lighter. There was no porch outside his apartment block, so they crossed the road and huddled outside the blue building, where the porch offered them some shelter. He pressed himself up against the wooden wall in order to avoid the rain whipping at his face. The wind tore at everything, and tossed the rain about. The raindrops felt like ice when they hit his skin. The tip of his cigarette lit up with every drag.

'You need to quit that crap,' Tupaarnaq said.

'I know, but not right now…I've only been smoking for a few years.'

'That's long enough. It was stupid to start in the first place, especially at your age.'

'Yes, I guess so.' He took a final drag of the cigarette. He had smoked it so far that he caught the sharp taste of the filter. 'I thought I might take up writing instead.'

'Don't you already make your living from writing?'

'Yes, but not like that. Privately. I want to write a book for my daughter.'

'If you had a daughter, you wouldn't be standing here.'

'No.' Matthew rubbed his face. There was an acrid smell about his fingers. 'But when my wife, Tine, was killed in a car crash, she was pregnant. We were expecting a little girl.'

'I'm sorry to hear that.' Tupaarnaq stared into the darkness. 'You would have made a good dad.'

Matthew stared out into the rain. 'Time to go back inside?'

'In a moment,' she said. 'I prefer being outside.'

'Freedom?' he asked, not taking his eyes off the rain.

'Yes.' She had turned her face and was looking at him now. 'Why did you come back to Greenland?'

He shrugged. 'My life in Denmark fell apart. I had nothing. One day I was looking through some pictures and I found one from when we saw my father for the last time.' Matthew raised his head and looked into her eyes. 'I remember him giving me a model aeroplane that he had built himself when I turned four. An American B-52. It was in a bag and it reeked of glue. I don't remember ever seeing him again. He promised to follow us, but he never did.'

'Do you think you'll find him? I mean, here, after today?'

Matthew shook his head. 'No, and I don't think it matters very much. I've been mad at him ever since I was a child.'

'And now you have a sister instead.'

'Yes…That hasn't quite sunk in yet.'

'Give it time and it'll all fall into place.'

He stared at his boots and shrugged again. 'I think she and I both really hate our father. Else, my half-sister's mother, texted me soon after my visit telling me that Arnaq doesn't want to have anything to do with a half-brother on her father's side, so she couldn't give me her mobile number. But at least they have mine now. We'll have to wait and see.'

He was about to add something more but was interrupted by his mobile, which had started to buzz in his pocket. 'Who on earth could that be?' he mumbled as he took it out. 'It's my editor. I didn't think he would be awake at this hour.'

'Hello? Matt? We can't print that. What the hell were you thinking? Nuuk is a small town, and you know it. It's out of the question!'

'I'm sorry for emailing you so late.'

'That's all right, I was up anyway. No, everything about that article is wrong—do you hear me? We just can't print it. We can't publish all those allegations. These are highly respected men you're slinging mud at, and you've managed to drag a dead Minister for Greenland into it as well. It just won't do. And I don't see how you can have any evidence to support your claims. Corrupt business practices, fair enough, but this! Jesus, Matthew. And Lyberth's body isn't even cold yet. I was expecting a respectful article about his death, and you send me this!'

'But it's true, all of it. Surely we have to—'

'*Sermitsiaq* isn't a tabloid. A great politician has been found murdered, and before we even announce his death to our readers, you're dragging his reputation through the mud…Along with that of Greenland's most powerful civil servant.'

'Every word I wrote is true. Read it again. I can produce a witness, and I have the police officer's notebook.'

'It's still no good. It goes against all press ethics.'

There was silence. The wind and the rain pushed and pulled at Matthew.

'Listen,' his editor continued in a softer tone of voice. 'When I get back to Nuuk, we can talk about it. I would like to see that notebook for myself. Let's meet tomorrow morning when I'm back. Until then, cobble together a few words about Lyberth's demise, but hold back the salacious details. The man is dead and the police are treating his death as suspicious. That's all we need to write right now. No—on second thought, I'll get one of the others to write his obituary.'

'Okay,' Matthew sighed. 'Where are you now?'

'Tasiilaq. My uncle's birthday party. I'm flying home tomorrow.'

The call ended, and Matthew dropped his mobile back into his pocket.

'The world is full of idiots,' Tupaarnaq said, and briefly put her hand on his shoulder.

'He's in Tasiilaq, just like Abelsen.'

'Greenland is a very small community.'

He nodded wearily. 'I need to watch some movies.'

'Movies? Right now?'

'Yes, eight-millimetre films. I believe they were recorded in '73 and show an eleven-year-old girl from the case back then. Najak—the one who was never found.'

Tupaarnaq clenched her fist, and her entire body tensed. The sinews on her neck stood out clearly. 'What if it's child porn? Can you cope with that?'

'I don't know, but I have to watch them.' He breathed deeply, all the way down to his stomach. 'I have to watch them. It's the least I can do.'

As soon as they were back at the apartment, he hooked up the projector and fitted the first reel. Tupaarnaq turned off the light. The film flickered. The light bulb. The darkness. The light. The tiny body of the curled-up little girl. Matthew changed reels without saying a word.

Tupaarnaq sat on the sofa with her legs pulled up in front of her, her face half-buried in her knees. Her arms were looped around her legs. Her eyes were distant.

'Wait!' Matthew exclaimed. 'There was a man. Did you see him?'

Tupaarnaq cleared her throat. 'I saw him. Rewind the film… quick.'

Matthew reached out his hand and flicked a switch so the film played backwards. The blanket. The shadow. The naked Najak.

'Stop,' Tupaarnaq whispered hoarsely.

Matthew stopped the film and restarted it in slow motion, taking pictures of it with his mobile at the same time. 'I'm going to send these to a friend at the newspaper. He might recognise something.' He looked at Tupaarnaq, who was still curled up on the sofa. 'Did you recognise anyone?'

She shook her head. 'Only what's happening.'

Matthew looked at her. 'Are you all right?'

She shrugged. 'No, but it's okay.' Then she leaned to the left and rested her head on his shoulder. 'Why do people do these things?'

'I don't know,' he said quietly, carefully leaning his head close to hers.

The film ran out. The rain was pelting the large windows and the balcony door.

'I'm glad that you're here,' he continued.

Tupaarnaq moved away. Not with a jerk. She just shifted.

Matthew looked down at the sofa. 'I'm sorry if I said the wrong thing.'

'It's okay…' She patted his thigh. 'You're a good man.'

Matthew pressed his lips together. 'Can you hack *Sermitsiaq*'s website, so that we can upload my article online ourselves?'

'Yes,' she said. 'Technically it's not difficult, but I gather from your conversation with your editor that it might cost you your job.'

'If Abelsen gets away with it, I'm guessing it'll cost me my life— and I wouldn't be surprised if he also gets you locked up for murder.'

Tupaarnaq shrugged.

'Too bad,' Matthew went on. 'They're not going to get away with this. They should have been stopped forty years ago.'

58

Matthew woke on the sofa under a blanket. It was morning, and the light had pierced the blanket fibres and found him. The wind was calm again.

He took out his mobile and brought up *Sermitsiaq*'s website. The article had already been taken down, but he knew it had been there. Some people must surely have seen it. Tupaarnaq had put it on the front page, along with photographs of the orphanage in Tasiilaq and two of Lyberth, one of which was taken when Lyberth was accused of sexual assault by a female government employee.

His mobile had been on silent, and Matthew could see that he had seven missed calls from his editor and a similar number of voicemails.

Leiff had called too, but only once. Rather than leave a message, he had sent him a text:

Matthew, please stop by the newspaper ASAP. Before noon. I've heard you'll be fired as soon as the boss is back, and you won't be allowed to clear your desk and your computer, so if I were you I would get here pronto. There's a parcel on your desk. It came in the post. If you're not here in an hour, I'll keep it for you. I believe it's Lyberth's handwriting on the cover.

Matthew then noticed another text from Leiff:

The other thing. The pictures you sent me. It looks like a very big shipping container, insulated on the inside. I don't recognise the girl in the picture, but I believe that the man is a young Abelsen. Now, watch your back and be careful what you get yourself mixed up in. This looks like a matter for the police.

It was still only nine-thirty in the morning, so he had plenty of time. Matthew didn't bother listening to the voicemails from his editor. He googled a couple of sentences from his article to see if anyone had managed to copy it before it was taken down, but found nothing.

He heard the toilet being flushed. Feet crossing the floor. He sat up and pushed the blanket to the far end of the sofa.

'You don't have to pretend that you were awake.'

He looked at her questioningly, and ran a hand through his hair.

'I heard you snoring a minute ago.'

'I don't snore.'

'If you say so.'

She headed for the kitchen. 'All right if I make some coffee?'

'Sure.' He cleared his throat, arched his back slowly and tilted his neck from side to side. 'If you can find some.'

'Well, you've got Nescafé,' she said, with her head halfway inside the cupboard to the right over the kitchen sink. 'That's good enough for me. Would you like a cup?'

'No, thanks—I don't drink coffee.'

'You should try it instead of cigarettes.'

The word *cigarettes* sent a frisson through his body, and he couldn't stop himself from glancing at the packet and the lighter on the coffee table. 'I need to go to the office to pick up something before my editor returns to Nuuk,' he said.

Tupaarnaq was standing with her back to him, stirring her cup. She nodded slowly. 'I saw that your article has been taken down,' she said, turning around with the cup in her hand. 'Are they up in arms about it?'

'I just need to clear my desk and then I'll get out of there. I've got some research to do—I want to check a few more things about the films.'

'Okay.'

'Someone from the paper has texted me to say that the man in the film is Abelsen.'

The coffee aroma reached his nostrils and slipped inside his mouth, where it unfurled and turned into an even stronger craving for a cigarette.

'Watch your step when you're outside,' was all she said.

59

It took Matthew just a few minutes to clear his desk, and as it was only ten o'clock in the morning, he decided he might as well delete his old emails as well. Not that he had anything to hide. He just didn't like the thought of other people going through his correspondence.

His parcel was in a drawer in Leiff's desk. It was the safest place, Leiff had texted him—and that was undoubtedly true, because Matthew soon surmised from his colleagues that they all knew what had happened.

Before lunchtime, he had finished going through his mailbox and deleting files and passwords, and he clicked *Shut down*. He picked up his bag and went downstairs to see Leiff, who opened the drawer and handed the parcel to Matthew.

'Take it home with you,' he said with a smile. 'And if you write another story, then send it to me and I'll try to get it published under my by-line.' He nodded in the direction of the parcel that was now in Matthew's bag. 'Looks like it might be exciting. You will text me once you open it, won't you?'

'Yes. I'll go through it and see what I find.'

'Sounds good. If things go wrong, then come over to my place.'

'Okay, thank you.' Matthew hesitated. 'The pictures I sent you.

Do you remember anything else? Might the container still be here?'

Leiff shook his head. 'I don't know. It could have been set down anywhere. Only I don't remember there being so many of that size in Nuuk in 1973. Then again, it's a long time ago, and it might have been left somewhere off the beaten track. I happen to know someone who has a container like that built into his house over on C.P. Holbøllsvej. I mean, from the outside it looks like a house. It has a roof, a window and everything, but it's just a shipping container with wooden cladding.'

'Could it be the same one?'

'No, that one came up here just under ten years ago, so it can't be. Only they're similar, and his is also insulated and shiny on the inside.' Leiff nodded to himself. 'I'll ask around.'

Matthew's apartment was only a few hundred metres from *Sermitsiaq*'s offices, but his legs and his mind felt as though it was much further away. He felt like everyone was staring at him. Did people know? Had Abelsen returned to Nuuk? Were the police looking for him? He still hadn't given the notebook back to Ottesen. Abelsen wanted it, but might well decide to have him killed anyway. Matthew spent several minutes looking about him before he inserted the key into his front door and let himself into the quiet, dry stairwell. He took the stairs rather than the lift, so that he would see if anyone was waiting on the landing.

He had bought himself some time by confirming that he would be outside Nipisa on Friday night with Jakob's notebook, but he was well aware that he had twenty-four hours at best in which to get Abelsen arrested, unless he wanted to end up like Lyberth and the men from 1973.

His thoughts began to calm down. There was no one on the landing or outside his door, and it took him only seconds to let himself in and lock the door behind him. He wondered whether he should go to see Tupaarnaq in the blue building across the road rather than stay in his apartment, where anyone could find him, but he decided nothing was likely to happen in the next few hours. And if the police or his editor turned up, he could always pretend to be out.

The files inside the parcel covered most of his coffee table when he had finished spreading them out. They were not at all what he had been expecting, because they weren't related to the orphanage, the girls, the medical experiments or anything that linked Lyberth to the 1973 case.

Matthew closed his eyes and slumped back on the sofa. The files contained nothing that would either support Jakob's case from '73 or acquit Tupaarnaq today. He couldn't even be sure that it was Lyberth who had sent him the parcel, although Leiff believed it to be his handwriting on the package. Matthew took out a cigarette and lit it, and then got up from the sofa and walked across to the balcony door.

Then again, he mused, the films might prove damning for Abelsen, if they could show conclusively that he was the man in front of the camera. Abelsen's habit of keeping trophies might very well have made him keep the container.

Matthew couldn't see if Tupaarnaq was inside the blue apartment, but she probably was. It was even riskier for her to venture around Nuuk than it was for him.

There were several different types of documents in the parcel. Notes, printed spreadsheets, accounts, photocopies of receipts and expense claims. It looked like something prepared by an accountant. They had been organised into twenty-three different bundles, with a strong clip on each. Matthew looked around, then stubbed out his cigarette on the buff envelope. There was a yellow Post-it note stuck on each file with a name on it. Lyberth's name was on one of them. On another was the name of the current Greenlandic prime minister, Aleqa Hammond, the country's first female leader. Abelsen's name featured too, as did several others whom Matthew recognised as senior government politicians.

Matthew fetched himself a beer from the fridge and sat down on the sofa with the files. He intended to review them one after the other, but was on only the second file when he twigged to what he had been sent. This wasn't a simple record of expenses, but a list of government expenditure for which there was either no receipt or a receipt that had been faked in order to disguise private expenditure as public. It was money spent on travel, artwork, expensive flat-screens and designer furniture. It was an economic and political scandal at a time when the Greenlandic economy was on its knees. Misuse of public funds. If this information was ever made public, it would destroy not only Lyberth but also many other politicians and civil servants, depending on how extensive the subsequent investigation turned out to be.

Matthew shook his head. It might even bring down Abelsen, but he wouldn't bet on it. Nothing beat a corpse, but this information was a start. It would undoubtedly have ended Lyberth's career; now it would merely be just another nail in his coffin. However, it would most definitely cost Lyberth's fellow party member Prime Minister Aleqa Hammond her job. Probably her entire government would fall. There was irrefutable evidence in the documentation of her personal use of public funds. She appeared to have spent public money on private plane tickets and hotel rooms for her family.

He smoothed his hair and stroked his stubble, then lit another cigarette and opened his laptop. There was more to this than he had first thought. It was a political scandal that would rock the whole of this small nation, which, with its first female leader, had otherwise been heading for unity and reconciliation. The outrage following in its wake would ruin everything and create division on several levels—the exact opposite of Hammond's stated vision.

If it really was Lyberth who had sent him the parcel, then Matthew had no doubt that he had chosen to expose the financial scandal in the hope that the ensuing chaos might act as a distraction from the other scandal involving him, which was about to come to light after more than forty years in the dark. It was a smokescreen, in which Lyberth would be sacrificing everyone else to save what he could for himself and his family. All in vain, sadly, but Lyberth probably hadn't expected to be killed soon after sending the parcel.

The smoke from Matthew's cigarette settled around the laptop when he exhaled heavily and began writing a new story. This time about the abuse of public office and of public funds.

This story would be uploaded onto the *Sermitsiaq* website, but in the official way this time, with Leiff credited as the reporter. It would undoubtedly be taken down as well in time, but someone would read it before that happened, and Leiff would hand over the contents of the parcel to the police and file a complaint based on the three most serious cases of abuse of public office and misuse of public funds.

Matthew closed the *Sermitsiaq* tab and checked his inbox one last time before going out to find Tupaarnaq. There was only one new email:

Don't forget our meeting tomorrow night, Matthew. Or the notebook. I came back early and I stopped by to see Paneeraq today. She remembered me well. She agrees that you should give me the notebook, and she's absolutely right. A middle-aged woman all alone with an old man in Block 2. Those rickety galleries are so dangerous. She could so easily have a bad fall. Ten o'clock tomorrow night. Come alone. You may have heard that I'm dead, but don't let that worry you. You just turn up. And I'll make sure that your new friend lives to see another week.

60

The aroma of freshly brewed coffee wafted soft and warm through Paneeraq's living room. The two candles had been lit again, and like the last time her grandfather was sitting in his anorak with the hood over his head. His armchair was turned so that it faced the yard between Blocks 1 and 2. It was nearly three o'clock in the afternoon, but the heavy clouds above Nuuk made it seem dark outside.

Paneeraq had let them in immediately, and Tupaarnaq had gone with Paneeraq to the kitchen to make coffee. Matthew heard them talking in Greenlandic.

'Impressive paintings,' Matthew said, trying to break the ice when the two women returned, each with a cup of steaming coffee.

'We brought them with us from Qeqertarsuatsiaat,' Paneeraq said, sitting down in an armchair. Tupaarnaq took a seat on the sofa.

Matthew frowned. 'Qeqertarsuatsiaat?'

'Yes—its Danish name is Fiskenæsset. It's a small village south of Nuuk. I've lived there ever since...well, you know.'

Matthew nodded slowly and absent-mindedly, while turning his attention to Tupaarnaq. 'Have you ever mentioned that village to me?'

'No, and I've never been there either.'

Then it dawned on Matthew where he had heard the name. Without thinking, he produced Jakob's notebook from his bag and flicked through to the days when Jakob's life imploded.

'Lisbeth—you travelled to Qeqertarsuatsiaat with Lisbeth.'

Paneeraq smiled briefly and looked down at the table, before turning her gaze to the man in the armchair.

The old man turned his upper body and pulled his hood down, so that his face and hair were exposed to the blueish light. 'You have my notebook, I see.'

Matthew nearly jumped out of his skin. He closed his eyes and clung to the notebook as if its contents were the last remains of his sanity. 'But you're—'

'Dead?'

'Yes.'

'It was a close call. Perhaps only a matter of minutes, but in such circumstances a minute is all it takes.' His fingers traced the drum skin. 'And now we find ourselves in the same boat. Forty years on.'

Matthew was silent. He looked furtively at the old man.

'Paneeraq has just had a visitor,' Jakob continued. 'Abelsen. He wanted the notebook.'

'I'm sorry,' Matthew croaked, rubbing his eyes and face with the heels of his hands. His stubble scratched his skin. 'I'm in shock.'

'There's no need.'

'But…I was so sure that you were dead.' He stared at the old man. His face was wrinkled and pale, his hair sparse and white.

'So were most people.'

'The man from the Faroe Islands,' Matthew then exclaimed. 'The one you wrote about. He's the one they found on the ice cap, isn't he?'

'I would think so,' Jakob said. 'But I haven't seen the mummy, so I can't say for sure. But it certainly scared Lyberth out of his wits—and now he's dead.'

'As are a young police officer and a fisherman,' Matthew added. 'They tried to pin the murders on Tupaarnaq because...' He came to a halt.

'I know about Tupaarnaq,' Jakob said, and he smiled at her. 'We had newspapers and the internet down in Qeqertarsuatsiaat.' He took a deep breath and looked at Tupaarnaq. 'I followed your case closely. You shouldn't have been on your own. I'm sorry.'

Tupaarnaq tilted her head a little and looked at him. 'Thank you. But I've always been alone.'

'I know. You're always welcome here, if you want to talk to someone.'

She gave a light shrug. 'I don't want to talk to anyone.'

'No, I know that too, but sometimes it can be nice just to chat about seals, the tide and the colours of the ice.' He gestured towards Paneeraq. 'Paneeraq also lived in Tasiilaq once, and her parents were killed. You can share your thoughts with her, if you need to.'

'You can,' Paneeraq joined in. 'My door is always open to you.'

'Thank you.' Tupaarnaq got up from the sofa. 'Where's the toilet, please?'

'Let me show you,' Paneeraq said.

Raindrops dotted the windows.

Matthew looked at Jakob in the armchair. 'Can I ask how you escaped alive?'

Jakob turned his face away from the window and smiled at Matthew. 'You must have been very confused after your visit here the other day. You should have said that you had read my notebook.'

'I was under the impression that it was the killer who had written the last few pages. Only I don't understand why he would do that... or her. The handwriting looks like a woman's.'

'It was actually the killer's.' Jakob turned his face back to the windows with a heavy sigh.

'But you didn't die,' Matthew said.

'That's true. I'm referring to the woman who killed the men. I was right all along: the motive for the killings was revenge.'

'But you didn't report it and clear your name so you could stay in Nuuk?'

'No, it was too late by then. And anyway, I couldn't have done that to her. She was just like Paneeraq, only she was an adult. And I had to get Paneeraq out of Nuuk.'

He hesitated, then spoke again. 'Ultimately, it was me who got the four men killed. My efforts to expose them. She heard everything. She read my files at the station without me noticing. Or maybe it never crossed my mind. All that coffee and cake. Her visit to my house.'

'Lisbeth? Lisbeth killed the four men? She flayed and gutted them? And she killed Paneeraq's mother?'

He nodded heavily. 'Indeed she did. As a result of her own childhood.' He looked up. 'Did you know that in Greenland one girl in three is raped? In some villages, it can be as many as all of them, and they have to live with the trauma for the rest of their lives.'

'Yes,' Matthew whispered hoarsely. 'I've read pretty much everything I could find of public reports and statistics.'

'How could I ever have done anything but take Lisbeth and Paneeraq with me to a place of safety? We had a good life in Qeqertarsuatsiaat. We kept mostly to ourselves. Paneeraq went to school until she was fifteen, and from then on we taught her ourselves. Lisbeth and me, I mean. There's a good library down there.'

'And no one ever worked out your true identities?'

'No, in that village the only thing people cared about was cod fishing. As far as they were concerned, I was just an eccentric Danish geologist, Lisbeth was my wife and Paneeraq our daughter.'

'It was that easy?'

'Yes, it was. I collected rocks, which was all the evidence they needed, and Lisbeth was Greenlandic.'

'But she killed four innocent men and a woman.'

'They weren't innocent—I'm even more certain of that now. Except for Paneeraq's mother. That haunts me to this day.'

Matthew shook his head and stared at the floor. 'I don't know what to say. She…she flayed those men and she gutted them. That's…' He shook his head again. 'What did she do with their skins?'

'She only did what she had been taught to do,' Jakob said through a quick sigh. 'She did exactly what her hands had done hundreds of times when she was a child. Nothing more. A dead body is a dead body.' He shrugged. 'We never spoke about it after that last night in Nuuk, so my knowledge is no greater than yours, and I've no idea what she did with their skins. Nor do I care, to be perfectly frank. My priority was the girls.'

'And what about the puzzle piece?'

'The puzzle piece?'

'From your jigsaw puzzle. The one placed on the forehead of the final victim. She was willing to sacrifice you.'

'Ah, the puzzle piece. I never asked her about it, but I don't think she was trying to frame me. No, I think she was trying to send me a message. A message meant only for me. She didn't think anyone else knew about the jigsaw.'

He glanced towards the hall. 'Paneeraq has never really opened up about what happened in the time between the orphanage and the murders. Nor have we discussed that Lisbeth was the killer.'

'So she doesn't know who killed her parents, or that you and Lisbeth killed the Faroese man and chucked him into a crevasse in the ice cap?'

'We've certainly never spoken about it. After I came round and realised what had happened, I was shocked and devastated. But what good was that? I couldn't turn back the clock—it was impossible. So I stole a boat and we sailed to the bottom of a fjord with him. I pulled him across the ice on a sleigh on my own. It was a hell of a trip.

We had to stop off at Kapisillit to refuel. I had wrapped him in some hides the Hemplers had left in the house, and I threw his intestines into the sea. We took Paneeraq with us, but she stayed in the wheelhouse and never saw what happened.'

He covered his face with his hands. They were thin and wrinkled. Shaped by a long life.

'I thought the ice would eat that stupid Faroese, given how close we were to the outskirts of the ice cap, but I must have thrown him into a crevasse in a location where the ice movement was minimal. Or perhaps it wasn't a crevasse, but just a crack in the rock with ice in it. It can be hard to tell in winter, and I didn't dare go too far in.'

'Well, whatever it was, he resurfaced,' Matthew said. 'Why did you move back to Nuuk?'

'Why? I'm over eighty now, and Lisbeth died two years ago. I thought the time had come.' He looked towards the door to the hall again. 'I think we both needed to come back and unburden ourselves, should the opportunity arise. In our different ways.'

'Are you hungry?'

Matthew looked up at Paneeraq, who was smiling at him from the doorway.

'A little, but don't you worry about that.' He took his mobile from his pocket. 'I have some pictures I'd like to show you. Perhaps you might recognise something. They may be of Najak when she was eleven years old. She's in distress. Do you mind?'

'Let me have a look.'

Matthew passed her his mobile.

Paneeraq took it and pressed her lips together. Then she nodded briefly before letting herself fall back into a chair. 'I never expected to see that again.'

'Can I get you anything?' Tupaarnaq said, putting her hand on Paneeraq's shoulder. 'Water?'

Paneeraq shook her head. Wiped her eyes with her fingers. 'No, thank you.'

'You were there?' Matthew said.

Paneeraq heaved a deep sigh. Her breathing trembled. 'Yes.'

Matthew looked from Paneeraq to Jakob.

The old man shook his head. 'I know nothing about that.'

'I've never told anyone,' Paneeraq said. 'But I've been there. Just like Najak. All four of us were kept there for a couple of weeks after we came back to Nuuk. They called it quarantine—they said they were afraid that we might still be infected, but it was all a lie.' She wrung her hands. 'I've repressed it as much as my nightmares will allow me.'

'So you too were imprisoned in the shipping container?'

'Yes—I'll never forget it, though I wish I could.'

'Was the light flashing inside?'

She nodded. 'There was a bright light bulb in the ceiling. It kept coming on and going off. All the time, although I soon lost any sense of day or night. There was only light or darkness. I was so scared of what they were going to do to me. Everything broke down inside me. And outside. In the end I wasn't even sure whether I was alive or dead because everything was a blur. I think I wanted to be dead.'

Matthew stared at the floor.

Tupaarnaq had sat down next to Paneeraq. 'Can you remember where it was?' she asked gently.

Paneeraq nodded. 'Yes.' Her voice was hoarse. Almost gone. 'I think so. I think maybe it was in Færingehavn. I'm not sure.'

'You should have told someone,' Jakob muttered from his chair.

'I know,' Paneeraq said. Now tears were streaming down her cheeks.

'Rubbish,' Tupaarnaq protested. 'She was eleven years old and trying to escape her monsters.'

Matthew looked at Jakob. 'Might it have been Færingehavn?'

'Yes, it sounds about right. Both in terms of the distance from Nuuk and their Faroese lackey. And no one would bother them out there.'

'We sailed for a few hours,' Paneeraq said. 'It wasn't that far away. I remember there was a whole little village of wooden houses there, and the harbour was made from the biggest timber logs I'd ever seen in my life. It went on forever.'

'That's definitely Færingehavn,' Jakob said.

'I spent some days in a big grey house.' Paneeraq stared at a distant point in space. 'I could see some huge round buildings on the far side of the fjord.'

'That will be Polaroil,' Jakob said. 'Those silos are still there... Everything is still there.'

'Including the shipping container?' Matthew said with raised eyebrows.

'I'm almost sure of it,' Jakob said. 'The town of Færingehavn wasn't abandoned until the early eighties, and since then everything has pretty much been left to rot.'

'Doesn't anyone live there?'

Jakob shook his head. 'Færingehavn was a fishing station that the Faroese were allowed to build in 1927. I don't know how many people lived there in its heyday, but it was quite lively the few times I visited it in '71 and '72. Today the place is deserted and the buildings are derelict.'

'So why do you think the shipping container would still be there?'

'Because everything was left behind. The inhabitants moved away over the course of a decade, and the last person to leave just turned the key and sailed off. It was too expensive to bring anything other than a suitcase. It's like that up here. When people move away, most of their stuff is left behind. It costs a fortune to clear a village or a town, and Greenland is so big that no one sees the rot.'

Matthew looked at Tupaarnaq. 'Can we go there? To Færingehavn?'

Tupaarnaq nodded. 'I don't know where it is, but yes, I guess we can.'

'Are you going to look for the shipping container?' Jakob asked.

'Yes,' Matthew said, turning his attention back to the older man. 'It's probably a long shot, but if everything really was left behind, it might still be there. And if we can identify it, we might find traces of the girls and connect them to Abelsen.'

Jakob straightened up. 'It's worth a try. And there's no statute of limitations for murder. You have a boat?'

Matthew shook his head.

'We'll get one,' Tupaarnaq said. 'It's not a problem. I just need the coordinates so I can find the location.'

'Shouldn't we contact the police?' Paneeraq said. 'So you don't go out there alone?'

'We can't.' Tupaarnaq looked at Matthew. 'No police—they... that'll have to wait.'

'That will have to wait,' Jakob echoed. 'But you should leave now if you want to get there before dark.' He turned to Tupaarnaq. 'Take a rifle. Just to be on the safe side.'

She smiled briefly. 'I never go anywhere without one.'

61

The bottom of the boat hit the waves hard as it ploughed its way across the water, bump by bump. Tupaarnaq was pushing hard—their speed had been around thirty-five knots most of the way.

The sun had broken through the clouds, but had also crawled closer to the horizon during the final stretch of their voyage, and when they turned into Buksefjorden, they only had a few hours of proper daylight left. The mountains soon enclosed the sea, and less than fifteen minutes into the fjord, the first big Polaroil silos came into view. Shortly after that, on the opposite shore, they saw Færingehavn's long timber quay.

'It really does look trashed,' Matthew said as his eyes scanned the quay and the warehouses. 'It's amazing that such places exist.'

The boat keeled slightly as it turned. Tupaarnaq peered at the shore. 'I don't think we can dock here. The quay is too high, and I can't risk ripping a hole in the boat by sailing too close to the rocks.' She looked over her shoulder. 'You drop the anchor, and I'll release the rubber dinghy.'

The anchor sank into the sea with a hollow plop and quickly hit the bottom. Matthew looked at the shore again. Most of the houses were medium-sized, made from wood and one or two storeys high, painted grey, red or green. They looked like old Swedish farmhouses. At first glance they seemed in good shape, but all the windows were smashed, the glass having been broken by bad weather or vandals. The wooden walls were peeling and dry. The metal roofing sheets were rusty and cracked in several places. Some sheets were missing altogether; Matthew could see the naked, pale wooden skeleton of one house whose rafters were exposed like a rib cage.

'Grab this!'

Matthew took the rope Tupaarnaq was holding out to him. She freed the dinghy and turned it over in the air so that it hit the sea the right way up. 'After you?'

He looked down at the water and nodded, then climbed into the small, grey rubber dinghy. It gave under his weight, and he could sense the sea through its soft bottom. He shifted to make way for Tupaarnaq.

'I'll row,' she said, placing her rifle on the floor of the dinghy. 'I want to get to that rusty ramp at the end of the quay.'

Matthew looked in the same direction as her. The end of the quay was thirty metres wide. Above it was a large, pale-grey building, partly constructed on huge iron posts immersed in the sea close to the shore. The metal roofing sheets were reddish-brown from rust. Several rusting oil barrels were stacked against the end of the building, and down by the rocks in the corner of the quay lay a torn green trawler net.

The iron ramp Tupaarnaq was aiming for wasn't far away, and the moment the rubber dinghy touched it Matthew jumped up on the ramp. Tupaarnaq followed him and pulled up the dinghy high enough to stop it being taken by the tide, which could come in swiftly.

'Do you think she's here?' she asked, as she pushed the boat under a rusty iron girder.

Matthew rubbed his chin, where his stubble felt increasingly dense, simultaneously soft and coarse. 'I don't know—it seems unlikely…Wow, this place really is a dump.' He shrugged. 'My friend Leiff told me it's not unusual to turn a shipping container into a house, or build one around the container.'

She nodded and slipped the strap of the rifle over one shoulder. 'I know about that from Tasiilaq. So are we checking every single house—is that your plan?'

'Yes, I think it's the only way.' Matthew looked around. They could see about thirty big buildings, quite a few of them several storeys high. Most were residential houses of one sort or another, while those along the harbour were mainly warehouses. He pointed to a grey house right in front of them. 'Let's start here.'

The house was as damaged on the inside as it was on the outside, possibly more. The ceilings were discoloured and bulging ominously in places. Most of the doors had come off their hinges. Toilet basins and sinks had cracked from frost. Cupboards and furniture were wrecked, as the broken windows had given storms, rain and snow free rein for decades. Old bits of paper were scattered about everywhere. Matthew picked up a 1962 Yellow Pages.

Behind him something heavy was pushed across the floor. 'This pile of crap is close to collapsing,' Tupaarnaq panted. 'Besides, these rooms are too small. I think they must have been offices.'

Matthew nodded. 'It looks like it.'

'Let's try the red house further up,' she said, and left through the front door.

Matthew followed her down the steps and across the tall, half-withered grass.

The next building was low, but fairly wide, and had an extension in the centre that looked like the main entrance. Every window had been smashed, and the only pieces of glass left in the frame were small, sharp teeth in a black mouth. The roofing felt was sun-bleached and weatherworn. The paint was peeling badly, but still identifiably red. The front door had been kicked in, and it had been a long time since it could shut properly.

'God almighty,' Matthew exclaimed. 'Any idea what this place used to be?'

'Maybe a club or something?' Tupaarnaq said, bending over a green velvet sofa whose cushions and upholstery had been ripped up. She nudged a pile of what looked like trash on the floor. 'Take a look. Someone's been knitting.' She looked up at Matthew.

'This is so weird.' He saw an old record-player on the floor, along with other broken things. 'They really did just walk out one day without taking anything.'

Tupaarnaq continued across the room and pressed a few keys on a collapsed piano. 'This place looks like it could have been a community hall. There's a stage and everything.' She turned to Matthew. 'I don't think we'll find your shipping container here.'

He shook his head.

Outside, the sun was approaching the mountains behind the furthest house. They could see approximately two hundred metres across the flat plain.

'I can see tracks,' Matthew exclaimed, looking down along a set of rusty metal rail tracks running inland. The tracks ended near some low, rusty wagons that stood close to a long concrete wall, similar to the kind of dam that generates electricity in Norwegian rivers. 'They have to be the only railway tracks in Greenland, surely?'

'I wouldn't know,' Tupaarnaq said. 'There are definitely no tracks on the east coast.' She looked towards the most built-up area. 'I don't think we're going to get back to Nuuk today.'

Matthew followed her gaze.

She looked back at him. 'It'll be dark before we're done searching, and sailing along a coast we don't know in the dark would be madness.'

'So what do we do?'

'Sleep here or on the boat, I guess.'

'Are there any sleeping bags on the boat, do you think?'

'No, but we can improvise.'

'Okay.' He looked around the abandoned town. Then he took a deep breath and shrugged. 'Let's walk down to the harbour and check out the big warehouses before it gets completely dark.'

They zigzagged through the scattered houses across the town on their way back to the harbour. A dozen buildings, all different, lay along the wooden quay, which stretched for over a hundred metres. Some were several storeys high and had windows, while others were entirely enclosed except for large gates at the ends.

While they searched the warehouses one after the other, Matthew's mind was working overtime. The hours had rushed by so fast that he hadn't had time to think about consequences or repercussions. He looked at the back of Tupaarnaq's neck. At the top of her rollneck jumper he could just make out the edge of the dark wilderness underneath her clothes. She had pushed down her hood and her head was exposed. 'If we find her,' he said hesitantly. 'Najak, I mean…Is that when we call the police?'

She turned around and glared so harshly at him that he could practically feel her fingers digging into the sinews along his collarbone.

'You're not going to be an idiot again, are you?'

'No, but I—'

'What? No matter what we find, you and I are both going straight to jail…Or at least I am.' She looked down. 'Join the dots, for fuck's sake.'

Matthew followed her gaze. In the dirt between them lay a faded green magazine. *Indre Missions Tidende*, Sunday, 25 September 1983. Issue 130: 'God is the Power and the Glory'.

'Besides, there's no mobile coverage here.' She kicked the magazine with her boot. 'Let's move on.'

Matthew bent down and picked up a sturdy copper hammer from the floor. It was heavy, probably weighing several kilos. He tried to imagine how strong the arms of the man who once wielded it must have been.

The next building they reached was windowless. It was a rectangular warehouse with an arched metal roof. The building was secured with a thick steel chain and a strong, rusty padlock, and they had to smash the door in order to get in. Each blow sounded like an explosion in the deserted town as the iron and corrugated metal slowly gave way and a gap opened up big enough for them to wriggle through.

Once inside, they could smell old oil and salt water. The floor was concrete to begin with, but about two-thirds of the way in it became worn wooden planks.

Matthew looked across the floor. 'I'm not sure that section is safe to walk on.'

Tupaarnaq switched on the torch on her mobile and pointed it across the floor. 'Look,' she whispered.

Matthew had spotted it at the same time, and quickly took out his own mobile and found the torch. At the far end of the room, up against the end wall, was an old, rusty freight container. 'That could be it.'

She nodded.

Matthew felt a chill go down his spine as he carefully stepped out onto the wooden floor.

When they reached the container, Tupaarnaq put her hand on one of the sturdy handles. She pulled it so hard that her entire body shook. 'It's completely rusted in place.'

Matthew put his mobile and the hammer on the floor and tried with both hands, but still the handle didn't budge. 'Could you light up the handle for me?'

Tupaarnaq nodded, and Matthew picked up the hammer. He

took a step forwards and gave the handle a good whack. 'My God, it's heavy,' he groaned. He swung the hammer again, this time holding it with both hands. The sound hurt their ears, and the echo bounced off the curved steel roof.

'Do it again,' Tupaarnaq said, kicking the cross member of the big metal gate. 'It'll shift in the end with a bit of luck.'

Matthew swung the hammer with all his strength a third time. When it collided with the handle, it felt like electric shocks were darting through his forearms. The handle of the hammer was two solid iron rods that were bent by the force with which it had been used back in the 1980s. The handle had been welded together with a bracket that ran around the copperhead itself. He struck the lock again. The recoil up through his arms was so severe that he dropped the hammer. He narrowed his eyes and rubbed his neck.

Tupaarnaq put her mobile on the floor and pushed the hammer away with her boot. Then she placed both hands on the handle and pushed it a couple of times. 'Help me, will you? On three, okay?'

She counted and they both pulled outwards as hard as they could, and finally they felt the lock give and the handle follow suit. The door behind the lock and the iron handle surrendered in squealing complaint.

Tupaarnaq grabbed the door, which was several metres high, and pulled it. She had to press all of her weight against the iron to create a gap wide enough for her to slip through.

Matthew heard her sigh.

'This is it,' she whispered.

He held up his mobile, letting the light sweep the floor and the shiny walls. There was a dry, metallic smell inside. He closed his eyes and his heart skipped a beat. Up against the wall, in the far corner of the container, was a green blanket. He heard Tupaarnaq's footsteps across the floor.

'There can't possibly be anything under that blanket,' she said.

Her voice was trembling. It felt heavy in the empty metal box.

'She was only eleven years old,' Matthew whispered and opened his eyes again. 'A little girl.'

Tupaarnaq bent over the blanket. Took hold of one of its folds.

Matthew heard her sigh again. He could see the white knuckles on her clenched hand on the fabric. She lifted it gently. It seemed dry. Stiff. Something crumbled. Scattered over the stiff folds. She stopped and let the blanket fall back. She turned around and walked towards Matthew, her eyes fixed on the narrow container exit. 'Time to go.' Her words were gusts of air.

'Najak?' He could barely hear his own voice.

'Just come with me. We need to find somewhere to spend the night.'

62

Matthew was woken by someone tugging his arm. The room was in total darkness, which meant it must be between midnight and three o'clock in the morning. He could feel the old, battered mattress through his clothing, the springs digging into his back.

Someone pulled his arm again, and he turned over. The jacket under his head hadn't been a good pillow and the stiff muscles in his neck complained.

'There's someone in the house,' Tupaarnaq whispered.

They had found a couple of rusty beds with mattresses in one of the houses. It lay away from the rest of the ghost town; it appeared to have had a canteen on the ground floor, while the first floor consisted of a long corridor with small rooms leading off it.

The night air blew in through the broken windows. The floor was covered by detritus. Plaster. Wallpaper. Fraying fabric. Shards of glass. Most doors were damaged, either by age, weather or vandals. He heard a crunching sound coming from the corridor.

'Did you hear that?' Tupaarnaq tugged at his arm again.

He nodded. His eyes adjusted to the darkness, and he could see her sitting upright with the rifle in front of her.

'There shouldn't be anyone here,' she said in a hushed voice, while she slowly loaded the weapon, letting something fall into place with a quiet click.

Matthew rose to his knees on the mattress. There was more than one pair of boots out in the corridor. Two, at least. He stood up and moved next to Tupaarnaq. 'Could it be people who got stranded, like we did?'

She shook her head. 'I think that's highly unlikely.'

'Maybe we can get out through the window?' Matthew continued, and took a step backwards so he could look out the window and down at the ground. There were shards of glass all around the window frame.

The crunching of the boots grew louder. Matthew looked at the rocky ground five to six metres below them and shook his head. 'We'll have to leave through the door.'

Tupaarnaq nodded. Matthew turned around. As he did, he could sense the sound through his boots before he heard it—a glass fragment breaking under his boot.

The corridor fell quiet.

'Why have you stopped?'

The voice was Danish. Adult. Sharp.

'I heard something.'

The other voice was deep and heavy.

Tupaarnaq looked towards Matthew's boot. 'Idiot.'

Matthew shrugged. 'They would have found us sooner or later.'

'Speak up,' the sharp voice said out loud. 'There's no point whispering anymore.'

'That sounds like Abelsen,' Matthew whispered.

Tupaarnaq raised the rifle to her shoulder. The muzzle was pointed at the open door.

'I bet you never thought you would run into me here, eh, Matthew? Did you really think this place was completely deserted? You're so naive. My friend Bárdur here lives just across the road. At the bunker fuel point.'

Matthew looked at Tupaarnaq's rifle. It was wedged in the hollow between her chin and neck. Her shoulders were calm. Her muscles tense.

'He doesn't care about the notebook, but I still want it. Did you bring it? You probably did—you're such a fool.'

Matthew shook his head. Tupaarnaq nodded grimly.

'Are you in there?' Abelsen went on. 'I'm getting bored out here.'

There was silence for a moment. Then the crunching resumed and grew closer. A few seconds later, a dark silhouette loomed at the doorway. He was enormous. He almost filled out the space completely.

The first shot sent a shock through the room, paralysing Matthew's thoughts. The silhouette disappeared with a short, deep roar.

'Run,' Tupaarnaq hissed.

Matthew leapt towards the door. 'Left?' The giant had come from the right.

'Yes—there are stairs going down at both ends.'

Matthew took a deep breath and ran out through the door. The corridor was dark. At one end, moonlight poured in through a broken door. Matthew didn't have time to see whether there were two or three silhouettes outside before Tupaarnaq fired another shot, this time into the darkness of the corridor. He completed the short distance to the corner by the stairs in a couple of long strides, then felt himself slip on the steps, the wood bashing against his back. He grabbed hold of the banister and scrambled to his feet. He continued stumbling down the stairs. Behind him he could hear running footsteps everywhere.

'It's only me,' Tupaarnaq shouted. 'Run, goddammit…Run towards the water!'

He took a sharp right at the bottom of the stairs and headed for the front door. Another rifle shot cut through the night. Her third.

Outside, the darkness seemed less solid. The sky was pink behind the mountains on the far side of the fjord.

'Run, damn you,' Tupaarnaq shouted behind him.

He sprinted down the short wooden footpath that connected the house to the rest of the town. His legs were going at full speed, and he knew they would soon be crippled by lactic acid. Everything began to cramp. His lungs were hurting. His blood boiling.

The buildings along the quay grew bigger with every step he took in the pink dawn. The damaged wooden walls and the black broken windows.

'We need to get to the boat now,' Tupaarnaq wheezed behind him. She was panting too.

He lunged forwards when they reached the iron posts and grabbed the dinghy, which fell limply into his hands.

Tupaarnaq crashed into him as she, too, reached for the dinghy. 'Shit.' She looked across the water. 'We'll have to swim.'

A shot was fired across the sea and they heard a hissing sound in the air close to them. They both threw themselves onto the ground.

'They must have someone on their boat,' Matthew gasped. His voice was trembling and black spots were dancing in front of his eyes. 'We need to get out of here.'

Tupaarnaq glanced over her shoulder. Not far behind them, Abelsen and Bárdur had emerged. Out on their boat was a man with a rifle.

'You missed him,' Matthew whispered.

'I fired at the ceiling.'

Another shot tore holes in the air above them.

'Stop shooting, for fuck's sake!' Abelsen shouted somewhere in the darkness.

'Come with me,' Tupaarnaq whispered.

Matthew followed her round the back of the warehouse at the end of the quay. They sought refuge behind the iron posts under the building. The darkness was dense down here. He could hear Tupaarnaq breathing in short, shallow gasps. Water sloshed around the posts.

She looked at him. 'We need to get to the boat...it's only thirty metres.'

'But the water can't be more than two degrees—what if we get cramps?'

'Then we drown. It'll be quick when the body is that cold. Now shut up.'

'Hello?' Abelsen's voice interrupted them. 'Bárdur kindly let the air out of that little rubber dinghy you used to get ashore.'

Matthew watched as Tupaarnaq sized up the sea. The water was black, so it was impossible to spot any rocks under the surface.

'You see, Matthew,' Abelsen went on, 'Bárdur is a very helpful man these days. He grew up here when this was a busy town, and he's the last one still hanging around. He has always believed that one day he would get the opportunity to avenge the death of his father. That's all that matters to me. He doesn't give a toss about the note-book...or your lives. He just wants Jakob, and I can help him with that, now that you have been kind enough to track him down for me.'

'Ignore him,' Tupaarnaq whispered. Her dark eyes gleamed like the sea below them.

Matthew shook his head.

'Matthew, are you there?' Abelsen called out. 'Bárdur has no use for you. He just wants Jakob. So if you give me the notebook and the film reels, I'll let you go.'

The water broke in silent ripples as Tupaarnaq let herself slip through the surface. She looked up. 'If they hear us, it's over,' she whispered.

Matthew nodded and lowered his feet and legs into the sea. The cold bit into his skin immediately, and he had to fight every instinct not to jump straight back out. Instead he submerged his whole body in the sea, leaving only his head free. Every part of him screamed in pain. His skin contracted. He gasped for air. Briefly. Silently.

'Think happy thoughts,' Tupaarnaq whispered. 'Distract your mind and relax, then your brain will leave your muscles alone.'

He nodded. 'Okay…Fuck…Okay.'

Her head started to glide slowly along the surface. She made no sound at all. Every movement happened underwater.

The rocks disappeared from under Matthew's boots and he began to tread water. He followed her slowly. The skin under his clothes burned from the cold.

'No sudden movements,' she warned him.

Matthew's throat was cramping too much to speak. He just carried on swimming. Carefully. As if drugged. Right under the surface. The salt water flowed around his face. It cut into his cheeks and lips. His thoughts were jumbling with thousands of images. Tine. Her belly. The red Mercedes. *I'm going to die out here*, he thought. *This is it.*

The cold ate him up. It tore chunks off his flesh. He closed his eyes. They were halfway at best. His legs stopped kicking. *I'm coming*, he thought. The blue Golf rolled over. His body surrendered. One ear hurt. Insanely. As if someone was trying to pull it off. His eyes opened. Tupaarnaq's hand.

'Get your shit together,' she whispered. 'We're nearly there. Come on, you wimp.'

He nodded. He shook his head to clear his mind.

Somewhere behind them Abelsen was calling out into the early summer dawn. Matthew heard the words 'bring in the boat'.

Seconds later, Abelsen's boat, which was anchored not far from them, started with a roar. Tupaarnaq pushed Matthew's head under the surface, and at the same time grabbed his jacket. They resurfaced soon afterwards. Matthew's face felt as if someone was stabbing it with icepicks.

'Come on,' she ordered him.

Abelsen's boat motored towards the shore. Matthew couldn't hear what the three men were saying to one another over the engine noise.

He grabbed the stern of their boat and slowly pulled himself up. His body was shaking so badly that he could barely support his own weight.

Tupaarnaq came out of the water right after him and collapsed on the deck close to him, near the wheelhouse.

'Do you know how to use a rifle?' she stuttered.

He shook his head.

'Well, now's your chance to learn,' she said, sitting up and taking the rifle from her shoulder. She pulled out the magazine and drained the water from it. Then she pulled the bolt back and checked the chamber, before she let the bolt slot into place again. She cocked the rifle and loaded it. 'Here.'

Matthew took it and struggled to his knees, while Tupaarnaq raised the anchor.

'I've just checked the battery,' she said. 'As soon as you hear me turn on the ignition, you fire at Abelsen's boat. The distance is very short—you can't miss.'

Matthew nodded. 'I understand.'

'Don't forget to press the butt hard against your shoulder before you pull the trigger. And don't drop it—all right?'

He nodded again.

A few minutes later their engine made a noise. And then another one. Deeper. The propeller started whipping up the black water. Matthew raised the rifle to his shoulder. The icy steel bit into his fingers as he aimed the rifle at the silhouette on the other boat. Then he fired. One shot. Two.

The boat beneath him roused itself from the water so forcefully that he nearly toppled over the stern, and he grabbed onto the frame that had held the rubber dinghy. He brought the rifle back up to his cheek, but they were already so far away that shooting again was pointless.

326

63

It was just past eight in the morning when Matthew and Tupaarnaq knocked on Paneeraq's door and hurried into the living room, where Jakob was waiting.

The first thing they had done on their return to Nuuk was to put on some dry clothes at Matthew's place. The heater had been on full blast in the boat, but it hadn't been enough to dry their clothing.

Tupaarnaq had pressed the boat harder than she'd wanted to, but the dawn light crawling lazily over the eastern mountains had helped her navigate the sea and the rocks.

As soon as they were close enough to Nuuk to have mobile coverage, Matthew had texted a summary of events to Malik, who had promised to forward it to Ottesen so that the police could despatch a helicopter to Færingehavn as quickly as possible. Matthew had then sent an email to jelly@hotmail.com:

You know that we saw Najak in the shipping container in Færingehavn—and we have the eight-millimetre films, one with you on it, from when she was alive. You're finished. The notebook is nothing compared to that.

Tupaarnaq hugged Paneeraq, while Matthew told them about Færingehavn, Bárdur, Abelsen and the shipping container.

'Did you see her?' Paneeraq wanted to know, looking from Matthew to Tupaarnaq. The tears that had welled up in her eyes began rolling down her cheeks. 'Did you see her. Properly?' Her voice cracked.

'It was her,' Tupaarnaq whispered. 'She was in the shipping container.'

Paneeraq dissolved in Tupaarnaq's arms and slipped down on the sofa. 'So she…she died…inside that thing…in that place.' She looked up with a jolt. 'How did she look?'

'Yes, she died,' Matthew said hoarsely. 'She died soon after the film was recorded.'

'But what did she die from?' Paneeraq wanted to know. 'How did she die?'

'I don't know,' Tupaarnaq said. 'But she was dressed, and I don't think that she had been beaten.'

Matthew glanced at Tupaarnaq.

Paneeraq slumped again. Her shoulders trembled. Tupaarnaq sat down next to her and pushed up her sleeves before putting her arms around Paneeraq.

Paneeraq looked up. 'That jumper is far too big for you, child.'

Tupaarnaq smiled wistfully. 'It's Matthew's—I borrowed it from him. My own clothes got wet.'

'Oh, dear.' Paneeraq straightened up and dried her eyes with her fingers. 'Why don't we go to my bedroom—I think I might have a jumper that would fit you.'

'All right, let's do that,' Tupaarnaq said.

Matthew turned to Jakob. 'Abelsen is finished. I have the note-book, the film reels and the fake expenses receipts, and then there's Najak's body.'

'Did she really look the way you told Paneeraq?'

Matthew stared at the floor. 'No.'

'I didn't think so.'

'I hope they catch Abelsen and the Faroese who wants to kill you.'

'All I ever did was hide the body, but he probably doesn't care about that.'

'It was Abelsen who said it. That he wanted to kill you.'

Jakob nodded and heaved a deep sigh. 'We'll have to wait and see.' He looked up. 'It wouldn't be the first time I've sat waiting for an angry Faroese who wants me dead.'

'No, but this time your odds are pretty poor.' Matthew hesitated briefly. 'Did you know that Karlo's son lives here in Nuuk?'

Jakob looked at him in surprise. 'No, I didn't know that. I'm afraid Karlo himself is dead.'

'Yes, but his son is a police officer. He's the one who gave me your notebook.'

'Aha—now I understand.'

'I've been thinking that we should contact him and ask him to come over so he can hear everything firsthand.'

Jakob tapped the drum by the side of his armchair. 'Karlo's son. Yes…yes. Do it. Let's do that.'

Matthew took out his mobile and texted Malik. He didn't have Ottesen's number, but asked Malik to contact Ottesen—and only him—and tell him that Matthew, Tupaarnaq and Jakob Pedersen were in Block 2 with Paneeraq and the notebook.

Malik replied immediately that he would get hold of Ottesen and tell him to come over.

'There, that's done,' Matthew sighed. He slumped back on the sofa.

Tupaarnaq and Paneeraq returned to the living room. Tupaarnaq was now wearing full Greenlandic national costume.

'Isn't she beautiful?' Paneeraq exclaimed in a bright and happy voice.

'Oh, so that's what you were up to,' Jakob said.

'I know it's a bit too small,' Paneeraq went on, 'but when I showed Tupaarnaq my national costume, she said she'd never worn one.'

'The boots are too tight,' Tupaarnaq said shyly. 'Apart from that, it's all right, I think.'

'You look amazing,' Jakob said loudly. 'Absolutely wonderful.'

Matthew stared at the young Inuit woman in the colourful, voluminous costume. The sturdy, beige leather boots with scalloped and patterned trimmings. The black sealskin trousers. The beautiful lilac shades of the cummerbund around the waist of her scarlet jacket. The glass bead shawl reaching from her neck down to her waist, covering her chest in a carpet of tiny beads sewn into fine, bright patterns.

His thoughts moved to her skin underneath it all. Her heavily tattooed body was now hidden beneath this explosion of colour and femininity. The contrast seemed infinite. If her hair had grown out in that very same moment, she would have looked like a completely different person. The costume reached up around her neck, where it ended in several overlapping collars. White, red and black.

'I made it myself,' Paneeraq said, still smiling. 'And I've offered to make one for Tupaarnaq too, although it'll be a West Greenland national costume for a girl from the east.'

'But I can't accept that,' Tupaarnaq objected. 'I told you, I know how expensive they are. So I've said no. Nor do I deserve it.'

'Deserve it?' Jakob exclaimed. 'You deserve everything, child.' He turned his attention to Matthew and pointed to a small, green-painted wooden box on the floor. 'Please, would you take a look inside that chest?'

Matthew slid aside a small metal bolt and opened the lid. Lots of little stones, but also a few bigger ones, lay at the bottom. They looked like dusty red granite. Some were redder and shinier than others.

'You can buy a lot of national costumes with that,' Jakob said, grinning.

Matthew looked up at him. 'Greenlandic rubies?'

'Yes—I told you I collected rocks, didn't I?' He was still smiling from ear to ear. 'In that chest you'll find rubies and pink sapphires, my friend. I began collecting rocks up here long before everybody else. Mount Aappaluttoq. The name alone drew me to it—it means the red mountain.'

Matthew's mobile buzzed in his pocket, so he closed the lid of the chest and took out his phone. It was a text message from Malik: *I couldn't get hold of Ottesen, but I got them to call him on the police radio, so now he knows to drive to your address.*

Matthew shook his head, but before he could tell the others, there was a knock on the door. He jumped; he hadn't had time to warn Tupaarnaq that Ottesen was coming. Now it was too late. Paneeraq was already making her way to the door, and Tupaarnaq was standing in the middle of the room, brightening it up in her national costume.

'Tupaarnaq.' Jakob's voice cut through the chaos that was Matthew's thoughts. 'I've only ever had one friend I could trust, and today his son is a police officer here in Nuuk. I've asked him to come over because I want to tell him everything, and so that you and Matthew can be eliminated from this enquiry and left in peace. We have plenty to tell the police, and it will acquit you both of all charges. I hope you can find it in your heart to trust me today.'

She glowered at him, but then her gaze softened. 'I'm not going back to prison.'

'You won't.'

At that moment they heard a scream from the front door, and then a bang as it was slammed shut. Another scream followed, but this time it was more strangled and suppressed.

Paneeraq was shoved into the living room. A hand holding a long knife was pressed up against her neck. The blade pushed so tightly against her throat that droplets of blood were running down the skin towards her collarbone.

'Ulrik?' Matthew exclaimed, staring at the angry young Greenlander. 'What the hell are you doing here?'

'Shut up,' Ulrik hissed through white, strained lips. 'I'll cut her if you move.' His gaze bored into Tupaarnaq, and he pulled out a bag of long, black strips from his pocket and tossed them onto the floor in front of Matthew. 'Tie her hands behind her back.'

Matthew hesitated.

'Fucking do it—or this old cow here is dead. Do you understand?' He tightened his grip on the knife.

Paneeraq squirmed, but didn't dare do anything other than whimper.

'It's all right,' Tupaarnaq said. 'Tie me up.'

Matthew moved towards her, and she placed her hands behind her back.

'I want you to use three strips,' Ulrik ordered him angrily. 'Have you done it?'

Matthew tightened another two strips around Tupaarnaq's wrists, then he nodded and straightened up.

In the meantime, Ulrik had tied a couple of strips around Paneeraq's wrists. Now he pushed her towards the sofa and faced Matthew. 'Turn around!' Ulrik grabbed Matthew's hands and had soon slipped a thin plastic strip so tightly around Matthew's wrists that it cut into the skin. Then he turned his attention to Jakob. 'Who are you?'

'A former officer with Nuuk Police.'

'Yeah? Well, screw you,' Ulrik grunted angrily.

Matthew felt Ulrik's boot collide with the back of his right leg, and he buckled and crashed onto the floor on both knees.

'Hey,' Tupaarnaq shouted, taking a step towards Ulrik. 'What the hell are you doing, you psycho?'

Ulrik punched her hard in the face with his clenched fist. 'You bitch,' he screamed. 'Shut your mouth, you fucking slag!' He leaned forward and followed up the punch with a blow to her stomach. 'I'm going to rip that fucking costume off you. You're no Greenlander anymore.'

Matthew tried getting to his feet, but received a hard kick to his thigh at the same time as Ulrik grabbed his head and yanked it backwards. The blow to his face made him black out.

64

Matthew woke to a fierce pain shooting through his body from the right side of his ribs.

Ulrik was bent over him, staring into his eyes. 'I'm going to beat you to a pulp,' he snarled as he drew back his clenched fist.

'Ulrik,' a voice interrupted him. 'I know why you're here.'

'Shut up, you old fool,' Ulrik hissed.

'But you're wrong,' Jakob continued from his armchair. 'I investigated your family's murder from a distance, based on all the evidence I could find, and I'm absolutely sure that your sister didn't kill your mother or your sisters.'

'That's it—I'm going to bloody well kill you first,' Ulrik bellowed, getting up from the floor. 'Don't you dare say another word about my mother, you bastard! Do you understand?'

He reached Jakob in seconds and pulled the hood from the old man's head, revealing his white hair and pale, wrinkled face. The old man's ice-blue eyes bored into the young Inuit's boiling brown void, even as Ulrik gripped Jakob's throat.

'What the hell?' Ulrik was suddenly taken aback. 'You...You... How would you...'

'Tupaarnaq never killed your family,' Jakob continued in a

wobbly voice as Ulrik's hand was still clamped around his soft neck. 'Your father shot your mother and your two sisters. Then Tupaarnaq came home and presumed that her father had been caught raping her sisters, just like he had raped her. And perhaps that was what had happened—I don't know. So she cut open your father like he had cut her open. Do you understand what I'm saying?'

He continued to fix the horrified young man with his eyes. 'Everyone assumed that Tupaarnaq had shot her mother and her sisters first. No one ever suspected your father of having raped them, because Tupaarnaq dressed your sisters before the police arrived. She didn't want them to be found naked. That explained why their blood was on her hands and arms. She dressed them after your father had killed them. Do you follow?'

Ulrik's grip tightened around Jakob's neck so that his fingernails dug into Jakob's skin. Something inside crunched.

'The case was a no-brainer,' Ulrik sneered. His mouth distorted and his nostrils flared. 'They were dead, and that...that fucking cunt was covered in everyone's blood...She was sitting on the floor, clutching an ulo, right next to my dad, who had been gutted...Fuck. Gutted. Like a seal.'

'That killing represented years of hatred and pain,' Jakob said hoarsely, still not taking his eyes off Ulrik for a second. 'Many hours of being pressed against the bed. But the killing wasn't prompted by her own violation. It was because your father had done to your two little sisters what he had done to her, and afterwards he had killed both them and your mother.'

The hand around Jakob's neck loosened and slipped away.

'Are you so blind, Ulrik, that you can't see the truth? Even when its blood is dripping from your own hands?'

Ulrik slumped back.

'Your father killed your mother and your sisters when he discovered that he wasn't your real father. I think he went berserk and killed them in a rage when your mother revealed that his only son wasn't his.'

'Now you're just guessing, you son of a bitch,' Ulrik said, straightening up. 'This is bullshit. Are you out of your mind?' He pressed his lips into two thin lines, while he stared at his clenched fists and a growl rose from deep within his throat.

'Look in the mirror,' Jakob continued calmly. 'Neither of your parents had so narrow a face or was as tall as you.'

'Shut up!' Saliva frothed around Ulrik's mouth as he raised his arm, preparing to deliver a blow. 'Fucking shut up!'

'Do you remember,' Jakob continued, still calm, 'that they were dressed? Your sisters. When they were found. Do you remember that there were no bullet holes in the clothing, even though they had been shot with a rifle right through their chests? Why would Tupaarnaq have taken off their clothes, shot them and then dressed them again? Can you tell me that?'

Matthew's mobile rang in his trouser pocket. He turned his attention to Paneeraq on the sofa. Her expression was distant and her cheeks streaked with tears. She was rocking back and forth, and staring at the white candles with Jesus and the Virgin Mary.

His mobile rang again.

'No one ever questioned that,' Jakob's voice continued. 'But for me that has always been the key to Tupaarnaq's innocence. Your sisters were killed naked, but found dressed. That is a fact. Your father raped your sisters. Your mother found out and told him, out of rage and impotence, that he wasn't your real father. Your father lost his temper and killed them all. She took his son, he took her daughters.'

Ulrik stepped back and stared frantically out into the yard below, while he wiped his palms hard on his shirt. 'It's too late!'

Matthew watched Ulrik before turning to look at the others in the room. 'Paneeraq,' he whispered towards the sofa. 'Paneeraq?'

336

There was no reaction from the curled-up figure, who continued rocking back and forth.

'Paneeraq?' he said again. 'Where's Tupaarnaq?'

'It was you who killed Aqqalu out on the ice cap, ilaa?' Jakob went on. 'They thought I was the mummy, didn't they? Abelsen and Lyberth? You were supposed to get rid of my body, but something went wrong, ilaa?'

The mobile buzzed again in Matthew's pocket. Refusing to be ignored.

Ulrik turned and glanced at Matthew. 'Shit...Lyberth told me that the guy on the ice cap wasn't an old mummy, and that I had to make sure that the body was never sent off for any tests.' Ulrik pounded his forehead with his fists. '*It can ruin everything and cause even greater division in Greenland*, he said. *Our careers are at stake*...I was meant to get rid of it. The body and the pictures and everything.' He looked up. 'I didn't know they were covering up a murder...I didn't know.'

Jakob took a deep breath and exhaled. 'I know. What about Aqqalu?'

'Aqqalu,' Ulrik groaned. His face was smeared with snot, and he kept wiping it with his hands. 'Fuck...He...he wouldn't let me take the body, even though I explained to him that it was essential for Greenland's future. He didn't want to...Bloody idiot...He banged his head on one of those crates with an iron edge...From the university. He...'

'And then he died?'

Ulrik nodded again and wiped more snot from his face, while he sniffled loudly and small sobs erupted from his throat. 'Abelsen...' He gasped for air. 'Abelsen promised to fix it. All I had to do was get out of there.'

'And so Aqqalu was gutted to make it look like your father's murder.'

Ulrik howled and rubbed his fists against his face. 'I didn't know…I didn't know…that…he was going to do that…I…*It's so we can pin the blame on your sister*, he said…My fucking sister. I didn't even know that she had been let out.'

'Did Abelsen do it?' Jakob looked towards the window and craned his neck.

Ulrik nodded. 'And the fisherman.'

Matthew had rolled onto his back and could feel his mobile buzz again.

'A police car with some of your colleagues has just pulled up,' Jakob announced in a voice louder than anything else he had said so far. He nodded in the direction of the window. 'They're here to interview Matthew and Tupaarnaq.'

'Shit,' Ulrik said. He pushed the curtain aside so that he could look down into the yard. 'I…I…' He quickly scanned the room, and then disappeared through the door.

Jakob got up from the armchair and made his way to Matthew. He bent down and cut the strips with a knife that had been lying in a fruit bowl on the coffee table.

'Where's Tupaarnaq?' Matthew said quietly as he felt the tight plastic strips come away. At last his arms were free to move again.

'Ulrik took her away while you were unconscious. I don't know where she is, or why he came back without her.'

'I think I know where she might be.' Matthew stood up, rubbing his wrists. 'They're in your old house.' He glanced towards the door. 'We haven't got time to explain all that to Ottesen now. Ulrik is in meltdown…He might very well kill her immediately.'

'If you go back to the stairs you came up, you can continue up another floor, then run to the end of the gallery and take another staircase down to the yard.'

As Matthew raced down the stairs at the far end of the apartment block, his mobile rang again. This time he managed to answer it.

'Hi, Matthew. What's happening?'

'I can't explain it now, Leiff. I'm on my way to Abelsen's house. Ulrik has gone mental, and I think he's going to kill his sister and Abelsen.' Matthew gasped for air as he sprinted down HJ Rinkip Aqqutaa. 'Jakob…the police officer from '73…he's alive…and he claims that Ulrik's father isn't his real father, and that it was Tupaarnaq's own father who killed the family back in Tasiilaq… And now…Ulrik has lost his mind.'

'Where are you?'

'I'm approaching Gertrud Rasks Vej…I'm heading for Abelsen's house.'

'Okay—are you able to listen while you run?'

'Yes…'

'The police went to Lyberth's home to go through his things in connection with his murder.' Leiff paused. 'By the way, I believe that Ulrik is currently suspended. He has been under a lot of stress. Anyway, that wasn't what I wanted to tell you. No, they found some old papers at Lyberth's place. Nothing relating to your case, but still relevant. Abelsen didn't move to Greenland from Denmark, as everyone thought. His father was a Danish doctor who worked here in the 1950s, but his mother was an underage Inuit girl from Tasiilaq, whom the doctor raped. Well, that particular fact wasn't mentioned in the papers at Lyberth's, but I took the liberty of ringing the world and his wife until I hit the jackpot. I managed to get a couple of names to follow up, you see. The girl died a long time ago, but she still has family in Tasiilaq who can remember that far back. Are you still there?'

'Yes,' Matthew wheezed. 'I'm just passing the lake.'

'Good. Abelsen lived with his young mother until he was ten years old, when he was sent to boarding school in Denmark— Daddy paid for it. As far as I could work out, that was the price for Abelsen Jr remaining a secret. You see, Daddy already had a wife and family in Denmark. At the age of twenty-four, Abelsen returned to Greenland, but this time to Nuuk, where he soon befriended another blatantly ambitious young man, Lyberth. Abelsen was a cold and calculating lawyer, Lyberth a politically active vicar who would sell his own mother to get to the top. The rest is history, as far as their partnership is concerned. But listen to this. Ulrik. You won't believe this, but it adds up with what you've just told me. Abelsen pulled the same stunt as his father and got a woman pregnant in Tasiilaq. Only this time it was a woman who already had a daughter.'

'And that daughter...was Tupaarnaq?' Matthew panted.

'Precisely, and the child that Abelsen had with Tupaarnaq's mother is Ulrik. That's why Lyberth took the boy in. One favour deserves another, as they say. Abelsen had no hint of family loyalty, but he cared enough to get Lyberth to take Ulrik in when his family was wiped out by Tupaarnaq's father, and Tupaarnaq was jailed for the murders.'

'Christ almighty...' Matthew wheezed. 'He's going to kill them... both of them.'

65

The windows in Jakob's old home were dark, but the house itself stood out more clearly now than in the dense, moist fog that had surrounded it the last time Matthew was there. There was only one row of houses further along, and then the rocks sloped steeply down to the North Atlantic, which lay calmer than it had done for several days.

The rough planks met Matthew's hand as he reached the end of the path between the rocks. He wiped his face on his sleeve and stepped sideways to look through the living room window. Abelsen was slumped in an old armchair in the middle of the room. His body was limp, but his eyes were open.

Matthew ducked immediately and pressed his back against the wall. With his eyes closed, he bumped the back of his head soundlessly against the wood. He turned around and pushed himself slowly up, in order to peer over the window ledge. He scanned the living room, but the only person he could see was Abelsen. The man's thin forearms were tied to the broad armrests with black strips.

Matthew heard a crash behind him. He spun around and looked across at the nearest houses, but there was nothing to see. Maybe a boat or a trailer had been knocked over. He turned his attention back to the window. An icy shiver crawled down his spine immediately.

Abelsen was staring right at him.

Matthew looked away, then took three steps to the front door, which he pushed open in a slow, gliding movement. The hall was small, and he quickly reached the living room, where the pale old man in the chair nodded for him to come over.

'Get a knife from the kitchen and free me,' he whispered between thin lips.

Matthew looked around the room. 'Where is your Faroese?'

'Forget about him,' Abelsen mumbled.

'Is Ulrik here?'

'I don't know,' Abelsen snarled irritably and grimaced. 'Why is that any of your business?'

'I think he's going to kill his sister, and that is my business.'

'Cut me free, then we can talk about it...Not a second before.' Abelsen moved his back from side to side and flexed his neck in a series of small cracks. 'Did you bring the notebook?'

'The notebook?' Matthew shook his head. 'No, I didn't bring the bloody notebook, but if you call off your Faroese and Ulrik, maybe we can talk about it.'

'Idiot,' Abelsen said, and wrinkled his nose. 'Reporters—you're vermin, the lot of you.' He heaved a deep sigh. 'I want that notebook...and that's final.'

'And I want Tupaarnaq.'

'Christ, don't tell me you've fallen for some Greenlandic slag? That bitch will bite off your dick, given half a chance.'

'Yes, you'd know all about Greenlanders, wouldn't you? With a mother and a son from Tasiilaq...The one you shagged wasn't Danish either, and she ended up getting killed because you couldn't keep your dick in your pants.'

'You think you're so clever, boy.' Abelsen jerked both arms, leaving red welts in the skin from the sharp strips. 'Now free me, goddammit.'

'Not without Tupaarnaq.'

'It's a pack of lies, all of it. I never lived in Tasiilaq, and as far as Ulrik is concerned, he's not my son. I don't know where you got that story from, but it's all lies. I never fathered a son, and certainly not a crybaby like Ulrik. My guess is he's the product of one of Lyberth's countless drunken one-night stands. They're like two peas in a pod, the pair of them.'

'I never said anything about Ulrik being your son.'

Abelsen's arms on the armrests relaxed for a moment, before tensing again when he clenched his fists. 'Now free me,' he commanded from deep down his throat.

'So you can kill me, like you killed Lyberth?'

Abelsen threw his head forward and grabbed the strips with his teeth. He shook his head and bit into the plastic. Blood started trickling from his mouth, down his wrist and onto the wood.

'Where are they?' Matthew shouted, kicking the armchair.

Abelsen looked up for a moment. His eyes were crazed. His chin and his thin lips were smeared with the blood that flowed from his teeth and gums. 'She's dead,' he sneered. 'Dead, like you, you bastard.' Then he resumed his attack on the plastic strip.

Somewhere above them they heard a thud.

Matthew kicked the armchair again. 'We found Najak in the shipping container in Færingehavn, you know,' he said, almost absent-mindedly, and then he looked back at Abelsen. 'You're finished, arsehole.'

'How big an idiot are you? That shipping container is empty now.'

Matthew shook his head. 'And I have the film reels. I told you that in my email, didn't I? And I'm sure the police will find plenty of DNA evidence out there.'

A new and much clearer sound from above drew Matthew's attention back towards the ceiling. 'Is that Ulrik?' he shouted. 'Are you up there, Ulrik, you piece of shit?'

66

Matthew pulled the harpoon off the wall; as far as he remembered from the notebook, it had been displayed there as an ornament since before Jakob lived there. He weighed it in his hand, sizing up the thin wooden spear that ended in a heart-shaped arrowhead. Once, many years ago, the wood had been polished as smooth as glass. The arrowhead felt cool against his skin. Then he snatched the ulo from the bookcase and ran towards the stairs.

Abelsen sensed nothing. His teeth chewed away at the hard plastic, while he panted and growled furiously.

The stairs leading up to the first floor were covered by a grey floral carpet, which was so faded that the flowers looked like brown patches. The steps disappeared under his feet two at a time, and in a few seconds he had reached the top and pushed open the first door.

The room lay in twilight, and he couldn't see very well, but he could hear that someone was in there. He took a firm hold of the harpoon and brandished it, ready to strike.

At the far end of the room was a solid wooden bed, and in the middle of a chaos of quilts and blankets Tupaarnaq lay on her back, her arms tied tightly to the bedposts. She was naked and tried to scream when she saw Matthew, but a piece of fabric had been stuffed into her mouth.

Ulrik was squatting on his haunches between her legs. His torso was lowered over her. He muttered incomprehensible words and saliva dripped from his chin. In his clenched right hand, which rested on the quilts on the mattress, he was clutching a knife, which flashed in the light from the passage. His trousers were pulled halfway down his thighs, and his dick stuck stiffly out into the air, right above the dark leaves between Tupaarnaq's hips.

'This slag needs to be punished,' he hissed, turning slowly to look at Matthew.

His hair was plastered to his face, and he was sweating profusely. His eyes shone as if he were in the grip of a violent fever. 'She killed my father…She killed all of them…Piss off, you Danish bastard.'

'Get away from her,' Matthew yelled. Everything inside him was shaking, and he raised the harpoon. 'Get away from her, you psycho! You're sick in the head!'

'She needs to be fucked,' Ulrik shouted back, his shoulders heaving and sinking rapidly.

Tupaarnaq spiralled her lower body violently and Ulrik was temporarily thrown off-balance.

'What the hell do you think you're doing, you cunt?' he screamed, turning back to her. He raised the knife and jammed it into the tattooed leaves on her left side.

She cried out behind the gag. Her body arched from the bed like a bow and twisted in agony from the blade, which was now buried deep under the roots of the plants. Her scream ebbed away, but rose again when Ulrik pulled out the knife and raised his arm to strike again.

Matthew roared at the top of his lungs.

The sound hung still in the air.

Ulrik's upper body jerked. His arm with the knife flopped onto the bed. His other hand travelled across his skin, and his fingers felt the bloody harpoon tip sticking out of the right side of his chest. For a moment he gritted his teeth and pressed his eyes shut, then he got up from the bed. The harpoon's wooden handle seesawed behind his back.

'I'm going to kill you,' he growled, and transferred the knife to his left hand.

Matthew could see Tupaarnaq turn and bend a leg, ready to kick. He clutched the ulo in his hand. The kick hit Ulrik's lower back and sent him flying. He let out a roar and nearly keeled over, but stayed on his feet. He raised his knife and lunged at Matthew, who managed to avoid the stumbling man and at the same time swung the ulo with all his strength in front of Ulrik. The soft, diagonal arc of the blade was stopped halfway by Ulrik's neck.

Ulrik fell to his knees, clutching his throat. The blood poured out between his fingers and his lips. Somewhere in his throat his breathing started to bubble. His gaze travelled in short leaps up to Matthew's face. His eyes were crazed. The noises coming from his throat grew sharper. Then they turned into hoarse gurgling.

There were voices coming from downstairs. Abelsen howled like an animal.

Matthew pushed Ulrik over with his foot. He dropped the ulo and heard it clatter onto the floor. Ulrik's arms and chest were covered in blood. His eyes were closed.

'Are you badly hurt?' Matthew whispered as he knelt down at the side of the bed to remove the gag from Tupaarnaq's mouth.

'Cut me free,' she croaked. She was sweating.

He reached for the ulo and rose to cut the strips that were keeping her restrained.

She wrapped the leaves of her arms around herself so they merged with the dark foliage of her body. 'Cover me up.'

Her voice was drowned out by the sound of boots stomping up the stairs. Matthew grabbed a blanket and put it around her shoulders.

The noise of the boots stopped and became movement in the air. 'Hello?' a voice called out from the stairs.

'I'm not going back to prison,' Tupaarnaq whispered, clutching Matthew's jumper.

He looked at the blood on the bed, and then into her eyes. 'Just hang in there.'

The heart-shaped freckle on her nose glowed, while her eyelids closed.

SKIN

67

Matthew raised his head when the door opened. He looked around in confusion, then sighed into the mattress, where the side of his face was still outlined in the sheet.

Ottesen closed the door softly behind him. 'The doctors say she's still unconscious. Were you asleep?'

'No,' Matthew said from the chair, then he shook his head and tilted his neck from side to side. 'Yes, maybe I was.' He looked up at Ottesen, who was wearing jeans and a black training top. 'I don't think she has woken up yet.'

'She will,' Ottesen said quietly, and came closer to the bed. 'You don't seem to be answering your mobile today, so I decided to stop by to see how you were. I thought I might find you here.'

In the hospital bed between the two men, Tupaarnaq was resting under a thick, white quilt that was wrapped tightly around her. Except for the spot where Matthew's head had dislodged it. On the other side there was a steel stand with two drips hanging from the crossbar. One contained blood, the other saline. Tupaarnaq's pulse ran in monotonous, green jumps across a small monitor.

'We need you to call in at the station to finalise your witness statement,' Ottesen said. Then he nodded towards the bed. 'The same goes for her when she wakes up.'

'If she wakes up,' Matthew whispered, his eyes returning to the quilt. 'And I told you everything yesterday.'

'Yes, I know, but…the body count is quite high, wouldn't you say? They'll double-check everything in Copenhagen, so I want to be sure that it all adds up one hundred per cent.'

Matthew rubbed his eyes and ran his hand over his nose and the fine, pale stubble on his chin. 'Abelsen?'

'Don't worry about him,' Ottesen said with a smile. 'We have quite a lot on him now. When we freed him from the armchair yesterday he was screaming and shouting about the murder and mutilation of Aqqalu. He's denying everything now, but several of us heard him so he'll get his just deserts once we get some people up here to gather technical evidence.'

'And Najak?'

Ottesen shook his head. 'We found nothing out there. The shipping container had been clinically cleaned and torched with petrol. It reeked to high heaven. But forensics will be taking samples of every inch of that warehouse, so who knows.'

Matthew nodded. 'Ulrik killed Aqqalu—you know that, don't you?'

'Yes.' Ottesen nodded grimly and looked past the bed and out through the window behind Matthew. 'Jakob said it was an accident.' He shook his head and looked up at the ceiling. 'It's a real shame we didn't work that out before Ulrik lost his mind. There was no need for it to go so wrong.'

'My guess is that Abelsen was putting pressure on him, and he probably had many more skeletons in the cupboard that you've yet to discover.'

'I'm sure you're right,' Ottesen said, exhaling heavily between his lips. He followed Matthew's gaze, which was fixed on Tupaarnaq.

'Listen…' Ottesen hesitated. 'Is there anything else you'd like to tell me about the murders in '73 and the mummy?'

'The Faroe Islands man?' Matthew asked, glancing up briefly.

'Yes, and the other dead men. I'm starting to realise that you have a better handle on this case than I thought.'

'If you know that he was Faroese, you know just as much as I do. Abelsen appears to be using his son, Bárdur, as his gorilla now.'

'The son has vanished without a trace, but we'll find him. No, I was thinking more about the other men. I want to know who killed them, because their killer might still be alive.'

'I don't know,' Matthew said wearily, burying his face in his hands.

'I think you do.'

'It's in the notebook.'

'But the notebook is gone.'

Matthew raised his head and looked at Ottesen, while his hands slipped slowly down the sides of the chair. 'Gone? How can it be gone?'

'You said you gave it to Jakob, but he thinks you took it with you when you ran down to Abelsen, so…well, it's gone.'

'That training top you're wearing,' Matthew said. 'Does it mean that anything I say will stay between the two of us, just like when we had pizza?'

'I'm Karlo's son, and I would like to know if my father…I would like to know if the killer from back then is still alive. Especially now that Jakob has resurfaced.'

'The killer is dead,' Matthew said.

'Are you sure?'

'The killer died a few years ago, yes.'

'Funny, that was about the time that…' Ottesen drummed his fingers on his trouser leg. 'Oh, okay. I get it now.' He shook his head.

'But they knew where she was all along. Everyone just thought that she had decided to move back to her village.' He smiled and shook his head. 'I think you might be right…Anyway, I'd better get going. Now, you won't forget to drop by the station, will you?'

Matthew nodded. His eyes began to close as he heard the door to the corridor open.

'Hey?'

Ottesen's voice made Matthew look up.

'I hear you lost your job at the newspaper,' the police officer said. 'We're still looking for a consultant, if you're interested.'

Matthew's eyes were focused on the green pulse, but he was staring without seeing. He nodded slowly.

'I would actually prefer to hire you as a kind of investigative assistant.' Ottesen smiled broadly. 'An external consultant, I mean.'

'I don't think I'd make a very good Sherlock,' Matthew said, shaking his head.

'Never mind…We'll talk about it some other time.' Ottesen drummed his fingers on the door. 'Take care, Matt Cave,' he said, and left.

Matthew's mobile had started vibrating in his pocket during Ottesen's visit. Now he took it out and looked at it. He was startled when the phone started buzzing again. He checked the number and rejected the call.

The room fell silent. Tupaarnaq lay locked in a faraway world of her own. The fluorescent tubes above them crackled faintly.

Matthew's mobile beeped again, but this time only briefly. He got up and walked to the window, opening the new text message.

Please drop by the office for a chat, Matthew. We'll work something out. Everyone wants to talk to you. KNR, Nuuk-TV, DR, TV2, CNN and CBC. Also Norway's TV2. You get the picture. It's gone viral. It's not every day that a country is hit by such extreme and overlapping scandals. See you soon. Ideally now. It's your story, all of it. Nothing is off-limits. We'll print everything.

There was a second text message. Matthew hadn't noticed it arrive.

Hi, this is Arnaq. Are you really my brother or are you taking the piss?

The light in the ward was so bright that he could see Tupaarnaq in the window. He pressed his forehead against her reflection. It was cold and she disappeared instantly in his shadow. He replied to Arnaq that they shared a father, and that he was indeed her half-brother. And that he was twelve years older than her.

As soon as he had sent the message, he put his mobile on the bedside table and went to turn off the light. The room didn't grow very dark but it was more peaceful. Almost without making a sound, he slipped down onto the chair beside the bed and took out a small, black notebook from his jacket.

'I'm going to read to you,' he said softly, without looking at Tupaarnaq. He wanted to hold her hand but he didn't have the courage. Instead, he placed his left hand on the sheet, close to hers. He held the notebook in his right hand. 'Perhaps you'll hear it.'

'I'll climb to the top of the mountain and let the serenity, the air and the loneliness enter my thoughts. Even though it might be the very loneliness and longing I'm trying to escape. But I think that's the beauty of the mountains and their peaks. Becoming one with loneliness. My soul is old. The mountain is its body, the brook its blood and the fog its breath. I can feel its breath. Its life. Its soul in me. And then I realise that there's no such thing as loneliness. We are all alive in the same world.'

The tears welled up in his eyes and rolled down his cheeks as he read on.

'If I stand still, I'll turn to stone. If I stand still, life can reach me and touch me. My deepest fear and longing are encompassed in the same thought. One day I will flee so high up the mountain that its pulsating

stone heart will take me in and let me feel what it means to be still. So still that I can't hear anything. But feel everything. While turning to stone.'

He closed the notebook. 'I've started writing down my thoughts to my daughter.'

He felt movement on his hand. Fingers searching. He turned over his hand and opened his palm. It was the first time he felt her skin.